Also by John Connolly
Every Dead Thing

DARK HOLLOW

A NOVEL

JOHN CONNOLLY

SIMON & SCHUSTER

NEW YORK LONDON TORONTO SYDNEY SINGAPORE

CON

SIMON & SCHUSTER
Rockefeller Center
1230 Avenue of the Americas
New York, NY 10020

Originally published in 2000 in Great Britain by Hodder and Stoughton

SIMON & SCHUSTER and colophon are registered trademarks
of Simon & Schuster, Inc.

Book design by Ellen R. Sasahara

Manufactured in the United States of America

1 3 5 7 9 10 8 6 4 2

Library of Congress Cataloging-in-Publication Data
Connolly, John, 1968-
Dark hollow / John Connolly.
p. cm.
1. Private investigators—New York (State)—New York—Fiction. 2. New York
(N.Y.)—Fiction. 3. Serial murders—Fiction. 4. Ex-police—Fiction. 5. Maine—
Fiction. I. Title.

PR6053.O48645 D37 2001
823'.914—dc21   Library of Congress Control Number: 2001027008
ISBN 0-7432-0332-1

For my father

DARK
HOLLOW

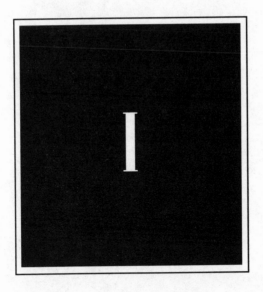

"Alone, alone, about a dreadful wood
Of conscious evil runs a lost mankind,
Dreading to find its Father."
—W. H. AUDEN, *FOR THE TIME BEING*

PROLOGUE

I dream dark dreams.

I dream of a figure moving through the forest, of children flying from his path, of young women crying at his coming. I dream of snow and ice, of bare branches and moon-cast shadows. I dream of dancers floating in the air, stepping lightly even in death, and my own pain is but a faint echo of their suffering as I run. My blood is black on the snow, and the edges of the world are silvered with moonlight. I run into the darkness, and he is waiting.

I dream in black and white, and I dream of him.

I dream of Caleb, who does not exist, and I am afraid.

The Dodge Intrepid stood beneath a stand of firs, its windshield facing out to sea, the lights off, the key in the ignition to keep the heater running. No snow had fallen this far south, not yet, but there was frost on the ground. From nearby came the sound of the waves breaking on Ferry Beach, the only noise to disturb the stillness of this Maine winter night. A floating jetty bobbed close to the shore, lobster pots piled high upon it. Four boats lay shrouded in tarpaulin behind the red wooden boathouse, and a catamaran was tied down close to the public access boat ramp. Otherwise, the parking lot was empty.

The passenger door opened and Chester Nash climbed quickly into the car, his teeth chattering and his long brown coat drawn tightly around him. Chester was small and wiry, with long dark hair and a sliver of a mustache on his upper lip that stretched down beyond the corners of his mouth. He thought the mustache made him look dashing. Everyone else thought it made him look mournful, thus the nickname "Cheerful Chester." If there was one thing guaranteed to make Chester Nash mad, it was people calling him Cheerful Chester. He had once stuck his gun in Paulie Block's mouth for calling him Cheerful Chester. Paulie Block had almost ripped his arm off for doing it, although, as he explained to Cheerful Chester while he slapped him repeatedly across the head with hands as big as shovels, he understood the reason why Chester had done it. Reasons just didn't excuse everything, that was all.

"I hope you washed your hands," said Paulie Block, who sat in the driver's seat of the Dodge, maybe wondering why Chester couldn't have taken a leak earlier like any normal individual instead of insisting on pissing against a tree in the woods by the shore and letting all of the heat out of the car while he did it.

"Man, it's cold," said Chester. "This is the coldest goddamn place I have ever been in my whole goddamn life. My meat nearly froze out there. Any colder, I'da pissed ice cubes."

Paulie Block took a long drag on his cigarette and watched as the tip flared briefly red before returning to gray ash. Paulie Block was aptly named. He was six-three, weighed two-eighty and had a face that looked like it had been used to shunt trains. He made the interior of the car look cramped just by being there. All things considered, Paulie Block could have made Giants Stadium look cramped just by being there.

Chester glanced at the digital clock on the dash, the green numerals seeming to hang suspended in the dark.

"They're late," he said.

"They'll be here," said Paulie. "They'll be here."

He returned to his cigarette and stared out to sea. He probably didn't look too hard. There was nothing to be seen, just blackness and the lights of Old Orchard Beach beyond. Beside him, Chester Nash began playing with a Game Boy.

Outside, the wind blew and the waves washed rhythmically on the beach, and the sound of their voices carried over the cold ground to where others were watching, and listening.

" . . . Subject Two is back in vehicle. Man, it's cold," said FBI Special Agent Dale Nutley, unconsciously repeating the words that he had just heard Chester Nash speak. A parabolic microphone stood beside him, positioned close to a small gap in the wall of the boathouse. Next to it, a voice-activated Nagra tape recorder whirred softly and a Badger Mk II low-light camera kept a vigil on the Dodge.

Nutley wore two pairs of socks, long johns, denims, a T-shirt, a cotton shirt, a wool sweater, a Lowe ski jacket, thermal gloves and a gray alpaca hat with two little flaps that hung down over the headphones and kept his ears warm. Special Agent Rob Briscoe, who sat beside him on a tall stool, thought the alpaca hat made Nutley look like a llama herder, or the lead singer with the Spin Doctors. Either way, Nutley looked like a clown in his alpaca hat, with its damn flaps to keep his ears warm. Agent Briscoe, whose ears were very cold, wanted that alpaca hat. If it got any colder, he figured he might just have to kill Dale Nutley and take the hat from his dead head.

The boathouse stood to the right of the Ferry Beach parking lot, giving its occupants a clear view of the Dodge. Behind it, a private road followed the shore, leading to one of the summer houses below the Neck. From the lot, Ferry Road snaked back to Black Point Road, leading ultimately to Oak Hill and U.S.1 to the north and the Neck to the southeast. The boathouse windows had received a reflective coating barely two hours before, in order to prevent anyone from seeing the agents inside. There had been a brief moment of apprehension when Chester Nash had peered in the window and tested the locks on the doors before running quickly back to the Dodge.

Unfortunately, the boathouse had no heating, at least none that worked, and the FBI had not seen fit to provide the two special agents with a heater. As a result, Nutley and Briscoe were about as cold as they had ever been. The bare boards of the boathouse were icy to the touch.

"How long we been here?" asked Nutley.

"Two hours," replied Briscoe.

"You cold?"

"What sort of a stupid question is that? I'm covered in frost. Of course I'm fucking cold."

"Why didn't you bring a hat?" asked Nutley. "You know, you lose most of your body heat through the top of your head? You should have brought a hat. That's why you're cold. You should have brought a hat."

"You know what, Nutley?" said Briscoe.

"What?" said Nutley.

"I hate you."

Behind them, the Nagra whirred softly, recording the conversation of the two agents. Everything was to be recorded, that was the rule on this operation: everything. And if that included Briscoe's hatred of Nutley because of his alpaca hat, then so be it.

The security guard, Oliver Judd, heard her before he saw her. Her feet made a heavy, shuffling noise on the carpeted floor and she was speaking softly to herself as she walked. Regretfully, he stood up in his booth and walked away from his TV and the heater that had been blasting warm air onto his toes. Outside, there was a kind of stillness that presaged further snow. There was no wind, though, which was something. It would soon get worse—December always did—but, this far north, it got worse sooner than it did anywhere else. Sometimes, living in northern Maine could be a bitch.

He walked swiftly toward her. "Hey, lady, lady! What are you doing out of bed? You're gonna catch your death."

The old woman started at the last word and looked at Judd for the first time. She was small and thin but carried herself straight, which gave her an imposing air among the other occupants of St. Martha's Home for the Elderly. Judd didn't think she was as old as some of the other folks in the home, who were so ancient that they'd bummed cigarettes from people who were later killed in World War I. This one, though, was maybe sixty at most. Judd figured that if she wasn't old then she was probably infirm, which meant, in layman's terms, that she was mad, plumb loco. Her hair was silver gray and hung loose over her shoulders and almost to her waist. Her eyes were bright blue and looked straight through Judd and off into the distance. She wore a pair of brown, lace-up boots, a nightgown, a red muffler and a long blue overcoat, which she was buttoning as she walked.

"I'm leaving," she replied. She spoke quietly but with absolute determination, as if it was nothing out of the ordinary that a sixty-year-old woman should try to leave a home for the elderly in northern Maine wearing only a nightdress and a cheap coat on a night when the forecast promised more snow to add to the six inches that already lay frozen on the ground. Judd couldn't figure out how she had slipped past the nurses' station, still less almost to the main door of the building. Some of these old folks were cunning as foxes, Judd reckoned. Turn your back on them and they'd be gone, heading for the hills or their former homes or off to wed a lover who had died thirty years before.

"Now you know you can't leave," said Judd. "Come on, you got to go back to bed. I'm going to call for a nurse now, so you stay where you are and we'll have someone down to take care of you before you know it."

The old woman stopped buttoning her coat and looked again

at Oliver Judd. It was then that Judd realized for the first time that she was scared: truly, mortally afraid for her life. He couldn't tell how he knew, except that maybe some kind of primitive sense had kicked in when she came near him. Her eyes were huge and pleading and her hands shook now that they were no longer occupied with her buttons. She was so scared that Judd began to feel a little nervous himself. Then the woman spoke.

"He's coming," she said.

"Who's coming?" asked Judd.

"Caleb. Caleb Kyle is coming."

The old woman's stare was almost hypnotic, her voice trembling with terror. Judd shook his head and took her by the arm.

"Come on," he said, leading her to a vinyl seat beside his booth. "You sit down here while I call the nurse." Who in hell was Caleb Kyle? The name was almost familiar, but he couldn't quite place it.

He was dialing the number for the nurses' station when he heard a noise from behind. He turned to see the woman almost on top of him, her eyes now narrow with concentration, her mouth set firmly. Her hands were raised above her head and he lifted his gaze to see what she was holding, his face rising just in time to see the heavy glass vase falling toward him.

Then all was darkness.

"I can't see a fucking thing," said Cheerful Chester Nash. The windows of the car had steamed up, giving Chester an uncomfortably claustrophobic feeling that the huge bulk of Paulie Block did nothing to ease, as he had just told his companion in no uncertain terms.

Paulie leaned across Chester and wiped the side window with his sleeve. In the distance, headlights raked the sky.

"Quiet," he said. "They're coming."

•   •   •

Nutley and Briscoe had also seen the headlights, minutes after Briscoe's radio had crackled into life to inform the agents that a car was on its way down Old County Road, heading in the direction of Ferry Beach.

"You think it's them?" asked Nutley.

"Maybe," replied Briscoe, brushing icy condensation from his jacket as the Ford Taurus emerged from Ferry Road and pulled up alongside the Dodge. Through their phones, the agents heard Paulie Block ask Cheerful Chester if he was ready to rumble. They heard only a click in response. Briscoe couldn't be certain, but he thought it was the sound of a safety clicking off.

In St. Martha's Home for the Elderly, a nurse placed a cold compress on the side of Oliver Judd's head. Ressler, the sergeant out of Dark Hollow, stood by with a reserve patrolman, who was still laughing quietly to himself. There was the faintest trace of a fading smile on Ressler's lips. In another corner stood Dave Martel, the chief of police in Greenville, five miles south of Dark Hollow, and beside him one of the Fisheries and Wildlife wardens from the town.

St. Martha's was technically in the jurisdiction of Dark Hollow, the last town before the big industrial forests began their sweep toward Canada. Still, Martel had heard about the old woman and had come to offer his help in the search if it was needed. He didn't like Ressler, but liking had nothing to do with whatever action needed to be taken.

Martel, who was sharp, quiet and only Greenville's third chief since the foundation of the town's small department, didn't see anything particularly funny about what had just happened. If they didn't find her soon, she would die. It didn't require too much cold to kill an old woman, and there was plenty to spare that night.

Oliver Judd, who had always wanted to be a cop but was too short, too overweight and too dumb to make the grade, knew the Dark Hollow cops were laughing at him. He figured that they probably had a right to laugh. After all, what kind of security guard gets coldcocked by an old lady? An old lady, what's more, who now had Oliver Judd's new Smith & Wesson 625 somewhere on her person.

The search team prepared to move off, headed by Dr. Martin Ryley, the director of the home. Ryley was wrapped up tightly in a hooded parka, gloves and insulated boots. In one hand he carried an emergency medical kit, in the other a big Maglite flashlight. At his feet lay a backpack containing warm clothing, blankets and a thermos filled with soup.

"We didn't pass her on the way in here, so she's moving across country," Judd heard someone say. It sounded like Will Patterson, the warden, whose wife worked in a drugstore in Guilford and had an ass like a peach waiting to be bitten.

"It's all hard going," said Ryley. "South is Beaver Cove, but Chief Martel didn't see her on his way up here. West is the lake. Looks like she may be just wandering aimlessly through the woods."

Patterson's radio buzzed and he moved away to talk. Almost immediately, he turned back. "Plane's spotted her. She's about one mile northeast of here, moving farther into the forest."

The two Dark Hollow cops and the warden, accompanied by Ryley and a nurse, moved off, one of the cops shouldering the backpack of clothing and blankets. Chief Martel looked at Judd and shrugged. Ressler didn't want his help, and Martel wasn't about to stick his nose in where it wasn't wanted, but he had a bad feeling about what was happening, a very bad feeling. As he watched the group of five heading into the trees, the first small flurries of snow began to fall.

•   •   •

"Ho Chi Minh," said Cheerful Chester. "Pol Pot. Lychee."

The four Cambodians looked at him coldly. They wore matching blue wool overcoats, blue suits with somber ties, and black leather gloves on their hands. Three were young, probably no more than twenty-five or twenty-six, Paulie reckoned. The other was older, with strands of gray seeping through his slicked-back dark hair. He wore glasses and smoked an unfiltered cigarette. In his left hand, he held a black leather briefcase.

"Tet. Chairman Mao. Nagasaki," continued Cheerful Chester.

"Will you shut up?" said Paulie Block.

"I'm trying to make them feel at home."

The senior Cambodian took a last drag on his cigarette and flicked it toward the beach.

"When your friend is finished making a fool of himself, perhaps we can begin?" he said.

"See," said Paulie Block to Cheerful Chester. "That's how wars start."

"That Chester sure is an asshole," said Nutley. The conversation between the six men carried clearly to them in the chill night air. Briscoe nodded in agreement. Beside him, Nutley adjusted the camera to zoom in on the case in the Cambodian's hand, clicked off a frame, then pulled back a little to take in Paulie Block, the Cambodian and the case. Their brief was to watch, listen and record. No interference. The interference part would come later, as soon as all of this—whatever "this" was, since all they had was the meeting point—could be traced back to Tony Celli in Boston. Two cars were waiting to pick up the Dodge at Oak Hill, while a third was positioned behind the Scarborough fire department in case either of the targets took the Spurwink Road to South Portland. A second pair of cars would follow the Cambodians. In addition, there was backup available from the police at both Scarborough and Portland, if required. Still, it was Nutley and Briscoe on point, and they knew it.

Briscoe picked up a Night Hawk scope and trained it on Cheerful Chester Nash.

"You see anything unusual about Chester's coat?" he said.

Nutley moved the camera a little to the left.

"No," he said. "Wait. It looks like it's fifty years old. He doesn't have his hands in his pockets. He's got them in those slits below the breast. Pretty awkward way to keep warm, don't you think."

"Yeah," said Briscoe. "Real awkward."

"Where is she?" said the Cambodian to Paulie Block.

Paulie gestured to the trunk of the car. The Cambodian nodded and handed the briefcase to one of his associates. The case was flicked open and the Cambodian held it, facing forward, so that Paulie and Chester could see what was inside.

Chester whistled. "Shit," he said.

"Shit," said Nutley. "There's a lot of cash in that case."

Briscoe trained the scope on the notes. "Ouch. We're talking maybe two mil."

"Enough to buy Tony Celli out of whatever jam he's in," said Nutley.

"And then some."

"But who's in the trunk?" asked Nutley.

"Well, son, that's what we're here to find out."

The group of five moved carefully over the hard ground, their breath puffing white as they went. Around them, the tips of evergreens scraped the sky and welcomed the flakes with their spread branches. The ground here was rocky, and the new snow had made it slick and dangerous. Ryley had already stumbled once, painfully scraping his shin. In the sky above them, they could hear the sound of the Cessna's engine, one of Currier's planes from Moosehead Lake, and could see its spotlight picking out something on the ground ahead of them.

"If this snow keeps up, the plane's going to have to turn back," said Patterson.

"Nearly there," said Ryley. "Another ten minutes and we'll have her."

A gunshot exploded in the darkness ahead of them, then a second. The light on the plane tilted and started to rise. Patterson's radio burst out with an angry blast of speech.

"Hell," said Patterson, with a look of disbelief on his face. "She's shooting at them."

The Cambodian stayed close to Paulie Block as he moved to the rear of the car. Behind them, the younger men pulled back their coats to reveal Uzis hanging from straps on their shoulders. Each kept a hand on the grip, one finger just outside the trigger guard.

"Open it," said the older man.

"You're the boss," said Paulie, as he inserted the key in the lock and prepared to lift the trunk. "Paulie's just here to open the trunk." If the Cambodian had been listening more intently, he would have noticed that Paulie Block said the words very loudly and very distinctly.

"Gun slits," said Briscoe suddenly. "Fucking gun slits, that's what they are."

"Gun slits," repeated Nutley. "Oh, Jesus."

• • •

Paulie Block opened the trunk and stepped back. A blast of heat greeted the Cambodian as he moved forward. In the trunk was a blanket, and beneath it was a recognizably human form. The Cambodian leaned in and pulled the blanket back.

Beneath it was a man: a man with a sawed-off shotgun.

"What is this?" said the Cambodian.

"This is good-bye," said Paulie Block, as the barrels roared and the Cambodian jerked with the impact of the shots.

"Fuck," said Briscoe. "Move! Move!" He drew his SIG and ran for the back door, flipping a switch on his handset and calling for the Scarborough backup to move in as he opened the lock and headed into the night in the direction of the two cars.

"What about noninterference?" said Nutley as he followed the older man. This wasn't the way it was supposed to happen. It wasn't supposed to go down like this at all.

Cheerful Chester's coat flew open, revealing the twin short barrels of a pair of Walther MPK submachine guns. Two of the Cambodians were already raising their Uzis when he pulled the triggers.

"Sayonara," said Chester, his mouth widening into a grin.

The 9mm parabellums ripped into the three men, tearing through the leather of the briefcase, the expensive wool of their coats, the pristine whiteness of their shirts, the thin shells of their skins. They shattered glass, pierced the metal of the car, pockmarked the vinyl of the seats. It took less than four seconds to empty sixty-four rounds into the three men, leaving them wrinkled and slumped, their warm blood melting the thin layer of frost on the ground. The briefcase had landed face down, some of the tightly packed wads scattering as it fell.

Chester and Paulie saw what they had done, and it was good.

"Well, what are you waiting for?" said Paulie. "Let's get the money and get the fuck out of here."

Behind him, the man with the shotgun, whose name was Jimmy Fribb, climbed from the cramped trunk and stretched his legs, his joints creaking. Chester loaded a fresh clip into one of the MPKs and dumped the other in the trunk of the Dodge. He was just leaning down to pick up the fallen money when the two shouts came almost together.

"FBI," said the first voice. "Let me see your hands now."

The other voice was less succinct, and less polite, but probably strangely familiar to Paulie Block.

"Get the fuck away from the money," it said, "or I'll blow your fucking heads off."

The old woman stood in a patch of clear ground, watching the sky. Snow fell on her hair, on her shoulders and on her outstretched arms, the gun clasped in her right hand, her left hand open and empty. Her mouth was gaping and her chest heaved as her aging body tried to cope with its exertions. She seemed not to notice Ryley and the others until they were only thirty feet from her. The nurse hung back behind the others. Ryley, despite Patterson's objections, took the lead.

"Miss Emily," he said softly. "Miss Emily, it's me, Dr. Ryley. We're here to take you home."

The woman looked at him and Ryley suspected, for the first time since they had set out, that Miss Emily was not mad. Her eyes were calm as she watched him, and she almost grinned as he approached.

"I'm not going back," she said.

"Miss Emily, it's cold. You're going to die out here if you don't come with us. We've brought you blankets and warm clothes, and I have a thermos of chicken soup. We'll get you warm and comfortable, then we'll bring you safely back."

The woman actually smiled then, a broad smile with no humor to it, and no trust.

"You can't keep me safe," she said softly. "Not from him."

Ryley frowned. He recalled something about the woman now, an incident with a visitor and a later report from one of the nurses after Miss Emily claimed that someone had tried to climb in her window. They'd dismissed it, of course, although Judd had taken to wearing his gun on duty as a result. These old folks were nervous, fearful of illness, of strangers, of friends and relatives sometimes, fearful of the cold, of the possibility of falling, fearful for their meager possessions, for their photos, for their fading memories.

Fearful of death.

"Please, Miss Emily, put the gun down and come back with us. We can keep you safe from harm. No one's going to hurt you."

She shook her head slowly. Above them, the plane circled, casting a strange white light over her frame, turning her long gray hair to silver fire.

"I'm not going back. I'll face him out here. This is his place, these woods. This is where he'll be."

Her face changed then. Behind Ryley, Patterson thought he had never seen an expression of such abject terror. Her mouth curled down at the edges, her chin and lips trembled and then the rest of her body began to shake, a strange, violent quivering that was almost like an ecstasy. Tears flowed down her cheeks as she began to speak.

"I'm sorry," she said. "I'm sorry, I'm sorry, I'm sorry, I'm sorry . . ."

"Please, Miss Emily," said Ryley, as he moved toward her. "Put the gun down. We have to take you back."

"I'm not going back," she repeated.

"Please, Miss Emily, you must."

"Then you'll have to kill me," she said simply, as she pointed the Smith & Wesson at Ryley and pulled the trigger.

• • •

Chester and Paulie looked first to their left and then to their right. To their left, in the parking lot, stood a tall man in a black jacket with a handset in one hand and a SIG held before him in the other. Behind him stood another, younger man, also holding a SIG, this time in a two-handed grip, with a gray alpaca hat on his head and flaps hanging down over his ears.

To their right, beside a small wooden hut used to collect parking fees during the summer, stood a figure dressed entirely in black, from the tips of his boots to the ski mask covering his head. He held a Ruger pump-action in his hands and he breathed heavily through the round slit in the mask.

"Cover him," said Briscoe to Nutley. Nutley's SIG shifted from Paulie Block to the black-garbed figure near the edge of the woods.

"Drop it, asshole," said Nutley.

The Ruger wavered slightly.

"I said, 'Drop it,'" repeated Nutley, his voice rising to a shout.

Briscoe's eyes moved briefly to take in the figure with the shotgun. It was all Chester Nash needed. He spun and opened fire with the MPK, hitting Briscoe in the arm and Nutley in the chest and head. Nutley died instantly, his alpaca hat turning red as he fell.

Briscoe opened fire from where he lay on the road, hitting Chester Nash in the right leg and the groin, the MPK tumbling from his hands as he fell. From the woods came the sound of the Ruger opening up and Paulie Block, his gun in his right hand, bucked as he was hit, the windshield behind him shattering as the shots exited. He slumped to his knees and then fell face down on the ground. Chester Nash tried to reach for the MPK with his right hand, his left hand clasping his injured groin, when Briscoe fired two more shots into him and he ceased moving. Jimmy Fribb dropped his shotgun and raised his hands, just in time to stop Briscoe from killing him.

Briscoe was about to rise when, from in front of him, he heard the sound of a shotgun shell being jacked.

"Stay down," said the voice.

He did as he was told, placing the SIG on the ground beside him. A black-booted foot kicked the gun away, sending it spinning into the undergrowth.

"Put your hands on your head."

Briscoe lifted his hands, his left arm aching as he did so, and watched as the masked figure moved toward him, the Ruger still pointing down. Nutley lay on his back close by, his open eyes staring out at the sea. Christ, thought Briscoe, what a mess. Beyond the trees, he could see headlights and hear the sound of approaching cars. The man with the shotgun heard them too, his head twisting slightly as he placed the last of the cash in the briefcase and closed it. Jimmy Fribb used the distraction to make a lunge for the discarded SIG but the gunman killed him before he could reach it, firing a shot into his back. Briscoe tightened his grip on his head, his injured arm aching, and started to pray.

"Stay flat on the ground and don't look up," he was told.

Briscoe did as he was told, but kept his eyes open. Blood flowed on the ground beneath him and he moved his head slightly to avoid it. When he looked up again, there were headlights in his eyes and the figure in black was gone.

Dr. Martin Ryley was forty-eight, and was anxious to see forty-nine. He had two children, a boy and a girl, and a wife called Joanie who cooked him pot roast on Sundays. He wasn't a very good doctor, which was why he ran an old folks' home. When Miss Emily Watts fired at him, he hit the ground, covered his head with his hands and began alternately praying and blaspheming. The first shot went somewhere to his left. The second sprayed wet dirt and snow on his face. Behind him, he heard the sound of safety catches clicking off and he shouted: "No, leave her, please. Don't shoot."

Once again the woods were silent, with only the high buzzing of the Cessna as a distraction. Ryley risked a glance up at Miss Emily. She was crying openly now. Carefully, Ryley rose to his feet.

"It's okay, Miss Emily."

Miss Emily shook her head. "No," she replied. "It will never be okay." And she put the mouth of the Smith & Wesson to her left breast and fired. The impact spun her backward and to her left, her feet tangling beneath her as she fell and the fabric of her coat igniting briefly from the muzzle flare. She shuddered once then lay still upon the ground, her blood staining the earth around her, the snow falling on her open eyes, her body lit by the light from above.

And around her, the woods watched silently, their branches shifting occasionally to allow the passage of the snow.

This is how it began for me, and for another generation: two violent occurrences, taking place almost simultaneously one winter's night, bound together by a single dark thread that lost itself in tangled memories of distant, brutal acts. Others, some of them close to me, had lived with it for a long, long time, and had died with it. This was an old evil, and old evil has a way of permeating bloodlines and tainting those who played no part in its genesis: the young, the innocent, the vulnerable, the defenseless. It turns life to death and glass to mirrors, creating an image of itself in everything that it touches.

All of this I learned later, after the other deaths, after it became clear that something terrible was happening, that something old and foul had emerged from the wilderness. And in all that would come to pass, I was a participant. Maybe, looking back into the past, I had always been a participant without ever really understanding how, or why. But that winter, a whole set of circumstances occurred, each incident separate yet ultimately connected. It opened a channel between what had been and what should never have been again, and worlds ended in the collision.

I look back over the years and see myself as I used to be, frozen in former times like a figure in a series of vignettes. I see myself as a young boy waiting for the first sight of my father as he returns from his day's exertions in the city, his policeman's uniform now put away, a black gym bag in his left hand, his once muscular form now running a little to fat, his hair grayer than it used to be, his eyes a little more tired. I run to him and he sweeps me up into the crook of his right arm, his fingers closing gently on my thigh, and I am amazed at his strength, at the muscles bunched below his shoulder, his biceps tight and hard. I want to be him, to emulate his achievements and to sculpt my body in his likeness. And when he begins to come apart, when his body is revealed only as the flawed shield for a fragile mind, then I, too, start to fall to pieces.

I see myself as an older boy, standing by my father's grave, only a handful of New York policemen straight and tall beside me, so that I too have to be straight and tall. These are his closest friends, the ones who are not ashamed to come. This is not a place where many wish to be seen; there is bad feeling in the city about what has taken place, and only a loyal few are willing to have their reputations frozen in the flare of a newsman's flashbulb.

I see my mother to my right, coiled in grief. Her husband— the man she has loved for so long—is gone, and with him the reality of him as a kind man, a family man, a father who could sweep his boy into the air like a leaf on the wind. Instead, he will forever be remembered as a murderer, a suicide. He has

killed a young man and a young woman, both unarmed, for reasons that no one will ever properly explain, reasons that lay in
the depths of those tired eyes. They had taunted him, this thug
making the transition from juvenile to adult courts and his mid-
dle-class girlfriend with his dirt under her manicured nails, and
he had killed them, seeing in them something beyond what they
were, beyond even what they might become. Then he had put
his gun in his mouth and pulled the trigger.

I see myself as a young man, standing at another grave,
watching as they lower my mother down. Beside me now is the
old man, my grandfather. We have traveled down from Scarborough, Maine—the place to which we fled after the death of my
father, the place in which my mother was born—for the funeral, so that my mother can be buried beside my father, as she
has always wished, for she has never stopped loving him.
Around us, old men and women have gathered. I am the
youngest person present.

I see snowfalls in winter. I see the old man grow older. I leave
Scarborough. I become a policeman, like my father, like my
grandfather. There is a legacy to be acknowledged, and I will not
be found wanting. When my grandfather dies, I return to Scarborough and fill in the grave myself, spadefuls of earth carefully
falling on the pine casket. The morning sun shines down on the
cemetery and I can smell the salt on the air, carried from the
marshes to the east and the west. Nearby, a golden-crowned
kinglet chases cluster flies, filthy gray insects that lay their eggs
inside living earthworms, their young eventually consuming the
host from within, and seek shelter from the winter in the chinks
and cracks of houses. Above, the first of the Canada geese fly
south for the winter, a pair of ravens flanking them like black
fighters escorting a flight of bombers.

And as the last patch of wood disappears, I hear the sound of
children's voices coming from the Lil Folks Farm nursery school
close by the cemetery, the noise of their games high and joyful,

and I cannot help but smile, for the old man would have smiled as well.

And then there is one more grave, one more set of prayers read from a tattered book, and this one tears my world apart. Two bodies are laid down to rest side by side, just as I used to find them resting close to each other when I returned at night to our Brooklyn home, my three-year-old daughter sleeping quietly in the curled quarter-moon of her mother's form. In one instant, I ceased to be a husband. I ceased to be a father. I had failed to protect them, and they had been punished for my failings.

All of these images, all of these memories, like the forged links of a chain, stretch back into the darkness. They should be put away, but the past is not so easily denied. Things left unfinished, things left unsaid, they all, in the end, come back to haunt us.

For this is the world, and the echo of worlds.

CHAPTER ONE

BILLY PURDUE'S KNIFE bit deeper into my cheek, sending a trickle of blood down my face. His body was pressed hard against mine, his elbows pinning my arms to the wall, his legs tensed against mine so I couldn't go for his groin. His fingers tightened on my neck and I thought:

Billy Purdue. I should have known better . . .

Billy Purdue was poor; poor and dangerous with some bitterness and frustration added to spice up the pot. The threat of violence was always imminent with him. It hung around him like a cloud, obscuring his judgment and influencing the actions of others, so that when he stepped into a bar and took a drink, or picked up a pool cue for a game, trouble would inevitably start. Billy Purdue didn't have to pick fights. Fights picked him.

It acted like a contagion, so that even if Billy himself managed to avoid conflict—he generally didn't seek it, but when he found it he rarely walked away—five would get you ten that he would have raised the testosterone level in the bar sufficiently to cause someone else to consider starting something. Billy Purdue could have provoked a fight at a conclave of cardinals just by looking into the room. Whatever way you considered it, he was bad news.

So far, he hadn't killed anybody and nobody had managed to kill him. The longer a situation like that goes on, the more the odds are stacked in favor of a bad end, and Billy Purdue was a bad beginning looking for a worse end. I'd heard people describe him as an accident waiting to happen, but he was more than that. He was a constantly evolving disaster, like the long, slow death of a star. His was an ongoing descent into the maelstrom.

I didn't know a whole lot about Billy Purdue's past, not then. I knew that he'd always been in trouble with the law. He had a rap sheet that read like a catalog entry for minor crimes, from disrupting school and petty larceny to DWD, receiving stolen goods, assault, trespassing, disorderly conduct, nonpayment of child support . . . The list went on and on; sometimes, it seemed like half the cops in Maine must have cuffed Billy at some point. He was an adopted child and had been through a succession of foster homes in his youth, each one keeping him for only as long as it took the foster parents to realize that Billy was more trouble than the money from social services was worth. That's the way some foster parents are: they treat the kids like a cash crop, like livestock or chickens, until they realize that if a chicken acts up you can cut its head off and eat it for Sunday dinner, but the options are more limited in the case of a delinquent child. There was evidence of neglect by many of Billy Purdue's foster parents, and suspicion of serious physical abuse in at least two cases.

Billy had at last found some kind of home with an old guy and his wife up in the north of the state, a couple that specialized in tough love. The guy had been through about twenty foster kids by the time Billy arrived and, when he got to know Billy a little, maybe he figured that this was one more too many. But he'd tried to straighten Billy out and, for a time, Billy was happy, or as happy as he could ever be. Then he started to drift a little. He moved to Boston and fell in with Tony Celli's crew, until he stepped on the wrong toes and got parceled back to Maine again, where he met Rita Ferris, seven years his junior, and they married. They had a son together, but Billy was always the real child in the relationship.

He was now thirty-two and built like a bull, the muscles on his arms like huge hams, his hands thick and broad, the fingers almost swollen in their muscularity. He had small pig eyes and uneven teeth, and his breath smelled of malt liquor and sourdough bread. There was dirt under his nails and a raised rash on his neck, the heads white, where he had shaved himself with an old, worn blade.

I was given the opportunity to observe Billy Purdue from close quarters after I failed to put an armlock on him and he pushed me hard against the wall of his silver Airstream trailer, a run-down thirty-footer out by the Scarborough Downs racetrack, that stank of unwashed clothes, rotting food and stale seed. One of his hands was clasped hard around my neck as he forced me upward, my toes barely touching the floor. The other held the short-bladed knife an inch beneath my left eye. I could feel the blood dripping from my chin.

The armlock probably hadn't been a good idea. In fact, on the scale of good ideas, it ranked somewhere between voting for Pat Buchanan and invading Russia in the winter. I would have had a better chance of successfully armlocking the trailer itself; even with all of my strength pulling on it, Billy Purdue's arm had stayed as rigid and immobile as the statue of the poet in Longfellow Square. While my mind was registering just how bad an idea it had been to go for the lock, Billy had pulled me forward and slapped me hard across the head, open palmed, with his enormous right hand, then pushed me up against the side wall of the trailer, his huge forearms holding my arms in place. My head was still ringing from the blow and my ear ached. I thought my eardrum had burst but then the pressure on my neck started to increase and I realized that I might not have to worry about my eardrum for much longer.

The knife twisted in his hand and I felt a fresh burst of pain. The blood was running freely now, dripping from my chin onto the collar of my white shirt. Billy's face was almost purple with rage and he was breathing heavily through clenched teeth, spittle erupting as he wheezed out.

He was completely focused on squeezing the life from me as I moved my right hand inside my jacket and felt the cool grip of the Smith & Wesson. I thought I was about to black out when I managed to wrench it free and move my arm enough to stick the muzzle into the soft flesh beneath Billy's jaw. The red light in his eyes flared briefly and then began to fade. The pressure on my neck eased, the knife slid out of the wound and I slumped to the floor. My throat ached as I pulled shallow, rattling breaths into my starved lungs. I kept the gun on Billy but he had turned away. Now that his tide of rage had begun to ebb, he seemed unconcerned about the gun, and about me. He took a cigarette from a pack of Marlboros, lit up, then offered the pack to me. I shook my head in refusal until the pain in my ear started raging again. I decided to stop shaking my head.

"Why'd you put the lock on me?" asked Billy in an aggrieved tone. He looked at me and there was genuine hurt in his eyes. "You shouldn't have put the lock on me."

The guy was certainly a character. I drew some more breaths, deeper now, and spoke. My voice sounded hoarse and my throat felt as if someone had rubbed grit into it. If Billy had been less of a child, I might have used the butt of the gun on him.

"You said you were going to get a baseball bat and beat the living shit out of me, as I recall," I said.

"Hey, you were being rude," he said and the red light seemed to glow again for a brief moment. I still had the gun pointed at him and he still didn't seem concerned. I wondered if he knew something about the gun that I didn't. Maybe the stench in the trailer was rotting the bullets as we spoke.

Rude. I was about to shake my head again when I remembered my ear and decided that it might be better, all things considered, to keep my head steady. I had come to visit Billy Purdue as a favor to Rita, now his ex-wife, who lived in a small apartment over on Locust Street in Portland with her two-year-old son, Donald. Rita had been granted her divorce six months before and since then Billy hadn't paid over a nickel of child support. I knew Rita's family when I was growing up in Scarborough. Her father had died in a botched bank raid in Bangor in '83 and her mother had struggled and failed to keep her family together. One brother was in jail, another was on the run from drug charges and Rita's elder sister was living in New York and had cut off all contact with her siblings.

Rita was slim and pretty and blonde but already the raw deal life had dealt her was taking its toll on her looks. Billy Purdue had never hit her or physically abused her, but he was prone to black rages and had destroyed the two apartments in which they had lived during their marriage, setting fire to one after a three-day binge in South Portland. Rita had woken up just in time to get her then one-year-old son out, before hauling Billy's unconscious body from the apartment and setting off the alarm to evacuate the rest of the building. She filed for divorce the next day.

Now Billy skulked in his bullet-shaped trailer and lived a life that was on nodding terms with poverty. During the winter he did some lumber work, cutting Christmas trees or heading farther north to the timber company forests. The rest of the time he did what he could, which wasn't a lot. His trailer stood on a patch of land owned by Ronald Straydeer, a Penobscot Indian from Old Town who had settled in Scarborough after returning from Vietnam. Ronald was part of the K-9 corps during the war, leading army patrols down jungle trails with his German shepherd dog Elsa by his side. The dog could smell Vietcong on the wind, Ronald once told me, even found freshwater once when a platoon ran dangerously low. When the Americans pulled out, Elsa was left behind as "surplus equipment" for the South Vietnamese army. Ronald had a picture of her in his wallet, tongue lolling, a pair of dog tags hanging from her collar. He figured the Vietnamese ate her as soon as the Americans left, and he never got himself another dog. Eventually, he got Billy Purdue instead.

Billy knew his ex-wife wanted to move to the West Coast and start a new life and that she needed the money Billy owed her to do that. Billy didn't want her to go. He still believed that he could salvage their relationship, and a divorce and an order preventing him from going within one hundred feet of his ex-wife hadn't altered this belief.

It was about the time that I told Billy Purdue that she wasn't coming back to him and that he had a legal obligation to pay her the money she was owed that Billy had gone for the baseball bat and things had fallen apart.

"I love her," he said, puffing on his cigarette and sending twin columns of smoke shooting from his nostrils like the exhalations of a particularly mean-tempered bull. "Who's gonna look out for her in San Francisco?"

I struggled to my feet and wiped some of the blood from my cheek. The sleeve of my jacket came back damp and stained. It was lucky my jacket was black, although the fact that I considered that lucky said a lot about the kind of day I was having.

"Billy, how can she and Donald survive if you don't pay her the money the judge told you to pay?" I replied. "How's she going to get by without that? If you do care about her, then you have to pay her."

He looked at me and then looked at his feet. His toe shifted on the filthy linoleum.

"Sorry I hurt you, man, but . . ." He reached behind his neck and scratched at his dark, unruly hair. "You gonna go to the cops?"

If I was going to the cops, I wouldn't tell Billy Purdue. Billy's regret was about as genuine as Exxon's when the *Valdez* went down. Plus, if I went to the cops Billy would be locked up and Rita still wouldn't get her money. But there was something in his tone when he asked about the cops, something that I should have picked up on but didn't. His black T-shirt was soaked with sweat, and there was mud caked at the cuffs of his pants. He had so much adrenaline coursing through his system, he made ants look calm. I should have known that Billy wasn't concerned about the cops because of some assault beef, or unpaid child support. Hindsight: it's a wonderful thing.

"If you pay the cash, I'll let it go," I said.

He shrugged. "I ain't got much. Ain't got a thousand dollars."

"Billy, you owe nearly two thousand dollars. I think you're missing the point here."

Or maybe he wasn't. The trailer was a dump, he drove a Toyota with holes in the floor and he made one hundred, maybe one-fifty, each week hauling junk and lumber. If he had two thousand dollars, he'd be someplace else. He'd also be somebody else, because Billy Purdue was never going to have two thousand dollars to his name.

"I got five hundred," he said eventually, but there was something new in his eyes as he said it, a kind of low cunning.

"Give it to me," I replied.

Billy didn't move.

"Billy, if you don't pay me the cops are going to come and lock you up until you do pay. If you're locked up, you can't make any cash to pay anyone and that looks like a vicious circle to me."

He considered that for a time, then reached beneath the filthy sofa at the end of the trailer and produced a crumpled envelope. He turned his back to me and counted out five hundred-dollar bills, then replaced the envelope. He handed over the cash with a flourish, like a magician producing someone's wristwatch after a particularly impressive conjuring trick. The bills were brand new, consecutively numbered. From the look of the envelope, they had left a lot of friends behind.

"You go to the cash machine over at Fleet Bank, Billy?" I asked. It seemed unlikely. The only way Billy Purdue would get money from a cash machine was by breaking it out of the wall with a bulldozer.

"You tell her something from me," he said. "You tell her that maybe there's more where this came from, understand? You tell her that maybe I ain't such a loser no more. You hear me?" He smiled a knowing smile, the kind of smile someone really dumb shoots at you when he thinks he knows something that you don't. I figured that if Billy Purdue knew it, then it wasn't anything that should concern me. I was wrong.

"I hear you, Billy. Tell me you're not still doing work for Tony Celli. Tell me that."

His eyes retained that gleam of dim cunning, but the smile faltered a little. "I don't know no Tony Celli."

"Let me refresh your memory. Tall wiseguy out of Boston, calls himself Tony Clean. Started off running whores, now he wants to run the world. He's into drugs, porn, shylocking, anything there's a statute against, so his hopes of a good citizen award are currently so low they're off the scale." I paused. "You used to work for him, Billy. I'm asking if you still do."

He twitched his head as if trying to dislodge water from his ears, then looked away. "Y'know, I did stuff, maybe, sometimes, y'know, for Tony. Sure, sure I did. It beat hauling junk. But I ain't seen Tony in a long time. *Long* time."

"You'd better be telling the truth, Billy, or else a lot of people are going to have some harsh words to say to you."

He didn't respond and I didn't push it. As I took the bills

from his hand he moved closer to me and I brought the gun up again. His face was an inch from mine, the muzzle of the gun against his chest.

"Why are you doing this?" he asked, and I could smell his breath and see the embers of that red glare flickering into life again. The smile was gone now. "She can't afford no private dick."

"It's a favor," I said. "I knew her family."

I don't think he even heard me.

"How's she gonna pay you?" His head turned to one side as he considered his own question. Then: "You fucking her?"

I held his gaze. "No. Now back off."

He stayed where he was, then scowled and moved slowly away.

"You better not be," he said as I backed out of the trailer and into the dark December night.

The money should have alerted me, of course. There was no way Billy Purdue could have come by it honestly, and maybe I should have pushed him on it, but I was sore and just glad to be getting away from him.

My grandfather, who was himself once a policeman, until he found the tree with the strange fruit far to the north, used to tell a joke that was more than a joke.

A guy tells his buddy that he's heading off to a card game.

"But it's crooked," protests his buddy.

"I know," says the guy. "But it's the only game in town."

That joke, a dead man's joke, would come back to me in the days that followed, as things began to fall apart. Other things that my grandfather had told me came back to me as well, things that were far from jokes for him, although many had laughed at them. Within seventy-two hours of the deaths of Emily Watts and the men at Prouts Neck, Billy Purdue would be the only game in town, and an old man's fancies would flame into violent being.

• • •

I stopped off at the bank at Oak Hill and withdrew two hundred dollars from my account through the automatic teller. The cut beneath my eye had stopped bleeding, but I figured if I tried to clean away the encrusted blood it would start bleeding all over again. I called into Ron Archer's office on Forest Avenue, where he saw patients two nights a week, and he put in three stitches.

"What were you doing?" he asked, as he prepared to give me a shot of anesthetic. I was going to ask him not to bother, but I figured he'd just think I was playing up to him. Dr. Archer was fifty, a handsome, distinguished-looking man with fine silver hair and the kind of bedside manner that made lonely women want him to climb into bed beside them and conduct intimate and unnecessary medical examinations.

"Trying to get an eyelash out," I said.

"Use eyedrops, you'll find they don't hurt as much and you'll still have an eye afterward."

He cleaned the wound with a swab, then leaned over me with the needle. I winced a little as he delivered the shot.

"That's the big, brave boy," he muttered. "If you don't cry I'll give you an M&M when it's all over."

"I'll bet you were the talk of med school with your doctor-patient wit."

"Seriously, what happened?" he asked, as he began to stitch. "Looks like someone stuck a sharp blade into this and you've got some bruising coming up on your neck."

"I tried to put an armlock on Billy Purdue. It wasn't a big success."

"Purdue? The crazy sonofabitch who nearly burned his wife and child to death?" Archer's eyebrows shot to the top of his forehead like a pair of startled crows. "You must be even more postal than he is." He began stitching. "You know, as your doctor, I should advise you that if you keep doing things like that you're likely to need more specialized treatment than I can offer." He slipped the needle through once more then cut the thread. "Although, given the dumb actions you're already taking, I imagine you'll find the transition to senility pretty smooth."

He stepped back and examined his handiwork proudly. "Wonderful," he said with a sigh. "A lovely piece of embroidery."

"If I look in the mirror and find you've stitched a little heart on my face, I'll have to burn your office down."

He wrapped the used needle carefully and dumped it in a protective container. "Those stitches will dissolve in a few days," he said. "And don't play with them. I know what you kids are like."

I left him laughing to himself and drove to Rita Ferris's apartment, close by the Cathedral of the Immaculate Conception and the Eastern Cemetery, where the two young fools Burrows and Blythe were buried. They died in an unneccessary naval combat between the American brig *Enterprise* and the British *Boxer*, of which they were the respective captains, off Monhegan Island during the War of 1812. They were interred in the Eastern Cemetery after a huge double funeral that paraded through the streets of Portland. Close by them is a marble memorial to Lieutenant Kervin Waters, who was mortally wounded in the same battle and took two agonizing years to die. He was just sixteen when he was injured, and eighteen when he died. I don't know why I thought of them as I approached Rita Ferris's apartment. Maybe, after meeting Billy Purdue, I was acutely conscious of young, wasted lives.

I turned into Locust, passing St. Paul's Anglican on my right and the St. Vincent de Paul thrift shop on my left. Rita Ferris's building was at the end of the street, across from the Kavanagh School. It was a run-down white three-story, with stone steps leading up to a door lined on one side with buzzers and apartment numbers and on the other with a row of unlocked mailboxes.

A black woman with a small girl, probably her daughter, opened the door of the building as I approached and looked at me with suspicion. There are comparatively few black people in Maine: in the early nineties, the state was still 99 percent white. It takes a long time to catch up on that kind of lead, so maybe she was right to be cautious.

I tried to give the woman my best smile to reassure her. "I'm here to see Rita Ferris. She's expecting me."

If anything, her features hardened even more. Her profile seemed to have been carved from ebony. "She's expecting you, then ring the buzzer," she said, as she closed the door in my face. I sighed and rang the buzzer. Rita Ferris answered, the door clicked and I headed up the stairs to the apartment.

Through the closed door of Rita's second-floor apartment I could hear the sound of *Seinfeld* on the TV and a child's soft cough. I knocked twice and the door opened. Rita stood aside to let me in, Donald, dressed in blue rompers, resting on her right hip. Her hair was tied back in a bun and she wore a shapeless blue sweatshirt over blue jeans with black sandals. The sweatshirt was stained with food and child spit. The apartment, small and neat despite the worn furniture, smelled of the child as well.

A woman stood a couple of feet behind Rita. As I watched, she placed a cardboard box filled with diapers, canned food and some fresh produce on the small couch. A plastic bag filled with secondhand clothes and one or two used children's toys lay on the floor, and I noticed that Rita was holding some bills in her hand. When she saw me, she blushed bright red, crumpled the cash and shoved it into the pocket of her denims.

The woman with her looked at me curiously and, I thought, with hostility. She was probably in her late seventies, with permed silver hair and large brown eyes. She wore a long wool coat that looked expensive, with a silk sweater and tailored cotton pants beneath it. Gold twinkled discreetly at her ears, her wrists and around her neck.

Rita closed the door behind me and turned to the older woman.

"This is Mr. Parker," she said. "He's been talking to Billy for me." She slipped her hands into the back pockets of her denims and nodded her head shyly to the older woman. "Mr. Parker, this is Cheryl Lansing. She's a friend."

I stretched out a hand in greeting. "Pleased to meet you," I said. After a moment's hesitation, Cheryl Lansing took my hand. Her grip was surprisingly strong.

"Likewise," she said.

Rita sighed, and decided to elaborate a little on her introduction. "Cheryl helps us out," she explained. "With food and clothes and stuff. We couldn't get by without her."

Now it was the older woman's turn to look uncomfortable. She raised a hand in dismissal and said, "Hush, child," once or twice. Then she pulled her coat tightly around her, and kissed Rita lightly on the cheek before turning her attention to Donald. She ruffled his hair, and the toddler smiled.

"I'll drop in on you again in a week or two," she said to Rita.

Rita looked a little pained, as if she felt that she was somehow being rude to her guest. "You sure you won't stay?" she asked.

Cheryl Lansing glanced at me, and smiled. "No, thank you. I have quite a ways to go tonight, and I'm sure you and Mr. Parker have a lot to talk about."

With that, she nodded a good-bye to me, and left. I watched her as she walked down the stairs: social services, I guessed, maybe even someone from St. Vincent de Paul. After all, they were only across the street. Rita seemed to guess what I was thinking.

"She's a friend, that's all," she said softly. "She knew Billy. She knew what he was like, what he's still like. Now, she tries to make sure that we're okay."

She closed and locked the door, then took a look at my eye. "Did Billy do that?"

"We had a misunderstanding."

"I'm sorry. I really didn't think he'd try to hurt you." There was genuine concern on her face and it made her seem pretty, despite the dark patches beneath her eyes and the frown lines that were working their way across her features like cracks through old plaster.

She sat down and balanced Donald on her knee. He was a large child, with huge blue eyes and a permanent expression of mild curiosity on his face. He smiled at me, raised a finger, then dropped it again and looked at his mother. She smiled down at him and he laughed, then hiccuped.

"Can I get you some coffee?" she asked. "I don't have any beer, otherwise I'd offer you a drink."

"It's okay, I don't drink. I just came by to give you this."

I handed her the seven hundred dollars. She looked a little shocked, until Donald tried to take a fifty-dollar bill and stick it in his mouth.

"Uh-uh," she said, moving the money beyond his reach. "You're expensive enough to keep as it is." She peeled away two fifties and offered them to me.

"Please, take it," she said. "For what happened. Please."

I folded her hand over the money and pushed it gently back toward her.

"I don't want it," I told her. "Like I told you, it's a favor. I've had a talk with Billy. I think he has a little cash right now and maybe he might start coming around to his obligations. If he doesn't, it may be a matter for the cops."

She nodded. "He's not a bad person, Mr. Parker. He's just confused, and he hurts a lot inside, but he loves Donnie more than anything in the world. I think he'd do just about anything to keep me from taking him away."

That was what worried me. The red flame in Billy's eyes flared up a little too easily, and he had enough rage and resentment inside him to keep it burning for a long, long time.

I stood up to leave. On the floor beside my feet I saw one of the toys that Cheryl Lansing had brought with her: a red plastic truck with a yellow hood that squeaked when I picked it up and placed it on a chair. The noise briefly distracted Donald, but then his attention returned to me.

"I'll drop by next week, see how you are." I reached out a finger to Donald and he gripped it in his little fist. I was suddenly seized by an image of my own daughter doing the same thing to me and a terrible sadness welled up inside me. Jennifer was dead now. She had died with my wife at the hands of a killer who believed that they were worthless enough to tear apart and display as a warning to others. He was dead as well, hunted to death in Louisiana, but it didn't make me feel any better. The books don't balance that way.

I gently removed my finger from Donald's grip and patted his head. Rita followed me to the door, Donald once again at her hip.

"Mr. Parker . . ." she began.

I stopped at the door.

"Please stay." With her free hand, she reached out and touched my cheek. "Please. I'm putting Donald to bed now. I got no other way to thank you."

I carefully removed her hand and kissed her palm. It smelled of hand cream and Donald.

"I'm sorry, I can't," I said.

She looked a little disappointed. "Why not? You don't think I'm pretty enough?"

I reached out and ran my fingers through her hair, and she leaned her head into my hand.

"It's not that," I said. "It's not that at all."

She smiled then, a small smile but a smile nonetheless.

"Thank you," she said and kissed me softly on the cheek. Suddenly Donald, whose face had darkened when I touched his mother, now began to strike at me with his little hand.

"Hey!" said his mother. "Stop that." But still he struck, until I took my hand away from her.

"He's very protective of me," she said. "He thought you were trying to hurt me." Donald buried his head in her breast, his thumb in his mouth, and looked out at me with suspicious eyes. Rita stood in the dark hallway as I went down the stairs, framed by the light of the apartment. She lifted Donald's hand to make him wave good-bye, and I waved back.

It was the last time I saw either of them alive.

CHAPTER TWO

I ROSE EARLY the day after Rita Ferris spoke to me for the last time. The darkness outside was still and oppressive as I drove to the airport to catch the first commuter flight to New York. There were early reports on the news bulletin of a shooting incident at Scarborough, but the details were still sketchy.

From JFK, I caught a cab, the Van Wyck and Queens Boulevard dense with traffic, to Queens Boulevard and 51st. There was already a small crowd gathered at the New Calvary Cemetery: groups of cops in uniform smoking and talking quietly at the gates; women in funeral black, their hair carefully arranged, their makeup delicately applied, nodding solemnly to one another; younger men, some barely out of their teens, uncomfortable in too-tight collars, with cheap, borrowed black ties knotted untidily at their necks, the knots too small, too thin. Some of the cops glanced at me and nodded, and I nodded back. I knew many of them by their last names, from my own former life as a policeman in New York.

The hearse approached from Woodside, three black limousines following, and entered the cemetery. The waiting crowd moved behind in twos and threes as, slowly, we made our way toward the grave. I saw a mound of earth, green matting thrown across it, wreaths and other floral tributes ranged against it. There was a larger crowd here: more police in uniform, others in plain clothes, more women, a sprinkling of children. I spotted some deputy chiefs, an assistant chief, half a dozen captains and lieutenants, all come to pay their last respects to George Greenfield, the old sergeant in the 30th Precinct, who had finally succumbed to his cancer two years before he was due to retire.

I knew him as a good man, a decent cop in the old mold who had the misfortune to work a precinct that had been plagued for years by rumors of shakedowns and corruption. The rumors eventually became complaints: guns and drugs, mainly cocaine, were routinely confiscated from dealers and resold; homes were raided illegally; threats were made. The precinct, over at 151st Street and Amsterdam Avenue, was investigated. In the end, thirty-three officers, who had been involved in two thousand prosecutions, were convicted, many for perjury. On top of the Dowd incident in the 75th—more arms and cocaine dealing, more payoffs—it made for bad coverage for the NYPD. I guessed that there was more to come: there were whispers that Midtown South was under the gun, the result of an ongoing deal with local prostitutes involving recreational sex for officers on duty.

Maybe that was why so many people had turned out for Greenfield's funeral. He represented something good and fundamentally decent, and his passing was something to mourn. I was there for very personal reasons. My wife and child were taken from me in December 1996, while I was still a homicide detective in Brooklyn. The ferocity and brutality of the manner in which they were torn from this world, and the inability of the police to find their killer, caused a rift to develop between me and my fellow officers. The murders of Susan and Jennifer tainted me in their eyes, exposing the vulnerability of even a policeman and his family. They wanted to believe that I was the exception, that somehow, as a drunk, I had brought it on myself, so that they would not have to consider the alternative. In a way, they were right: I did bring it on myself, and on my family, but I had never forgiven them for forcing me to confront this alone.

I resigned from the NYPD barely one month after the deaths. Few people had tried to argue me out of my decision, but one of them was George Greenfield. He met me one bright Sunday morning at John's on Second Avenue, close by the UN building. We ate pink grapefruit and English muffins while sitting in a booth by the window, Second Avenue quiet with little traffic and few pedestrians. Slowly, patiently, he listened to my reasons for leaving: my growing isolation; the pain of living in a city where everywhere reminded me of what I had lost; and my belief that maybe, just maybe, I could find the man who had stolen everything I held dear.

"Charlie," he said (he never called me Bird), thick gray hair topping a full-moon face, eyes dark like craters, "those are all good reasons, but if you quit then you're alone and there's a limit to the help anyone can give you. With the force, you still have family, so stay. You're a good cop. It's in your blood."

"I can't, I'm sorry."

"You leave, and maybe a lot of people will think you're running away. Some of them will probably be glad that you are, but they'll hate you for caving in."

"Let them. Those ones aren't worth worrying about anyway."

He sighed, sipped his coffee. "You were never the easiest man to get along with, Charlie. You were too smart, too likely to go off the handle. We all have our demons, but you wore yours for everyone to see. I think you made people nervous, and if there's one thing a cop doesn't like, it's being made to feel nervous. It goes against the grain."

"But I don't make you nervous?"

Greenfield twisted his mug on the table with his little finger. I could tell that he was debating whether or not to tell me something. What he said when he spoke made me feel a little ashamed, and increased my admiration for him tenfold, if such a thing was possible with a man like this.

"I have cancer," he said quietly. "Lymphosarcoma. They tell me I'm going to get real sick in the next year, and I've got maybe another year after that."

"I'm sorry," I said, the words so small that they were quickly lost in the enormity of what he was facing.

Greenfield raised a hand and gave a little shrug. "I'd like to have more time. I got grandchildren. I'd like to watch them grow. But I've watched my own kids grow, and I feel for you because that's been taken away from you. Maybe it's the wrong thing to say, but I hope that you get a second chance at that. In the end, it's the best thing you get in this world.

"As for you making me nervous, the answer's no. I got death coming for me, Charlie, and that puts things in perspective. Every day I wake up and thank God that I'm still here and that the pain isn't too bad. And I go into the 30th, and I take my seat at the muster desk and watch people piss their lives away for nothing, and I envy them every minute they waste. Don't you go doing that, Charlie, because when you're angry and grieving and you're looking for someone to blame, the worst thing you can do is turn on yourself. And the next worst thing is to turn on someone else. That's where the structure, the routine can help. That's why I'm still at that desk, because otherwise I'd tear myself and my family to pieces."

He finished his coffee and pushed the mug away. "In the end, you'll do what you have to do, and nothing I can say will change that. You still drinking?"

I didn't resent the bluntness of the question, because it contained no deeper implication. "I'm trying to quit," I said.

"That's something, I guess." He raised his hand for the check, then scribbled a number on a napkin. "My home number. You need to talk, you give me a call." He paid the check, shook my hand and walked out into the sunlight. I never saw him again.

At the graveside, a figure raised its head and I felt its attention focus on me. Walter Cole gave a small nod in my direction, then returned his attention to the priest as he read from a leather-bound prayer book. Somewhere, a woman cried softly, and in the dark skies above, a hidden jet roared its way through the clouds. And then there were only the low, muted tones of the priest, the soft rustle as the flag was folded, and the final, muffled echo as the first handfuls of earth hit the casket.

I stood by a willow as the mourners began to move away. And I watched, with bitterness, sorrow and regret, as Walter Cole walked away with them without saying a word to me. We had been close once; partners for a time, then friends and, of all those whose friendship I had lost, it was Walter that I missed the most. He was an educated man. He liked books, and movies that didn't star Steven Seagal or Jean-Claude Van Damme, and good food. He had been best man at my wedding, the box holding the rings clutched so hard in his hand that it had left deep ridges in his palm. I had played with his children. Susan and I had enjoyed dinners, the theater and walks in the park, with Walter and his wife, Lee. And I had sat with him for hours and hours, in cars and bars, in courtrooms and back rooms, and felt the deep, steady pulse of life throbbing beneath our feet.

I remembered one case in Brooklyn, when we were trailing a painter and decorator whom we believed to have killed his wife and somehow disposed of her remains. We were in a bad neighborhood, just northeast of Atlantic Avenue, and Walter smelled so much of cop they could have named a scent after him, but the guy didn't seem to suspect we were there. Maybe nobody told him. We weren't bothering the junkies or the pushers or the whores, and we were so obvious that we couldn't be undercover, so the local color decided that the best thing would be to let us be and not to interfere in whatever we were doing.

Each morning, the guy filled his van with paint cans and brushes and headed off to work, and we followed him. Then, from a distance, we watched as he painted first a house and, a day or two later, the storefront on which he was working, before he dumped the empty cans and headed home.

It took a few days to figure out what he was doing. It was Walter who took a screwdriver and flipped open the lid, as the can lay with its fellows in a Dumpster. It took him two tries, because the paint had dried along the edge. That was what had alerted us, of course: the fact that the paint on the can was dry, not wet.

Inside the can was a hand, a woman's hand. There was still a wedding ring on one of the fingers, and the stump had adhered to the paint at the bottom of the can, so the hand seemed to be emerging from the base. Two hours later we had our warrant and, when we kicked in the door of the painter's place, there were paint cans stacked almost to the ceiling in one corner of the bedroom, each containing a section of his wife's body. Some of them were packed tight with flesh. We found her head in a two-gallon can of white gloss.

That night, Walter had taken Lee out for dinner, and when they went home he held her the whole night through. He didn't make love to her, he said, he just held her, and she understood. I couldn't even remember what I did that night. That was the difference between us; at least, it *was*. I knew better now.

I had done things since then. I had killed in an effort to find, and avenge myself upon the killer of my family, the Traveling Man. Walter knew this, had even used it for his own ends, recognizing that I would tear apart whoever stood in my way. I think that, in some ways, it was a test, a test to see if I would realize his worst fears about me.

And I did.

I caught up with him near the cemetery gate, with the roar of the traffic in our ears, the city's answer to the sound of the sea. Walter was talking with some captain who used to be with the 83rd: Emerson, who was now with Internal Affairs, which maybe explained the look he gave me as I approached. The murder of the pimp Johnny Friday was now a cold case, and I didn't think they'd ever get the guy who killed him. I knew, because I was the guy. I had killed him in a burst of black rage in the months following the deaths of Jennifer and Susan. By the end, I didn't care what Johnny Friday knew or didn't know. I just wanted to kill him for what he had helped to do to a hundred Susans, a thousand Jennifers. I regretted the manner of his death, like I regretted so much else, but regrets weren't going to bring him back. There had been rumors since then, but nothing would ever be proved. Still, Emerson had heard the rumors.

"Parker," he nodded. "Didn't think we'd see you back here."

"Captain Emerson," I replied. "How are things in Infernal Affairs? Being kept busy, I'm sure."

"Always time for one more, Parker," he said, but he didn't smile. He raised a hand to Walter and walked toward the gates, his back straight, his spine held tight by the cords of righteousness.

Walter looked at his feet, his hands in his pockets, then raised his eyes to me. Retirement didn't seem to be doing him much good. He looked uncomfortable and pale, and there were burn marks and cuts where he had shaved that morning. I guessed that he was missing the force, and occasions like this just made him miss it more.

"Like the man said," Walter muttered at last, "I didn't think we'd see you back here."

"I wanted to pay my respects to Greenfield. He was a good man. How's Lee?"

"She's good."

"And the kids."

"They're good." Walter and Emerson were proving to be tough crowds to play one after the other. "Where are you now?" he asked, although his tone said he was only inquiring out of awkwardness.

"I'm back in Maine. It's peaceful. I haven't killed anyone in weeks."

Walter's eyes remained cold. "You should stay up there. You get itchy, you can shoot a squirrel. I've got to go now."

I nodded. "Sure. Thanks for your time."

He didn't reply. As I watched him walk away, I felt a deep, humiliating grief, and I thought: they were right. I should not have come back, not even for a day.

I took the subway to Queensboro Plaza, where I changed onto the N train for Manhattan. As I sat opposite a man reading a self-help book, the sound of the subway and the smell in the train set off a chain of memories, and I recalled something that had happened seven months before, in early May, just as the heat of the summer was beginning to tell. They had been dead for almost five months.

It was late, very late, one Tuesday night. I was taking the subway from Café Con Leche at 81st and Amsterdam back to my apartment in the East Village. I must have dozed off for a time, because when I awoke the car was empty, and the light in the next car down was flickering on and off, black to yellow to black again.

There was a woman sitting in the car, looking down at her hands, her hair obscuring her face. She wore dark pants and a red blouse. Her arms were spread, her palms raised upward, as if she were reading a newspaper, except that her hands were empty.

Her feet were bare and there was blood on the floor beneath them.

I stood and moved down the car until I came to the connecting door. I had no idea where we were, or what the next stop might be. I opened the door, felt the rush of heat from the tunnel, the taste of filth and smog in my mouth as I stepped across the gap and into the darkness of the next car.

The lights flickered on again, but the woman was gone, and

there was no blood on the floor where she had been sitting only moments before. There were three other people in the car: an elderly black woman clutching four oversized plastic bags; a slim, neatly dressed white male wearing glasses, a briefcase on his knees; and a drunk with a ragged beard who lay across four seats, snoring. I was about to turn to the woman when, ahead of me, I saw a shape in black and red briefly illuminated. It was the same woman, sitting in the same position—arms spread, palms up—as she had been when I first saw her. She was even occupying more or less the same seat, except one car farther down again.

And I noticed that the flickering light seemed to have moved down with her, so that once more she was a figure briefly frozen by the faulty lighting. Beside me, the old woman looked up and smiled; and the executive with the briefcase gazed at me unblinking; and the drunk shifted on his seat and awoke, and his eyes were bright and knowing as he watched me.

I moved down the car, closer and closer to the door. Something about the woman was familiar, something in the way she held herself, something in the style of her hair. She did not move, did not look up, and I felt my gut tighten. Around her, the lights weakened, and then were gone. I stepped into the car, the last car before the driver, and I could smell the blood on the floor. I took one step, then another, and another, until my feet slid on something wet and I knew then who she was.

"Susan?" I whispered, but the blackness was silent, a silence broken only by the rushing of the wind in the subway, the rattle of the wheels on the tracks. As the tunnel lights flashed by, I saw her silhouetted against the far door, head down, her arms raised. The light flickered for a second, and I realized that she was not wearing a red blouse. She was not wearing anything. There was only blood: thick, dark blood. The light shone dimly through the skin that had been pulled back from her breasts and arrayed like a cloak over her outstretched arms. She lifted her head, and

I saw a deep-red blur where her face had been, and the sockets of her eyes were empty and ruined.

And the brakes shrieked and the car rocked as the train approached the station. All light left the world and there was only a void until we burst into Houston Street, unnatural illumination flooding the darkness. The smell of blood and perfume lingered in the air, but she was gone.

That was the first time.

The waitress brought us dessert menus. I smiled at her. She smiled back. What's seldom is wonderful.

"She's got a fat ass," remarked Angel, as she walked away. He was dressed in the traditional Angel garb of faded denims and wrinkled check shirt over a black T, and sneakers that were now a filthy mockery of their original white. A black leather jacket hung on the back of his chair.

"I wasn't looking at her ass," I replied. "She has a pretty face."

"So she could be like the spokeswoman for the lardasses, the one they wheel out when they want to look good on TV," offered Louis. "Folks look at her and say, 'Hey, maybe them lardasses ain't so bad after all.'"

As always, Louis looked like a deliberate riposte to his lover. He wore a black, single-breasted Armani suit and a snow-white dress shirt with the collar unbuttoned, the virgin white of the shirt in stark contrast to his own dark features and his shaven, ebony head.

We were sitting in J. G. Melon's at the corner of 74th and Third. I had not seen them in over two months, but these men, this diminutive, white ex-burglar and his enigmatic, soft-spoken boyfriend, were now the closest things to friends I had left. They had stood by me when Jennifer and Susan died, and they had been with me in those last, terrible days in Louisiana as we drew closer to a final confrontation with the Traveling Man. They were outsiders—perhaps that was one of the reasons for our closeness—and Louis in particular was a dangerous man, a hired killer now enjoying a murky, indefinite form of semiretirement, but they were on the side of the angels, even if the angels were not entirely sure that this was a positive development.

Angel laughed loudly—"Spokeswoman for the lardasses," he repeated to himself—and scanned the menu. I tossed a discarded french fry at him.

"Hey, Slim," I said. "Looks like you could skip a couple of sundaes every now and then. You tried to burgle somewhere you'd get stuck in the door. The only places you could break into would be ones with big windows."

"Yeah, Angel," said Louis, stone-faced. "Maybe you could specialize in cathedrals, or the Met."

"I can afford to fill out," replied Angel, throwing him a glare.

"Man, you fill out any more, you be twins."

"Funny, Louis," shrugged Angel. "She's still two tokens on the subway, if you see what I mean."

"What does it matter to you anyway?" I said. "You don't have any right to pass comments about the opposite sex. You're gay. You don't *have* an opposite sex."

"That's just prejudice, Bird."

"Angel, it's not prejudice when someone points out that you're gay. It's just a statement of fact. It's prejudice when you start baiting the wider members of society."

"Hey," he said. "Doesn't change the fact that if you're looking for company, maybe we can help."

I stared at him, and raised an eyebrow. "I think that's unlikely. I get that desperate, I'll blow my head off."

He smiled. "Well, you know, you got that look. I hear that Web site Womenbehindbars.com, is worth a visit."

"Excuse me?" I replied. His smile widened so much you could have slotted toasting bread into it.

"Lot of women out there looking for a guy like you." He turned his right hand into a little gun and fired his index finger at me with a movement of his thumb. It made him look like the cabaret act from gay hell.

"What exactly is Womenbehindbars.com?" I asked. I knew I was being baited, but I sensed something more as well from both Angel and Louis. You're up there alone, Bird, they seemed to say. You don't have too many people you can fall back on, and we can't look out for you from New York City. Sometimes, maybe even before you think you're ready, you have to reach out and find something on which you can rely. You have to try to find a foothold, otherwise you're going to fall and you're going to keep falling until it all goes dark.

Angel shrugged. "Y'know, it's one of those Internet dating services. Some places have more lonely women than others: San Francisco, New York, state prisons . . ."

"You're telling me there's a dating service for women in jail?"

He raised his hands wide. "Sure there is. You know, cons have needs too. You just log on, take a look at the pictures and pick your woman."

"They're in jail, Angel," I reminded him. "It's not as if I can invite them out for dinner and a movie without committing a felony. Plus, I might have put them in jail. I'm not going to try to date anyone I jailed. It'd be too weird."

"So date out of state," said Angel. "You declare anywhere from Yonkers to Lake Champlain a no-go zone, and the rest of the Union's your oyster." He toasted me with his glass, then he and Louis exchanged a look, and I envied them that intimacy.

"Anyway, what are these women in for?" I asked, resigned by now to playing the role of straight man.

"The site don't say," replied Angel. "All it says is their ages, what they're looking for in a guy, and then it gives you a picture. One without numbers underneath it," he added. "Oh, and it tells you whether or not they're willing to relocate, although the answer's pretty obvious. I mean, they *are* in jail. Relocation's probably top of their list of priorities."

"So what does it matter why they're in there?" asked Louis. I noticed that his eyes were watering. I was glad I was providing amusement for him. "The ladies do the crime, do the time, then their debt to society is paid. Long as they ain't cut off a guy's dick and tied it to a helium balloon, you're home free."

"Yeah," said Angel. "You just set some ground rules, and then dip your toes in the pool. Suppose she was a thief. Would you date a thief?"

"She'd steal from me."

"A hooker?"

"Couldn't trust her."

"That's a terrible thing to say."

"Sorry. Maybe you could start a campaign."

Angel shook his head in mock sorrow, then brightened. "How about an assault case? Broken bottle, maybe a kitchen knife. Nothing too serious."

"A kitchen knife and it's nothing too serious? What planet do you live on, Angel? Plastic silverware world?"

"Okay then, a murderer."

"Depends who she killed."

"Her old man."

"Why?"

"The fuck do I know why? You think I was wearing a wire? Do you date her or not?"

"No."

"Shit, Bird, if you're going to be fussy you're never going to meet anyone."

The waitress returned. "Would you gentlemen like to order dessert?"

We all declined, Angel adding: "Nah, I'm sweet enough as it is."

"Cheesy enough, too," said the waitress, and flashed me another grin. Angel reddened and Louis's mouth twitched in an approximation of a smile.

"Three coffees," I said, and grinned back at her. "You just earned yourself a substantial tip."

After the meal, we took a walk in Central Park, stopping to rest by the statue of Alice on the mushroom by the model boat pond. There were no kids sailing their boats on the water, although one or two couples sat huddled together by the bank, watched impassively by Louis. Angel hoisted himself up onto the mushroom, his legs dangling beside me, Alice in turn watching over him.

"How old are you?" I said.

"Young enough to appreciate this," he replied. "So how you doin'?"

"I'm okay. I have good days and bad days."

"How do you tell them apart?"

"On the good days, it doesn't rain."

"The house coming along?" I was completing the renovations on my grandfather's old house in Scarborough. I had already moved in, although there were some repairs still needed.

"Nearly finished. Roof just needs fixing, that's all."

He stayed quiet for a time. "We were only yanking your chain back in the restaurant," he said at last. "We know this is maybe not such a good time for you. It'll be the first anniversary soon, won't it?"

"Yeah, December twelfth."

"You okay with that?"

"I'll visit the grave, have a mass said. I don't know how difficult it will be." In truth, I was dreading the day. For some reason, it was important to me that the house should be finished by then, that I should be firmly established there. I wanted its stability, its links to a past that I remembered with happiness. I wanted a place that I could call home, and in which I could try to rebuild my life.

"Let us know the details. We'll come up."

"I'd appreciate it."

He nodded. "Until then, you need to look out for yourself, you know what I mean? You spend too much time alone, you're likely to go crazy. You hear from Rachel?"

"No." Rachel Wolfe and I had been lovers, for a time. She had come down to Louisiana to assist in the hunt for the Traveling Man, bringing with her a background in psychology and a love for me that I did not understand and that I was unable to fully return, not then. She had been hurt that summer, physically and emotionally. We had not spoken since the hospital, but I knew she was in Boston. I had even watched her cross the campus one day, her red hair glowing in the late morning light, but I could not bring myself to intrude upon her solitude, or her pain.

Angel stretched and changed the subject. "Meet anyone interesting at the funeral?"

"Emerson."

"The Internal Affairs schmuck? That must have been a joy."

"Always a pleasure meeting Emerson. Guy just stopped short of measuring me up for a set of manacles and a suit with stripes on it. Walter Cole was there too."

"He have anything to say to you?"

"Nothing good."

"He's a righteous man, and they're the worst kind."

I glanced at my watch. "I've got to go. I have a flight to catch."

Louis turned and strolled back to us, the muscles on his slim, six-six frame obvious even beneath the suit and overcoat. "Angel," he said, "I found you on a mushroom, I'd burn the crop. You makin' Alice look ill."

"Uh-huh. Alice saw you coming for her, she'd figure she was going to be mugged. The White Rabbit you ain't." I watched as

Angel eased himself down, using his hands to arrest his slide. Then he raised them, the palms now lightly coated with grime, and approached Louis's immaculate form.

"Angel, you touch me, man, you be wavin' good-bye with a stump. I'm warnin' you . . ."

I walked past them and looked out over the park and the stillness of the pond. I had a growing feeling of unease for which I could find no cause, a sense that, while I was in New York, events were happening elsewhere that somehow affected me.

And in the water of the pond, dark clouds gathered, forming and reforming, and birds flew through the shallows as if to drown. In the dimness of this reflected world, the bare trees sent searching branches down into the depths, like fingers digging deeper and deeper into a half-remembered past.

CHAPTER THREE

FOR ME, the first sign that winter is coming has always been the change in the coloration of the paper birches. Their trunks, usually white or gray, turn yellow-green in the fall, blending into the riot of chimney red, burning gold and dying amber as the trees turn. I look at the birches and know that winter is on its way.

In November, the first heavy frosts arrive and the roads become treacherous, the blades of grass fragile as crystal, so that when you walk the ghosts of your footsteps trail behind like the ranks of lost souls. In the skeletal branches above, tree sparrows huddle together; cedar waxwings trapeze from bough to bough; and, at night, the hawk owls come, hunting for prey in the darkness. In Portland harbor, which never entirely freezes, there are mallards, and harlequin ducks, and eiders.

Even in the coldest weather, the harbor, the fields, the woods, all are alive. Blue jays fly, and brown winter wrens; finches feed on birch seed. Tiny, unseen things crawl, hunt, live, die. Lacewings hibernate under the loose bark on the trees. Caddis-fly larvae carry houses made from plant debris on their backs, and aphids huddle on the alders. Wood frogs sleep frozen beneath piles of leaf mold, and beetles and back swimmers, newts and spotted salamanders, their tails thick with stored fat, all flicker in the icy waters above. There are carpenter ants, and snow fleas, and spiders, and black mourning cloak butterflies that flit across the snow like burned paper. White-footed mice and woodland voles and pygmy shrews scurry through the slash, ever-wary of the foxes and weasels and the vicious, porcupine-hunting fishers that share the habitat. The snowshoe hare changes its coat to white in response to the diminishing daylight hours, the better to hide itself from its predators.

Because the predators never go away.

It is dark by four when winter comes, and lives are compressed to meet the new restrictions set by nature. People return to a lifestyle that would have been familiar in ways to the earliest settlers who traveled along the great river valleys toward the interior in search of timber and farmland. Folks move about less, preferring to remain in their homes. They complete their daily tasks before the darkness sets in. They think of seeding, of the welfare of animals, of children, of their old. When they do leave their houses they wrap up warm and keep their heads down, so that the wind does not blow the sand from the road into their eyes.

On the coldest nights, the branches of the trees crack in the darkness, the sky is lit by the passing angels of the aurora borealis, and young calves die.

There will be false thaws in January, more in February and March, but the trees will still be bare. The ground turns to mud in the warmth after the dawn, then freezes again at night; tracks become impassable by day, and dangerous by dark.

And still the people will gather in the warmth of their homes, and wait for the ice to crack in April.

•   •   •

At Old Orchard Beach, south of Portland, the amusement parks stand silent and empty. Most of the motels are closed, the AC vents covered with black plastic bags. The waves break gray and cold, and the wheels of the cars make a deep thudding sound as they cross the old railroad tracks on the main street. It has been this way for as long as I can remember, ever since I was a boy.

When the trees began to turn, before the paper birches changed from bone white to the colors of a beautiful decay, the grifter Saul Mann would pack his bags and prepare to leave Old Orchard for Florida.

"Winter is for rubes," he would say, as he laid his clothes— his huckster's ties, his bright JC Penney jackets, his two-tone shoes—into a tan suitcase. Saul was a small, dapper man, with hair that was jet black for as long as I knew him and a small belly that strained only slightly the buttons of his vest. His features were relentlessly average, strangely unmemorable, as if they had been expressly ordered for that purpose. His manner was friendly and unthreatening, and he wasn't greedy, so he rarely, if ever, overstepped his own limits. He took people for tens and twenties, sometimes a fifty, occasionally, if he thought the mark could take the loss, for a couple of hundred. He generally worked alone although, if the con required it, he would hire a steerer to draw in the pigeons. Sometimes, if things were not going well, he would find work with the carnies and fleece folk with rigged games.

Saul had never married. "A married man's a mark for his wife," Saul would say. "Never marry, unless she's richer than you, dumber than you and prettier than you. Anything less than that, you're a pigeon."

He was wrong, of course. I married a woman who took walks in the park with me, who made love to me and gave me a child, and whom I never really knew until she was gone. Saul Mann never had that joy; he was so worried about becoming a mark that life swindled him without him even noticing.

Beside Saul as he packed, in a second, smaller, black patent-leather bag, were the tools of the bunco, the armory of the short-con artist. There was the wallet stuffed with twenty-dollar bills that, on closer examination, revealed themselves to be one twenty dollar bill plus half of the *Maine Sunday Telegram* carefully cut up to the size of twenty-dollar bills and packed beneath the single genuine article. The con artist "finds" the wallet, asks the mark's advice on what to do with it, agrees to entrust it to his safekeeping until the legal obligation to hand it over is negated by the passage of time, encourages him to give over a one-hundred-dollar deposit as a gesture of goodwill, just to be sure that he's not going to swindle anyone out of a share of the cash and, hey, the con man is up eighty bucks on the deal, minus the cost of a new wallet and another copy of the *Maine Sunday Telegram* for the next mish roll.

There were fake diamond rings, all glass and paste and metal so cheap it took a week to get the green stain from your finger, and bottle caps for the three-shell game. There were cards with more marks than Omaha Beach on D-Day. And there were other, more elaborate cons too: papers heavy with official seals which promised the bearer the sun, the moon and the stars; lotteries that guaranteed the winner precisely zero percent of nothing; checks for ten or twenty different accounts, each with barely enough in them to keep them active but still sufficiently open to enable checks to be successfully written on them on a Friday night, giving them a whole two days of fiscal respectability before they bounced.

During the summer months, Saul Mann would trawl the resorts of the Maine coast looking for pigeons. He would arrive at Old Orchard Beach religiously on the third day of July, hire himself the cheapest room he could find, and work the beach for a week, maybe two at most, until his face started to become familiar. Then he would head up toward Bar Harbor and do the same, always moving, never staying too long, picking his marks carefully. And when he had amassed sufficient funds and the crowds began to peter away after Labor Day, when the trees slowly began to turn, Saul Mann would pack his bags and move to Florida to scam the winter tourists.

My grandfather didn't like him or, at least, he didn't trust him, and trust and like were the same thing in my grandfather's book. "He asks you to lend him a dollar, don't do it," he warned me, time and time again. "You'll get back ten cents if you get back anything at all."

But Saul never asked me for a thing. I met him first when I was doing summer work in the arcades at Old Orchard, taking money from little kids in exchange for soft toys whose eyes were held in place by half-inch-long pins and whose limbs were connected to the torso by the will of God. Saul Mann told me about the carny, about the joint scams: the basketball shoot with the overinflated ball and the too-small ring, the balloon darts with the soft balloons, the shooting gallery with the skewed sights on the rifles. I watched him work the crowds, and I learned as I watched. He targeted the elderly, the greedy, the desperate, the ones who were so uncertain of themselves that they would trust another man's judgment above their own. He sometimes went for the dumb ones, but he knew that the dumb ones could turn mean, or that maybe they wouldn't have enough cash to make the scam worthwhile, or that they might possess a low cunning that made them naturally distrustful.

Better still were the ones who thought they were smart, the ones who had good jobs in medium-sized towns, who believed that they could never be taken in by a grifter. They were the prime targets, and Saul relished them when they came. He died in 1994, in a retirement home in Florida, among the people he used to take as his marks, and he probably swindled them at canasta until the last breath left his body, until God reached down and showed him that, in the end, everybody is a mark.

Here is what Saul Mann told me.

Never give the suckers a break: they'll run if you do. Never have pity: pity is the mother of charity, and charity is giving money away, and a grifter never gives money away. And never force them to do anything, because the best scams of all are the ones where they choose to come to you.

Lay the bait, wait, and they will always come to you.

The snows came early that December to Greenville and Beaver Cove and Dark Hollow and the other central towns on the very rim of the great northern wilderness. The first flurries fell and people looked to the skies before hurrying on, a new quickness in their steps, spurred on by the cold they could already feel in their bones. Fires were lit, and children were wrapped up warm in bright red scarves and mittens colored like rainbows, and warnings were given about staying out late, about hurrying home before darkness fell, and stories were told in school yards about little children who had strayed from the path and were found cold and dead when the thaws came.

And in the woods, among the maples and birches and oaks, through the spruce and hemlock and white pine, something moved. It walked slowly and deliberately. It knew these woods, had known them for a long, long time. Every footfall was surely placed, every fallen tree anticipated, every ancient stone wall, long overtaken by the renewed forests and lost amid the undergrowth, was a place to rest, to draw breath, before moving on.

In the winter blackness, it moved with a new purpose. Something that had been lost had now been found again. Something unknown had been revealed, as if a veil had been drawn back by the hand of God. It passed by the derelict remains of an old farmhouse, its roof long collapsed, its walls now no more than a shelter for mice. It reached the crest of a hill and moved along its edge, the moon bright above it, the trees whispering in the darkness.

And it devoured the stars as it went.

CHAPTER FOUR

I T HAD BEEN three months since I returned to Scarborough, following the death of the man who had taken my wife and child from me. I was back in the house where I had spent my teenage years after my father died, and that my grandfather had left to me in his will. In the East Village, where I lived for some time after my wife and child died, the old lady who owned my rent-controlled apartment had ushered me out with a smile on her face as she calculated the potential increase she could apply to the next tenant. She was a seventy-two-year-old Italian-American who had lost her husband in Korea, and she was usually about as friendly as a hungry rat. Angel suggested that her husband had probably handed himself over to the enemy to avoid being sent home to her again.

The Scarborough house was where my mother had been born and where my grandfather still lived at the time of my father's death, a widower alone but for his dog and his memories. Scarborough was changing when I arrived at the end of the seventies. Economic prosperity meant that it was becoming a satellite town for Portland and, although some of the older residents still held on to their land, land that had been in some families for generations, the developers were paying premium prices and more and more people were selling up. But Scarborough was still the kind of community where you knew your mailman and who his family was and he, in turn, knew the same about you.

From my grandfather's house on Spring Street, I could cycle north into Portland or south to Higgins Beach, Ferry Beach, Western Beach or Scarborough Beach itself, or down to the head at Prouts Neck to look out on Bluff Island and Stratton Island and the Atlantic Ocean.

Prouts Neck is a small point of land that protrudes into Saco Bay about twelve miles south of Portland itself. It was where the artist Winslow Homer set up house near the end of the nineteenth century. His family bought up most of the land on the Neck and Winslow vetted his prospective neighbors carefully since, by and large, he wanted to be left to his own devices. The folks out on the Neck are still that way. There's been a fancy yacht club there since 1926 and a private beach club with membership limited to those who live or rent summer homes in the area and who belong to the Prouts Neck Association. Scarborough Beach remains public and free and there's public access to Ferry Beach, close by the Black Point Inn on the Neck. Since it was beside Ferry Beach that Chester Nash, Paulie Block and six other men had lost their lives, the Neckers were going to have a lot to talk about when they returned in the summer.

In the old house, the past hung in the air like motes of dust waiting to be illuminated by the sharp rays of memory. It was there, surrounded by remembrances of a happier youth, that I hoped to set about putting old ghosts to rest: the ghosts of my wife and child, who had haunted me for so long but had maybe now achieved a kind of peace, a peace not yet mirrored in my own soul; of my father; of my mother, who had taken me away from the city in an effort to find solace for both of us; of Rachel, who now seemed lost to me; and of my grandfather, who had taught me about duty and humanity and the importance of making enemies of whom a man could be proud.

I had moved out of the Inn at St. John on Congress Street in Portland as soon as most of the house had been made habitable. At night, the wind made the plastic on the roof slap like the beating of dark, leathery wings. The final job left to do was the shingling, which was why I was sitting on my porch with a cup of coffee and *The New York Times* at 9 A.M. the next morning, waiting for Roger Simms. Roger was fifty, a straight-backed man with long, thin muscles and a face the color of rosewood. He could do just about anything that involved a hammer, a saw and a natural craftsman's ability to bring order out of the chaos of nature and neglect.

He arrived right on time, his aged Nissan belching blue fumes that tainted the air like nicotine on a lung. He stepped out of the car wearing paint-splattered jeans, a denim shirt and a blue sweater that was little more than an assortment of holes held together by yarn. A pair of brown cowhide work gloves hung from one of the ass pockets of his jeans and a black watch cap was pulled down over his ears. From beneath it, strands of dark hair hung like the legs of a hermit crab. A cigarette dangled from his lips, a gravity-defying pillar of ash forming at the tip.

I gave him a mug of coffee and he drank it while examining the roof critically, as if seeing it for the first time. He had been up there about three times already, checking the rafters and the roof supports and measuring the angles, so I didn't think it was likely to hold any surprises for him. He thanked me for the coffee and handed back the mug. "Thanks" was the first word he had said to me since he arrived; Roger was a great worker but the amount of air he wasted on unnecessary small talk wouldn't have saved a gnat's life.

We had already laid down strips of lath in preparation for the shingles, using pieces of two-by-four cut lengthways in half and oiled with wood preservative. Now, with the air crisp and cold and no promise of rain in the sky, we began our work. There was something in the placing of shingles, its rhythms and routines, that made it an almost meditative exercise. Traveling methodically across the face of the roof, I reached for a shingle, placed it on the one below, adjusted its exposure using a notch on the handle of my hammer, nailed down the shingle, reached for another and began the process again. I found a kind of peace in it and the morning passed quickly. I decided not to share my meditative speculations with Roger. Somehow, those who do jobs like roofing for a living tend to resent the musings of amateurs on the nature of the task. Roger would probably have thrown his hammer at me.

We worked for four hours, each of us resting when the mood took him, until I climbed carefully down and told Roger that I was heading up to the Seng Thai on Congress to get us some food. He grunted something that I took as an okay and I started up the Mustang and drove toward South Portland. As usual, there were plenty of cars on Maine Mall Road, people nosing about in Filene's or heading for the movies, eating in the Old Country Buffet or sizing up the motels on the strip. I drove past the airport, along Johnson and, finally, onto Congress. I parked in the lot behind the Inn at St. John between a Pinto and a Fiat, then headed down a block, bought the food and dumped it on the backseat of the car.

There was still a crate of my stuff behind the reception desk at the inn and I figured I might as well pick it up while I was in the area. I opened the door and entered the ornate, old-style lobby, with its ancient radio and its neat piles of tourist brochures. Mark, who was manning the desk, hauled the crate out, gave me a smile and then went back to counting receipts. I left him to it.

When I stepped back into the lot, I saw that someone had boxed me in. A huge black Cadillac Coupe De Ville, forty years old and virtually an antique, was parked behind the Mustang, leaving me with no way to get out. The car had whitewall tires and restored tan upholstery, and the distinctive pontoon bumpers at the front were shiny and intact. A map of Maine lay on the backseat and it had Massachusetts plates but, apart from that, there was nothing about the car to identify its owner. It could have come straight from a museum exhibit.

I placed the crate in the trunk of the Mustang and headed back into the inn, but Mark said he'd never seen the Cadillac before. He offered to have it towed but I decided to try to track down the owner first. I asked in Pizza Villa across the street but they didn't know anything about it either. I tried the Seng Thai and the local bars until, still unsuccessful, I recrossed the street and slapped the roof of the Cadillac in frustration.

"Nice car," said a voice, as the echo of the slap faded. The voice was high, almost girlish, the words drawn out with what sounded more like malice than admiration, the sibilance in the first word almost menacing.

At the entrance to the inn's back lot, a man was leaning against the wall. He was short and squat, probably no more than five-five and maybe 230 pounds. He wore a tan raincoat, belted at the front, with brown pants and a pair of brown brogues.

He had a face from a horror movie.

His head was completely bald, with a rounded crown that ran into wrinkles of fat at the back. The head seemed to grow wider instead of narrower from the temples to the mouth, before it lost itself in his shoulders. He had no neck, or at least nothing that was worthy of the name. His face was deathly pale, apart from his long, thick, red lips, which were stretched into a rictus of a grin. He had wide dark nostrils, set in a flattened snout of a nose, and his eyes were so gray as to be almost colorless, the pupils like black pinpoints at their center, tiny dark worlds in a cold, hostile universe.

He pulled himself from the wall and advanced slowly and

steadily, and as he did so I caught the smell. It was indistinct and masked by some cheap cologne, but it caused me to hold my breath and take a step back from him nonetheless. It was the smell of earth and blood, the stench of rotting meat and stale animal fear that hangs in a slaughterhouse at the end of a long day's butchering.

"Nice car," he repeated, and a fat white hand emerged from one of his pockets, the fingers like thick, pale slugs that had spent too long in dark places. He caressed the roof of the Mustang appreciatively, and it seemed as if the paint would corrode spontaneously beneath his fingers. It was the touch a child molester would give a kid in a playground when his mother's back was turned. For some reason, I felt the urge to push him away, but I was stopped by a stronger instinct that told me not to touch him. I couldn't have explained why, but something foul appeared to emanate from him that discouraged any contact. To touch him, it seemed, would be to blight oneself, to risk contamination or contagion.

But it was more than that. He exuded a sense of extreme lethality, a capacity for inflicting hurt and pain that was so profound as to be almost sexual. It seeped from his pores and flowed viscously over his skin, seeming almost to drip visibly from the tips of his fingers and the end of his ugly, brutish nose. Despite the cold, tiny beads of perspiration glittered on his forehead and upper lip, spangling his soft features with moisture. Touch him, I sensed, and your fingers would sink into his flesh, the skin yielding clammily to the pressure as it sucked you in.

And then he would kill you, because that was what he did. I was certain of it.

"Your car?" he asked. Those gray eyes glittered coldly and the tip of a pink tongue appeared between his lips, like a snake testing the air.

"Yes, it's my car," I replied. "That your Cadillac?"

He didn't seem to notice the question, or decided not to notice it. Instead, he passed another long caressing movement along the roof of the Mustang.

"Good car, the Mustang," he said, nodding to himself, and again there was that intense sibilance on the *S* sound, like water dropped on a hot stove. "Me and the Mustang, we got a lot in common."

He moved closer to me, as if to share some deep, darkly funny secret. I could smell his breath on me, sweet and overripe as late-summer fruit.

"We both went to hell after nineteen seventy."

And then he laughed, a low hissing sound like gas escaping from a corpse. "Better take care of that car, make sure nothing happens to it," he said. "A man's got to look out for what's his. He should take care of his own business, and keep his nose out of other people's." He walked around the back of the car before entering the Cadillac, so I had to turn to watch him.

"Be seeing you again, Mr. Parker," he said. Then the Caddy started with a low, confident rumble and the car made an illegal left onto Congress and headed in the direction of downtown Portland.

CHAPTER FIVE

ROGER DIDN'T LOOK too happy about being kept waiting for his food, because the permanent frown lines on his forehead had dipped by about half an inch by the time I got back.

"You were a coon's age," he muttered as he took the food. It was one of the longest sentences I had ever heard him speak.

I picked at my chicken and rice, but my appetite was gone. I was bothered by the appearance of the fat, bald man on Congress, although I couldn't tell why, exactly, apart from the fact that he knew my name and made my skin crawl.

Roger and I returned to the roof, a chill wind now forcing the pace a little so that we finished just as the light was starting to fade. I paid Roger and he nodded his thanks, then headed back to town. My fingers were numb from working on the roof but the job had to be done before the heavy snows came, or else I'd be living in an ice castle. I took a hot shower to remove the grit from my hair and fingers, and was just making a pot of coffee when I heard a car pull up outside.

For a moment, I didn't recognize her as she stepped from the Honda Civic. She had grown since I last saw her, and her hair was lighter, tinted with some kind of coloring. She had a woman's body, large-breasted and generous at the hips. I felt a little embarrassed noticing the changes in her. After all, Ellen Cole was barely into her twenties, and Walter Cole's daughter to boot.

"Ellen?" I stepped from the porch and opened my arms to her as she hugged me.

"It's good to see you, Bird," she said softly, and I hugged her tightly in response. Ellen Cole: I had watched her grow up. I could remember dancing with her at my wedding, the shy grin she threw back at her younger sister, Lauren, her tongue stuck out teasingly between her lips at Susan in her bridal gown. I remembered, too, sitting on the steps of Walter's porch with a beer, and Ellen beside me, her hands clasped around her knees, as I tried to explain why boys sometimes behaved like assholes to even the most beautiful of girls. I liked to think that was one area in which my expertise was beyond doubt.

She had been a friend to Susan, and Jennifer had loved her. My daughter never cried out when Susan and I left her for an evening, as long as Ellen was there to baby-sit her. The child would sit in the older girl's arms, toying with her fingers, eventually falling asleep with her head on her lap. Ellen had about her a kind of strength that had its roots in an immense store of kindness and compassion, a strength that inspired trust in those smaller and weaker than she.

Two days after Susan and Jennifer had died, I found her waiting for me alone at the funeral home as I arrived to make arrangements for the bodies. Others had offered to accompany me, but I didn't want them there. I think I was already retreating into my own strange world of loss at that point. I didn't know how long she had been waiting for me there, her little Honda parked in the lot, but she came to me, and she held me for a long, long time, and then she stood beside me as I looked at pictures of caskets and cars, never letting go of my hand. In her eyes, I saw the depths of my own pain reflected and I knew that, like me, she felt the loss of Jennifer as an absence in her arms, and the loss of Susan as a silence in her heart.

And when we left, the strangest thing happened. I sat with her in her car, and for the first time in days, I cried. That deep, still, placid thing inside Ellen drew the pain and hurt and grief from me, like the lancing of a wound. She held me again, and for a time, the clouds cleared, and I was able to go on.

Behind Ellen, a young man stepped from the driver's side of the car. He had dark skin and long black hair that hung lankly to his shoulders. His dress code was slacker chic, apart from his Zamberlan hiking boots: jeans, T-shirt loose over the top of his jeans, denim shirt hanging open over everything else. He shivered a little as he watched me with suspicious eyes.

"This is Ricky," said Ellen. *"Ricardo,"* she added, with a vaguely Spanish inflection on the word. "Ricky, come meet Bird."

He shook hands firmly, then put one arm protectively around Ellen's shoulders. It seemed to me that Ricky was territorial and insecure, a bad combination. I kept an eye on him as we went into the house, just in case he decided to make his mark by taking a leak against my door.

We sat in my kitchen and drank coffee from big blue mugs. Ricky didn't say a whole lot, not even "Thanks." I wondered if he'd ever met Roger. Put the two of them together and you'd have the world's shortest conversation.

"What are you doing here?" I asked Ellen.

She shrugged. "We're heading north. I've never been far north before. We're going to make for Moosehead Lake, see Mount Katahdin, whatever. Maybe we'll rent some Ski-Doos."

Ricky stood up and asked where the john was. I directed him and he sloped off, slouching from side to side as he walked like a man with his feet in parallel ditches.

"Where did you find the Latin lover?" I asked.

"He's a psychology major," she replied.

"Really?" I tried to keep the cynicism out of my voice. Maybe Ricky was trying to kill two birds with one stone by taking psychology so he could analyze himself.

"He's really nice, Bird. He's just a little shy with strangers."

"You make him sound like a dog."

She stuck her tongue out at me in response.

"School finished?"

She dodged the question. "I have some study time coming."

"Hmm. What are you planning on studying? Biology?"

"Ha-ha." She didn't smile. I guessed that Ricky had pushed thoughts of semester exams from her mind.

"How's your mom?"

"Good."

She stayed silent for a moment.

"She worries about you and Dad. He told her you were at the funeral in Queens yesterday, but that you didn't have much to say to each other. I think she feels that you should sort out whatever happened between you."

"It's not that easy."

She nodded. "I've heard them talking," she said softly. "Is what he says about you true?"

"Some of it, yes."

She bit down on her lip, then seemed to reach a decision. "You should talk to him. You were his friend, and he doesn't have many of those."

"Most of us don't," I replied. "And I've tried talking to him, Ellen, but he's judged me and found me wanting. Your father's a good man, but not everything good fits his definition."

Ricky came back into the room and the conversation sort of died. I offered them my bed for the night but was kind of glad when Ellen declined. I'd probably never be able to sleep there again if I had visions of Ricky humping in it. They decided to spend the night in Portland instead of Augusta, with the intention of heading straight for the Great North Woods the next morning. I suggested the Inn at St. John, and told them to say that I had sent them. Apart from that, I left them to it, although I was pretty sure I didn't want to know what "it" was. Somehow, I didn't imagine Walter Cole would want to know either.

After they had gone, I got in the car and drove back into Portland to work out in the Bay Club at One City Center. Slating the roof had been exercise in itself, but I was trying to work off the little handles of fat that were clinging to my sides like determined children. I spent forty-five minutes doing peripheral hard-flow circuits, constantly alternating leg and upper-body exercises until my heart was pounding and my shirt was soaked with sweat. When I had finished, I showered and looked at the little fat deposits in the mirror to see if they were getting any smaller. I was almost thirty-five, I had gray hairs invading the blackness of my hair, and I was two hundred pounds of insecurity in a five-eleven frame. I needed to get a life—that, or liposuction.

The white Christmas lights glowed in the trees of the Old Port as I left the Bay Club, so that, from a distance, they seemed to be burning. I walked to Exchange to pick up some books in Books Etc., then continued down to Java Joe's to nurse a large one and read the newspapers. I rustled through the *Village Voice* to find out Dan Savage's latest views on sex with eggs or urinary games. This week, Dan was dealing with a guy who said he wasn't homosexual, he just liked having sex with men. Dan Savage didn't seem to see the difference. Frankly, neither did I. I tried to imagine what Angel would have said to the guy and then figured even the *Voice* wouldn't print what Angel would have said to him.

It had started to rain and wet streaks marked the windows

like cuts on crystal. I watched the rain for a time, then returned to the *Voice*. As I did so, I was conscious of a figure moving toward me and a rank smell in my nostrils. My skin prickled with unease.

"Can I ask you a question?" said a distinctive voice. I looked up and started. The same coldly amused eyes watched me from the doughlike face, rain glistening on the bald head. The mingled scents of blood and cologne were stronger now, and I drew back a little from the table.

"Do you want to find God?" he continued, with the kind of concerned look that doctors give smokers when they start patting their pockets for cigarettes in the waiting room. In his pale hand, he held a crumpled Bible pamphlet, a crude pen drawing of a child and its mother visible on one side.

I looked at him in puzzlement, then my face cleared. I thought for a moment that he might be some kind of Jesus freak, although if he was then Jesus was scraping the bottom of the barrel for recruits. "When God wants me, he'll know where to find me," I replied and went back to reading the *Voice*, my eyes on the page but my attention riveted to the man before me.

"How do you know that this isn't God looking for you now?" he said, as he sat down across from me.

I realized that I should have kept my mouth shut. If he was a religious nut, then talking to him would only encourage him. These types act like monks who've just been given a weekend off from their vows of silence. Except this guy didn't seem like the religious kind, and I got the feeling that there was a subtext to his questions that I hadn't quite grasped.

"I'd always hoped He'd be taller," I told him.

"There's a change coming," said the bald man. His eyes had a kind of intense look to them now. "There'll be no place for sinners, for divorcees, for fornicators, for sodomites, for women who don't respect their husbands."

"I think you've just covered some of my hobbies, and all of

my friends," I said, folding the paper and taking a last, regretful sip of my coffee. It just wasn't my day. "Wherever they end up sounds good to me too."

He watched me carefully, like a snake preparing to strike if it saw an opening. "No place for a man who comes between another man and his wife, or his little boy." There was audible menace in his words now. He smiled and I could see his teeth, small and yellow like the fangs of a rodent. "I'm looking for someone, Mr. Parker. I think you may be able to help me find him." His obscenely soft red lips stretched so far that I thought they might burst and shower me with blood.

"Who are you?" I asked.

"It doesn't matter who I am."

I looked around the coffee shop. The kid behind the counter was distracted by a girl at the window table and there was no one else sitting down here at the rear of the shop.

"I'm looking for Billy Purdue," he continued. "I was hoping you might know where he is."

"What do you want with him?"

"He has something that belongs to me. I want to claim it."

"I'm sorry, I don't know any Billy Purdue."

"I think you're telling lies, Mr. Parker." The tone and volume of his voice didn't change, but the threat of danger it contained rose a notch.

I flipped back my jacket to reveal the butt of my gun.

"Mister, I think you have the wrong person," I said. "Now I'm going to leave and if you get up before I've gone, I'll use this gun on your head. You understand me?"

The smile didn't flicker, but his eyes were now dead. "I understand," he said, and again there was that terrible sibilance in his voice. "I don't think you can be of help to me after all."

"Don't let me see you again," I said.

He nodded to himself. "Oh, you won't see me," he replied, and this time the threat was explicit. I kept him in sight until I reached the door, then watched as he took the pamphlet and set it alight with a brass Zippo. All the time, his eyes never left my face.

I retrieved my car from the parking garage at Temple and took a ride by Rita Ferris's place, but the lights were out and there was no reply when I rang the bell. Then I drove from Portland to Scarborough Downs until I came to Ronald Straydeer's place close by the junction of Payne Road and Two Rod Road. I pulled in beside Billy Purdue's silver trailer and knocked on the door, but the trailer was quiet and no lights burned inside. I peered in the window, cupping my fingers at the glass, but the place still looked a mess. Billy's car stood to the right of the trailer. The hood was cold.

I heard a noise from behind me and turned, half expecting to see that strange head erupting like a white sore from its tan raincoat. Instead, there was only Ronald Straydeer, dressed in black denims, sandals and a Sea Dogs T-shirt, his short dark hair hidden by a white baseball cap decorated with a red lobster. He held an AK-47 in his hands.

"I thought you were someone else," he said, looking at the gun with embarrassment.

"Like who? The Vietcong?" I knew that Ronald swore by his AK. A lot of men who had served in Vietnam did likewise. Ronald once told me that their standard-issue rifle, the M1, used to jam in the rains of Southeast Asia, and they would routinely replace them with AK-47s stolen from the bodies of Vietcong. Ronald's gun looked old enough to be a war souvenir, which it probably was.

Ronald shrugged. "Ain't loaded anyhow."

"It's okay, Ronald. I'm looking for Billy. You see him?"

He shook his head. "Not since yesterday. He hasn't been around." He looked unhappy, as if he wanted to say more.

"Has anyone else been looking for him?"

"I don't know. Maybe. I thought I saw someone last night looking in the trailer, but I could be mistaken. I didn't have my glasses on."

"You're getting old," I said.

"Yuh, he could have been old," replied Ronald, seemingly mishearing me.

"What did you say?"

But he had already lost interest. "I ever tell you about my dog?" he began, and I figured that Ronald had told me just about everything I might find useful.

"Yeah, Ronald," I said, as I walked back to the car. "Maybe we'll talk about him again, another time."

"You don't mean that, Charlie Parker," he said, but he smiled as he spoke.

"You're right," I smiled back, "I don't."

That night, cold rain fell like nails on my newly shingled roof. It didn't leak, not even from the parts that I had done. I felt a deep satisfaction as I drifted off to sleep, the wind rattling the windows and causing the boards of the house to creak and settle. I had spent many years falling asleep to the sounds of those boards, to the gentle murmur of my mother's voice in the living room beyond, to the rhythmic tapping of my grandfather's pipe on the porch rail. There was still a mark on the rail, an ocher stain of tobacco and worn wood. I had not painted over it, a sentimental gesture that surprised me.

I can't recall why I awoke, but some deep sense of disquiet had penetrated through my REM sleep and drawn me back into the darkness of night. The rain had stopped and the house seemed peaceful, but the hairs on the back of my neck were almost rigid and my perceptions were immediately razor-sharp, the mugginess of sleep dispelled by the instinctive knowledge that some danger was near.

I slipped silently from my bed and pulled on a pair of jeans. My Smith & Wesson lay in its holster by my bed. I removed the gun and thumbed the safety. The bedroom door was open, the way I had left it. I pulled it a little farther, the well-oiled hinges moving silently, and carefully placed a foot on the bare boards of the hallway.

My foot hit something soft and damp and I drew it back immediately. The moonlight shone through the windows beside the front door, bathing the hallway in a silvery light. It illuminated an old coatrack, and some paint cans and a ladder that lay to my right. It also shone on a set of muddy footprints that ran from the back door, through the kitchen, up to my bedroom door and then into the living room. The mark of my bare foot lay in the print nearest the bedroom door.

I checked the living room and the bathroom before making my way to the kitchen. I could feel my heart thumping in my chest and my breath was white as the cold night air invaded my home. I counted to three in my head then came in fast through the kitchen door, the gun panning around the room.

It was empty, but the back door was open slightly. Someone had jimmied the lock then made his way—I assumed it was male by the size of the boot prints—through the house, and watched me while I slept. I recalled the bald-headed grotesque I had encountered the day before and the thought of him observing me from the shadows made me sick to my stomach. I opened the back door fully and scanned the yard. Leaving the kitchen and porch light off, I slipped on a pair of work boots that I kept in the kitchen beside the door, then stepped outside and walked once around the house. There were more prints on the porch and in the mud below. At my bedroom window they turned slightly, where the visitor had stood watching me from outside.

I went back into the house, dug out my Maglite and threw on a sweater, then traced the tracks through the mud and out onto the road. There had been little traffic and it was still possible to see where the boot marks petered out on the tarmac. I stood on the empty road, looking left and right, then returned to the house.

It was only when I turned on the kitchen light that I noticed what lay on the table in the corner of the room. I picked it up using a piece of paper towel and turned it over in my hand.

It was a small wooden clown, its body made up of a series of brightly painted rings that could be removed by twisting the clown's smiling head off. I sat looking at it for a time, then placed it carefully in a plastic bag and left it by the sink. I locked the back door, checked all the windows and returned to bed.

I must have drifted off into an uneasy sleep at some point, because I dreamed. I dreamed that I saw a shape moving through the night, black against the stars. I saw a tree standing alone in a clearing and shapes moving beneath it. I smelled blood and sickly sweet perfume. Squat, white fingers moved across my bare chest.

And I saw a light die, and I heard a child crying in the darkness.

CHAPTER SIX

THE FIRST GRAY LIGHT of dawn had appeared at the window and the ground had frozen again when I rose and returned to the kitchen. I looked at the shape of the clown in the bag, its contours masked, its long red nose jutting through the white plastic, its colors dimly visible like a faded ghost of itself.

I slipped on my running gear and started for U.S. 1. Before I left, I made sure all the doors and windows were locked, something that I didn't ordinarily do. I turned onto Spring Street and headed down to the Mussey Road intersection, the red-brick exterior and white wood steeple of the Scarborough First Baptist Church to my left and the 8 Corners store straight ahead. I continued on Spring to 114 and kept going, the road quiet, the pine trees whispering above me. I passed Scarborough High School on my right, where I had attended school after moving to Maine, even getting a few games with the Redskins one spring when half the team went down with flu. To my left, the parking lot of the Shop n Save was silent, but there was already traffic ahead on the untidy strip of U.S. 1. It had always been untidy: by the time zoning began in the

1980s, it was too late to save it. Then again, maybe it's in the nature of U.S.1 to be this way, because it looks the same in just about every place I've ever been.

When I first arrived in Scarborough there was only one mall in the town, the Orion Center. It had the Mammoth Mart department store, which was kind of like a Woolworth, and Martin's grocery store, and a Laundromat and a liquor store, the kind my grandfather used to refer to as a "Dr. Green's" from the days when they were all painted uniformly green in compliance with the regulations of the state liquor commission. At Dr. Green's we bought Old Swilwaukee and Pabst Blue Ribbon—the legal drinking age was still eighteen then, not that it mattered—to drink on Higgins Beach, down at the quiet end beside the bird sanctuary, where the piping plover marks its territory with a song like small bells tolling.

I remember, in the summer of eighty-two, trying to convince Becky Berube to lie down on the sand there with me. I was unsuccessful, but it was that kind of summer, the kind that makes you think you're going to die a virgin. Becky Berube has five kids now, so I guess she learned to lie down pretty quickly after that. We drove sixties automobiles: Pontiac convertibles, MGs, Thunderbirds, Chevy Impalas and Camaros with big V-8 engines; even, in one case, a Plymouth Barracuda convertible. We took summer jobs at the ClamBake at Pine Point, or as waiters and busboys at the Black Point Inn, and the sound of the sea was as familiar to us as our own voices.

I crossed Route 1 at Amato's Italian restaurant and continued down Old County Road, through the salt marshes that flooded once a month with the phases of the moon, and past the Maximilian Kolbe Catholic Church until I reached the cemetery. My grandfather was buried on Fifth Avenue, a joke he liked to share with my grandmother after they bought the plot. They lay there together now, and while I rested I cleared some of the weeds away and said a small prayer for them.

When I got back to the house I put on a pot of coffee, ate some grapefruit and thought again about what had happened the night before. It was almost nine by the clock on the wall when Ellis Howard arrived at my door.

Ellis looked like lard poured into a flexible, vaguely human-shaped mold and left to set. Wrapped in a brown sheepskin coat, the deputy chief in charge of the Portland Police Department's Bureau of Investigation climbed, with some difficulty, from his car. The detective division of the Portland PD was divided into sections dealing with Drugs, Crimes Against Persons, Crimes Against Property, and Administration. Ellis was in charge, assisted by a detective lieutenant named Kramer—who was currently on sick leave with kidney trouble—and four sergeants, each with responsibility for a section. In total, there were maybe twenty detectives and four evidence technicians involved. It was a small, efficient operation.

Ellis rolled up to the porch, like a bowling ball that someone had wrapped in fur. He didn't look like he could move at even half the pace of a bowling ball, didn't look like he could run to save his life or anyone else's. But then Ellis's job wasn't to run around and, anyway, looks could be deceptive. Ellis watched and thought and asked questions and watched and thought some more. Little got past Ellis. He was the kind of man who could eat soup with a fork and not spill a drop.

His wife was a fearsome woman named Doreen, who wore her makeup so thick that you could have carved your initials into her face without drawing blood. When she smiled, which wasn't too often, it was as if someone had just stripped a section of peel from an orange. Ellis seemed to tolerate her the way saints tolerated their martyrdom, although I guessed that, deep down, really deep down, he still didn't like her very much.

I stood aside to let him enter the house. I didn't have a whole lot of choice. "Looking good, Ellis," I said. "The all-fat diet is really paying dividends."

"I see you got someone to fix your roof," he replied. "Know you were from the city, only man in the durned state doing roofing in the winter. Do any of it yourself?"

"As a matter of fact, yes."

"Jesus, maybe we'd be safer talking outside."

"Funny guy," I said, as he sat down heavily in a kitchen chair. "Maybe you should be more concerned about the floor collapsing under you."

I poured him some coffee. He sipped it and I noticed that his face had grown serious, almost sad.

"Something wrong?"

He nodded. "Very. You know Billy Purdue?"

I guessed that he knew the answer to that question already. I fingered the scar on my cheek. I could feel the edges of the stitches beneath my finger.

"Yeah, I know him."

"Heard you had a run-in with him a few days back. He say anything to you about his ex-wife?"

"Why?" I wasn't about to get Billy into trouble unnecessarily, but I already had a sinking feeling in the pit of my stomach.

"Because Rita and her child turned up dead this morning in her apartment. No sign of forced entry and no one heard a thing."

I breathed out deeply and felt a sharp pang of sorrow as I recalled Donald's hand on my finger, as I remembered the touch of his mother's palm on my cheek. A burning anger at Billy Purdue coursed through my system as I briefly, instinctively, assumed his guilt. The feeling didn't last long but the intensity of it remained with me. I thought: why couldn't he have stood by them? Why couldn't he have been there for them? Maybe I didn't have the right to ask those questions; or maybe, given all that had happened in the last year, nobody else had a greater right.

"What happened to them?"

Ellis leaned forward and rubbed his hands together with a soft, rustling sound.

"From what I hear, the woman was strangled. The boy, I don't know. No obvious signs of sexual assault on either."

"You haven't been at the apartment?"

"No. This was supposed to be my day off, but I'm on my way now, what with Kramer being sick and all. The ME's already on the scene. Unlucky for him, he was in Portland for a wedding."

I stood up and walked to the window. Outside, the wind brushed the evergreens and a pair of black-capped chickadees flew high into the sky.

"You think Billy Purdue killed his own child and his ex-wife?" I said.

"Maybe. He wouldn't be the first to do something like it. She called us three nights ago, said he was hanging around outside, shouting, roaring drunk, demanding to be let in to see her. We sent a car and took him in, let him cool off for a time, then told him to keep away from her or we'd lock him up. Could be he decided that he wasn't going to let her leave him, whatever it took."

I shook my head. "Billy wouldn't do that." But I had some doubts, even as I said it. I recalled that red glare in his eyes, the way that he had almost choked the life from me in his trailer, and Rita's belief that he would do anything to stop her from taking his son away from him.

Ellis was keeping pace with my thoughts. "Maybe, maybe not," he said. "That's a nice scar you got on your cheek. You want to tell me how you came by it?"

"I went to his trailer to try to get some child-support money. He threatened to take a baseball bat to me, I tried to stop him and things got a little out of hand."

"Did she hire you to get her money?"

"I did it as a favor."

Ellis turned his mouth down at the corners. "A favor," he repeated, nodding to himself. "And when you were doing this . . . *favor,* did he say anything to you about his ex-wife?" There was an edge to Ellis's voice now.

"He said he wanted to look out for her, for them both. Then he asked me if I was sleeping with her."

"What did you tell him?"

"I told him no."

"Probably the right answer, under the circumstances. Were you sleeping with her?"

"No," I said, and looked hard at him. "No, I wasn't. You pick up Billy yet?"

"He's gone. No sign of him at the trailer and Ronald Straydeer hasn't seen him since day before yesterday."

"I know. I was out there last night."

Ellis arched an eyebrow. "Want to tell me why?"

I told him about my encounter with the white-faced freak at the inn and later at Java Joe's. Ellis took out his notebook and wrote down the number of the Coupe De Ville. "We'll run it through the system, see what comes up. Anything else I should know?"

I went to the sink unit and handed him the plastic bag with the clown toy in it. "Someone came into the house last night when I was sleeping. He took a look around, watched me for a time, then left this."

I opened the bag and placed it on the table in front of Ellis. He took an evidence glove from his pocket, then reached in and touched the toy clown gently.

"I think you'll find that it's Donald Purdue's."

"Did you handle it?"

"Not directly."

He nodded. "We'll check it, run anything we find through AFIS." AFIS was the Automated Fingerprint Identification System. If that didn't yield anything, any prints would be submitted to the FBI for further analysis.

Ellis looked at me and paused before he asked the next question. "And where were you last night?"

"Jesus, Ellis, don't ask me that." I could feel a huge surge of anger welling up inside me. "Don't even imply that."

"Take it easy. Don't cry before you're hurt. You know I have to ask. May as well get it done now as have to go through it later."

He waited.

"I was here during the afternoon," I said through gritted teeth. "I went into Portland yesterday evening, worked out, bought some books, had a coffee, dropped by Rita's apartment . . ."

"What time?"

I thought for a moment. "Eight. Eight-thirty at the latest. There was no reply."

"And then?"

"I headed out to Ronald Straydeer's place, came back here, read, went to bed."

"When did you find the toy?"

"Maybe 3 A.M. You might want to get someone down here to take molds of the boot prints outside my house. The frost will have held the marks in the mud."

He nodded. "We'll do that." He stood to leave, then stopped. "I had to ask. You know that."

"I know."

"And here's something else: the presence of this—" He raised the bag containing the clown. "—means someone has marked you out. Someone's drawn a line between you and Rita Ferris, and it seems to me that there's only one likely candidate."

Billy Purdue. Still, it just didn't sit right, unless Billy had decided that I was to blame for the events leading up to the death of his son; that, by my actions in helping Rita, I had forced him to act as he did.

"Look, let me go with you to the apartment, see if there's anything about it that strikes a chord," I said, at last.

Ellis leaned against the door frame and considered what I had said for a moment, until at last he seemed to reach a decision. "Just don't touch anything and, if anyone asks, you're assisting us in our investigation," he said, then added: "I hear you applied to Augusta for a PI license."

That was true. I still had some cash left from Susan's insurance policy and the sale of our home, and from some work I had undertaken in New York, but I figured that sooner or later I'd have to make a living somehow. I'd already been offered some work in "corporate competitive intelligence," a euphemism for tackling industrial espionage. It sounded more interesting than it was: a sales rep suspected of selling a competitor's goods in violation of a noncompetition agreement; sabotage of a production line in a software factory in South Portland; and the leaking of information on bids for a new public housing development in Augusta. I was still debating whether or not to take on any of them.

"Yeah, the license came through last week."

"You're better than that. We all know what you did, the people you've hunted down. We could do with someone like that."

"What are you saying?"

"I'm saying there's a badge waiting, if you want it. There's something coming up in CAP pretty soon."

"Property or Persons?"

"Don't be a jerk."

"A minute ago you were implying that I might be a suspect in a double homicide. You sure are a changeable man, Ellis."

He smiled. "So how about it?"

I nodded. "I'll think about it."

"You do that," he said. "You do that."

Rita Ferris lay facedown on the floor of her apartment, close to the TV. The coiled ends of a rope hung at her neck, and the tip of one ear, visible through the twisted strands of her hair, was blue. Her skirt was pushed up almost to her waist but her panty hose and panties were in place and undamaged. I felt a rush of pity for her, and something more: a kind of love born out of a brief feeling of intense loss. It made my stomach tighten and my eyes burn and, on my face, I could feel, once again, her last, brief touch, as if I had been branded by her hand.

And in that small room, clean and neat but for the toys and clothes, the diapers and pins, the everyday beauty of her child's slow-forming life, I made myself feel her last moments. I felt—*I see—the blur of movement as the ligature is flipped over her head, the sudden instinctive shifting of her own hands to her throat in an effort to slip her fingers beneath the rope, the brief burn at her fingertips as she fails and the rope tightens around her.*

It is a long death, this slow choking of life from her body. It is a bitter, terrible struggle against the gradual, remorseless crushing of her throat, the slow destruction of the cricoid cartilage and the eventual soft death knell as the fragile hyoid bone snaps.

She panics as her pulse rate increases; her blood pressure soars as she struggles and gasps for breath. She tries to kick back at the body behind her, but the action is anticipated and the rope is pulled tighter. Her face becomes congested, her skin gradually turning blue as cyanosis develops. Her eyes bulge and her mouth froths and she feels as though her head must explode under the pressure.

Then her body convulses and she can taste the blood in her mouth, can feel it flowing from her nose and over her lips. Now she knows that she is going to die and she makes a final desperate effort to release herself, to save her child, but her body is already failing, her mind darkening, and she can smell herself as the light fades, as she loses control of her bodily functions and she thinks to herself:

but I have always been so clean . . .

"You finished?" said a voice. It was the medical examiner, Dr. Henry Vaughan, speaking to the police photographer. Vaughan was gray haired and erudite, a philosopher as much as a doctor, and had been the ME for over twenty years. The post of ME was a appointed job with a seven-year term, which meant that Democrat governors, Republican governors and independent governors had all appointed, or reappointed, Vaughan down the years. He was due to retire soon, I knew, and was set to leave his storage room in Augusta lined with old peanut, mayonnaise and sauce bottles, each now containing some small part of someone's remains. He wasn't too unhappy about it: according to Ellis, he wanted "more time to think."

The photographer took one final photograph of the knot, then nodded his assent. The preliminary sketches had already been made and the measurements taken. Rita's hands had been covered with plastic bags to preserve any possible samples of her attacker's skin, blood or hair. The evidence technician with responsibility for this room had finished his work around the bodies and had moved on to the periphery of the crime scene.

"We're going to flip her," said Vaughan. Two detectives, both wearing plastic gloves, took up positions beside the body, one at her legs, one at her torso, their feet at the edge of the taped outline surrounding her, while Vaughan held her head.

"Ready?" he said, then: "Here we go."

They turned the body, gently but expertly, and I heard one of the cops, a muscular, balding man in his forties, softly whisper: "Ah, Jesus."

Her eyes were wide open and filled with blood where the tiny capillaries had burst under the pressure of the rope, the pupils like dark suns in a red sky. Her fingertips were blue and her nostrils and mouth were covered in blood and dried white froth.

And her lips, the lips that had kissed me softly barely three nights before, that once were red and welcoming and now were cold and blue,

say bye-bye

her lips had been sewn together with thick black thread, the stitches crisscrossing from top to bottom in ragged V shapes, a tangled knot of thread at one corner so that it would not work itself through the hole while the stitches were still being put in place.

I moved closer and it was only then that I saw the child. His body had been obscured by the couch but, as I walked, his small, covered feet became visible, and then the rest of his body, dressed in purple Barney the dinosaur rompers. There was blood around his head, blood caked in his fine blonde hair and blood on the corner of the windowsill where his head had impacted.

Ellis was beside me. "There's bruising to his face. We figure whoever did this hit him, maybe while he was crying, maybe because he got in the way. The force of the blow knocked him into the windowsill and broke his skull."

I shook my head and remembered how the little boy had flailed at me as I touched his mother the night before.

"No," I said, and I squeezed my eyes shut hard as the burning became too much. And I thought of my own child, lost to me now, and the others, their bodies wrapped in plastic, bodies buried beneath the earth of a damp cellar in Queens, tiny faces in jars, a small host of the lost stretching into the darkness, walking hand in hand to oblivion.

"No, he didn't just cry," I said. "He was trying to save her."

While the bodies were placed in white body bags to be taken to Augusta for autopsy, I walked through the apartment. There was only one bedroom, although it was wide and long and held a double bed and a smaller bed with retractable side bars for Donald. There was a pine chest of drawers and a matching pine wardrobe, and a box piled high with toys beside a small bookshelf stacked with picture books. In one corner, beside the open closet door, an evidence technician dusted for fingerprints.

And the sight of the clothes stacked neatly on the shelves,

and the toys packed away in their box, brought back a memory that speared me through the heart. Less than one year before, I had stood in our small house on Hobart Street in Brooklyn and, in the space of one night, had gone through the possessions of my dead wife and child, sorting, discarding, smelling the last traces of them that clung to their clothing like the ghosts of themselves. My Susan and my Jennifer: their blood was still on the kitchen walls and there were chalk marks on the floor where the chairs had stood, the chairs to which they had been tied and in which they had been mutilated while the husband and father who should have protected them was propping up a bar.

And I thought, as I stood in Rita's bedroom: who will take their clothes and sort them now? Who will feel the cotton of her blouse between his fingers, caressing it until the material holds the stains of his prints like a seal? Who will take her underwear, her pink bras without the support wiring (for her breasts were so very small), and hold them carefully, recalling, before he puts them away forever, how he used to undo the clasps with just one hand, the weight of her forcing the straps apart, the cups gently falling?

Who will take her lipstick and run his finger along the edge, knowing that this, too, was a place she touched, that no lips but hers had ever touched it before, or would ever touch it again. Who will see the small traces of a fingertip in her blusher, or carefully unwind each strand of hair from her brush, as if by doing so he might begin to remake her again, piece by piece, atom by atom?

And who will take the child's toys? Who will spin the wheels on a bright, plastic truck? Who will test a button nose, the glass eyes of a bear, the upraised trunk of a white elephant? And who will pack away those small clothes, those little shoes, with laces that young fingers had not yet learned to master?

Who will do all these things, these small services for the dead, these acts of remembrance more powerful in their way than the most ornate memorial? In parting with what was once theirs they became, in that moment, intimately, intensely present, for the ghost of a child is still, for all that, a child, and the memory of a love is still, even decades later, love.

I stood outside the apartment in the cold winter sunlight and watched as the bodies were removed. They had been dead for no more than ten hours, according to Vaughan, possibly less; the precise time of death would take longer to establish, for a number of reasons, including the cold in the drafty old apartment and the nature of Rita Ferris's death. Rigor mortis had set into the small muscles at the eyelids, the lower jaw and the neck, gradually spreading to the other muscles of their bodies, although in Rita Ferris the process of rigor mortis was hastened by her death struggles.

Rigor mortis is caused by the disappearance of the energy source for muscle contraction, called adenosine triphosphate, or ATP. ATP usually dissipates entirely four hours after death, leaving the muscles rigid until decomposition starts to occur. But if the victim struggles before death, then the ATP energy source becomes depleted during the struggle and rigor mortis sets in more quickly. That would have to be taken into account in the case of Rita, so Vaughan reckoned that Donald Purdue would provide a more accurate estimate of the time of death.

There was fixed lividity on the underside of both bodies, where gravity had drawn the blood down, which normally occurs six to eight hours after death, and pressure applied to the area of lividity did not cause "blanching" or whitening, since the blood had already clotted, meaning that they had been dead for at least five hours. Thus the window for a time of death was certainly greater than five hours but probably not in excess of eight hours to ten hours. There was no fixed lividity on the backs of either body, which meant that they had not been moved after death. They had not been dead when I had tried to find Rita the night before. Maybe she had been shopping, or visiting friends. If I had found her, could I have warned her? Could I have saved her, saved them both?

Ellis walked over to me, where I stood away from the throng of curious onlookers.

"Anything strike you about it?" he asked.

"No," I said. "Not yet." I began to remove the set of overalls I has been wearing to prevent me from contaminating the crime scene.

"You think of anything, you let us know, y'hear?"

But my attention had already been distracted. Two men in plainclothes flashed ID at the cop keeping the crowds back and made their way into the building. I didn't need to see what was in their wallets to know what they were.

"Feds," I said.

Behind them, a taller figure with jet-black hair and wearing a conservative blue suit followed.

"Special Agents Samson and Doyle, out of Boston" said Ellis. "And the Canadian cop, Eldritch. They were here earlier. Guess they don't trust us."

I turned to him. "What do I not know here?"

He reached into his pocket and removed a clear plastic evidence bag. It contained four hundred-dollar bills, consecutively numbered, still crisp and new but with a fold where Rita Ferris had stored them in her purse.

"Let's barter," said Ellis. "Know anything about these?"

There was no way to avoid the issue. "They look like the bills Billy Purdue gave me for Rita as part of the child-support payments."

"Thanks," he said, and started to walk away. I could see that he was angry at me, although I wasn't sure why.

I reached out and gripped him by the upper arm. He didn't

look happy about it but I didn't care. My gesture attracted the attention of two uniformed cops, but Ellis waved them away.

"Don't be presuming on my good humor, Bird," he warned, looking at my hand on his arm. "Why didn't you tell me that he gave you this money?"

I didn't release my grip. "I couldn't have known that the money was important," I said. "Come on, Ellis, I liked Rita a lot. Help me out here."

He frowned, then replied: "Just testing, I guess. You want to let go of my arm now? My fingers are going numb."

I took away my hand and he rubbed his arm gently.

"Still working out, I see." He glanced back toward the apartment building, but the feds and the Canadian cop were still inside.

"That business out at Prouts Neck a couple of nights back?" he began.

"Yeah, I watch the news. A dead Irish-American fed, three dead Italians and four dead Cambodians: an equal-opportunity slaughter. What about it?"

"There was another player. Took out Paulie Block and Jimmy Fribb with a pump-action, and that's not all he took."

"Go on."

"There was a trade going on at the Neck, cash in exchange for something else. The feds were tipped off to it when Paulie Block and Chester Nash turned up in Portland. They figure a ransom, for someone who was already dead. Norfolk County Sheriff's Office down in Massachusetts dug up a body out by the Larz Anderson Park yesterday, a Canadian national named Thani Pho. A dog sniffed her out."

"Let me guess," I interrupted. "Thani Pho was of Cambodian extraction."

Ellis nodded. "Seems she was a freshman student at Harvard; her bag was found with her. Autopsy indicated that she'd been raped, then buried alive. They found earth in her throat. The way the feds and this guy Eldritch figure it, Tony Celli's crew kidnapped the girl, pulled a double cross on the Cambodians and then blew them away under the noses of the feds. It's their mess, and the Scarborough PD has been sidelined. Now the main focus of the investigation is Boston and the feds are concentrating their attention on Tony Celli. Those two agents are just clearing up loose ends."

"Who paid the ransom?"

He shrugged. "The FBI Free Information Store closed for business at that point, but they believe that the exchange and the murder of Thani Pho are connected: there has to be a Canadian angle if this guy Eldritch is involved. Feds have a record of the numbers on the bills. They came from a bank in Toronto, and they match the bills that fell from the ransom stash out at the Neck and the hundred dollar bills you gave to Rita Ferris. Trouble is, the rest of the cash is gone, and that's where the other player comes in."

"How much?"

"I heard two mil, maybe more."

I pushed my hands through my hair and kneaded the muscles on the back of my neck. Billy Purdue: the guy was like some kind of infernal ricocheting bullet, bouncing off people and destroying lives until he ran out of energy or something stopped him. If what Ellis said was true, then Billy had somehow heard of Tony Celli's deal at the Neck, may even have been involved somewhere lower down the scale, and decided to make a big score, maybe in the hope of getting his ex-wife and son back and carving out a new life somewhere else, somewhere he could leave the past behind.

"You still think Billy killed Rita and his own son?" I asked quietly.

"Possibly," shrugged Ellis. "I don't see anyone else on the horizon."

"And sewed her mouth shut with black thread?"

"I don't know. If he's crazy enough to cross Tony Celli, he's crazy enough to sew up his old lady."

But I knew that he didn't believe what he was saying. The money changed everything. There were people who would cause a lot of pain to get their hands on that kind of cash, and Tony Celli was one of them, especially since he probably felt that it was his money to begin with. Still, the damage to Rita's mouth didn't fit. Neither did the fact that she hadn't been tortured. Whoever killed her didn't do it in the course of trying to find out something from her. She was killed because someone wanted her dead, and her mouth was sewn up because that same someone wanted to send a message to whoever found her.

Two million dollars: that money was going to bring a storm of trouble down on everybody's head—from Tony Celli, maybe from the guys he tried to double-cross. Jesus, what a mess. I didn't know it then, but the money had attracted others too, individuals who were anxious to secure it for their own ends and didn't care who they killed to get it.

But Billy Purdue, by his actions, had also drawn someone else, someone who didn't care about money, or the Boston crew, or a dead child, or a young woman who was trying to make a better life for herself. He had come back to claim something as his own, and to avenge himself on all those who had kept him from it, and God help anyone who got in his way.

Winter had come howling down from the north, and he had come with it.

CHAPTER SEVEN

WHEN ELLIS HAD LEFT I stood for a time, considering whether or not to leave the police to their work. Instead of simply driving away, I reentered the apartment building and walked up to the third floor. The door to apartment five had been freshly painted a bright, cheerful yellow, small paint flecks still freckling the brass numeral. I knocked gently and the door opened on a chain. In the gap, a small dark face appeared about four feet from the ground, its features framed by black curls, its eyes wide and wondering.

"Come away from there, child," said a voice and then a taller, darker figure filled the gap. I could see the resemblance in the two faces almost instantly.

"Mrs. Mims?" I asked.

"*Ms.* Mims," she corrected. "And I just finished talking to a police officer not twenty minutes ago."

"I'm not with the police, ma'am." I showed her my ID. She examined it carefully without touching it, her daughter straining up on her toes to do the same, then glanced back at my face. "I remember you," she said. "You called here, couple of nights back."

"That's right. I knew Rita. Can I come in for a moment?"

She bit down gently on her lower lip, then nodded and closed the door. I could hear the chain being removed before the door swung open again, revealing a bright, large-ceilinged room. The couch inside was blue and decorated with yellow throws, its legs set on a bare varnished floor. Two tall bookshelves crammed with paperbacks stood at either side of an old, stained marble fireplace, and there was a portable stereo on a stand by the window close to a combination TV and VCR. The room smelled of flowers and opened to the right onto a short hallway, presumably leading to the bedroom and bathroom, and on the left into a small, clean kitchen. The walls had been newly painted a soft yellow, so that the room seemed to be bathed in sunlight.

"You have a nice place. You do all this yourself?"

She nodded, proud despite herself.

"I helped her," piped the girl. She was maybe eight or nine, and it was possible to see in her the seeds of a beauty that would eventually grow to outshine her mother's.

"You'll have to start hiring yourself out," I said. "I know people who'd pay a lot of money for a job as good as this. Including me."

The girl giggled shyly and her mother reached out and gave her a little hug around the shoulders. "Go on now, child. Go and play while I talk with Mr. Parker here."

She did as she was told, casting a small, anxious look back as she entered the hallway. I smiled to reassure her, and she gave a little smile back.

"She's a beautiful girl," I said.

"Takes after her father," she replied, her voice thick with sarcasm.

"I don't think so. He around?"

"No. He was a worthless sonofabitch, so I kicked him out. Last I heard, he was a drain on the economy of New Jersey."

"Best place for him."

"Amen to that. You want coffee? Tea maybe?"

"Coffee would be fine." I didn't really want it, but I figured it might take the strain out of the situation a little. Ms. Mims seemed like a pretty tough woman. If she decided to be unhelpful, a steel hull wouldn't be enough to break the ice.

After a few minutes, she emerged from the kitchen with two mugs, placed them carefully on coasters on a low pine table, then went back to the kitchen for milk and sugar. When she returned we sat, and I noticed for the first time that, as she held her coffee, her hand was shaking. She caught my look, and raised her left hand to try to still the mug.

"It's not easy," I said softly. "When something of this kind happens, it's like a stone dropped in a pool. It ripples out, and everything gets tossed in its wake."

She nodded. "Ruth's been asking me about it. I haven't told her that they're dead. I haven't figured out how to tell her yet."

"Did you know Rita well?"

"I knew her a little. I knew more by reputation. I knew about her husband, knew he almost killed them in a fire." She paused. "You think he did this?"

"I don't know. I hear he was around lately."

"I've seen him, once or twice, watching the place. I told Rita, but she only called the police that last time he got roaring drunk. The rest of the time, she seemed content to let him be. I think she felt sorry for him."

"Were you here last night?"

She nodded, then paused. "I went to bed early—women's troubles, you know? I took two Tylenol, drank a shot of whiskey and didn't wake up until this morning. I went downstairs, saw Rita's door was open, and went in. That's when I found them. I can't help thinking that if I hadn't taken the pills, hadn't had a drink . . ." She swallowed loudly and tried not to cry. I looked away for a moment, and when I turned back she seemed to have composed herself.

"Was there anything else bothering her, any*one* else?" I continued.

Again, there was a pause, but this one spoke volumes. I waited, but she didn't speak. "Ms. Mims . . ." I began.

"Lucy," she said.

"Lucy," I said gently. "You can't say anything to hurt her now. But if you do know something that might help to find whoever did this then, please, tell me."

She sipped her coffee. "She was short of money. I knew, because she told me. There was a woman helped her out, but it still wasn't enough. I offered her some, but she wouldn't take it. Said she had found a way to make a little on the side."

"Did she say how?"

"No, but I looked after Donnie while she was gone. Three times, each at short notice. The third time, she came back and I could see she'd been crying. She looked scared, but wouldn't tell me what had happened, just said that she wouldn't need me to watch Donnie no more, that the job hadn't worked out."

"Did you tell the police this?"

She shook her head. "I don't know why I didn't. It was just that . . . she was a good person, you know? I think she was just doing what she had to do to make ends meet. But if I told the police, it would have become something else, something low."

"Do you know who she was working for?"

She rose and went into the hallway, and I could hear her footsteps on the bare floor as she walked. When she appeared again, there was a piece of paper in her hands.

"She told me that if there was any trouble with Donnie or Billy, or if she didn't come back on time, I was to call this number and talk to this man." She handed me the piece of paper. On it, written in Rita Ferris's tight, neat script, was a telephone number and the name Lester Biggs.

"When did the crying incident happen, Lucy?"

"Five days ago," she said, which meant that Rita had called me the day after looking for help and money to get out of Portland.

I held up the piece of paper. "Can I keep this?"

She nodded and I placed it in my wallet. "Do you know who he is?" she asked.

"He runs an escort service out of South Portland," I replied. There was no point in sugaring it. Lucy Mims had already guessed the truth.

For the first time, tears glistened in her eyes. A drop hung from her eyelash, then slowly trickled down her cheek. At the hallway, her daughter appeared and ran to her mother to hug her tight. She looked at me, but there was no blame in her eyes. She knew that, whatever had happened, it was not my fault that her mother was crying.

I took my card from my wallet and handed it to Lucy. "Call me if you think of anything else, or if you just want to talk. Or if you need help."

"I don't need help, Mr. Parker," she said. In her voice, I could hear the echo of someone being kicked all the way to New Jersey.

"I guess not," I said, and opened the door. "And most people call me Bird."

She walked across the room to close the door behind me, her daughter's arms still clutched tightly around her.

"You will find the man who did this, won't you?" she asked.

Passing clouds dappled the winter sunshine, creating movement on the walls behind her. And, for a moment, it seemed to assume a human shape, the shape of a young woman passing through the room, and I had to shake my head slightly to make it disappear. It lingered for a second, then the clouds cleared and it was gone.

I nodded. "Yes, I'll find him."

Lester Biggs operated out of an office on Broadway, above a hairdressing salon. I rang the intercom on the door and waited about thirty seconds before a male voice answered.

"I'm here to see Lester Biggs," I said into the speaker.

"What's your business with Mr. Biggs?" came the reply.

"Rita Ferris. My name's Charlie Parker. I'm a private investigator."

Nothing happened. I was about to ring again when the door buzzed and I pushed it open to reveal a narrow staircase carpeted in faded green, with a small, grimy window on the landing. I went up two flights of stairs to where a door opened on to an office overlooking the street. There was the same green carpet on the floor, a desk with a telephone, two wooden chairs without cushions and a pile of skin magazines on the floor, twin stacks of videocassettes beside them. Three sets of filing cabinets stood along the wall. Opposite them, beneath and alongside the two big windows that looked out onto Broadway, stood a selection of electrical items in boxes: microwave ovens, hair dryers, cookware, stereos, even some computers, although they were made by no company that I knew. The writing on the box appeared to be Cyrillic: trust Lester Biggs to buy and sell Russian computers.

Behind the desk, in a leather seat, sat Lester himself, and to his right, on one of the chairs, sat a bearded man with a huge pot belly and biceps the size of melons. His buttocks hung over the edges of the chair, like balloons filled with water.

Lester Biggs was slim and kind of well groomed, if your definition of well groomed was a disc jockey at his sister-in-law's wedding. He looked about forty and was dressed in a cheap three-button pinstripe suit, a white shirt and a slim pink tie. He wore his hair in a mullet-cut, the top short, the back long and permed. His face was tanning-salon brown, his eyes slightly hooded, like a man caught between sleeping and waking. In his right hand he held a pen, which he tapped lightly on the desk as I entered, causing the gold bracelet on his arm to jangle.

Biggs wasn't a bad man by the standards of his profession, according to some. He had started out running a used electronics store, had progressed rapidly into buying and selling stolen goods, then branched out into a number of other areas. The escort service was a recent one, maybe six or seven months old. From what I heard, he took the calls, contacted the girl, provided a car to take her to the address and a guy, sometimes the big man Jim who sat beside him, to make sure everything went smoothly. For that, he took 50 percent. He wasn't morally bankrupt, just overdrawn.

"The local celebrity sleuth," he said. "Welcome. Take a seat." He gestured with the pen to the remaining unoccupied wooden chair. I sat. The back creaked a little and started to give way, so I leaned forward to take the pressure off.

"Business is booming, I see."

Biggs shrugged. "I do okay. It doesn't pay to maintain a high profile in my line of work."

"And that would be . . .?"

"I buy and sell things."

"Like people?"

"I provide a service. I don't force anybody to do what they do. Nobody, apart from Jim here, works for me. They work for themselves. I just act as the facilitator."

"Tell me how you facilitated Rita Ferris."

Biggs didn't reply, just twisted in his seat to look out the window. "I heard about it. I'm sorry. She was a nice woman."

"That's right, she was. I'm trying to find out if her death was connected in any way to what she was doing for you."

He flinched a little. "Why should it matter to you?"

"It just does. It should matter to you too."

He exchanged a look with Jim, who shrugged. "How'd you find me?" he said.

"I followed the trail of cheap porn."

Biggs smiled. "Some men need a little something extra to get them going. There are a lot of screwed-up people out there, and every day I thank God for them."

"Did Rita Ferris meet one of those screwed-up people?"

Biggs kicked back from his desk until his chair came to rest against the wall. He didn't say anything, just sat sizing me up.

"Tell me, or tell the cops," I said. "I'm sure they'd be happy to discuss the nature of facilitation with you."

"What do you want to know?"

"Tell me about last Monday night."

Again, he exchanged a look with Jim, then seemed to resign himself to talking. "It was a freak call, that's all. Guy rang from the Eastland over on High Street, wanted a girl. I asked him if he had any preferences and he gave me short, blonde, small tits, neat ass. Said that was what he liked. Well, that was Rita. I gave her a call, offered her the job, and she said yes. It was only her third time, but she was keen to make some cash. Cash for gash." He smiled emptily.

"Anyway, Jim picked her up, dropped her off, parked the car and waited in the lobby while she went up to the room."

"What room?"

"Nine-twenty-seven. Ten minutes later Rita comes down, runs into the lobby and straight over to Jim, demands to be taken home. Jim hauls her into a corner and tries to calm her down, find out what happened. Seems she got to the room and an old guy opened the door and let her in. She said he was dressed kind of funny—" He looked to Jim for confirmation.

"Old," said Jim. "He was dressed old-fashioned, like his suit was thirty, forty years out of date."

For the first time, Biggs looked uneasy. "It was strange, she said. There were no clothes in the room, no cases or bags, nothing but the old guy in his old suit. And she got scared. She couldn't say why, but the old guy frightened her."

"He smelled bad," said Jim. "That's what she told me. Not bad like rotten fish or eggs, but bad like there was something rotten inside him. Bad like . . . like if evil had a smell, it would have smelled like him." He looked embarrassed by his own words, and started examining his fingers.

"So he puts his hand on her shoulder," continued Lester, "and, immediately, she just wants to run. She pushes out at him and he falls back on the bed, and while he's down there she makes for the door, but he's locked it and she loses some time trying to get it open. By the time she gets it unlocked, he's behind her so she starts to scream. He's pulling at her dress, trying to cover her mouth, and she strikes out at him again, catches him on the head. Before he can recover, she has the door open and she's running down the corridor. She can hear him behind her, too, pounding after her, and he's gaining. Then she turns a corner and there's a group of people getting in the elevator. She reaches them just before the doors close, jamming her foot in the opening. The door opens and she gets in. There's no sign of the old guy, but she can still smell him, she says, and knows that he's close. She was lucky, I guess. The Eastland only had one functioning elevator that night. If she'd missed it, he'd have gotten her, no question. Then the elevator brings her down to the lobby, and to Jim."

Jim was still looking down at his hands. They were big and heavily veined, with scars on the knuckles. Maybe he was wondering if Rita Ferris might still have been alive if he'd had a chance to use them on the old man. "I told her to wait for me in the lobby, by the reception desk," he said, as he took up the story. "I went up to the room, but the door was open and the room was empty. Like she said, there were no bags, nothing. So I went back down to the desk, told them that I was supposed to meet a friend of mine who was staying in the hotel. Room nine-twenty-seven."

He pursed his lips, and tugged at one of his scars with a long fingernail. "There was no guest in room nine-twenty-seven," he said at last. "The room was unoccupied. The old guy must have bullshitted one of the staff so he could get in. I took Rita to the bar, bought her a brandy and waited until she had calmed down before taking her home. That's all there is."

"You find any way to tell the cops about this guy?"

Biggs shook his head. "How could I?"

"You have a telephone."

"I have a business," he replied.

Not for long, I thought. Biggs, for all his posturing, was no better than a cluster fly, insinuating himself into young women's lives and then draining them from the inside. "He could try again," I said. "Maybe he did try, and Rita Ferris ended up dead because of it."

Biggs shook his head. "Nah, these things happen. The freak probably went home and jerked off instead." His eyes told me that he didn't believe his own lies. Beside him, Jim still hadn't lifted his face. Guilt rolled off him like a fog.

"She give you a description?"

"Like we told you: old, tall, gray hair, smelled bad. That's it."

I rose. "Thanks, you've been a big help."

"Anytime," he said. "You ever want to party, you give me a call."

"Yeah, you'll be the first to know."

When I stepped outside, a car drew up: Ellis Howard's car. He didn't look overly happy to see me.

"What are you doing here?" he asked.

"Same thing you are, I guess."

"We got an anonymous tip-off."

"Lucky you." I guessed that Lucy Mims's conscience had got the better of her in the end.

Ellis rubbed his hand across his face, dragging his skin down so I could see the red beneath his eyes. "You still haven't answered the question," he said. "How did you know she was working as a prostitute?"

"Maybe the same way you did. It doesn't matter."

"But you weren't going to tell us?"

"I would have, eventually. I didn't want her labeled as a whore, that's all, not with the press around and not before I had a chance to find out if it was true."

"I didn't know you were so sentimental," said Ellis. He wasn't smiling.

"I have hidden shallows," I replied, as I turned and walked to my car. "See you around, Ellis."

CHAPTER EIGHT

FTER I LEFT Lester Biggs's office, I headed down to the Bagel Works at Temple Street, where I ate a muffin, drank some French roast and watched the cars go by. A handful of people queued to see cheap movies in the Nickelodeon movie theater next door, or took the air around Monument Square. Nearby, Congress Street was bustling: it had suffered when the suburban malls drew the retail businesses out of the city, but now had restaurants and new stores and the Keystone movie theater and diner, and was pretty much Portland's cultural district

This was a survivor's city: it had burned twice at the hands of the Indians in 1676 and 1690, burned again under the guns of the Englishman Henry Mowatt in 1775 following a dispute over masts, and burned once more in 1866 when someone threw a firecracker into a boatbuilder's yard on Commercial Street and turned the eastern half of the city to ash. And still the city remained, and still it grew.

I felt about the city as I felt about the house in Scarborough: it was a place where the past was alive in the present, where a man could find a place for himself as long as he understood the fact that he was a link in the chain, for a man cut off from his past is a man adrift in the present. Maybe that was part of Billy Purdue's problem. There had been little stability in his life. His past was a series of unconnected episodes, united only by unhappiness.

In the end, I figured that Billy Purdue was probably none of my business. Whatever he had done to Tony Celli, for whatever reason, was a matter for them both to resolve. Billy was a big boy now and his actions at Ferry Beach meant that he was playing by big boys' rules. So if Billy Purdue was none of my business, why did I feel that I should try to save him?

If I stretched the point then Rita and Donald were none of my business either, but it didn't feel that way. In their apartment, as the two bodies lay on the floor, frozen briefly by the flashbulbs of the camera, I felt something ripple through me, something I recognized from before, something that had come to me as a gift from another. In the crowded coffee shop, as people sheltered from the cold, talked about their children, gossiped about their neighbors, touched the hands of girlfriends, boyfriends, lovers, I moved the fingers of my left hand gently over the palm of my right and recalled a touch more intense than that of any lover, and I smelled again the rich heady odor of the Louisiana swamps.

Almost eight months before, I had sat in the bedroom of an old, blind woman named Tante Marie Aguillard, a huge ebony form with dead, sightless eyes whose consciousness moved through the darkness of her own life, and the lives of others. I wasn't sure what I was looking for from her, except that she said she could hear the voice of a dead girl calling her from the swamps. I believed then that the man who killed the girl might also have been responsible for the deaths of my own wife and child—assuming the old woman wasn't crazy, or vindictive, or just plain lonely and seeking attention.

But when she touched my hand in that darkening room,

something shot through me like a jolt of electricity and I knew that she was not lying, that somehow she heard that girl crying amid the rotting vegetation and the deep green waters, and that Tante Marie had tried to comfort her as she died.

And through Tante Marie, I heard the voices also of Susan and Jennifer, faint but distinct, and I took those voices away with me, and on a subway train a week later my wife appeared to me for the first time. That was Tante Marie's gift to me: I saw and heard my dead wife and child, and I saw and heard others too. Eventually, Tante Marie was among them. That was her gift, passed in the touch of a hand, and yet I could not explain it.

I think that it may be a kind of empathy, a capacity to experience the suffering of those who have been taken painfully, brutally, without mercy. Or perhaps what I experience is a form of madness, a product of grief and guilt; maybe I am disturbed, and in my disturbance I have imagined alternative worlds where the dead seek reparation from the living. I do not know for certain. All I can say is that those who are absent, by its means become present.

But some gifts are worse than curses, and the dark side of the gift is that they know. The lost, the stragglers, those who should not have been taken but were, the innocents, the struggling, tormented shades, the gathering ranks of the dead, they know.

And they come.

Despite my misgivings, I spent that afternoon moving from bar to bar, talking to those who had known Billy Purdue, who might have some idea of where he had gone. In some cases, the Portland police had been there before me, which usually meant that my welcome was pretty frosty. No one could, or would, tell me anything, and I had almost given up hope when I found James Hamill.

I guessed that there weren't too many forks in Hamill's family tree. He was a scrawny piece of lowlife, 120 pounds of bitterness, repressed anger and redneck mentality, the kind of guy who wouldn't willingly do someone a good turn if he could do a bad one instead. Hamill's position was pretty low down on the food chain: where he existed, they ate it raw.

He was playing alone in Old Port Billiards down on Fore Street when I came upon him, his baseball cap turned backward on his head as he lined up a shot, his scrawny mustache curled in concentration. He missed the shot and swore loudly. If the ball had been iron and the pocket magnetized, he still would have missed the shot. Hamill was just that kind of guy.

Someone in Bubba's Sulky Lounge over on Portland Street had told me that Hamill hung out with Billy Purdue on occasion. I couldn't imagine why. Maybe Billy just wanted to be with someone who could make him look good.

"James Hamill?" I asked.

He scratched his ass and offered me his hand. His smile was a dentist's nightmare.

"Pleased to meet you, whoever you are. Now go fuck yourself."

He went back to his game.

"I'm looking for Billy Purdue."

"Get in line."

"Someone else been asking after him?"

"Just about anyone with a uniform and a badge, from what I hear. You a cop?"

"Nope."

"Private?" He drew back his cue slowly, aiming to put a stripe in the center pocket.

"I guess."

"You the one he hired?"

I lifted the stripe and the cue ball went straight into the pocket.

"Hey!" said Hamill. "Gimme back my ball." He sounded like

a small, spoiled child, although I figured you'd have a hard time getting any mother to claim Hamill as her own.

"Billy Purdue hired a private investigator?" I said.

My tone betrayed me, for the look of profound unhappiness disappeared from Hamill's face to be replaced by a greedy leer.

"What's it to you?"

"I'm interested in talking to anyone who can help me to trace Billy. Who's the PI?" If Hamill didn't tell me, I could probably find out by calling around, assuming that whoever he had hired would admit to working for him.

"I wouldn't want to get my amigo into trouble," said Hamill, rubbing his chin with a rough approximation of a thoughtful expression. "What's your angle?"

"I worked for his ex-wife."

"She's dead. Hope you got paid up front."

I hefted the pool ball in my hand and thought about letting fly at Hamill's head. Hamill saw the intent in my face.

"Look, I need some cash," he said, his manner softening. "Let me have something, I'll give you his name."

I took out my wallet and put a twenty on the table.

"Shit, twenty bucks," spat Hamill. "What are you, on welfare? It'll cost you more than that."

"I'll give you more. I want the name."

Hamill considered for a moment. "I don't know his first name, but he's called Wildon or Wifford or something."

"Willeford?"

"Yeah, yeah, that's it. Willeford."

I nodded my thanks and moved off.

"Hey! Hey!" shouted Hamill, and I could hear his sneakered feet shuffling across the floor behind me. "What about my extra?"

I turned back. "Sorry, I almost forgot."

I put a dime on top of the twenty and gave him a wink as I returned the ball to the table.

"That's for the crack about his ex-wife. Enjoy it in good health."
I walked away and headed for the stairs.

"Hey, Mr. Trump," shouted Hamill at my retreating back. "You hurry back now, y'hear?"

Marvin Willeford wasn't in his office, a one-desk job above an Italian restaurant across from the blue Casco Bay ferry terminal, but a handwritten sign on the door said he had gone to lunch— a long lunch, obviously. I asked in the restaurant where Willeford usually hung out and the waiter gave me the name of a waterfront bar, the Sail Loft Tavern at Commercial and Silver.

During the eighteenth and nineteenth centuries, Portland harbor was a thriving center for fishing and shipping. In those days, the wharves would be piled high with lumber bound for Boston and the West Indies. There would be lumber on them again soon, but now that wood was bound for China and the Middle East. Meanwhile, the redevelopment of the harbor, the building of new condos and stores to attract the tourists and the young professionals, was still the subject of controversy. It's hard to have a proper working harbor when folks in tie-dyes and sandals are hanging around taking pictures of one another and eating snow cones. The Sail Loft looked like a throwback to the old days, the kind of place some people liked to call home.

I knew Willeford to see but I had never spoken to him and knew almost nothing about his past. He looked older than I remembered when I found him at the dark bar, watching the rerun of a basketball game on TV surrounded by sea horses and starfish on the walls. I figured he must be in his early sixties by now, jowly and bald, with a few strands of white hair flicked across his skull like seaweed on a rock. His skin was pale, almost translucent, with a fine tracery of veins at his cheeks and a bulbous red nose pitted with craters, like a relief map of Mars. His features seemed misty and inexact, as if they were slowly dissolving into the alcohol that coursed through his system, gradually becoming blurred versions of their original form.

He held a beer in one hand, an empty shot glass beside it, and the remains of a sandwich and potato chips lay on a plate before him as he watched the screen above the bar. He didn't slouch at the bar, though; he sat tall and straight, leaning slightly into the rest at the back of the chair.

"Hi," I said as I took a seat beside him. "Marvin Willeford?"

"He owe you money?" asked Willeford, without removing his gaze from the screen.

"Not yet," I replied.

"Good. You owe him money?"

"Not yet," I repeated.

"Pity. Still, I'd keep it that way if I were you." He turned himself toward me. "What can I do for you, son?"

It felt odd to have someone call me "son" at thirty-four. I almost felt compelled to show some ID. "My name's Charlie Parker."

He nodded in recognition. "I knew your granddaddy, Bob Warren. He was a good man. Hear you may be moving in on my patch, Charlie Parker."

I shrugged. "Maybe. Hope there'll be enough work for both of us. Buy you a beer?"

He drained his glass and called for a refill. I ordered coffee.

"'The old order changeth, yielding place to new,'" said Willeford sadly.

"Tennyson," I said.

He smiled approvingly. "Nice to see there are still some romantics left." There was more to Willeford than long lunches in a dark bar. With his kind, there usually is.

He smiled and saluted with his new beer. "Well at least you're not a total philistine, son. Y'know, I've been coming to this place for too many years. I look around and wonder how much longer it'll be here, now that they're building fancy apartments and cute little stores on the port. Sometimes I think I ought to chain myself to some railings in protest, 'cept I got a bad hip and the cold hurts my bladder." He shook his head sadly. "So, what brings you to my office, son?"

"I was hoping you could tell me about Billy Purdue."

He pursed his lips as he swallowed his beer. "This professional, or personal? 'Cause if it's personal, then we're just talking, right? But if it's professional, then you got your ethics, you got your client confidentiality, you got your poaching, although—and here I'm speaking personally, you understand—you want to take Billy Purdue as a client, then be my guest. He lacked some of the basic qualities I look for in a client, like money, though from what I hear he needs a lawyer more'n a PI."

"Let's call it personal, then."

"Personal it is. He hired me to find his birth parents."

"When?"

"Month or so back. He paid me two-fifty up front—in ones and fives, straight out of the cookie jar—but then couldn't pay anything more, so I dropped him. He wasn't real pleased about it, but business is business. Anyway, that boy was more trouble than arthritis."

"How far did you get?"

"Well, I took the usual steps. I applied to the state for non-identifying information—you know, ages of the parents, professions, birth states, ethnicity. Got zilch, nada. The kid was found under a cabbage leaf."

"No birth records at all?"

He held up his hands in mock amazement, then took another huge mouthful of beer. I reckoned it took him three mouthfuls to a glass. I was right.

"Well, I headed up to Dark Hollow. You know where that is, up north past Greenville?" I nodded. "I had some other business up by Moosehead, figured I'd do Purdue a favor and carry on some of his work on my other client's time. The last guy who fostered him lives up thataways, though he's an old man now, older than me. His name's Payne, Meade Payne. He told me that, far as he knew, Billy Purdue's was originally a private adoption arranged through some woman in Bangor and the sisters at St. Martha's."

St. Martha's rang a bell, but I couldn't remember why. Willeford seemed to sense my struggle. "St. Martha's," he repeated. "Where that old lady killed herself last week, the one who ran away. St. Martha's used to be a convent and the nuns took in women who had, you know, fallen by the wayside. Except now all the nuns are dead, or Alzheimered out, and St. Martha's is a private nursing home, strictly low end. Place smells of pee and boiled vegetables."

"So no records?"

"Nothing. I looked through whatever files remained, which wasn't a whole lot. They kept a record of the births and retained copies of the relevant documents, but there was nothing that matched Billy Purdue. It didn't go through the books or, if it did, then somebody made sure to hide the traces. No one seemed to know why."

"You talk to this woman, the one who arranged the adoption?"

"Lansing. Cheryl Lansing. Yeah, I spoke to her. She's old too. Jeez, even her kids were getting old. All I seem to meet is old people—old people and clients. I think I need to make some young friends."

"People will talk," I said. "You'll get a reputation."

He laughed to himself. "Can you be a sugar daddy without having any cash?"

"I don't know. You could try, but I don't think you'd get very far."

He nodded and finished his beer. "Story of my life. Dead folks get more action than I ever did."

So Cheryl Lansing was the woman who had arranged Billy Purdue's adoption. She obviously had more than a professional interest in him if she was still trying to help out his ex-wife and his son three decades later. I pictured the bag of clothes, and the box of food, and the small wad of bills in Rita Ferris's hand. Cheryl Lansing had seemed like a nice woman. The news of the two deaths would hit her hard, I thought.

I called for another beer and Willeford thanked me. He was pretty stewed by now. I felt like a great guy, getting him so drunk that he wouldn't be able to work for the rest of the day just so I could satisfy my crusading urge.

"What about Cheryl Lansing?" I pressed.

"Well, she didn't want to talk about Purdue. I kept at her but it was no use. All she would say was that the mother was from up north, that she arranged the adoption at the request of the sisters, and that she didn't even know the woman's name. Apparently, she made some money brokering adoptions for the nuns and passed on a portion of the proceeds to them, except this one was pro bono. She had a copy of a birth certificate, though, but the parents were John and Jane Doe. I figured there had to be a record of the birth somewhere."

"What did you do?"

"Well, through what Payne could tell me and by checking the records, I found that most of the people who fostered Billy Purdue also came from up north. Farthest south he got was Bangor, until he left for Boston when he was old enough. So I asked questions, put up notices with approximate dates of birth, even took out an advertisement in some of the local papers, then sat around and waited. Anyway, the money had run out by then and I didn't see as how Purdue would be able to come up with any more.

"Then I got a call, saying I should talk to a woman in the old folks' home up in Dark Hollow, which brought the focus back to St. Martha's." He paused and took a long slug of beer. "Well, I told Billy that I might have something and asked him if he wanted me to continue. He told me he had no more money, so I told him that, regrettably, I would have to terminate our business relationship. Then he chewed me out some, threatened to smash up my office if I didn't help him. I showed him this—" He pushed back his jacket to reveal a Colt Python with a long, eight-inch barrel. It made him look like an aging gunfighter. "And he went on his way."

"Did you give him the name of the woman?"

"I would have given him the coat off my back to get rid of him. I figured it was time to beat a strategic retreat. If I'd retreated any faster, I'd have been going forward again."

My coffee was cold in the mug before me. I leaned over the bar and poured it into a sink.

"Any idea where Billy might be now?"

Willeford shook his head. "There is one more thing," he said.

I waited.

"The woman in St. Martha's? Her name was Miss Emily Watts or, least, that's what she called herself. That name ring a bell with you?"

I thought for a while but came up with nothing. "I don't think so. Should it?"

"She's the old lady who died in the snow. Strange stuff, don't you think?"

I remembered the full story now. The deaths of the men at Prouts Neck had forced it from the forefront of my memory.

"You think Billy Purdue went to see her?"

"I don't know, but something spooked her enough to make her run off into the woods and kill herself when they tried to take her back."

I stood and thanked him, then shrugged on my overcoat.

"It was my pleasure, son. You know, you look something like your granddaddy. You act like him too and you'll give no one cause to regret meeting you."

I felt another pang of guilt. "Thanks. You want me to give you a ride somewhere?"

He shook his glass to order another beer, and called for a whiskey chaser as well. I put down ten bucks on the bar to cover it, and he raised the empty glass in salute.

"Son," he said, "I ain't goin' nowhere."

It was already growing dark when I left the bar and I pulled my coat tightly around me to protect myself from the cold. From off the harbor a wind came, running icy hands through my hair and rubbing my skin with chill fingers. I had parked the Mustang in the lot at One India, a corner of Portland with a dark history. One India was the original site of Fort Loyal, erected by the colonists in 1680. It only survived for ten years, before the French and their native allies captured it and butchered the 190 settlers who had surrendered. Eventually, the India Street Terminal was built on the same spot, marking milepost 0.0 for the Atlantic and St. Lawrence Railroad, the Grand Trunk Railway of Canada and the Canadian National Railways, when Portland was still an important rail center. At One India, now occupied by an insurance company, it was still possible to see the sign for the Grand Trunk and Steamship Offices over the door.

The railroads had been gone for almost three decades now, although there was talk of rebuilding Union Station and reopening the passenger railway from Boston. It was strange how things from the past, once thought lost and gone forever, should now be resurrected and made vivid once again in the present.

The windows of the Mustang were already beginning to frost over as I approached it, and a mist that dulled every sound hung over the warehouses and the boats on the water. I was almost at the car when I heard the footsteps behind me. I began to turn, my coat now open, my right hand making a leisurely movement toward my gun, but something jammed into the small of my back and a voice said:

"Let it go. Keep them wide."

I kept my hands horizontally away from my sides. A second figure limped from my right, his left foot curved slightly inward, distorting his walk, and took my gun from its holster. He was small, maybe five-four, and probably in his late forties. His hair was thick and black over brown eyes and his shoulders were wide beneath his overcoat, his stomach hard. He might even have been handsome, but for a harelip that slashed his soft cupid's bow like a knife wound.

The second man was taller and bulkier, with long dark hair that hung over the collar of a clean white shirt. He had hard eyes and an unsmiling mouth that contrasted with the bright Winnie the Pooh tie neatly knotted at his neck. His head was almost square, set on wide, rectangular shoulders, with the barest hint of a neck intervening. He moved the way a kid moves an action figure, loping from side to side without bending his knees. Together, the two made quite a pair.

"Jeez, fellas, I think you may be a little late for trick or treat." I leaned conspiratorially toward the shorter guy. "And you know," I whispered, "if the wind changes direction, you'll be left that way."

They were cheap shots, but I didn't like people sneaking around in the mist poking guns in my back. As Billy Purdue might have said, it was kind of rude.

The shorter guy turned my gun over in his hand, examining the third-generation Smith & Wesson with an expert's appreciation.

"Nice piece," he said.

"Give it back and I'll show you how it works."

He smiled a strange, jagged smile.

"You gotta come with us." He waved me in the direction of India Street, where a pair of headlights had just flashed on in the darkness.

I looked back at the Mustang.

"Shit," said Harelip, with a look of mock concern on his face. "You worried about your car?"

He flicked the safety on my gun and fired at the Mustang, blowing out the front and rear tires on the driver's side. From somewhere close by, a car alarm began to sound.

"There," he said. "Nobody's gonna steal it now."

"I'll remember you did that," I replied.

"Uh-huh. You want me to spell my name for you, you let me know."

The taller guy gave me a shove in the direction of the car, a silver Seven Series BMW, which moved over to us and swung to the right, the rear door popping open. Inside sat another handsome devil with short brown hair and a gun resting on his thigh. The driver, younger than the rest, popped bubble gum and listened to an AOR station on the car stereo. Bryan Adams came on as I climbed into the car, singing the theme song from *Don Juan DeMarco.*

"Any possibility we could change the station?" I asked, as we drove off.

Beside me, Harelip prodded me hard with his gun.

"I like this song," he said, humming along. "You got no soul."

I looked at him. I think he was serious.

We drove to the Regency Hotel on Milk Street, the nicest hotel in Portland, which occupied what was once a redbrick armory in the Old Port. The driver parked in back and we walked to the rear entrance on Fore Street, where another young guy in a neat black suit opened the door for us before speaking in a mike on his lapel to advise that we were on our way up. We took the stairs to the top floor, where Harelip knocked respectfully at the end door on the right. When it opened, I was led in and brought to meet Tony Celli.

Tony sat in a big armchair with his shoeless feet on a matching footstool. His black stockings were silk and his gray trousers were immaculately pressed. He wore a blue-striped shirt with a white collar and a dark red tie marked with an intricate pattern of black spirals. Gold gleamed at his white cuffs. He was clean shaven and his black hair was neatly combed and parted to one side. His eyes were brown beneath thin, plucked eyebrows. His nose was long and unbroken, his mouth a little soft, his chin a little fat. There were no rings on his fingers, which lay clasped in his lap. In front of him, the TV was turned to the nightly financial report. On a table beside him lay a pair of headphones and a bug detector, indicating that the room had already been searched for listening devices.

I knew Tony Celli by reputation. He had worked his way up through the ranks, running porn shops and whores in Boston's Combat Zone, paying his dues, gradually building up a power base. He took cash from the people below him and paid a lot of it to the people above him. He met his obligations and was now regarded as a hot tip for the future. I knew that he already had a certain amount of responsibility in money matters, based on a perception that he was gifted with financial acumen, a perception he now reinforced with his striped shirt and the attention he was paying to the stock prices that flashed past at the bottom of the screen.

I guessed that he was forty by now, certainly no more than that. He looked good. In fact, he looked like the sort of guy you could bring home to meet your mother, if you didn't think that he'd probably torture her, fuck her, then dump her remains in Boston harbor.

The nickname Tony Clean had stuck for a number of reasons: his appearance was part of it, but mainly it was because Tony never got his hands dirty. People had washed a lot of blood off their hands for Tony's sake, watching it spiral down into cracked porcelain bathtubs or stainless steel sinks, but Tony never got so much as a speck of it on his shirt.

I heard a story about him once, back in 1990 when he was still slashing up pimps who forgot how territorial Tony could be. A guy called Stan Goodman, a Boston real estate developer, owned a weekend house in Rockport, a big old gabled place with vast green lawns and an oak tree that was about two centuries old out by the boundary wall. Rockport's a pretty nice place, a fishing village north of Boston at Cape Ann where you can still park for a penny and the Salt Water trolley will haul you around town for four dollars a day.

Goodman had a wife and two teenage children, a boy and a girl, and they loved that house as well. Tony offered Stan Goodman a lot of money for the house, but he refused. It had belonged to his father, he said, and his father had bought it from the original owner back in the forties. He offered to find Tony Clean a similar property nearby, because Stan Goodman figured that if he kept on the good side of Tony Clean then everything would turn out okay. Except Tony Clean didn't have a good side.

One night in June, someone entered the Goodman house, shot their dog, bound and gagged the four members of the family and took them out to the old granite quarries at Halibut Point. My guess is that Stan Goodman died last, after they had killed his wife, his daughter and his son by placing their heads on a flat rock and cracking them open with a sledgehammer. There was a lot of blood on the ground when they were found the next morning, and I reckon it took the men who killed them a long time to wash it from their clothes. Tony Celli bought the house the following month. There were no other bidders.

The mere fact that Tony was here after what had taken place at Prouts Neck indicated that he wasn't screwing around. Tony wanted that money, and he wanted it bad, and he was willing to risk bringing down heat on himself to find it.

"You watch the news?" he said at last. He didn't look away from the screen, but I knew that the question was directed at me.

"Nope."

He looked at me for the first time.

"You don't watch any news?"

"Nope."

"Why not?"

"It depresses me."

"You must depress easy."

"I have a sensitive nature."

The financial report ended. He clicked off the TV using a manicured finger on the remote, then turned his full attention to me.

"You know who I am?" he said.

"Yeah, I know who you are."

"Good. Then, being an intelligent man, you probably know why I'm here."

"Christmas shopping? Looking to buy a house?"

He smiled coldly. "I know all about you, Parker. You're the one that took down the Ferreras." The Ferreras were a New York crime family, *were* being the operative word. I had become mixed up in their business, and it had ended badly for them.

"They took themselves down. I just watched."

"That's not what I heard. A lot of people in New York would be happier if you were dead. They think you lack respect."

"I'm sure."

"So why aren't you dead?"

"I brighten up a dull world?"

"They want to brighten up their world, they can turn on a light. Try again."

"Because they know I'll kill whoever comes after me, then I'll kill whoever sent them."

"I could kill you now. Unless you can come back from the dead, your threats aren't going to disturb my sleep."

"I have friends. I'd give you a week, maybe ten days. Then you'd die too."

He pulled a face, and a couple of the men around him snickered. "You play cards?" he asked, when they had finished laughing.

"Only solitaire. I like playing with someone I can trust."

"You know what 'fucking the deck' means?"

"Yeah, I know." Fucking the deck was something neophyte gamblers did: they screwed up the cards by making dumb calls. That was why experienced gamblers didn't play with amateurs, no matter how much money they had. There was always the chance that they'd fuck the deck so badly that the risk of losing increased to the extent that it wasn't worth gambling.

"Billy Purdue fucked my deck, and now I think you might be about to fuck my deck too. That's no good. I want you to stop. First I want you to tell me what you know about Purdue. Then I'll pay you to walk away."

"I don't need money."

"Everybody needs money. I can pay whatever debts you owe, maybe make some others disappear."

"I don't owe anybody."

"Everybody owes somebody."

"Not me. I'm free and clean."

"Or maybe you figure you got debts that money can't pay."

"That's very perceptive. What does it mean?"

"It means I am running out of reasonable ways to alter your current course of action, Bird-*man*." He made a little quotation marks sign with his fingers as he spoke the last syllable, then his voice lowered and he stood up. Even in his stocking feet, he was taller than I was.

"Now you listen to me, Birdman," he said, when he was only inches from me. "Don't make me tear your wings off. I hear you did some work for Billy Purdue's ex-wife. I hear also that he gave you money, my money, to give to her. That makes you a very interesting individual, because I figure you were one of the last people to talk to both of them before they went their separate ways. Now, do you want to tell me what you know so that you can go back to your little birdhouse and curl up for the night?"

I held his gaze. "If I knew anything useful and told you, my conscience wouldn't let me sleep," I said. "As it happens, I don't know anything, useful or otherwise."

"You know that Purdue has my money?"

"Has he?"

He shook his head, almost in sorrow. "You're going to make me hurt you."

"Did you kill Rita Ferris and her son?"

Tony took a step back then punched me hard in the stomach. I saw it coming and braced myself for the blow, but the force was strong enough to send me to my knees. As I gasped for breath I heard a gun cock behind me and felt cold steel against my skull.

"I don't kill women and children," said Tony.

"Since when?" I replied. "New Year's?"

A clump of my hair was gripped in someone's hand and I was dragged to my feet, the gun still behind my ear.

"How stupid are you?" said Tony, rubbing the knuckles of his right hand. "You want to die?"

"I don't know anything," I repeated. "I did some work for his ex-wife, crossed swords with Billy Purdue and walked away. That's all."

Tony Clean nodded. "What were you talking to the rummy in the bar about?"

"Something else."

Tony drew his fist back again.

"It was something else," I said again, louder this time. "He was a friend of my grandfather's. I wanted to look him up, that's all. You're right, he's just a rummy. Leave him be."

Tony stepped back, still rubbing his knuckles.

"I find out you're lying to me, you'll die badly, you understand? And if you're a smart guy, and not just a guy with a smart mouth, you'll stay out of my affairs."

The tone of his voice grew gentler, but his face hardened as he spoke again: "I'm sorry we have to do this to you, but I need to be sure that you understand what we've discussed. If at any point you feel you have something to add to what you've told me, just moan louder."

He nodded at whoever was behind me and I was forced down to my knees again. A rag was stuffed in my mouth, and my arms were pulled back and secured with cuffs. I looked up to see Harelip limping toward me. In his hand, he held a short metal rod. Crackling blue lightning danced along its length.

The first two shots from the cattle prod knocked me backward and sent me spasming to the ground, my teeth gritted in pain against the rag. After the third or fourth contact I lost control of myself and blue flashes moved through the blackness of my mind until, at last, the clouds took me and all went quiet.

When I came to, I was lying behind my Mustang, hidden from anyone walking on the street. The tips of my fingers were raw and my coat glittered with crystals of frost. My head ached badly, my body still trembled and there was dried blood and vomit on the side of my face and the front of my coat. I smelled bad. I got unsteadily to my feet and checked my coat pockets. My gun was in one, its clip gone, and my cell phone was in the other. I called a cab and, while I waited for it to arrive, made a call to a mechanic with a tow truck over by the Veteran's Memorial Bridge and asked him to take care of the car.

When I got back to Scarborough, the right side of my face had swollen badly and there were small burn marks where the prod had touched my skin. There were also two or three gashes on my head, one of them deep. I reckoned that Harelip had kicked me a couple of times for good measure. I put ice on my head and spray on the burns, then swallowed some painkillers, pulled on a pair of sweatpants and a T-shirt to guard against the cold, and tried to sleep.

I don't recall why I awoke, but when I opened my eyes the room seemed to hang between darkness and brightness, as if the universe had paused to draw a breath when the morning sun first sent shafts of light through the dark winter clouds.

And from somewhere in the house came a sound like the scuffling of feet, as if small delicate steps were padding over the floorboards. I drew my gun and rose. The floor was cold and the windows rattled gently. I opened the door slowly and stepped into the hallway.

To my right, a figure moved. I caught the motion out of the corner of my eye, so that I was not sure that I even saw a figure as such or merely a shifting of shadows in the kitchen. I turned and walked slowly to the back of the house, the floor creaking slightly beneath my feet.

Then I heard it: a soft burst of childlike laughter, a giggle of amusement, and the padding of feet again, moving to my left. I reached the entrance to the kitchen, the gun half raised, and turned in time to see another flash of movement by the door frame that connected the kitchen to the living room, to hear another cry of childish delight at the game we were playing. And I felt certain that what I had seen was a child's foot, its sole protected by the enclosures of purple rompers. And I knew too that I had seen that tiny foot before and the remembrance of it made my throat go dry.

I entered the dining room. Something small waited for me beyond the far door. I could see its form in the shadows and the light in its eyes, but no more than that. As I moved in its direction, the form shifted and I heard the front door creak open on its hinges and impact against the wall, the wind now rushing through the house, pulling at the drapes, setting frames rattling, raising spirals of dust in the hallway.

I walked faster now. As I reached the door, I caught another glimpse of the little figure, a shape dressed in purple that flitted between the trees, moving farther and farther into the darkness beyond. I stepped from the porch and into the yard, felt the grass beneath my feet, the small stones digging into the soles, and tensed as something light and multilegged scuttled across my toes. I stood at the verge of the woods, and I was afraid.

She was waiting for me there. She stood unmoving, masked by bushes and trees that hid her body from me, her face now obscured by the shadows of branches, now clear again. Her eyes were full of blood and the thick black thread wove back and forth across her face like the crudely constructed mouth of an old cloth doll. She stood there unspeaking, watching me from the woods, and behind her the smaller figure danced and skipped in the undergrowth.

I closed my eyes and concentrated, trying to wake myself, but the cold in my feet was real, and the throbbing pain in my head, and the sound of the child's laughter carrying on the wind.

I felt movement behind me and something touched me on the shoulder. I almost turned, but the pressure on my shoulder increased and I knew that I must not turn, that I was not meant to see what stood at my back. I looked to my left, to the point of pressure, and I could not restrain the shudder that ran through my body. I closed my eyes instantly but what I had seen was imprinted on my mind like an image seen against bright sunlight.

The hand was soft and white and delicate, with long, tapering fingers. A wedding band gleamed in the strange, predawn light.

bird

How many times had I heard that voice whisper to me in the darkness, a prelude to the soft caress of a warm hand, the feel of her breath against my cheek, my lips, her small breasts hard against my body, her legs like ivy curling around me? I had heard it in times of love and passion when we were happy together, in moments of anger and rage and sadness as our marriage fell apart. And I had heard it since in the rustling of leaves on the grass and the sound of branches rubbing against one another in the autumn breezes, a voice that carried from far away and called to me from the shadows.

Susan, my Susan.

bird

The voice was close now, almost beside my ear. It had the sound of earth in it, as if dirt had caught in her throat.

help her

In the woods beyond, the woman watched me, her red eyes wide and unblinking.

How?

find him

Find who? Billy?

The fingers tightened their grip.

yes

He's not my responsibility.

they are all your responsibility

And in the patches of moonlight beneath the trees, shapes twisted and turned, suspended above the earth, their feet not touching the ground, and their ruined stomachs shone dark and wet. All of them, my responsibility.

Then the pressure on my shoulder eased and I sensed her moving away. Ahead of me came a sound from the undergrowth and the woman who had been Rita Ferris receded into the trees. I caught a final glimpse of purple moving swiftly beyond the line of trees, laughter like music carrying back to me.

And I saw something else.

I saw a small girl with long blond hair who looked back at me with something like love before she followed her playmate into the darkness.

CHAPTER NINE

I WOKE TO a bright room, winter sunlight spearing through a gap in the drapes. My head ached and my jaw felt stiff and sore where I had gritted my teeth as the shocks hit my body. It was only when I sat up and the pain in my head increased that I remembered my dream from the night before, if a dream was what it was.

There were leaves in my bed, and I had mud on my feet.

I had some homeopathic remedies that Louis had recommended to me, so I took them with a glass of water while I waited for the shower to heat up. I downed a combination of phosphorus, to combat nausea, and hypericum, which was supposed to act as a natural painkiller. Frankly, I felt like a flake taking the stuff but there was no one around to see me do it, so that made it okay.

I started a pot of coffee, poured a cup and watched it grow cold on the kitchen table. I felt pretty low and was considering taking up a different profession—gardening, maybe, or lobster fishing. After the coffee had developed a nice film, I called Ellis Howard. I figured that, in the absence of his lieutenant and given the federal angle, Ellis was taking a hands-on approach to the case. It took a while for him to come to the phone. He was probably still sore over the Biggs affair.

"You're awake early," were his first words when he got to the phone. I could hear him sigh as he eased his bulk into a chair. I could even hear the chair squeaking in protest. If Ellis had sat on me, I'd have squeaked too.

"I could say the same about you," I said. "You sound like you slept as well as I did."

"Yeah, like the bed was made of broken glass. You aware that Tony Celli turned up in town yesterday?"

"Yeah. Bad news travels fast." Particularly when it's being passed into your jaw in the form of an electric current.

"He blew out again this morning. Looks like he's gone to ground."

"It's a shame. I thought he was going to move here and open a florist's."

At the other end of the phone there was the sound of the receiver being covered, a muffled exchange and then the rustling of papers. Then: "So what do you want, Bird?"

"I wanted to know if there was any movement on Rita Ferris, or Billy Purdue, or on that Coupe De Ville."

Ellis laughed dully. "Ixnay on the first two, but the third one is interesting. Turns out the Coupe De Ville is a company car, registered to one Leo Voss, a lawyer in Boston." There was a pause on the other end of the line. I waited until I realized that, once again, I was supposed to be playing the role of straight man in a conversation.

"But . . .?" I said at last.

"*But*," said Ellis, "Leo Voss is no longer with us. He's dead, died earlier this week."

"Damn, a dead lawyer. Only another million to go."

"We live in hope," said Ellis.

"Did he fall, or was he pushed?"

"That's the interesting part. His secretary found him and called the cops. He was sitting behind his desk still dressed in his running outfit—sneakers, socks, T-shirt, sweatpants—with an opened bottle of water in front of him. Their first impression was that he'd had a heart attack. According to the secretary, he'd been feeling ill for a couple of days. He thought it might be flu.

"But when he was autopsied, there was evidence of inflammation of the nerves in the hands and feet. He'd also lost some hair, probably only in the previous day or two. Tests on a hair sample turned up traces of thallium. You know what thallium is?"

"Uh-huh." My grandfather had used it as rat bait, until its sale was restricted. It was a metallic element, similar to lead or mercury, but far more poisonous. Its salts were soluble in water, almost tasteless and produced symptoms similar to influenza, meningitis or encephalitis. A lethal dose of thallium sulfate, maybe eight hundred milligrams or more, could kill in anything from twenty-four to forty hours.

"So what sort of work did this Leo Voss do?" I asked.

"Fairly straightforward stuff, mainly corporate, although what he did must have been pretty lucrative. He had a house in Beacon Hill, a summer place in the Vineyard, and still had some money in the bank, probably because he was single and there was no one putting fur coats on *his* credit card."

Doreen, I thought. If Ellis could have afforded it, he'd have pasted pictures of her outside churches as a warning to bridegrooms.

"They're still going through his files, but he seems to have been squeaky clean," concluded Ellis.

"Which probably means that he wasn't."

Ellis tut-tutted. "Such cynicism in one so young. Now I've got something for you: I hear you were talking to Willeford."

"That's right. Is that a problem?"

"Could be. He's gone, and I'm starting to resent arriving in places to find that you've already been there. It's making me feel inadequate, and I get enough of that at home."

I felt my grip tighten on the phone. "Last I saw of him, he was sitting in the Sail Loft nursing a drink."

"Willeford never nursed a drink in his life. They don't survive in the glass long enough to be nursed. He give any indication that he might be planning to go away somewhere?"

"No, nothing." I recalled Tony's Celli's interest in Willeford and felt my mouth go dry.

"What did you two talk about?"

I paused before I spoke. "He did some work for Billy Purdue: tracing of birth parents."

"That it?"

"That's it."

"He have any luck?"

"I don't think so."

Ellis went quiet, then said distinctly: "Don't hold back on me, Bird. I don't like it."

"I'm not." It wasn't quite a lie, but I'm not sure that it qualified as the truth either. I waited for Ellis to say something more, but he didn't push the issue.

"Stay out of trouble, Bird," was all he said, before he hung up.

I had just finished cleaning off the table and was in my bedroom slipping on my boots when I heard the sound of a car pulling up outside. Through the gap in the drapes I could see the rear of a gold Mercury Sable parked near the side of the house. I took my Smith & Wesson, wrapped it in a towel and walked onto the porch. And as I stepped into the cold morning sunlight, I heard a voice that I knew say:

"Why would anybody plant so many trees? I mean, who has that kind of time? I can't even find time to get my laundry done."

Angel stood with his back to me, staring out at the trees at the edge of my property. He wore a Timberland fleece top, a pair of brown corduroy pants and tan work boots. At his feet was a hard plastic suitcase which was so pitted and battered that it looked like it had been dropped from an airplane. A piece of blue climbing rope and the whim of fortune held it closed.

Angel breathed in deeply then bent over as his body was racked by a fit of coughing. He spat something large and unpleasant on to the ground before him.

"That's the clean air getting the shit out of your lungs," said a deep, drawling voice. From behind the raised trunk door of the car Louis appeared holding a matching Delsey case and suit carrier. He wore a black Boss overcoat beneath which a gray double-breasted suit shimmered. A black shirt was buttoned to the neck and his shaved head gleamed. In the open trunk, I could see a long, metal storage case. Louis never went anywhere without his toys.

"I think that *was* my lung," said Angel, using the tip of his boot to poke with interest at whatever piece of matter had expelled itself from his body. As I looked at them both, my spirits lifted. I wasn't sure why they were here instead of back in New York, but, whatever the reason, I was glad. Louis glanced at me and nodded, which was usually as close as Louis ever came to looking pleased about anything.

"You know, Angel," I said, "you make nature look untidy just by standing there."

Angel turned and raised an arm in a sweeping gesture.

"Trees," he said, shaking his head in bafflement and smiling. "So many trees. I ain't seen this many trees since I got thrown out of the Indian Scouts."

"You know, I don't think I even want to know why," I said.

Angel picked up his case. "Bastards. And I was just about to get my explorer's badge too."

"Didn't think they had badges for the shit you was exploring," said Louis, from behind. "Badge like that could get a man thrown in jail in Georgia."

"Funny," barked Angel. "It's just a myth that you can't be gay and do macho things."

"Uh-huh. Just like it's a myth that all homosexuals wear nice clothes and take care of their skin."

"That better not be aimed at me."

It was nice to see that some things hadn't changed.

"How you doin' today?" said Angel, as he pushed past me. "And lose the gun. We're staying, like it or not. You look like shit, by the way."

"Nice suit," I remarked to Louis, as he followed Angel.

"Thanks," he replied. "Never forget: no such thing as a brother with no taste, just a brother with no money."

I stood on the porch for a moment, feeling a little stupid holding the towel-wrapped gun. Then, figuring that the matter had obviously been decided long before they got to Maine, I followed them into the house.

I showed them to the spare bedroom, where the furniture consisted only of a mattress on the floor and an old closet.

"Jesus," said Angel. "It's the Hanoi Hilton. If we knock on the pipes, someone better answer."

"You gonna supply sheets, or we have to roll some drunks and steal their coats?" asked Louis.

"I can't sleep here," said Angel, with an air of finality. "If the rats want to feed on me, fuckers should at least have to go to the trouble of climbing up a bedframe."

He brushed past me again, and seconds later, I heard his voice call:

"Hey, this one's much nicer. We'll take this."

There came the unmistakable sound of someone bouncing up and down on my bed. Louis looked at me.

"Might need that gun after all," he said. Then he shrugged and followed the sound of the springs.

When I eventually got them out of my bedroom and had arranged to have some extra furniture, including a bed, taken out of the Kraft Mini-Storage on Gorham Road and delivered to the house, we sat around the kitchen table and I waited for them to tell me why they were here. It had begun to rain: hard, cold drops that spoke of the coming of snow.

"We're your guardian angels," said Angel.

"Why doesn't that fill me with a sense of blessing?" I replied.

"Or maybe we just heard that this is the place to be," continued Angel. "Anybody who's anybody is here right now. You got your Tony Celli, you got your feds, you got your local shit-kickers, you got your dead Asians. Shit, this place is like the UN with guns."

"What do you know?" I asked.

"We know that you've been pissing people off already," he replied. "What happened to your face?"

"Guy with a harelip tried to educate me with a cattle prod, then rearranged my hairline with his shoe."

"That's Mifflin," said Louis. "He have another guy with him, looked like someone dropped a safe on his head and the safe lost?"

"Yeah," I said. "He didn't kick me, though."

"That's 'cause the message probably got halfway from his brain to his foot then forgot where it was going. His name's Berendt. He's so dumb he makes dodos look smart. Tony Clean was with them?" While he spoke, he balanced one of my carving knives on the tip of his index finger and amused himself by tossing it in the air and catching it by the handle. It was a pretty neat trick. If the circus came to town, he was a shoo-in.

"They were staying at the Regency," I said. "I got to visit Tony's room."

"Was it nice?" asked Angel, pointedly running a hand along the underside of the table and examining the accumulated dust on the tips of his fingers.

"Yeah, pretty nice, apart from the kicks in the head and the electric shocks."

"Fuck him. We should make him stay here. The squalor would put him back in touch with his roots."

"You criticize my house again, you can sleep in the yard."

"Probably be cleaner," he muttered. "And warmer."

Louis tapped a long, slim finger gently on the tabletop. "Hear there's a lot of money got misdirected around these parts. A lot of money."

"Yeah, so I gather."

"Any idea where it is?"

"Maybe. I think it's with a guy called Billy Purdue."

"That's what I hear too."

"From Tony Celli's end?"

"Disaffected employees. They figure this Billy Purdue's so dead, someone should name a cemetery after him."

I told them about the deaths of Rita and Donald. I noticed Angel and Louis exchange a glance and I knew that there was more to come.

"Billy Purdue take out Tony's men?" asked Angel.

"Two of them, at least. Assuming he's the one who took the money, and that's what Tony Celli and the law have assumed."

Louis stood and carefully washed his mug. "Tony's in trouble," he said at last. "Got involved in some deal on Wall Street that fell through." I had heard stories that the Italians had moved into Wall Street, establishing paper companies and getting crooked brokers to float them and rip off investors. There was a lot of money to be made if it was done right.

"Tony screwed up," continued Louis, "and now you got a guy whose days are numbered in single figures."

"How bad is it?"

Louis placed the mug upside down to drain, then leaned against the sink. "You know what PERLS is?"

"PERLS *are*," I corrected him, incorrectly as it turned out. "Something found in an oyster?"

"Easy to know you never had no money to invest," said Louis. "PERLS stands for Principal Exchange Rate Linked Security. It's a structured note, a kind of bond sold by investment banks. It's packaged to look safe, except it's risky as sex with a shark. Basically, the buyer bets a certain amount of money and the return is based on the changes in the exchange rate of a number of different currencies. It's a formula, and if things go right, you can make a killing."

I always found it fascinating that Louis could drop the monosyllabic black gunman shtick if the subject required it, but I didn't point it out to him.

"So Tony Celli thinks he's a financial wizard, and some people in Boston believe him," he went on. "He takes care of laundering, passes a lot of money through offshore banks and paper companies, until it finds its way back into the right accounts. He deals with the accountants, but he's also the first point of contact for any cash. He's like the thinnest part of an hourglass: everything has to go through him to get to somewhere else. And sometimes, Tony makes investments on the side using other people's money, or makes a little on currency exchanges, and keeps what he makes. No one cares, long as he doesn't get too greedy."

"Let me guess," I interrupted. "Tony got too greedy."

Louis nodded. "Tony's tired of being an Indian and now he wants to be a chief. He figures he needs money to do that, more than he's got. So he gets talking to some derivatives salesman who doesn't have a fucking clue who Tony is beyond the fact that he's a wop in a striped shirt with money to spend, because Tony is trying to keep his dealings as low-key as possible. He convinces Tony to buy a variation on these PERLS, linked to the difference between the value of some Southeast Asian currencies and a basket of other currencies—dollars, Swiss francs, German marks, I heard—and pockets the commission. The thing is so dangerous it should be ticking, but Tony buys in for one and a half million dollars, most of which isn't his own money, because there are midwestern insurance companies and pension funds in on the deal too and Tony figures wrongly that they're too conservative to bet on a risky hand. It's purely a short-term investment, and Tony figures he'll have his money made before anybody notices he's holding onto the cash for longer than usual."

"So what happened?"

"You read the papers. The yen plummets, banks fail, the whole economy of Southeast Asia starts to come unstuck. The value of Tony's bonds falls by 95 percent in forty-eight hours, and his life expectancy falls by roughly the same amount. Tony sends some people to look for the salesman and they find him in Zip City down on 18th Street, laughing about how he ripped some guy's face off. That's what these salesmen call it when they sell someone an exploding bond."

And with those words, according to Louis, the salesman had signed his own death warrant. He was taken when he went to the bathroom, brought to a basement in Queens and tied to a chair. Then Tony came in, stuck his fingers in the soft flesh beneath the guy's chin, and started to pull. It took him less than two minutes to tear the guy's face apart, then they put him in a car and beat him to death in some woods upstate.

Louis picked up the knife again, gave it a couple of extra spins for good luck, then put it back in its wooden block. There was no blood on his fingertip, despite the pressure of the knifepoint. "So

Tony's in the hole for the cash, and some people higher up start getting concerned about the length of time it's taking for their money to reach them. Then Tony gets lucky: a mook in Toronto, who owes Tony big time, tells him about this old Cambodian guy living the quiet life in Hamilton, south of the city. It seems the old man was Khmer Rouge, used to be a deputy director in the Tuol Seng camp in Phnom Penh."

I had heard of Tuol Seng. It had once been a school in the Cambodian capital, but was converted into a place of torture and execution by the Khmer Rouge when they took over the country. Tuol Seng had been run by the big-eared camp director known as Comrade Deuch, who had used whips, chains, poisonous reptiles and water to torture and kill maybe sixteen thousand people, including Westerners who strayed too close to the Cambodian coast.

"Seems like this old man had friends in Thailand, and made a lot of money on the side by acting as a conduit for heroin smuggling," said Louis. "When the Vietnamese invaded, he disappeared and reinvented himself as a restaurateur in Toronto. His daughter had just started school in Boston, so Tony targeted her, took her and sent her old man a ransom demand to cover his debts, and then some. The old man couldn't go to the cops because of his past, and Tony gave him seventy-two hours to comply, though his daughter was already dead by then. The old man comes up with the money, sends his men down to Maine for the drop and—bam!—it all goes haywire."

That explained the presence of the Toronto cop, Eldritch. I mentioned him to Louis and he raised a slim finger. "One more thing: at the same time that the killings were going down here, the old man's house in Hamilton burned to the ground, with him, the rest of his family and his personal guards still in it. Seven people, all told. Tony wanted it to be clean, because he's a clean kind of guy."

"So Tony's got a price on his head and then Billy Purdue takes his get-out-of-jail-free card," I remarked. "Now, you want to tell me what that look that passed between you and Angel was about?" When Louis had finished talking, Angel had once again glanced at him in a way that told me that there was something more to hear, and it wasn't good.

Louis watched as the rain speckled the window.

"You got more problems than Tony and the law," he said quietly. His face was serious, his expression mirrored by the usually ebullient Angel.

"How bad?"

"Don't think it gets any worse. You ever hear of Abel and Stritch?"

"No. What do they do, make soap?"

"They kill people."

"With all due respect, that hardly makes them unique in the present company."

"They enjoy it."

And for the next half hour, Louis traced the path of the two men known only as Abel and Stritch, a trail marked by torture, burnings, gassings, casual sexual homicide, paid and unpaid assassinations. They broke bones and spilled blood; they electrocuted and asphyxiated. Their trail wound its way around the world like a coil of barbed wire, stretching from Asia and South Africa to South and Central America, through every trouble spot where people might pay to have their enemies, real or imagined, terrorized and killed.

Louis told me of an incident in Chile, when a family suspected of harboring Mapuche Indians was targeted by agents of Pinochet's National Intelligence Directorate. The family's three sons, all in their early twenties, were taken to the basement of an abandoned office building, gagged and tied to the concrete supports of the building. Their mother and sisters were led in and forced at gunpoint to sit facing the men. Nobody spoke.

Then a figure had appeared from the darkness at the back of

the room, a squat, pale man with a bald head and dead eyes. Another man remained in the shadows, but they could see his cigarette flare occasionally and could smell the smoke he exhaled.

In his right hand, the pale man held a large, five-hundred-watt soldering iron, adapted so that its glowing tip was almost half an inch long and burned at two or three hundred degrees. He walked to the youngest son, pulled back his shirt and applied the tip to his breast, just below the sternum. The iron hissed as it entered the flesh, and the smell of burning pork filled the room. The young man struggled as the iron went deeper and deeper, and muffled noises of panic and pain came from his mouth. His tormentor's eyes had changed now, had become bright and alive, and his breathing came in short, excited gasps. With his free hand, he fumbled at the zipper of the man's pants, and he reached in and held him as the iron moved upward toward his heart. As it pierced the wall of muscle, the pale man's grip tightened and he smiled as his victim shook and died.

The women told them what they knew, which was little, and the other men died quickly, as much because the pale man had spent himself as because of what had been revealed.

Now these two killers had come north, north as far as Maine.

"Why are they here?" I said at last.

"They want the money," said Louis. "Men like them, they make enemies. If they're good at what they do, most of those enemies don't live long enough to do them any harm. But the longer they keep working, the more the chances of someone slipping through the net increase. These two have been killing for decades. The clock is ticking on them now. That money would help to provide a pretty cool retirement fund, maybe help them escape the net that's closing in on them. I got a feeling they may be calling on you, which is why we're here."

"What do they look like?" I asked, but I already had my suspicions.

"That's the problem. Nothing on Abel, 'cept he's tall with silver, almost white, hair. But Stritch, the torturer . . . The guy is a fucking freak show: small, with a wide, bald head, a mouth long as the slit in a toaster. Looks like Uncle Fester but without the good nature."

I thought of the strange, goblinlike man outside the inn, the same man who had later turned up at Java Joe's ostensibly proselytizing for the Lord, with his crudely drawn picture of a mother and child and his soft, implicit threats.

"I've seen him," I said.

Louis wiped his hand across his mouth. I had never before found him so concerned about the threat posed by anyone. In my mind, I still had an image of the darkness coming alive in an old warehouse back in Queens and one of the city's most feared killers rising up on his toes, his mouth wide, as Louis's blade entered the base of his skull. Louis didn't frighten easily. I told him about the car and the encounter in the coffee shop, and the lawyer named Leo Voss.

"My guess is that Voss was their point of contact, the guy people came to if they wanted to hire Abel and Stritch," said Louis. "If he's dead, then they killed him. They're closing down the operation, and they don't want any loose ends. If Stritch is here, then so is Abel. They don't work separately. He make any other move?"

"No. I got the feeling he just wanted to make his presence felt."

"Takes a special guy to drive around in a dead man's Caddy," said Angel. "Kind of guy who wants to draw attention to himself."

"Or away from someone else," I said.

"He's watching," said Louis. "So is his partner, somewhere. They're waiting to see if you can lead them to Billy Purdue." He thought for a moment. "The woman and the boy, were they tortured?"

I shook my head. "The woman was strangled. No sign of other injuries or sexual assault. The boy died because he got in the way." I recalled the sight of Rita Ferris's mouth as the cops turned her over. "There was one thing: the killer sewed the woman's mouth shut with black thread after she died."

Angel screwed up his face. "Makes no sense."

"Makes no sense if it's Abel and Stritch," agreed Louis. "They'd have ripped her fingers off and hurt the boy to find out what she knew about the money. Doesn't sound like their work."

"Or Tony Celli's," added Angel.

"The cops think Billy may have killed them," I said. "It's possible, but there's still no reason for him to mutilate the mouth."

We were silent then as we balanced and weighed what we knew. I think we all moved toward the same conclusion, but it was left to Louis to voice it:

"There's someone else."

Outside, the rain fell hard, hammering on the tiles and raking at the windowpanes. I felt a coldness at my shoulder, or perhaps it was just the memory of a touch, and the voice of the rain seemed to whisper to me in a language that I could not comprehend.

A couple of hours later, a truck arrived with some of my furniture and we set up a bed in the spare room, added some throw rugs and generally made the place look like a home away from home, as long as the original home was nothing too fancy. Then, when we had all freshened up, we drove into Portland, past the blue-and-white lights of the Christmas tree at Congress Square and the second, larger tree at Monument Square. We parked the car, then strolled down to the Stone Coast Brewing Company on York Street, where Angel and Louis drank microbrew beer while we decided where to eat.

"You got a sushi bar around here?" asked Louis.

"I don't eat seafood," I said.

"You don't eat seafood?" Louis's voice rose an octave. "The fuck you mean, you don't eat seafood? You live in Maine. Lobsters practically hand you a knife and fork and invite you to chew on their ass."

"You know I don't eat seafood," I replied patiently. "It's just a thing."

"It's not just a thing, man, it's a *phobia*."

Beside me, Angel smiled. It was good to be out like this, to be acting in this way, after what we had spoken of earlier.

"Sorry," I continued, "but I draw the line at anything with more than four legs, or no legs at all. I bet you even eat the lungs out of crabs."

"Lungs, the crab juice . . ."

"That's not juice, Louis, it's the contents of their digestive system. Why do you think it's yellow?"

He waved a hand dismissively. "Ain't no crab shit in sushi anyways."

Angel drained the last of his beer. "Well I'm with Bird on this one," he said. "Last time I was in L.A. I ate in a sushi bar. Pretty much ate them out of anything that had gills. Went outside, took one last look in the window, and the place had a 'C' grading from the health department. A fucking 'C'! I might eat in a burger joint with a C grade, worst you could expect would be a dose of Ronald McDonald's Revenge, but C-graded sushi . . . Man, that stuff'll kill you. Damn fish was so bad, it almost pulled a gun and tried to steal my wallet."

Louis put his head in his hands and prayed to whoever it was that people like Louis prayed to—Smith & Wesson, probably.

We ate in David's on Monument Square. As it happened, sitting three tables away from us were Samson and Doyle, the two feds I had seen at Rita Ferris's apartment, and the Toronto policeman, Eldritch. They gave us interested but unfriendly looks, then went back to their food.

"Friends of yours?" said Angel.

"The federal boys, plus their cousin from north of the border."

"Feds got no reason to like you, Bird. Not that they need a reason not to like anyone."

Our own food came: fish for Louis and beef for Angel and me. We ate in silence. The feds and Eldritch left in the course of our meal. I got the feeling that I'd be hearing from them again. When they were gone, Louis dabbed his lips carefully with a napkin and drained the last of his beer. "You got a plan of campaign on the Billy Purdue thing?"

I shrugged. "I've asked around, but he's gone to earth. Part of me says that he's here, but another part tells me that he may be heading north. If he's in trouble, my guess is that he may look for someone who's been sympathetic to him in the past, and those people are precious few. There's a guy up by Moosehead Lake in a place called Dark Hollow, acted as Billy Purdue's foster parent for a time. It may be that he knows something, or has heard from him."

I told them about my conversation in the bar with Willeford and his subsequent disappearance. "I'm also going to pay a call on Cheryl Lansing, see if she can add anything to what she told Willeford."

"Sounds like your curiosity's been sparked," remarked Angel.

"Maybe, but . . ."

"But?"

I didn't want to tell him about my experience the night before, no matter how much I trusted him. That was the stuff of madness. "But I owe something to Rita and her son. And, anyhow, it seems like other people have decided to involve me whether I like it or not."

"Ain't that always the way?"

"Yeah." I reached into my wallet, took out the bill from the furniture removal firm and waved it pointedly at Angel. "Ain't that always the way?" I echoed.

He smiled. "Take that attitude and we might never leave."

"Don't even go there, Angel," I warned. "And pick up the check. It's the least you can do."

CHAPTER TEN

I WOKE EARLY and refreshed for the trip to Bangor. Angel and Louis were still in bed, so I drove to Oak Hill, intending to stop off at the bank to withdraw some cash for the trip north. But when I had finished, I headed on down Old County Road and onto Black Point Road, past the White Caps Sandwich Shop until I reached Ferry Road. To my left was the golf course, to my right the summer homes, and ahead of me was the parking lot where the men had died. The rain had washed away the evidence, but lengths of tattered crime scene tape still fluttered on one of the barriers as the wind howled in off the sea.

As I stood, taking in the scene, a car pulled up behind me: a cruiser driven by one of the Scarborough reserve cops, probably drafted in since the killings to keep rubberneckers away.

"You okay, sir?" he asked, as he stepped from the car.

"Yeah, just looking," I replied. "I live up on Spring Street."

He sized me up, then nodded. "I recognize you now. Sorry, sir, but after what happened here, we have to be careful."

I waved a hand at him, but he seemed to be in the mood for conversation. He was young, certainly younger than I was, with straw-colored hair and soft, serious eyes. "Strange business," he said. "It's usually pretty quiet and peaceful here."

"You from around these parts?" I asked.

He shook his head. "No, sir. Flint, Michigan. Came east after GM screwed us over, and started again here. Best move I ever made."

"Yeah, well, this place hasn't always been so peaceful." My grandfather could trace his family's roots back to the mid-seventeenth century, maybe two decades after Scarborough was first settled in 1632 or 1633. Back then, the whole area was called Black Point and the settlement was abandoned twice because of attacks by the natives. In 1677, the Wabanaki had attacked the English fort at Black Point on two occasions. Forty English soldiers and a dozen of their Indian allies from the Protestant mission village at Natick, near Boston, died in the second assault alone. Maybe ten minutes by car from where we were standing was Massacre Pond, where Richard Hunnewell and nineteen others died in an Indian attack in 1713.

Now, with its summer homes and its yacht club, its bird sanctuary and its polite police, it was easy to forget that this was once a violent, troubled place. There was blood beneath the ground here, layer upon layer of it like the marks left in rock faces by seas that had ceased to exist hundreds of millions of years before. I sometimes felt that places retained memories—houses, lands, towns, mountains, all holding within themselves the ghosts of past experiences—and sometimes those places acted just like magnets, attracting bad luck and violence to them like iron filings. In other words, once a lot of blood was spilled somewhere, then there was a pretty good chance that it would be spilled there again.

It wasn't strange that eight men should have ended their lives so bloodily here. It wasn't strange at all.

• • •

When I returned to the house I toasted some English muffins, made coffee and had a quiet breakfast in the kitchen while Louis and Angel showered and dressed.

We had decided the night before that Louis would stay at the house, maybe take a look around Portland and see if he could find any signs of Abel and Stritch. Also, in the event that anything developed while we were away, he could call me on the cell phone and let me know.

Portland to Bangor is 125 miles north on I-95. As we drove, Angel flipped through my cassette tape collection impatiently, listening to something for one or two songs then discarding it on the back seat: The Go-Betweens, The Triffids, The Gourds out of Austin, Jim White, Doc Watson, they all ended up in the pile, so that the car started to look like a music business nightmare. I put on a Lampchop cassette, and the gentle, sad chords of *I Will Drive Slowly* filled the car.

"What'd you say this is?" asked Angel.

"Alternative country," I replied.

"That's when your truck starts, your wife comes back and your dog gets resurrected," he snickered.

"Willie Nelson heard you talking like that, he'd whip your ass."

"This the same Willie Nelson whose wife once tied him up in a bedsheet and beat him unconscious with a broom handle? That pothead comes after me, I reckon I can handle myself."

Eventually, we settled for a discussion of local news on PBS. There was some talk of a timber company surveyor who might have gone missing up north, but I didn't pay a whole lot of attention to it. At Waterville, we took the off-ramp and stopped for soup and coffee. Angel toyed with saltine crumbs as we waited for the check. He had something on his mind, and it didn't take long for it to emerge.

"Remember when I asked you about Rachel, back in New York?" he said at last.

"I remember," I replied.

"You weren't too keen on talking about it."

"I'm still not."

"Maybe you should."

There was a pause. I wondered when Louis and Angel had discussed Rachel and me, and guessed that it might have come up between them more than once. I relented a little.

"She doesn't want to see me," I said.

He pursed his lips. "And how do you feel about that?"

"You going to charge me by the hour for this?"

He flicked a crumb at me. "Just answer the question."

"Not so good but, frankly, I've got other things on my mind."

Angel's eyes glanced up at me, then back down again. "Y'know, she called once, to ask how you were."

"She called *you*? How'd she get your number?"

"We're in the book."

"No, you're not."

"Well, then, we must have given it to her."

"You're so helpful." I sighed, and ran my hands over my face. "I don't know, Angel. The whole thing is screwed up. I don't know if I'm ready yet and, anyway, I frighten her. She's the one who pushed me away, remember?"

"You didn't need a whole lot of pushing."

The check came, and I put down a ten and some ones on top of it. "Yeah, well . . . I had my reasons. Just like she did."

I stood, and Angel stood with me.

"Maybe," he said. "Pity neither of you could come up with one good reason between you."

As we drove back onto I-95, Angel stretched contentedly beside me, and as he did so, the sleeve of his oversized shirt fell down to his elbow. On his arm, a scar, white and ragged, ran from the hollow curve beneath his stringy biceps to within an inch or two of his wrist. It was maybe six inches long in total and I couldn't imagine why I hadn't noticed it before but, as I thought about it, I realized it was a combination of factors: the fact that Angel rarely wore only a T-shirt or, if he did so, it was one with long sleeves; my own self-absorption while we were in Louisiana hunting the Traveling Man; and Angel's basic lack of inclination to discuss anything about past pains.

He caught me looking at the scar and reddened, but he did not try to hide it immediately. Instead, he looked at it himself and went quiet, as if recalling its making.

"You want to know?" he asked.

"You want to tell?"

"Not particularly."

"Then don't."

He didn't respond for a time, then: "It kind of concerns you, so maybe you got a right to know."

"If you tell me you've always been in love with me, I'm stopping the car and you can walk to Bangor."

Angel laughed. "You're in denial."

"You have no idea how deep."

"Anyway, you ain't that good lookin'." He touched the scar gently with the index finger of his right hand. "You been in Rikers, right?"

I nodded. I'd been at Rikers Island in the course of investigations. I had also been there while Angel was a prisoner, when another inmate named William Vance had threatened to take Angel's life and I had intervened. Vance was dead now. He had died from injuries received after persons unknown poured detergent down his throat, after they learned that he was a suspected sex killer who would never stand trial for his crimes because of a lack of evidence. I had provided the information on which his attackers had acted. I had done it to save Angel, and Vance was no loss to the world, but it still weighed on my conscience.

"First time Vance came at me, I knocked out one of his teeth," Angel said quietly. "He'd been threatening it for days, saying how he was gonna fuck me up bad. Fucking guy just had it in for me, you know that. The blow wasn't bad or nothing, but a screw found him bleeding and me standing over him and I got twenty days in the bing."

The "bing" was solitary confinement: twenty-three-hour lockdown, with one hour's exercise permitted in the yard. The yard was basically a cage, not much bigger than a cell, and prisoners were kept handcuffed while they walked. The yard had basketball hoops but no basketballs, even assuming anyone could play basketball with cuffs on. The only thing the prisoners could do was fight, which is what they did when they were let out.

"Most of the time, I didn't leave my cell," said Angel. "Vance had been given ten days, just for getting his mouth cut, and I knew he was waiting for me out there." He went quiet, his teeth working at his bottom lip. "You think it's going to be easy—you know, peace and quiet, sleep, safe most of the time—but it isn't. You can't bring nothing in with you. They take your clothes and give you three jumpsuits instead. You can't smoke, but I boofed the best part of a pack of tobacco in three condoms, rolled it in toilet paper to smoke it." "Boofing" meant taking contraband and inserting it in the anus in order to transport it.

"The tobacco was gone in five days, and I never smoked again. After those five days in that cell, I couldn't take it any more: the noise, the screams. It's psychological torture. I went out into the yard for the first time and Vance came at me straight off, caught me on the side of the head with his balled fists, then started kicking me on the ground. He got five, maybe six good ones in before they hauled him off, but I knew then that I couldn't take any more time in that place. There was no way I could do it.

"I was taken to the infirmary after the beating. They looked me over, decided nothing was broken, then sent me back to the bing. I brought a screw back with me, maybe three inches long, that I'd worked out of the base of a medicine cabinet. And when they put me in the cell, and the lights went out, I tried to cut myself."

He shook his head and, for the first time since he started the story, he smiled. "You ever try to cut yourself with a screw?"

"Can't say that I have."

"Well, it's kinda hard to do. Screws just weren't designed with that particular purpose in mind. After a lot of effort, I managed to get some serious blood flowing, but if I was hoping to bleed to death I'd probably have finished my twenty days before it happened. Anyway, they found me hacking away at my arm and hauled me off to the infirmary again. That's when I called you.

"After some talk, and a psychological profile, and whatever you told them, they put me back in the general population. They figured I wasn't going to harm no one, except maybe myself, and they needed the bing space for someone more deserving."

I had spoken to Vance shortly afterward, before he was due to be released from solitary, and told him what I knew about him, and what I would tell the others if he made a move on Angel. It didn't do any good, and Vance's first act on release was to try to kill Angel in the showers. After that, he was a dead man.

"If they'd put me back in the bing, I'd have found a way to kill myself," concluded Angel. "Maybe I'd have let Vance do it, just to get done with it. There are some debts that will never be paid, Bird, and that's no bad thing sometimes. Louis knows, and I know. The fact that you do what you do because it's right makes it easier to take your side, but you decide you want to take out Congress and Louis will find a way to light the fuse. And I'll hold his coat while he does it."

• • •

Cheryl Lansing lived in a clean, white, two-story house at the western edge of Bangor itself, surrounded by neat lawns and twenty-year-old pine trees. It was a quiet neighborhood with prosperous-looking homes and new cars in the drives. Angel stayed in the Mustang while I tried the bell. No one answered. I cupped my hands and peered in through the glass, but the house was quiet.

I walked around the side and into a long garden with a swimming pool at the end nearest the house. Angel joined me.

"Baby-brokering business must have paid good," he remarked. Smiling, he waved a black wallet, maybe six inches by two inches: the tools of his trade. "Just in case," he said.

"Great. The local cops drop by and I'll tell them I was making a citizen's arrest."

The back of the house had a glass-walled extension that allowed Cheryl Lansing to look out on her green lawn in the summer and watch the snow fall on it in the winter. The pool hadn't been cleaned in a while, and there was no cover over it. It didn't look too deep, sloping from maybe three feet at one end to six or seven feet at the other, but it was full of leaves and dirt.

"Bird."

I walked over to where Angel was looking into the house. There was a kitchen area to one side and a large oak table across from it surrounded by five chairs, with a doorway behind leading into a living room. On the table stood cups, saucers, a coffee pot and an assortment of muffins and breads. A bowl of fruit stood in the center. Even from here, I could see the mold on the food.

Angel pulled a pair of double-thick gloves from his pocket and tried the sliding door. It opened to his touch.

"You want to take a look around?"

"I guess."

Inside, I could smell sour milk and the lingering stench of food gone bad. We moved through the kitchen and into the liv-

ing room, which was furnished with thick couches and arm-
chairs with a pink floral motif. I searched downstairs while Angel went through the upper rooms. When he called me, I was
already on the stairs to follow him up.

He stood in what was obviously a small office, with a dark
wood desk, a computer and a pair of filing cabinets. On the
shelves along the wall sat a series of expanding files, each
marked with a year. The files for 1965 and '66 had been removed
from the shelves and their contents lay scattered on the floor.

"Billy Purdue was born early in '66," I said quietly.

"You figure he came calling?"

"Someone did."

How badly did Billy Purdue want to trace his roots, I wondered? Bad enough to come here and ransack an old woman's office to find out what she knew?

"Check the cabinets," I said to Angel. "Then see if there's
anything relating to Billy Purdue that we can salvage from those
files. I'm going to have another run through the house, see if I
can find anything that might have been discarded."

He nodded and I went through the house again, searching
bedrooms, the bathroom and eventually ending up once again in
the downstairs rooms. In the kitchen, the rotting fruit on the
table was surrounded by the compass points of four settings,
three with coffee cups, one with a glass of rancid milk. Four settings: four people unaccounted for.

I went back out into the yard. At the far eastern side stood a
toolshed, an open lock hanging below the bolt. I walked down,
took a handkerchief from my pocket and slipped the bolt. Inside, there was only a gas-powered mower, flowerpots, seeding
trays and an assortment of short-handled garden tools. Old paint
cans sat on the shelves beside jars filled with brushes and nails.
An empty birdcage hung from a hook on the roof. I closed the
shed and started back toward the house.

As I walked, a breeze arose and pulled at the branches of the trees and the blades of the grass beneath my feet. It lifted the leaves in the unfilled pool, sending them tumbling softly over one another with a crisp, rustling sound. Amid the greens and browns and soft yellows at the deep end, something bright red showed.

I squatted by the edge of the pool and looked down at the shape. It was a doll's head, topped by a tuft of red hair. I could make out a glass eye and the edge of a set of ruby lips. The pool was wide and I thought for a moment of going back to the shed and trying to find a tool long enough to grip the doll, but I couldn't remember seeing anything there that might serve my purpose. Of course, the doll might mean nothing. Kids lost things in the oddest places all of the time. But dolls . . . They tended to look after their dolls. Jennifer had one that she called Molly, with thick dark hair and a movie-star pout, that would sit beside her at the dinner table and stare emptily at the food. Molly and Jenny, friends forever.

I moved to the end of the pool nearest the house, where a set of steps led into the shallow end, the bottom step obscured by leaves. I walked down and stepped carefully into the pool itself, anxious not to lose my footing on the slope. As I progressed, the depth of the leaves began to increase, covering first the toes of my shoes, then the cuffs of my pants, then rising almost to my knees. By the time I came close to the doll, they were halfway up my thighs and I was conscious of a sense of dampness from the rotting vegetation and the feel of water seeping into my shoes. I was walking with caution now, the tiles slick beneath my feet and the slope more pronounced.

The glass eye looked to the heavens, a spread of brown leaves and dirt masking the other side of the doll's face. I reached down carefully, dug into the leaves and lifted the doll's head free from below. As it came away, the leaves fell and the doll's right eye, which had been held closed by the pressure, clicked open gently. Its blouse, slowly revealed, was blue and its skirt green. Its chubby knees were filthy with mud and decaying vegetation.

The entire body of the doll came away from the leaves with a soft sucking sound, and something else came with it. The hand clutching the doll was quite small and delicate, but decay had swollen it and mottled it with winter colors. Two nails had begun to come loose and there were tears in the skin exposing long striations of muscle. At the elbow, above a large gas blister, I could see the end of a rotting sleeve, its pretty pink pattern now almost black with leaf mold, dirt and dried blood.

And I knew that they were down there.

They were all down there.

Angel called Louis, then I called the Bangor police. Angel left before they arrived; with his record, his presence would only complicate matters. I told him to take a cab, check into the Days Inn by the huge Bangor Mall out of town and wait for me there. And then I stood by the side of the pool, the doll and the exposed arm now clearly visible amid the wind-danced leaves, and waited for the police to come.

I met Angel back in the Days Inn four hours later. I had told the cops everything, including the fact that I had made a search of the house. They were none too pleased, but Ellis Howard reluctantly vouched for me from back in Portland, then asked for me to be put on the line.

"So you weren't holding anything back?" The receiver almost vibrated with the depth of the anger in his voice. "I should have let them lock you up for interfering with a crime scene."

There was no point in apologizing, so I didn't. "Willeford told me about her. She arranged Billy Purdue's adoption. She was with Rita Ferris a couple of nights before Rita and Donald were killed."

"First his wife and child, now this adoption woman. Looks like Billy Purdue has a grudge against the world."

"You don't believe that, Ellis."

"Fuck do you know what I believe? You want to be a bleeding heart, go bleed somewhere else. We're all full up here." He was so annoyed it took him three noisy tries to hang up. I gave the Bangor cops my cell phone number and told them I'd help in any way I could.

As I left, the bodies were being fully revealed. Cheryl Lansing was at the bottom of the deep end, beneath the body of her daughter-in-law Louise. Beside them were Lansing's two granddaughters. The leaves had been heaped on them from all around the yard, and topped off with a pile of mulch from behind the toolshed.

The throats of all four had been cut, left to right. Cheryl Lansing's jaw had also been broken by a blow to the left side of her face and her mouth gaped strangely as her head was revealed by the men working in the empty pool. And as she lay beneath the body of her daughter-in-law, mouth wide, it became clear that her killer had visited one final indignity on her body.

Before she died, Cheryl Lansing's tongue had been ripped out.

If Cheryl Lansing was dead, then someone—Billy Purdue, Abel and his partner Stritch, or an individual as yet unrevealed—was tracing a path through Billy's life, a path that appeared now to be related to the abortive investigation into his roots carried out by Willeford. I decided then to continue north. Angel offered to come with me but I told him instead to catch a commuter flight back to Portland the next morning, while I used the Mustang to move on.

"Bird?" he asked, as I started the car. "You've told me about Billy Purdue, about his wife and his kid. What I don't get is: how did she end up with a guy like that?"

I shrugged. She came from a dysfunctional family, I guessed, and she seemed to be repeating the cycle by starting her own dysfunctional family with Billy Purdue. But there was more to it than that: Rita Ferris had something good inside her, something that had remained untouched and uncorrupted despite all that had happened to her. Maybe, just maybe, she believed that she saw something similar in Billy and thought that if she could find the place where it was, and touch him there, she could save him; that she could make him need her as much as she needed him, because she thought that love and need were the same. A host of abused wives and beaten lovers, bruised women and unhappy children, could have told her that she was wrong, that there is a willful blindness in believing that one person can somehow redeem another. People have to redeem themselves, but some of them just don't want redemption, or don't recognize it when it shines its light upon them.

"She loved him," I said, at last. "In the end, it was all she had to give, and she needed to give it."

"It's not much of an answer."

"I don't have the answers, Angel, just different ways of phrasing the questions." Then I pulled out of the parking lot and headed north to the junction of I-95 and 15, toward Dover-Foxcroft, and Greenville, and Dark Hollow. Looking back, it was the first step on a journey that would force me to confront not only my own past, but also my grandfather's; that would disturb old ghosts long believed to have been laid to rest; and that would lead me at last to face what had waited for so long in the darkness of the Great North Woods.

CHAPTER ELEVEN

FOR MUCH OF ITS HISTORY, Maine was little more than a series of fishing settlements clinging to the Atlantic coastline. Beneath the sea off that coast lay the remains of another world, a world that had ceased to exist when the waters rose. Maine has a drowned coastline: its islands were once mountains, and forgotten fields lie on the bed of the ocean. Its past lies submerged, fathoms deep, beyond the reach of the sunlight.

And so the present came into existence at the very precipice of the past, and the people clung to the coast of the region. Few ventured into the wilderness at its heart, apart from French missionaries seeking to bring Christianity to the tribes—which never numbered much more than three thousand to begin with, and most of them also lived along the coast—or trappers trying to make a living from the fur trade. The soil that covered the bedrock of the coast was good and fertile and the Indians farmed it using rotting fish as fertilizer, the smell of it mixing with the scents of wild roses and sea lavender. Later came the saltwater farms, the digging for clams in the flats, the gathering of dulse to chew or to turn into puddings, the huge icehouses where Maine ice was stored before being exported to the farthest reaches of the globe.

But as the possibilities offered by the forests came to be realized, settlers pushed deeper and deeper north and west. On the king's orders, they harvested those white pines which measured over twenty-four inches in diameter one foot from the ground for use as masts on his ships. The masts of Admiral Nelson's ship HMS *Victory,* which fought Napoléon's forces at the Battle of Trafalgar, were grown in Maine.

But it was not until the early nineteenth century, when the financial opportunities represented by Maine's forests were recognized, that the interior was fully explored and surveyed, leading the way into the Great North Woods. Mills were built in the wilderness to produce paper, pulp and two-by-fours. Schooners sailed up the Penobscot to load pine and spruce timber that had been brought downstream from the farthest reaches of the north. Sawmills lined the river's banks and those of the Merrimack, the Kennebec, the Saint Croix, the Machias. Lives were ended in the struggle to break jams or hold a million board feet of logs together, until the era of the industrial river drives came to an end in 1978. The land was remodeled to meet the demands of the timber barons. The paths of rivers were altered, lakes raised, dams built. Fires ravaged the dry slash left behind by the loggers and entire streams were denuded of life by the sawdust waste left behind. The first growth of pine has been gone for two centuries; the hardwood second growth of birch, maple and oak soon followed.

Now much of the north country is industrial forest owned by the timber companies, and lumber trucks make their way along the roads carrying stacks of freshly cut trees. The companies cut swaths through acres of forest in the winter, removing every tree in their path and piling them during March and April. Wood is the state's wealth. and even my grandfather, like many on the coast, used to grow spruce and fir for sale as Christmas trees, harvesting and selling them from November 1 to mid-December.

But there are still a few places where the mature forest remains untouched, with animal trails and moose droppings leading to secluded watering holes fed by waterfalls that tumble over rocks and stones and fallen trees. This was one of the last regions to have wolves and mountain lions and caribou. There are still ten million uninhabited acres in Maine and the state is greener now than it was one hundred years ago, when the exhaustion of the thin soil caused agriculture to decline and the forest reclaimed the land, as is its way, and walls that had once sheltered families now sheltered only hemlock and pine.

A man could lose himself in that wilderness, if he chose.

Dark Hollow lay about five miles north of Greenville, close by the eastern shore of Moosehead Lake and the two hundred thousand acres of protected wilderness in Baxter State Park, where Mount Katahdin dominates the skyline at the northern end of the Appalachian Trail. I had half-considered stopping off in Greenville—the road was dark and the evening cold—but I knew that finding Meade Payne was more important. People who had been close to Billy Purdue—his wife, his child, the woman who had organized his adoption—were dying, and dying badly. Payne had to be warned.

Greenville was the gateway to the north woods, and wood had sustained this town and the surrounding area for many years. There had even been a lumber mill in the town providing jobs for the people of Greenville and its surrounds, until it closed in the mid-seventies when the economic situation made it unprofitable to operate. A lot of people left the area then and those that remained tried to make new lives in tourism, fishing and hunting, but Greenville and the smaller towns scattered farther north—Beaver Cove, Kokadjo and Dark Hollow, where the power lines ended and the wilderness truly began—were still poor. When the golf club at Greenville had raised its fees from ten dollars to twelve dollars per round, there had been an uproar.

I drove up Lily Bay Road, for many years the winter road used for hauling heavy supplies to the logging camps, snow piled high on each side, the woods stretching beyond, until I came to Dark Hollow. It was a small town, barely more than two blocks at its center, with a police department at the farthest limit of the northern end. Dark Hollow got some of the tourism and hunting overflow from Greenville, but not much. There was no view of the lake from its streets, only the mountains and the trees. There was one motel, the Tamara Motor Inn, which looked like a relic from the fifties, with a high arched frontage across which its name glowed in red and green neon. There were one or two handicraft shops selling scented candles and the kind of furniture that left pieces of bark on your pants if you sat on it. A bookstore-cum-coffee shop, a diner and a drugstore made up a considerable part of the town's commercial area, where piles of icy snow still lay in the gutters and in the shadows of the buildings.

Only the diner was still open. Inside, there were reproductions of old concert posters and landscapes by what I took to be local artists. In one corner there was a framed photo of a kid in an army uniform beside an older man, some faded red, white and blue ribbon around it, but I didn't look too closely. A couple of old folks sat in a booth drinking coffee and shooting the breeze and four young guys tried to look cool and vaguely menacing without bursting their pimples when they sneered.

I ordered a club sandwich and a mug of coffee. It was good and almost made me forget, for a moment, what had happened back in Bangor. I asked the waitress, whose name was Annie, for directions to the Payne place and she gave them to me with a smile, although she told me that there was frost and maybe more snow expected and that the road was poor at the best of times.

"You a friend of Meade's?" she asked. Annie seemed keen to talk, more keen than I was. She had red hair and red lipstick, and dark blue makeup around her eyes. Combined with her naturally pale features, the total effect was of an unfinished drawing, like something abandoned by a distracted child.

"No," I replied. "I just want to talk to him about something."

Her smile faltered a little. "It's nothing bad, is it? Because that old man has had his share of bad times."

"No," I lied. "It's nothing bad. I'm sorry to hear that things haven't been going so good for Meade."

She shrugged, and the smile regained some of its vigor. "He lost his wife a couple of years back, then his nephew died in the Gulf during Desert Storm. He's kept pretty much to himself since then. We don't see him around here much anymore."

Annie leaned over, her breasts brushing my arm as she took away the remains of my sandwich. "You want anything else?" she asked brightly, bringing an end to the Meade Payne conversation. I wasn't sure if there was a subtext to the question. I decided that there wasn't. Life tended to be simpler that way.

"No, thanks."

She tore the check from her pad with a flourish. "Then I'll just leave you with this." She flashed me another smile as she slipped the check beneath the bowl of creamers. "You take care now, sugar," she said, as she sashayed away.

"I will," I replied. I felt kind of relieved when she was gone.

Meade Payne didn't have a phone, or at least his name wasn't in the book. Reluctantly, I decided not to talk to him until the morning. I got a room at the Tamara for twenty-eight dollars and slept in an old bed with a high, thick mattress and a carved wood bedstead. I woke once during the night, when the smell of rotting leaves and the sound of heavy decaying things moving beneath them became unbearable.

· · ·

The waitress had been right: a heavy frost covered the ground when I left the Tamara the next morning and the blades of grass on the motel's narrow strip of lawn were like carved crystal as I walked. In the bright morning sunlight, cars passed slowly down the main street and folks in coats and gloves puffed their way along like steam engines. I left the car at the Tamara and made my way on foot to the diner. From outside, I could see that most of the booths were already full and there was a welcoming air of community, of belonging, among those seated inside. Waitresses—Annie didn't seem to be among them—flitted from table to table like butterflies and a fat, bearded man in an apron chatted with patrons beside the register. I was almost at the door when a voice behind me said—gently, softly, familiarly—"Charlie?" I turned around and the past and the present collided in the memory of a kiss.

Lorna Jennings was six years older than I was and lived a mile from my grandfather's house. She was small and lithe, no taller than five-two and certainly no more than one hundred pounds, with short, dark hair cut in a bob and a mouth that always seemed to be entering into, or emerging from, a kiss. Her eyes were blue-green and her skin was porcelain white.

Her husband's name was Randall, but his friends called him Rand. He was tall and had been a hockey hopeful once, even getting a trial with the Portland Pirates. He was a cop, still in uniform but angling for a transfer to the Bureau of Investigation. He had never hit his wife, never hurt her physically and she believed that their marriage was sound until he told her about his first, and, he said, his only, affair. That was before I knew her, before we became lovers.

It was my first summer out of the University of Maine, where I had majored, barely, in English. I was twenty-three. I had worked some after I finished high school—lousy jobs mainly—

then taken some time out to travel to the West Coast before taking up a place at college. Now I had returned to Scarborough for what would be my final summer there. I had already applied to the NYPD, using what few contacts remained with those who had some fond memories of my father. Maybe I had some idealistic notion that I could remove the stain from his name by my presence there. Instead, I think I just stirred up old memories for some people, like mud disturbed from the bottom of a pond.

My grandfather got me a job in an insurance firm, where I worked as an office boy, a runner. I made the coffee and swept the floors and answered the phones and polished the desks and learned enough about the insurance business to know that anybody who believed what he was told by an insurance salesman was either naive or desperate.

Lorna Jennings was the personal assistant to the office manager. She was never less than polite to me but we spoke little in the beginning, although once or twice I found her looking at me in a kind of amused way before she went back to studying her papers or typing her letters. I spoke to her properly for the first time during a retirement party for one of the secretaries, a tall woman with blue-rinsed hair who was committed a year later after she killed one of her dogs with an ax. Lorna strolled up to me as I sat at the bar, drinking a beer and trying to pretend that the insurance business and I were not even remotely acquainted.

"Hi," she said. "You look kind of lonesome. You trying to keep your distance from us?"

"Hi," I replied, twisting the glass. "No, not really."

She arched an eyebrow, and I confessed.

"Well, maybe just a little. Although not from you."

The eyebrow moved up another notch. I wondered if it was possible to burst a blood vessel from embarrassment.

"I saw you reading something today," she said, taking the stool across from me. She was wearing a long, dark wool dress that hugged her body like a sheath and she smelled of flowers:

body lotion, I later learned. She rarely wore perfume. "What was it?"

I was still embarrassed a little, I guess. I had been reading Ford Madox Ford's *The Good Soldier*. I'd picked it up thinking it was something other than what it was: an examination of a series of characters who were unfaithful to one another in their various ways. In the end, as our relationship developed, it came to seem more like a textbook than a novel.

"It's Ford Madox Ford. Have you read him?"

"No, I just know the name. Should I?"

"I guess." This didn't seem like a particularly hearty recommendation and, as literary criticism, it left a lot to be desired, so I pressed on. "If you want to read about weak men and bad marriages."

She winced a little at that and, although I knew almost nothing about her, not then, a little piece of my world fell off and bounced across the floor amid the cigarette butts and the peanut shells. I figured if I dug a hole halfway to China and pulled the earth down on top of me, then I might be far enough underground to hide my discomfort. I had hurt her in some way, and I wasn't sure how.

"Really?" she said at last. "Maybe you might let me borrow it sometime."

We talked a little more, about the office, about my grandfather, before she stood to leave. As she did so, she moved her hand across the material of her dress, above the knee, rubbing at a tiny piece of white lint that had caught in the fabric. It made the material stretch and tighten further against her thighs, revealing the shape of her almost to her knees. And then she looked at me curiously, her head to one side, and there was a light in her eyes that I had never seen until then. No one had ever looked at me that way before. She touched my arm gently, and the touch burned.

"Don't forget that book," she said.

Then she left.

That was how it began, I suppose. I gave her the book to read and, somehow, it gave me a strange pleasure to know that her hands were touching my book, her fingers caressing the pages gently. I left the job a week later. More accurately, I was fired after an argument with the office manager in the course of which he called me a lazy sonofabitch and I told him he was a cocksucker, which he was. My grandfather was kind of angry at first that I had lost the job, although he was secretly pleased that I had called the office manager a cocksucker. My grandfather thought he was a cocksucker too.

It was another week before I worked up the courage to call Lorna. We met for coffee in a little place near the Veterans Memorial Bridge. She said she had loved *The Good Soldier,* although it made her unhappy. She had brought the book back to give to me but I told her to keep it. I think I wanted to believe that she might be thinking of me as she looked at it. That's what infatuation does to a person, I suppose, although the infatuation soon became something more.

We left the coffee shop and I offered her a ride home in the MG my grandfather had bought for me as a graduation present, one of the American-built models made before British Leyland bought the company and screwed it up. It was kind of a chick car, but I liked the way it moved. She declined.

"I have to meet Rand," she said. I think the hurt must have shown in my face, because she leaned forward and kissed me softly on the cheek.

"Don't leave it so long the next time," she said. I didn't.

We met often after that day but it was a warm August night when we kissed properly for the first time. We had been to see some lousy movie and we were walking to our separate cars. Rand didn't like the movies, lousy or not. She didn't tell Rand that she was going to a movie with me and she asked me if I thought that was okay. I said that I guessed it was, although it probably wasn't. Certainly Rand didn't see it that way, when things started to come apart toward the end.

"You know, I don't want to stop you from meeting some nice girl," she said. She didn't look at me when she said it.

"I won't," I lied.

"Because I don't let us come between me and Rand," she lied back.

"That's okay then," I lied again.

We were at the cars by that point and she stood with her keys in her hands, staring ahead, her eyes on the sky. Then, still holding her keys, she put her hands in her pockets and bowed her head.

"Come here," I said. "Just for a moment."

And she did.

The first time we made love was in my bedroom, one Saturday afternoon when Rand had gone to Boston to attend a funeral. My grandfather was in town with some of his old cop buddies, remembering old times and catching up on the obituaries. The house was quiet.

She walked from her home. Even though we had agreed that she would come, I was still surprised when I saw her standing there, dressed in jeans and a denim shirt with a white T-shirt underneath. She didn't say anything as I led her to my room. We kissed awkwardly at first, her shirt still buttoned, then harder, and with more confidence. My stomach danced with nerves. I was acutely conscious of her presence, of her scent, of the feel of her breasts beneath her shirt, of my own inexperience, of my desire for her, of, even then, I think, my love for her. She stepped back and unbuttoned her shirt, then pulled off her T-shirt. She wasn't wearing a bra and her breasts rose slightly with the movement. Then I was beside her, fumbling at her jeans as she pulled at my shirt, my tongue slipping and coiling around her own, my hips hard against her.

And in the dappled sunlight of an August afternoon, I lost

myself in the warmth of her kiss and the soft yielding of her flesh as I entered her.

I think we had five months together before Rand found out about us. We would meet whenever she could get away. I was working by then as a waiter, which meant my afternoons were pretty much free, and two or three nights as well if I decided I didn't want to work flat out. We made love where we could and when we could, and communicated mostly by letter and snatched phone conversations. We made love on Higgins Beach once, which kind of made up for my lack of success with the Berube girl, and we made love when my letter of acceptance came through from New York, although I could feel her regret even as we moved together.

My time with Lorna was different from any of the previous relationships I had had. They were short, abortive things blighted by the small-town environment of Scarborough where guys would come up to you and tell you how many ways they had screwed your girl when she was with them, and how good she was with her mouth. Lorna seemed beyond those things, although she had been touched by them in another way, evident in the gradual, insidious corrosion of a marriage between high school sweethearts.

It ended when some friend of Rand's spotted us in a coffee shop, holding hands across a table covered with doughnut sugar and creamer stains. It was that mundane. They fought and, in the end, she decided not to throw away seven years of marriage on a boy. She was probably right, although the pain tore through me for two years after and stayed as a lingering ache for longer than that. I didn't call or see her again. She was not among the mourners at my grandfather's funeral, although she had been his neighbor for almost a decade. It turned out that she and Rand had left Scarborough, but I didn't bother trying to find out where they might have gone.

There is a kind of postscript to this. About one month after our relationship ended I was drinking in a bar on Fore Street, catching up with a few people who had stayed on in Portland while the rest moved on to college, or out-of-state jobs, or marriage. I went to the men's room and was washing my hands when the door opened behind me. I looked in the mirror to see Rand Jennings standing there, out of uniform, and behind him a fat, burly guy who leaned back against the door to hold it closed.

I nodded at him in the mirror; after all, there wasn't a whole lot else I could do. I dried my hands on the towel, turned and took his knee in my groin. It was a hard blow, with the full force of his body behind it, and the pain was almost unbearable. I fell to my knees, curled into myself and feeling like I was about to die, and he kicked me hard in the ribs. And then, as I lay there on the filth and piss of the floor, he kicked me again and again and again: on my thighs, my buttocks, my arms, my back. He stayed away from my head until the end, when he lifted it up by the hair and slapped me hard across the face. Throughout the whole beating he never said a word, and he left me there, bleeding, for my friends to find. I was lucky, I suppose, although I didn't believe it then. Worse things happened to people who messed with a cop's wife.

And now, in this small town on the edge of the wilderness, the years tumbled away and she was before me again. Her eyes were a little older, the lines streaking away from them more pronounced. There were tiny striations around her mouth too, as if she had spent too long with her lips pinched closed. Yet, when she smiled cautiously, there was that same look in her eyes and I knew that she was still beautiful and that a man could fall in love with her all over again, if he wasn't careful.

"It is you, isn't it?" she said, and I nodded in reply. "What in the Lord's name are you doing in the Hollow?"

"Looking for someone," I replied, and I could see in her eyes that, for one brief moment, she thought it might be her. "You want to get a cup of coffee?"

She appeared doubtful for a moment, looking around as if to make sure that Rand wasn't watching from somewhere, then smiled again. "Sure, I'd like that."

Inside, we found an empty booth away from the window and ordered mugs of steaming coffee. I had some toast and bacon, which she nibbled at in spite of herself. For those few seconds, the years fell away and we were back in a coffee shop in South Portland, talking about a future that would never be and stealing touches across the table.

"How've you been?" I asked.

"Okay, I guess. It's a nice place to live; a little isolated, maybe, but a nice place."

"When did you come here?"

"In ninety-one. Things weren't going so well for us in Portland, Rand couldn't get his detective's badge, so he took a post up here. He's chief now."

Heading up to the edge of nowhere to save your marriage seemed like a dumb thing to do, but I kept my mouth closed. They'd stayed together this long, so I figured that they knew what they were doing.

I figured wrong, of course.

"So you two are still together?"

For the first time, something flickered across her face: regret or anger, maybe, or a recognition that this was true yet with no idea why it should be so. Or it may simply have been my own memories of that time transferred on to her, like recollecting an ancient injury and wincing at the recall.

"Yeah, we're together."

"Kids?"

"No." She looked flustered, and pain flashed across her face. She took a sip of her coffee, and when she spoke again the pain was hidden, put back in whatever box she used to hide it away. "I'm sorry. I heard about what happened to your own family, back in New York."

"Thanks."

"Someone paid for it, didn't they?"

It was a curious way of putting it. "A lot of people paid."

She nodded, then looked at me with her head to one side for a time. "You've changed. You look . . . older, *harder* somehow. It's strange seeing you this way."

I shrugged. "It's been a long time. A lot of things have happened since I saw you last."

We moved on to talk of other things: about life in Dark Hollow, about her job teaching part-time in Dover-Foxcroft, about my return to Scarborough. To anyone passing by, we must have looked like old friends relaxing together, catching up, but there was a tension between us that was only partly to do with our past. Maybe I was wrong, but I sensed a need within Lorna, something unsettled and unfocused that was looking for somewhere to alight.

She drained the last of her coffee in a single mouthful. When she put the mug down, her hand was shaking a little. "You know," she said, "after it ended between us, I still thought about you. I'd listen for snatches of information about you, about what you were doing. I spoke to your gramps about you. Did he tell you that?"

"No, he never said."

"I asked him not to. I was afraid, I guess, afraid that you might take it the wrong way."

"And what way would that be?"

I meant it lightly, but instead her lips tightened and she held my gaze with a look half of pain, half of anger. "You know, I used to stand at the edge of the cliffs out at the Neck and pray that a wave would come, one of the big twenty-footers, and wash me away. There were times when I'd think of you and Rand and the whole sad fucking business and dream about losing myself beneath the ocean. Do you know what that kind of pain is like?"

"Yes," I said. "Yes, I do."

She stood then, and buttoned her coat, and gave me a little half smile before she left. "Yes," she said. "I guess you do. It was good seeing you, Charlie."

"And you."

The door closed behind her with a single, soft slap. I watched her through the windows, looking left and right, running a little as she crossed the street, her hands deep in her pockets, her head low.

And I thought of her standing at the end of the black cliffs at Prouts Neck, the wind blowing her hair, the taste of salt on her lips; a woman dark against the evening sky, waiting for the sea to call her name.

Meade Payne lived in a red wood house overlooking Ragged Lake. A long, poorly kept driveway wound up to the yard, where a Dodge pickup was parked, old and partially eaten by rust. There were no chairs on the porch and no dog barked as I drew the Mustang up alongside the truck.

I knocked on the door, but no one answered. I was about to go around to the back of the house when the door opened and a man peered out. He was in his late twenties or early thirties, I guessed, with dark hair and sallow, windblown skin. There was a hardness about him, and his hands were tough and pitted with scars across the backs of the fingers. He wore no rings, no watch and his clothes looked like they didn't fit him quite as well as they should. His shirt was a little too tight on his shoulders and chest, his jeans a little too short, revealing heavy wool socks above black, steel-toed shoes.

"Help you?" he said, in a tone of voice that indicated that, even if he could, he'd prefer not to.

"I'm looking for Meade Payne."

"Why?"

"I want to talk to him about a boy he fostered once. Is Mr. Payne around?"

"I don't know you," he said. For no reason, his tone was becoming belligerent.

I kept my temper. "I'm not from around these parts. I've come from Portland. It's important that I talk to him."

The young man considered what I had said, then left me to wait in the snow as he closed the door behind him. A few minutes later, an elderly man appeared from the side of the house. He was slightly bent over and walked slowly, shuffling a little as if the joints in his knees hurt him, but I guessed that he might once have been close to my own height, maybe even six feet. He wore a pair of dungarees over a red check shirt and dirty white sneakers. A Chicago Bears cap was pulled down low on his head and wisps of gray hair tried to escape from beneath the rim. His eyes were bright blue and very clear. He kept his hands in his pockets and looked me over, his head slightly to one side, as if trying to place me from somewhere.

"I'm Meade Payne. What can I do for you?"

"My name's Charlie Parker. I'm a private investigator out of Portland. It's about a boy you fostered some years back: Billy Purdue."

His eyes widened a little as I said the name and he waved me in the direction of a pair of old rocking chairs that stood at the end of the porch. Before I sat down, he took a rag from his pocket and carefully cleaned the seat. "Sorry, but I don't get many visitors. Always tried to discourage them, mostly for the sake of the boys."

"I'm not sure I understand."

He indicated the house with a movement of his chin. His skin was still quite taut, its color a reddish brown. "Some of the boys I fostered down the years, they were troublesome types. They needed a firm hand to guide them and they needed to be kept away from temptations. Out here"—he waved a hand toward the lake and the trees—"only temptations are hunting rabbits and jacking off. I don't know how kindly the Lord takes to either, but I don't reckon they count for much in the great scheme of things."

"When did you stop fostering?"

"Back a ways," he said, but added nothing more. Instead, he reached out a hand and rapped a long finger on the arm of my chair. "Now, Mr. Parker, you tell me: is Billy in some kind of trouble?"

I told him as much as I felt that I could: that his wife and child had been killed; that he might be a suspect in the killings but that I didn't think that he was; that certain people outside the law believed that he might have stolen some money belonging to them and they would hurt him to get it back. The old man listened silently to all that I said. The hostile young man leaned on the frame of the open door, watching us.

"Do you know where Billy might be now?" he asked.

"I was hoping you might have some idea."

"I ain't seen him, if that's what you're asking," he said. "And if he comes to me, I can't say as I'll hand him over to anyone, 'less I'm sure he'll get a fair hearing."

Out on the lake, a motor boat was moving through the waters. Birds flew from its path, but they were too far away to identify.

"There may be something more to this," I said, weighing carefully what I was going to say next. "You remember Cheryl Lansing?"

"I recall her."

"She's dead. She was murdered along with her daughter-in-law. I'm not sure how long ago; certainly only a few days. If there's a connection to Billy Purdue, then you could be in danger."

The old man shook his head gently. He pinched his lips with

his fingers and said nothing for a time. Then: "I appreciate you taking the time to come up here, Mr. Parker, but, like I said, I ain't heard from Billy and, if I do, I'll have to think long and hard about what to do next. As for being in danger, I can handle a gun and I've got the boy with me."

"Your son?"

"Caspar. Cas, to them what knows him. We can look out for each other and I don't fear no man, Mr. Parker."

There didn't seem to be anything more I could say. I gave Meade Payne the number of my cell phone and he stuffed it into one of the pockets of his dungarees. He shook my hand and walked slowly, stiffly, back to the door, humming softly to himself. It was an old song, I thought. I seemed to recall it from somewhere but couldn't place it, something about tender ladies and a handsome gambler and memories haunting the mind. I found myself whistling a little of it as, through the rearview, I saw Caspar help the old man into the house. Neither of them looked back as I drove away.

CHAPTER TWELVE

BACK IN DARK HOLLOW, I stopped off at the diner and went through the phone book. I got Rand Jennings's address and the chef gave me directions to his house. Rand and Lorna lived about two miles out of town, in a two-story house painted yellow and black with a neat garden and a black fence at its boundary. Smoke rose from the chimney. Behind the house, a river ran from the lakes to the west of town. I slowed as I drove by, but didn't stop. I wasn't even sure why I was there: old memories stirred up, I supposed. I still felt something for Lorna, I knew, although it wasn't love. I think, and I had no reason to feel it, that it was a kind of sorrow for her. Then I turned back to head south for Greenville.

I found the Greenville Police Department at the town's Municipal Building on Minden Street, where it occupied an unattractive tan-sided office with green shutters and Christmas wreaths on the windows in an effort to make it look prettier. There was a fire department office close by, and a police car and a green Department of Conservation forest ranger truck in the lot.

Inside, I gave my name to a pair of cheerful secretaries, then took a seat on a bench across from the door. After twenty minutes, a stocky man with dark hair and a mustache and brown, watchful eyes came out of an office down the hall, his blue uniform neatly pressed, and extended his hand in greeting.

"Sorry for keeping you waiting," he said. "We have a contract for policing Beaver Cove. I've been out there most of the day. My name's Dave Martel. I'm chief of police."

At Martel's instigation, we left the police building and walked past the Union Evangelical Church to the Hard Drive Café at Sanders Store. There were a couple of cars in the parking lot across the street, the white hull of the steamboat *Katahdin* looming behind them. A mist hung over the lake and created a white wall at the end of the street through which cars occasionally burst. Inside the café, we ordered French vanilla coffee and took a seat close by one of the computer terminals that folks used to pick up their e-mail.

"I knew your granddaddy," said Martel, as we waited for the coffee to arrive. Sometimes it was easy to forget how close the ties still were in parts of the state. "Knew Bob Warren from back in Portland, when I was a boy. He was a good man."

"You been here long?"

"Ten years now."

"Like it?"

"Sure. This is an unusual place. You got a lot of people in this part of the country who don't care much for the law, who've maybe come up here because they don't like being regulated. Funny thing is, here they've got me, they've got the game wardens, they've got the county sheriff and the state police all keeping an eye on 'em. Mostly we get along just fine but, still, enough things happen to keep me busy."

"Anything serious?"

Martel smiled. "Serious is shooting a moose out of season, if you talk to the wardens."

I winced. Grouse, pheasant, rabbit, maybe even squirrel I could understand—at least squirrels moved fast enough to constitute a challenge—but not moose. The moose population in the state had risen from about three thousand in the thirties to its present level of thirty thousand, and moose hunting was now allowed for one week in October. It brought in a lot of revenue at a time when there weren't too many tourists around, but it also brought in its share of assholes. That year, about one hundred thousand people had applied for maybe two thousand permits, every one of them trying to put a moose head above the fireplace.

It's not difficult to kill a moose. In fact, the only thing easier to hit than a moose is a dead moose. Their sight is poor, although their sense of smell and hearing are good, and they don't move unless they have to. Most hunters get their moose on their first or second day out, and boast about it to all the other morons. Then, after all the hunters have gone with their fat bikes and their orange caps, you can head out and, if you're lucky, you can look at the animals that have survived, the glory of them as they come down to lick salt from the rocks by the side of the road, put there to melt the snow and instead used by the moose to supplement their diet.

"Still," continued Martel, "if you're asking what's current, there's a timber company man, a freelance surveyor name of Gary Chute, who hasn't delivered his report yet."

I recalled the PBS news program, although I hadn't noticed any sense of urgency in its discussion of the situation. "I heard them talking about it on the radio," I said. "How bad is it?"

"Hard to say. Seems his wife hasn't seen him in a while, although that's not unusual. He had a couple of projects to work on, and was set to spend some time away from home. Plus rumor has it he has some sweet stuff stashed over in Troy, Vermont. Add to that his fondness for the bottle, and you got a guy who maybe isn't the most reliable. He doesn't turn up in the next twenty-four hours, there may have to be a search organized. It'll probably be down to the wardens and maybe the Piscataquis sheriff and the state police, but could be we'll all have to lend a hand. Talking of serious, I hear you want to know about Emily Watts?"

I nodded. I figured that it would be easier to talk to Martel first and then try to deal with Rand Jennings than to try to find out what I wanted to know by talking to Jennings alone. I thought I might slip it past Martel without him noticing, but he was too good for that.

"Can I ask why you're not talking to Rand Jennings up in Dark Hollow about this?" There was a smile on his face, but his eyes were still and watchful.

"Rand and I have some history," I replied. "You get on with him?" Something in the way that Martel asked the question told me that I wasn't the only one with a little history behind him.

"Have to try," said Martel diplomatically. "He's okay, I guess. He's not the most sympathetic of men, but he's conscientious in his way. His sergeant, Ressler, now he's another matter. Ressler's so full of shit his eyeballs are brown. Haven't seen too much of him lately, which is fine by me. They've been kept busy, what with the trouble over Emily Watts dying and all."

Outside, a car crawled sluggishly up the street, heading north, but there didn't appear to be anybody walking around. Farther beyond, I could see the shapes of pine-covered islands out on the lake, but they were little more than dark patches in the mist.

The coffee arrived and Martel told me about what took place the night Emily Watts died, the same night that Billy Purdue took some two million dollars for which a lot more people had died. It was a strange death, out there in the woods. She would have died anyway from the cold, if they hadn't tracked her down, but to kill herself out in the woods at the age of sixty . . .

"It was a mess," said Martel. "But these things, they happen sometimes and there's no way to call them before they go down. Maybe if the security guard hadn't been packing, and the nurse on the old woman's floor had been watching less TV, and the doors had been locked more securely, and a dozen other things hadn't been out-of-sync that night, then it might have been different. You want to tell me what your interest is in all this?"

"Billy Purdue."

"Billy Purdue. Now there's a name to warm your heart on a winter's night."

"You know him?"

"Sure I know him. He got rousted not so long ago. Ten days, maybe. He was out at St. Martha's, kicking and screaming with an ass pocket of whiskey. Said he wanted to speak to his momma, but no one knew him from Cain himself. He was hauled in, allowed to cool off in one of Jennings's cells, then packed off home. They told him that, if he came back, he'd be charged with trespassing and disturbing the peace. He even made the local papers. From what I hear, the last few days haven't made him a reformed character."

It looked like Billy Purdue had followed up on the information supplied by Willeford. "You know his wife and child were killed?" I asked.

"Yeah, I know. Never figured him for a killer, though." He gave me a thoughtful look. "My guess is, you don't either."

"I don't know. You think he could have been looking for the woman who was shot?"

"Why would you think that?"

"I'm not overfond of coincidences. They're God's way of telling you that you're not seeing the big picture." Plus, I knew that Willeford, for good or bad, had given Emily Watts's name to Billy.

"Well, you see that picture and you let me know, because I sure as hell don't know why that old woman did what she did. Could be it was her nightmares that drove her to it."

"Nightmares?"

"Yeah, she told the nurses that she saw the figure of a man

watching her window and that someone tried to break into her room."

"Any sign of an attempt at forced entry?"

"Nothing. Shit, the woman was on the fourth floor. Anyone trying to get in would have had to climb up the drainpipe. There might have been someone on the grounds earlier in the week, but that happens sometimes. Could have been a drunk taking a leak, or kids fooling around. In the end, I think she was just starting to lose it, because there's no other way to explain it, or the name she called when she died."

I leaned forward. "What name did she call?"

"She called the bogeyman," said Martel with a smile. "She called the guy that mothers use to scare their children into bed, the hobgoblin."

"What was the name?" I repeated.

Martel's smile gave way to a look of puzzlement as he said it.

"Caleb," he said. "She called on Caleb Kyle."

"For the thing which
I greatly feared is come upon me,
and that which I was afraid of
is come unto me."
—JOB 3:25

CHAPTER THIRTEEN

THE YEARS TUMBLE BY like leaves driven before the breeze, intricate and veined, fading from the green of recent memory to the gold autumnal shades of the distant past. I see myself as a child, as a young man, as a lover, a husband, a father, a mourner. I see old men around me in their old men pants and their old men shirts; old men dancing, their feet moving delicately, following a pattern lost to those younger than them; old men telling tales, their liver-spotted hands moving before the fire, their skin like crumpled paper, their voices soft as the rustle of empty corn husks.

An old man walks through the lush August grass with wood in his arms, brushing away loose bark with a gloved hand; an old man, tall and unbowed, with a halo of white hair like an ancient angel, a dog stepping slowly beside him, older, in its way, than the man himself, its gray-beard muzzle flecked with foam, its tongue lolling, its tail swinging gently through the warm evening air. The first patches of red are showing in the trees, and the clamor of the insects has begun to subside. The ash trees, the last to unfurl their leaves in spring, are now the first to let them fall to the ground. Pine needles decay on the forest floor and the blackberries are ripe and dense as the old man passes by, at one with the rhythms of the world around him.

These are the things he does, open-coated, firm footsteps leaving the clear imprint of his passing as he goes: the woodcutting, relishing the weight of the ax in his hands, the perfection of the swing, the fresh crack as the blade splits the sugar maple log, the sweep of the head to clear the two halves, the careful positioning of the next log, the heft of the ax, the feel of his old man muscles moving, stretching, beneath his old man shirt. Then the piling, wood on wood, fitting one to the other, shifting, turning, forming the pile so that it remains steady, so that none will fall, so that not even one will be lost. Finally, he stretches the sheeting, a brick at each corner to hold it in place, always the same bricks for he is, and has ever been, a methodical man. And when the time comes in winter to set the fire, he will return to his pile and bend down, the buckle of the belt on his old man pants digging into the softness of his belly, and he will remember that it was firm once, when he was a young man, when the belt held a gun and a nightstick and cuffs, and his badge shone like a silver sun.

I will be old too, and I will be this man, if I am spared. I will find a kind of happiness in repeating his motions, in the aptness of the action as I feel the circle closing, as I become him, as he made her, who made me. And in doing what he once did, in front of that same house, with the same trees moving in the wind, the same ax in my hand cleaving the wood beneath its blade, I will create an act of remembrance more powerful than a thousand prayers. And my grandfather will live in me, and the ghost of a dog will taste the air with its tongue, and bark at the joy of it.

Now it is his hands that I see moving before the fire, his voice that tells the tale, about Caleb Kyle and the tree with the strange fruit at the edge of the wilderness. He has never told me the tale before and he will never tell me how it ends, because it has no end, not for him. It is I who will finish the tale for him, and I who will complete the arc.

Judy Giffen was the first to disappear, in Bangor in 1965. She was a slim girl, nineteen, with a mane of dark hair and soft red lips with which she tasted men, savoring them like berries. She worked in a hat shop and went missing on a warm April evening redolent with the promise of summer. They searched and they searched, but they didn't find her. Her face looked out from ten thousand newspapers, frozen in her years as surely as if she had been trapped in amber.

Ruth Dickinson from Corinna, another thin beauty, with long blonde hair that hung to her waist, was next to go, in late May when she was just short of her twenty-first birthday. To their names would be added Louise Moore from East Corinth, Laurel Trulock from Skowhegan, and Sarah Raines from Portland, all disappearing within a period of not more than a few days in September. Sarah Raines was a schoolteacher and, at twenty-two, the eldest of the women to disappear. Her father, Samuel Raines, had been to school with Bob Warren, my grandfather, and Sarah was Bob's goddaughter. The last to go missing was an eighteen-year-old student named Judith Mundy, who disappeared after a party in Monson in the first week of October. Unlike the others, she was a chubby, plain girl, but by then people had figured out that there was something very wrong and the break in the pattern didn't seem so important. A search was organized for the Mundy girl to the north and a lot of folks helped out, some, like my grandfather, from as far south as Portland. He drove up on a Saturday morning but, by then, all hope was pretty much gone. My grandfather joined a small party out by Sebec Lake, a few miles east of Monson. There were only three men, then two, then just my grandfather.

That evening, he got himself a room in Sebec and had dinner in a bar outside town. It was bustling, what with all the people who had been out looking for Judith Mundy, and the newspapermen and the police. He sat drinking a beer at the counter when a voice beside him said:

"You know what all this fuss is about?"

He turned and saw a tall, dark-haired man with a knife slash for a mouth and bleak, unloving eyes. There was a trace of the south in his voice, he thought. He wore tan corduroy pants and a dark sweater pitted with holes, through which patches of a dirty yellow shirt were visible. A brown slicker hung to his calves, and the toes of heavy black boots peered from under the too-long cuffs of his pants.

"They're looking for the girl who's gone missing," replied my grandfather. The man made him uneasy. There was something in his voice, he recalled, something sour-sweet, like syrup laced with arsenic. He smelled of earth and sap and something else, something he couldn't quite place.

"You think they're gonna find her?" A light flickered in the man's eyes, and my grandfather thought that it might have been amusement.

"Maybe."

"They ain't found the others."

He was watching my grandfather now, his face solemn but the strange glimmer still in his eyes.

"No, they haven't."

"You a cop?"

My grandfather nodded. There was no point in denying it. Some people just knew.

"You're not from around here, though?"

"No. I'm from Portland."

"Portland?" said the man. He seemed impressed. "And where you been searching?"

"Out by Sebec Lake, the south shore."

"Sebec Lake's nice. Me, I prefer the Little Wilson Stream, up there by the Elliotsville Road. It's pretty, worth a look if a man had the time. Lot of coverage on the banks." He gestured for a whiskey, tossed some coins on the bar, then drained the glass in a single mouthful. "You going back out there again tomorrow?"

"I guess."

He nodded, wiping the back of his right hand across his mouth. My grandfather saw scarring on the palm, and dirt beneath the fingernails. "Well, maybe you'll have better luck than them other fellas, seeing as how you're from Portland and all. Sometimes it takes new eyes to see an old trick." Then he left.

That Sunday, the day when my grandfather found the tree with the strange fruit, dawned crisp and bright, with birds in the trees and blossoms by the shining waters of Sebec Lake. He left his car by the lake at Packard's Camps, showed his badge and joined a small party, made up of two brothers and a cousin from the same family, that was heading for the northern shore. The four men searched together for three hours, not talking much, until the family returned home for Sunday lunch. They asked my grandfather if he wanted to join them, but he had wrapped sourdough bread in a napkin with some fried chicken, and he had a thermos of coffee in his backpack, so he turned down their offer. He returned to Packard's Camps and ate seated on a stone by the bank, the water lapping behind him, and watched rabbits skipping through the grass.

When the other men didn't return, he got in his car and began to drive. He took the road north till he came to a steel bridge that crossed the waters of the Little Wilson. Its roadway was a series of grilles through which could be seen the brown rushing torrent of the stream. Across the bridge the road sloped upward before splitting in two, heading for Onawa and Borestone Mountain along the Elliotsville Road to the northwest and Leighton to the east. On each side of the river, the trees grew thickly. A hermit thrush shot from a birch and looped across the water. Somewhere, a warbler called.

My grandfather did not cross the bridge, but parked his car by the side of the road and followed a rough trail of stones and dirt down to the riverbank. The water was fast moving, and there were rocky outcrops and fallen branches to negotiate as he began to walk, so that he had to step into the flow at times to by-pass them. Soon, there were no more houses on the slopes above him. The bank grew increasingly wild, and he was forced more and more often to take to the water in order to continue upriver.

He had been walking for almost thirty minutes when he heard the flies.

Ahead of him, a huge slab of rock rose up from the bank, its end almost tapering to a point. He climbed it, using its ridges and alcoves for footholds and handholds, until he reached the plateau. To his right was the river, to his left a space in the trees through which the buzzing sounded louder. He walked through the gap, over which the trees hung in an arch like the entry into a cathedral, until he reached a small clearing. The sight that met him made him stop short and caused his food to erupt from his gut in a rush.

The girls hung from an oak, an old, mature tree with a thick, gnarled trunk and heavy extended branches like splayed fingers. They turned slowly, black against the sun, their bare feet pointing at the ground, their hands loose by their sides, their heads lolling. A fury of flies surrounded them, excited by the stench of decay. As he moved toward them, he could make out the color of their hair, the twigs and leaves caught in the strands, the yellowing of their teeth, the eruptions on their skin, their mutilated bellies. Some were naked, while tattered dresses still clung to the others. They pirouetted in midair, like the ghosts of five dancers no longer restricted by the pull of gravity. A heavy, rough rope around the neck of each anchored the girls to the branches above.

There were only five. When the bodies were taken down and identified, Judith Mundy's was not among them. And when she didn't appear, when no trace was ever found of her, it was decided that whoever was responsible for the deaths of the five others had probably had nothing to do with the disappearance of the Mundy girl. It would be more than thirty years before that piece of reasoning was proved wrong.

My grandfather told the police about the man in the bar and what he had said. The details were taken down and it was found that a man roughly fitting that description had been seen in Monson about the time of Judith Mundy's disappearance. There were similar descriptions of a fellow in Skowhegan, although folks differed about his height, or the color of his eyes, or the cut of his hair. This anonymous man was a suspect, for a time, until something broke in the case.

Ruth Dickinson's clothes, soiled with blood and grime, were found in a shed in Corinna owned by the family of Quintin Fletcher. Fletcher was twenty-eight and somewhat retarded. He made a little money by selling handicrafts he created from wood picked up in the forest, traveling around the state by Greyhound bus with his case of wooden dolls, toy trucks and candlesticks. Ruth Dickinson had complained to his family and, later, to the police, that Fletcher had followed her on occasion, leering and making lewd suggestions. After he tried to touch her breast at a county fair the police told his family that they would have him put away if he approached the Dickinson girl again. Fletcher's name came up in the course of the investigation into the girls' deaths. He was questioned, the house searched, and the discovery made. Fletcher started crying, claiming that he didn't know where the clothing came from, that he hadn't hurt anybody. He was remanded for trial and placed in a secure unit in Maine State Prison, for fear that someone might try to get to him if he was kept locally. He might still have been there now, making toys and nautical gifts for the store out on U.S.1 that sells prisoners' crafts, but for the fact that a trusty, who was related distantly to Judy Giffen, attacked Fletcher when he was undergoing a checkup in the prison infirmary and stabbed him three times in the neck and chest with a scalpel. Fletcher died twenty-four hours later, two days before his case was due to go to trial.

And there it lay, for most people at least: the killings ended with Fletcher's capture and subsequent death. But my grandfather couldn't forget the man in the bar, and the glimmer in his eyes, and the reference to the Elliotsville Road. For months afterward, he countered hostility and the desire to mourn and forget with quiet persistence and sensitivity. And what he got was a name, which folks had heard but couldn't quite remember how, and sightings of the man from the bar in each town where a girl had been lost. He mounted a campaign of sorts, speaking to any newspaper or radio show that would listen, putting across his view that the man who had killed the five girls and used them to decorate a tree was still at large. He even convinced some people, for a time, until the family of Quintin Fletcher weighed in behind him and folks took a turn against the whole affair, even his old friend Sam Raines.

In the end, the hostility and indifference became too much for him. Under some pressure, my grandfather left the force and took up construction and then woodworking to support his family, carving lamps and chairs and tables and selling them through the H.O.M.E. service for cottage industries run by the Franciscan nuns in Orland. He carved each piece of work with the same care and sensitivity he had used to question the families of the girls who died. He only spoke of the affair once thereafter, that night in front of the fire with the smell of the wood on him and the dog sleeping at his feet. The discovery he had made on that warm day had blighted his life. It haunted him in his sleep, the possibility that the man who had killed those girls had somehow escaped justice.

After he told me the tale, I knew that on those occasions when I found him sitting on the porch, his pipe cold between his lips, his eyes fixed somewhere beyond the sunset, he was thinking about what had taken place decades before. When he pushed away food almost untouched, after reading in the papers about some young girl who had strayed from home and not yet been found, he was back on the Elliotsville Road, his feet wet in his boots and the ghosts of dead girls whispering in his ear.

And the name that he found all those years before had, by then, become a kind of talisman in towns in the north, although no one could figure out how that might have happened. It was used to scare bad children who wouldn't do what they were told, who wouldn't go to sleep quietly or who headed off into the woods with their friends without telling anyone where they were going. It was a name spoken at night, before the light was switched off and the hair tousled by a familiar hand, the soft scent of a mother's perfume lingering after a final good night kiss: "Be good now and go to sleep. And no more trips into the forest, else Caleb will get you."

I can see my grandfather poking at the logs in the fire, letting them settle before he adds another, the sparks flying up the chimney like sprites, the melting snow sizzling in the flames.

"Caleb Kyle, Caleb Kyle," he intones, repeating the words of the children's rhyme, the fire casting shadows on his face. "If you see him, run a mile."

And the snow hisses, and the wood cracks, and the dog whimpers softly in his sleep.

CHAPTER FOURTEEN

S T. MARTHA'S stood on its own grounds, surrounded by a stone wall fifteen feet in height and guarded by wrought-iron gates from which black paint bubbled and flaked in preparation for a slow, fluttering fall to the earth and snow below. The ornamental pond was filled with leaves and trash, the lawn was overgrown and the trees had not been pruned for so long that the branches of some intertwined with those of their neighbors, creating a woven canopy beneath which the grass had probably died. The building itself was grimly institutional: four floors of gray stone with a gabled roof beneath which a carved cross betrayed its religious origins.

I drove to the main entrance and parked in a space reserved for staff, then walked up the granite steps and into the home itself. To one side stood the security guard's booth where the old woman had cold-cocked Judd before racing off to her death. Straight ahead was a reception desk where a female attendant in a white coat was busy rearranging some papers. Behind her, a door opened into an office lined with books and files. The attendant was a plain-faced woman with white, doughy cheeks and dark eye shadow that made her look like a Mardi Gras skeleton.

She had no name tag on her lapel; close up, her coat was stained at the breast and white threads hung like cobwebs from the fraying collar. Willeford had been right: the place smelled of over-boiled vegetables and human waste, unsuccessfully masked by disinfectant. All things considered, Emily Watts might have done the smart thing by making a break for the woods.

"Can I help you?" said the woman. Her face was neutral but her voice had the same tone as the young man at Meade Payne's place. It made "help" sound like a dirty word. The way she said "you" wasn't much better.

I gave her my name and told her that Chief Martel had called ahead to arrange for me to talk to someone about the death of Emily Watts.

"I'm sorry, but Dr. Ryley, the director, is at a meeting in Augusta until tomorrow." She sounded superficially pleasant, but her face told me that anyone asking about Emily Watts was about as welcome as Louis Farrakhan at a Klan dinner. "I told the chief, but you'd already left." Now her face matched her tone, with the addition of a look of malicious amusement at the trip I'd been forced to make unnecessarily.

"Let me guess," I said. "You can't let me talk to anyone without the director's permission, the director isn't here and you have no way of contacting him."

"Exactly."

"Happy to save you the trouble of saying it."

She bristled and gripped her pen tightly, as if in preparation for ramming it into my eye. From out of the security booth stepped a pudgy guy in a cheap, badly fitting uniform. He pulled on his hat as he walked toward me, but not quickly enough to hide the scars at the side of his head.

"Everything okay here, Glad?" he asked the woman behind the desk. Glad: some people were just like a big finger raised to the universe.

"Now I *am* scared," I said. "Big security man and no old lady to protect me."

He blushed a deep red and sucked in his stomach a little.

"I think you'd better leave. Like she said, there's nobody here who can help you."

I nodded and pointed to his belt. "I see you got a new gun. Maybe you should get a lock and chain for it. A passing child might try to steal it."

I left them in the reception area and walked back into the grounds. I felt a little petty for picking on Judd but I was tired and antsy and the mention of the name Caleb Kyle after all those years had thrown me. I stood on the grass and looked up at the stained, unlovely facade of the home. Emily Watts's room was at the western corner, top floor, according to Martel. The drapes were drawn and there were bird droppings on the window ledge. In the room beside it, a figure moved at the window and an elderly woman, her hair pulled back in a bun, watched me. I smiled at her but she didn't respond. When I drove away, I could see her in the rearview, still standing at the window, still watching.

I had planned to stay another day in Dark Hollow, since I hadn't yet spoken to Rand Jennings. The sight of his wife had stirred up feelings in me that had been submerged for a long time: anger, regret, the embers of some old desire. I remembered the humiliation of lying on the toilet floor as Jennings's kicks rained down on me, his fat friend snickering as he held the door closed. It surprised me, but part of me still wanted a confrontation with him after all that time.

On my way back to the motel I tried to call Angel using the cell phone but I seemed to be out of range. I called him instead from a gas station, where I was told that Dark Hollow was a virtual black spot for cell phone communications due to ongoing problems with trees and aerials. The newly installed telephone in the Scarborough house rang five times before he eventually picked up.

"Yeah?"

"It's Bird. What's happening?"

"Lots, none of it good. While you've been doing your Perry Mason thing up north, Billy Purdue was spotted in a convenience store down here. He got away before the cops could pick him up but he's still in the city, somewhere."

"He won't be for long, now that he's been seen. What about Tony Celli?"

"Nothing, but the cops found the Coupe De Ville in an old barn out by Westbrook. Louis picked it up on the police band. Looks like the freak show ditched his wheels for something less showy."

I was about to tell him what little I had learned when he interrupted.

"There's something else. You got a visitor here, arrived this morning,"

"Who is it?"

"Lee Cole."

I was surprised, given the deterioration of my friendship with her husband. Maybe she had hopes of rebuilding bridges between Walter and me, but that didn't seem a good enough reason to track me down in Maine.

"Did she say what she wanted?"

There was a hesitation in Angel's voice, and I immediately felt my stomach turn. "Kinda. Bird, her daughter Ellen is missing."

I drove back immediately, doing a steady eighty as soon as I hit I-95. I was almost on the outskirts of Portland when the cell phone rang. I picked it up, half expecting it to be Angel again. It wasn't.

"Parker?" I recognized the voice almost immediately.

"Billy? Where are you?"

Billy Purdue's voice was panicky and scared. "I'm in trouble, man. My wife, she trusted you, and now I'm trusting you too. I didn't kill them, Parker. I wouldn't do that. I couldn't kill her. I couldn't kill my little boy."

"I know, Billy, I know." As we spoke, I kept repeating his name in an effort to calm him and develop whatever tentative trust he might have toward me. I tried to put Ellen Cole out of my mind, at least for the present. I would deal with that as soon as I could.

"The cops are after me. They think I killed 'em. I loved 'em. I'd never have hurt 'em. I just wanted to keep 'em." His voice bubbled on the edge of hysteria.

"Okay, Billy," I said. "Look, tell me where you are and I'll come and get you. We'll take you somewhere safe and we can talk this thing through."

"There was an old guy at their place, Parker. I saw him watching it, that night the cops picked me up. I was trying to look out for them, but I couldn't." I wasn't even sure that he had heard my offer of help, but I let him talk as I drove past the Falmouth exit about three miles from the city.

"Did you recognize him, Billy?"

"No, I never seen him before, but I'd know him if I saw him again."

"Okay, Billy, that's good. Now tell me where you are and I'll come and get you."

"I'm at a phone box on Commercial, but I can't stay here. There's people, cars. I've been hiding out in the Portland Company complex at Fore Street, down by the locomotive museum. There's a vacant building just inside the main entrance. You know it?"

"Yeah, I know it. Go back inside. I'll be there as soon as I can."

I called Angel again and told him to meet me, with Louis, at the corner of India and Commercial. Lee Cole was to be left at Java Joe's. I didn't want her at the house in case Tony Celli, or anyone else, decided to pay a visit.

There was no one else around when I arrived at the corner of India and Commercial. I pulled into the parking lot of the old India Street Terminal at One India, the car nestling in the shadow of the old three-story building. As I stepped from the car, the first drops of rain began to fall, a heavy, skin-soaking volley that exploded dramatically on the hood of the car and left splashes the size of quarters on the windshield. I walked around the terminal, past a picnic table and a single-story office building, painted red, until I was on the harbor side, looking out over the dark waters. Thunder rumbled, and on Casco Bay, a ship was frozen in a flash of lightning. Ahead of me, on a restored stretch of line used to give tourists a taste of a narrow-gauge railway, stood a flatbed car with a storage tank on top, marking the start of the line. A row of locked cargo containers was ranged behind the car. To my right was the Casco Bay ferry terminal, the dinosaur body of a blue eighteen-ton crane standing above it on four spindly legs like a mutilated bug.

I was about to turn back to my car when, from behind me, I heard a noise on the gravel and a familiar voice said: "Bad weather for birds. You should be curled up in your coop." The voice was accompanied by the cocking of a hammer on a pistol.

I slowly raised my hands from my coat and turned to see Mifflin, Tony Celli's harelipped enforcer, smiling crookedly at me. He held a Ruger Speed Six in his hand, the rounded butt gripped hard in his stubby fist.

"It's like déjà vu all over again," I said. "I'll have to park someplace else in the future."

"I think your parking problem is about to be solved. Permanently. How's your head feel?" The smile was still fixed in place.

"Pretty good. Hope I didn't hurt your foot too badly."

"I get the soles made special to absorb impact. I didn't feel a thing." He was close to me, maybe only six or seven feet away. I didn't know where he had come from; maybe he had been waiting in the shadows behind One India all along, or had followed me to the meeting place, although I couldn't figure out how he might have known about it. Behind me, the rain made cracking noises as it hit the water.

Mifflin nodded in the direction of the lot. "See you got your Mustang fixed."

"Accidents will happen. That's why I have insurance."

"You should have saved your money, spent it on dames. You ain't gonna need a car no more, unless they have demolition derbies in hell."

He raised the gun and his finger tightened on the trigger. "Bet your insurance doesn't cover you for this."

"Bet it does," I said, as Louis appeared from behind the red office building, his dark hand gripping Mifflin's gun arm tightly as I moved quickly to my left. Louis's right hand pressed the barrel of a SIG into the soft jowl of the would-be assassin.

"Gently," said Louis. "Wouldn't want that thing to go off and scare somebody, make them loose off a shot into someone else's fat jaw."

Mifflin carefully removed his finger from within the guard and slowly eased the hammer down. Angel joined Louis and took the Ruger from the gunman's hand.

"Hi, gorgeous," he said, pointing it at Mifflin's head. "That's a big gun for a little guy."

Mifflin said nothing as Louis eased the SIG away from his mouth and slipped it into the side pocket of his dark overcoat, his hand still gripping the gunman's arm. Louis made a sudden, swift movement and there was a hard, sharp crack as he broke

Mifflin's right arm at the elbow, then struck the smaller man's head twice against the side of the building. The gunman folded to the ground. Angel disappeared and returned a minute later driving the Mercury. He flipped the trunk and Louis dumped Mifflin's prone form inside. Then we followed the car as Angel drove to the end of the Island parking lot, close by a gap in the fencing that led to the edge of the dock. When we had stopped, Louis took Mifflin's body from the trunk, dragged him to the edge, and threw him into the sea. There was a loud splash as he hit the water, the noise quickly drowned by the steady sound of the rain.

Louis would have regarded me as weak, I think, if I had said it, but I regretted the death of Mifflin. Certainly, the fact that he had been about to kill me indicated that Tony Celli felt my limited usefulness was now at an end. If we had let him live, he would have come back and tried again, probably with more guns to back him up. But the finality of that soft splash made me weary.

"His car's parked a block away," said Angel. "We found this on the floor." In his hand was a mobile VHF three-channel receiver, maybe five inches wide and an inch and a half in width, designed to draw power from the car battery. If there was a receiver, then there had to be a transmitter.

"They bugged the house," I said. "Probably while I was in Celli's room. I should have known, when they didn't kill me."

Angel shrugged, and tossed the receiver into the sea. "If he was here, then his friends are already on their way to the complex," he said. To my left, Fore Street wound north, parallel to the harbor, and I could see the silhouettes of the Portland Company buildings in the distance.

"We'll follow the railway line, come in from the harbor side," I said. I drew my gun and clicked off the safety, but Louis tapped me on the shoulder as I did so and withdrew a Colt Government Model .380 from his right coat pocket. From his inside pocket, he produced and fitted a suppressor. "You use your Smith & Wesson and anything goes down, they can trace it back to you," he said. "Use this, and we can dump it later. Plus, it'll be a whole lot quieter." Not surprisingly, Louis knew his guns: semiautomatics chambered for subsonic ammunition are about the only pistols that function effectively with a suppressor. If the Hertz people knew the kind of luggage Louis was keeping in their car, they'd have suffered a collective seizure.

Louis handed his SIG to Angel, took a matching .380 from his left pocket and once again fitted a suppressor. His actions should have alerted me to what would happen later—not even Louis just "happened" to be carrying a pair of silenced weapons—but I was too concerned about Billy Purdue to give it much thought.

Louis and I walked down the line, Angel behind us. Rust-red railroad tracks lay in forgotten piles beside ties that were pitted and knotted, the wood almost black in places. Beyond the storage yards, where old wrecking balls lay side by side and concrete supports bled rust from their innards, wooden pilings moved in the tide like the remains of a primeval forest.

The Portland Company complex stood across from the marina, its entrance marked by the Sandy River Railroad car used to carry the tourists, its red guard's car and green carriages now standing silent. The complex had served the railroads once, when the Portland Company had built engines and steam locomotives, but it closed in the seventies and the buildings had now been redeveloped as a business park. Inside the yard, an old black steel tractor with a restored chimney stood at the entrance to the Narrow Gauge Railroad Museum. The building, like all those in the complex, was redbrick, and three stories at its highest point, with a machine tool company housed in a similar, though larger, structure behind it, the two connected by a closed walkway. To the left of the museum was a long building that housed some kind of yacht service, I seemed to remember, and a second, similar building used by a fiberglass company.

At the southern end of the yard was another, three-story building, the windows on the ground floor boarded up, the windows on the other levels obscured by wire screens, where Billy Purdue had said he was hiding. There was no doorway on the harbor side but the northern end had a wooden, shedlike structure that housed the main door. A roadway wound past the doorway and sloped upward to the visitor entrance to the complex on Fore Street. The whole place appeared deserted and the rain fell hard and unforgiving upon it. The drops sounded like stones beating on the roof of the museum, where a side door stood open. Silently, I indicated it and Louis, Angel and I made our way into the building.

Inside, beneath a vaulted ceiling, deserted railroad cars stood in rows: green Wicasset and Quebec cars, green and red Sandy River cars from Franklin County, a green-and-yellow Bridgton and Saco, and, to our right, an old Railbus with an REO Speedwagon chassis from the Sandy River line.

Beside the Railbus, a body lay curled, its long dark coat gathered around it like a shroud. I turned it over, steeling myself for the sight of Billy Purdue. It was not him. Instead, the contorted features of Berendt, Mifflin's square-headed sidekick, stared back at me, a dark, ragged exit wound in his forehead. I could smell singed hair. On the floor of the museum, blood and dust congealed.

Louis's shadow fell across me. "You think Billy Purdue did this?"

I swallowed, and the sound was huge in my ears. I shook my head and he nodded silently to himself.

We made our way left, passing between two Edaville cars on our way to the museum office. There was no one else in the building, but the steel door at the front entrance banged noisily against the frame as the wind blew and the rain continued to fall.

In the darkness beneath the walkway connecting the tool

works and the museum building, a black Ford sedan was parked, its windows obscured by the falling rain. I recognized it from the crime scene outside Rita Ferris's apartment.

"It's the feds," I said. "They must have found Celli's guys."

"That, or they were listening in on you as well," muttered Louis.

"Great," said Angel. "Is there anybody who isn't here? Billy Purdue's so fucking popular, he should have his own holiday."

The rear door of the car opened and a figure in a dark raincoat stepped out, head down, closing the door softly behind him. He walked quickly in our direction, one hand deep in his pocket, the other holding a black umbrella above his head. A light from the tool works briefly illuminated him as he passed through its beam.

"And this would be . . .?" said Angel wearily.

"Eldritch, the Canadian cop. Stay here."

I stepped from the shadows and Eldritch stopped, a puzzled look on his face as he tried to place me.

"Parker?" he said at last. "You want to bring your friends out of the shadows too?"

From behind me, Louis and Angel appeared and stood beside me, Louis regarding Eldritch with relaxed interest.

"Well, you going to get out of this rain?" asked the Canadian.

"After you, officer," I replied. Something had caught my eye over by the Ford when Eldritch stepped from the car, the interior light casting a faint glow on the ground below. There was a small pool of red beneath the driver's door, which was not fully closed, and, as I watched, something dripped steadily from the crack.

Eldritch stepped by me, one hand still holding the umbrella, exposing a gold cuff link and a white shirtsleeve. There was a dark spot spreading on the cuff as he turned to watch my progress toward the car.

I glanced back at Louis but something else had caught his eye.

"You got something on your collar, officer," he said quietly, as Eldritch stood beneath the light.

Eldritch's shirt collar showed above the lapel of his coat. At its edge, and just above the knot of his tie, there were spots of black, like soot. But as Louis spoke, Eldritch lowered his umbrella, trying to block my view as he made his move, the gun visible to me only briefly as he removed his right hand from his pocket. I could see Louis already raising his own gun as Eldritch began to turn, the umbrella now tumbling in midair between them, Angel to one side looking on. But I fired first, the bullet tearing a hole in the umbrella and hitting Eldritch low on the thigh, the gunshot masked by the suppressor and the driving rain. I fired again, this time hitting him in the side. The gun fell from his hand and he tumbled against the wall of the museum, sliding down with his back against it until he sat on the ground, his teeth gritted in pain and his hand clutching at the red stain which was spreading across the front of his raincoat. Beside him, Louis picked up his gun by slipping a pen through the trigger guard and examined the weapon with professional detachment.

"Taurus," he said. "Brazilian. Looks like our friend might have vacationed in South America."

I walked to the car. There were two star-shaped bullet holes in the windshield surrounded by twin sunbursts of blood. I opened the driver's door with a gloved hand and stepped back as Agent Samson fell sideways onto the ground, a dark hole at the bridge of his ruined nose where the bullet had exited. Beside him, Agent Doyle's forehead rested against the dashboard, blood pooling at his feet. Both were still warm.

Carefully, I lifted Samson into the car, closed the door and walked back to where Angel and Louis stood over the bleeding man.

"Abel," said Louis. Despite his pain, the man on the ground regarded us with dark, hateful eyes, but didn't speak.

"He's not going anywhere," I said. "We put him in the trunk of the Ford, call the cops, let them take care of him after we're done."

But neither Angel nor Louis appeared to be listening to me. Instead, Angel shook his head and tut-tutted: "A man your age dyeing his hair," he said to Abel. "That's just vanity."

"And you know what they say about vanity," said Louis softly.

Abel looked up at him, his eyes widening.

"Vanity kills," concluded Louis. Then he shot him once, the Colt jumping in his hand. Abel's head bumped against the wall behind him, his eyes closed tightly, and then his chin slumped forward on his chest.

For the first time in my life, I touched Louis in anger. Reaching out, I pushed him hard on the chest. He took a step back, his expression unchanged.

"Why?" I shouted. "Why did you kill him? Jesus, Louis, do we have to kill everybody?"

"No," said Louis. "Just Abel and Stritch."

And then I understood why Louis and Angel had come here, and the realization was like a punch in the stomach.

"It's a contract," I said. "You took on the hit." I knew now why Leo Voss had been killed, why Abel and Stritch had chosen this time to recede into the shadows, and it was only partly to do with the opportunity offered by Billy Purdue and the money he had stolen. Abel and Stritch were running, and they were running from Louis.

He nodded once. Beside him, Angel looked at me with a kind of sorrow, but also determination. I knew whose side he was on.

"How much?" I asked.

"A dollar," said Louis simply. "I'd have taken fifty cents, but the man didn't have no change."

"A *dollar?*" It was strange, but I almost smiled despite myself. He had taken a dollar, yet their lives were worth even less than that. I looked back at Abel's body and thought of the two agents in the car and the real Eldritch, who had probably never made it as far as Maine.

"They're that bad, Bird," said Angel. "These guys are the fucking worst. Don't let them come between us."

I shook my head. "You should have told me, that's all. You should have trusted me."

Now Louis spoke. "You're right. It was my call. I called wrong."

He stood before me, waiting for me to respond, and I knew why he had kept it from me. After all, I was an ex-cop, with cop friends. Maybe Louis still had doubts. I had saved Angel's life while he was in prison and, in return, they had stood by me when Jennifer and Susan were killed, had put their own lives on the line in the hunt for their killer and the killers of others, and asked nothing in return. I had no reason to doubt them; they, on the other hand, a burglar and an assassin, could be forgiven for having concerns about me.

"I understand," I said at last.

Louis nodded his head once in response, but in that gesture and the look in his eyes he said all that he needed to say.

"Okay," I said. "Time to find Billy Purdue." And as we walked to the vacant building, the rain falling heavily now, I took a last look at Abel's body and shivered slightly. His huddled form, and the remains of Berendt in the railroad museum, were mute testament to the fact that the squat, grotesque figure of Stritch could not be far away.

There were two cars parked farther up on Fore Street, across from a new development of gray wood houses half-clad in red brick. It was too dark to see if anyone remained inside the vehicles. When we reached the main door to the unoccupied building, the lock had already been broken open and the door stood slightly ajar. Staying close to the wall, I peered around the corner to the front of the building. There, the windows on the top floor were boarded up, while a wooden walkway led from the grass border to a locked door on the second story. Because of the gradient of the slope, the ground floor was actually below the grass, its windows masked with more screens.

I came back to where Angel and Louis were waiting by the door, where we agreed that Angel should leave us and return in the Mercury, so that if we came out with Billy Purdue we could leave quickly.

Inside the door was a flight of stairs, dusty and littered with old newspaper. They led up to the second floor, to a kind of storage bay supported by steel columns. Behind the stairs was a series of empty offices and work areas, all quiet and unlit. The warehouse still smelled faintly of wood, although now the pervading odor was one of dampness and decay. Louis had a flashlight but didn't light it for fear of drawing attention to us.

From where we stood, I could see that mounds of rotted timber still lay in one corner near the stairs. Water dripped from the ceiling as the rain fell through the warehouse roof and gradually leaked through to the floors below. We moved behind the stairway and into the first of the series of workshops, empty apart from some wooden benches and a broken plastic chair. Through the sound of the pouring rain and dripping water I could hear a noise from the other side of the wall as we neared a doorway. I motioned Louis to the left and took up a position at the right wall until I could partially see into the room beyond. Then, slowly, I inched my way forward, peering in quickly and then carefully progressing when nobody tried to blow my head off.

I was in one of a pair of what were once adjoining offices. There was a faint smell of smoke from the room, which came from a pile of smoldering wood and trash in the far corner. In the corner opposite, something moved.

I spun quickly and tightened my finger on the trigger.

"Don't shoot," said a raw, cracked voice, and a figure gradually emerged from where it had been crouching in the darkness. It wore plastic bags over its feet, its legs were encased in dirt-encrusted denims and a coat with no elbows was tied around its waist with a length of string. Its hair was long and unkempt, its beard gray but streaked with nicotine yellow. "Please, don't shoot. I didn't mean no harm by starting the fire."

"Move to your right. Quickly." Through a crack in one of the wooden panels on the windows, a weak glow shone from a streetlight. The old man moved until he was caught in its beam. His eyes were small and dull. Even from twelve feet away I could smell the booze, and other things too.

I held him in my sights for a moment longer, then gestured to my right with the gun as Louis appeared in the doorway. "Get out of here," I said. "It's not safe."

"Can I collect my stuff?" He pointed at a heap of meager possessions stacked in a shopping cart.

"Take what you can carry, then go." The old guy nodded his thanks and began to pick up items from the cart: a pair of boots, some soda cans, a pile of copper wire. Some he put back again, others he seemed to want to think about. As he considered a single Reebok sneaker, a deep voice behind me said: "Old man, you got five seconds to get your shit out of here, else the coroner be sorting it for you." Louis's comment seemed to focus the old guy's mind; seconds later he was running past us with a tangled collection of wire, boots and cans in his arms.

"You won't steal anything, will you?" he asked Louis as he prepared to go.

"No," replied Louis. "You done took all the good stuff."

The old guy nodded happily and started to scurry out, Louis shaking his head as he went. The old man paused at the doorway. "Them other fellas went upstairs," he said simply, then left.

We moved quickly but carefully through that level until we reached a pair of parallel staircases at the far end of the building, one at each corner. I heard footsteps above us, moving carefully across the floor. Between the stairs was a set of twin doors to the yard outside. A length of broken chain lay on the ground and a half brick held one of the doors open. Louis took the right-hand stairway, I took the left. As I climbed, I kept to the sides of the stairs to minimize the risk of stepping on a weak or rotted step. I needn't have bothered. The rain was falling with a renewed ferocity and the old building echoed and hummed with its sound.

We met at a kind of mezzanine, where a single wide set of steps led up to the second story. Louis moved ahead, while I stayed a little farther behind. I watched as he pushed open a swinging door, a dirty, wire-mesh window at head level, and began his search of the floor. I had decided to move on to the third story when there was the sound of movement from below. I looked down over the stair rail and a man stepped into my line of vision, striking a match to light a cigarette. In the flash of illumination I recognized him as one of Tony Celli's crew from the hotel room, left to guard the door from outside, but instead taking shelter from the rain. Above me, a floorboard creaked gently, then another: at least one of Celli's men had progressed to the top floor.

As I watched Tony Clean's man smoke his cigarette, something caught my attention to my left. The windows on the mezzanine, which would once have looked out onto the lot below, were now boarded up and no light shone through them. The only illumination came from a jagged hole in the wall, ringed with damp where the plaster surrounding an old air-conditioning unit had given way and fallen in a heap to the floor below, taking the unit with it. The hole created a kind of murky pool of light between two masses of dark at either side. In one of those unlit areas, I sensed a presence. A pale figure flickered, like a piece of paper gently tumbling. I moved forward, my heart pounding and the gun heavy in my hand.

From out of the blackness, a face appeared. Its eyes were dark, with no whites showing, and a dark necklace seemed to hang around its neck. Slowly, its mouth became visible, the zigzagging black thread sealing it shut. Beneath it, the mark left by the rope was deeply indented on her skin. She watched me for a moment, then seemed to turn in on herself, and there was only emptiness where she had been. I felt a cold sweat on my back and a feeling of nausea swept over me. I gave one more look at the patch of darkness, then turned away just as a sudden soft cry of pain came from below me.

I paused on the first step, and waited. Around me the rain fell and water dripped. There was the sound of a shoe softly scuffing on the wood below and then a man drifted into view on the right-hand stairway, wearing a tan raincoat from which a bald head emerged like a toadstool. Stritch raised his strange, melted-wax features and his strange, colorless eyes regarded me for a moment. Then his too-wide mouth broke into a smile from which all humor was absent and he withdrew back beneath the mezzanine. I wondered if he knew yet that Abel was dead, or how much of a threat he considered me.

The answer came within seconds as the rounds tore through the soft damp wood of the stair rail, splinters spearing the gloom. I sprang up the remaining steps, the bullets following me as Stritch tried to gauge my position from the sounds I made. I felt something tug at the tail of my coat as I reached the top of the steps and knew that he had come close, very close, with at least one of his shots.

I got to the second floor and headed the same way Louis had gone. There was in a kind of lobby inside the door, with an old raised receiving desk to my right behind which lay another storage bay, part of a succession of small bays that led to the back of the building, each connected by a single doorway so that, if the light had permitted, I could have seen straight through to the far wall of the warehouse. Even from where I was standing, I could see that the bays still contained battered desks and broken chairs, rolls of rotting matting and boxes of discarded paper-work. Two corridors stretched away on either side, one directly in front of me and one to the right. I guessed that Louis was already making his way down the right-hand corridor so I moved quickly down the other, casting anxious glances over my shoulder to see if Stritch had appeared yet.

A burst of gunfire came from ahead of me and to my right, answered by two softer shots fired in close succession. I heard voices shouting and running footsteps, the noises echoing around the old building. At a doorway to my right, a figure in a black leather jacket lay slumped on the floor, blood pooling around its head. Louis was already making his mark but he didn't know that Stritch was somewhere behind us, and it was important that he was told. I moved back into the corridor in time to see a flash of tan move behind the receiving desk. I stepped sideways, moving past the prone form of Tony Celli's man until I could see beyond the top of the desk, but there was no sign of Stritch. I stepped quickly to the doorway of the next bay and peered around the door frame in time to receive the muzzle of a silenced pistol in my right temple.

"Shit, Bird, I almost blew your head off," said Louis. In the semidarkness he was almost invisible in his dark clothes, with only his teeth and the whites of his eyes showing.

"Stritch is here," I said.

"I know. Caught a glimpse of him, then got distracted by you."

Our discussion was interrupted by the sound of more firing ahead of us, the same gun shooting each time, loosing off three shots with no return of fire. There was more shouting and then a burst of automatic fire, followed by footsteps running up a flight of stairs. Louis and I exchanged a nod and began to make our way toward the back of the building, one of us at each side of every door frame to give us a clear view of the room beyond and the section of corridor at either side. We kept moving until we reached an open service elevator, in which another of Tony Celli's men lay dead. Alongside the elevator, a single flight of stairs wound up to the top level, where Stritch had presumably gone ahead of us. We were on the second step when I heard a sound behind me that was chillingly familiar: the twin clicks of a cartridge being jacked into a pump-action shotgun. Louis and I turned slowly, our guns held up and away to our sides, to find Billy Purdue standing before us. His face was streaked with dirt, his clothes soaked through, and on his back was a black knapsack.

"Put your guns down," he said. Somehow, he had found a way to hide from his pursuers, and from us, among the old furniture and office waste. We did as we were told, casting cautious looks both at Billy's gun and the staircase above us.

"You brought them here," he said, his voice shaking with anger. "You sold me out." There were tears running down his cheeks.

"No, Billy," I said. "We came to get you to safety. You're in a lot of trouble here. Put the gun down and we'll try to get you out of it."

"No. Fuck you. There's nobody here for me now." With that, he fired two bursts from the shotgun, spraying the wood and plaster behind us and forcing us to dive to the ground. When we looked up again, splinters and grit in our hair, Billy was nowhere to be seen but I could hear his running footfalls as he headed back in the direction in which we had come. Louis immediately sprang to his feet and moved after him.

More shots came from the floor above as I rose, automatic fire followed by a single shot. I took the steps slowly, my neck craned to one side, my hands slick with sweat. At the top of the stairs, beside the elevator, another of Celli's men lay huddled in a corner. Blood flowed from the bullet wound in his neck. There was something else about him too, something I almost did not see.

His trousers were opened, the zipper pulled down, and his genitals partially exposed.

Before me was a doorway, and beyond the doorway was total darkness. In that darkness, I knew that Stritch waited. I could smell his cheap, sickly cologne and the dark, earthy odor he used it to conceal. I could sense his watchfulness, the tendrils he sent out to test the air around him for prey. And I could feel his desire, the sexual charge he took from hurting and bringing lives to an end, the aberrant sexuality that had led him to touch and expose the young man in the corner as he lay dying.

And I knew with absolute certainty that if I set foot beyond that doorway Stritch would take me and kill me, and that he would touch me as I died. I felt the shadows move around me, and a child laughed in the dim reaches below. It seemed to summon me back from the brink, or perhaps it was my own fear making me believe that was the case. I chose to leave Stritch in the darkness and return to the light.

Louis approached as I made my way backward down the stairs. His pants were torn at the knee, and he was limping slightly. "I slipped," he said, spitting the words from his mouth. "He got away. What about Stritch?"

I indicated the floor above. "Maybe Tony Celli will do you a favor."

"You think?" said Louis, in a tone that said he didn't believe it was likely. He looked at me more closely. "You okay, Bird?"

I moved past him so that he could not see my face. I was ashamed at my weakness, but I knew what I had felt, and what I had seen in the blood red eyes of a dead woman.

"My concern is Billy Purdue," I said. "When Stritch finds out that his buddy is dead, he won't go anywhere until he's settled the score. You'll get another chance."

"I'd prefer to take this one," he replied.

"It's pitch black up there. You set foot on that top floor, and he'll kill you."

Louis remained standing, watching me, but he did not speak. In the distance, I heard the wail of approaching sirens. I saw Louis hesitate, balancing the risk of the police and the shadows on the floor above with the opportunity to try to take out Stritch. Then slowly, with just one glance back to the stairs leading up to the darkness of the third floor, Louis followed me.

We reached the main bay where we had met the old man. "We go out the front, we may run into Tony Celli's wheelmen, or the cops," I said. "And if Billy went out that way, then he's already dead."

Louis nodded in agreement and we headed down to the door at the back of the warehouse, where the man Stritch had killed lay half in, half out of the doorway, one arm across his eyes as if he had glimpsed the heart of the sun. Across the lot, I could see the Mercury. It growled into life as Angel shot across the lot and turned the car, then stopped to allow us to get in.

"Any sign of Billy?"

"No, least none that I saw. You two okay?"

"Fine," I said, although I was still shaken by the fear I had felt on the top floor. "Stritch was in there. Came from the back of the building."

"Seems like everybody knows your business except you," remarked Angel as we tore out of the lot and followed the tracks back in the direction of India Street. Just before they ended, he swung the wheel to the right and sped through the gap in the wire fence to bring us into the parking lot at One India. He killed the lights as sirens wailed and two black and white police cars raced up Fore Street. Then we waited to see if Billy Purdue might show.

While we sat in silence, I tried to piece together what had happened. The feds had either been monitoring my phone or had managed to find some trace of Tony Celli's crew. When they moved, Abel contacted Stritch and told him where to go, with the intention of joining him after taking care of the feds. With three different groups of men after him in one enclosed space, Billy Purdue had still managed to get away.

And I thought too of the figure I had glimpsed in the shadows. Rita Ferris was dead and, soon, the snow would be falling on her grave. Yet something of her still remained, her presence like a ripple on still water.

No one came toward us on foot from the direction of the complex. If any of Tony Celli's men had survived, I figured that they would head north instead of coming straight back into town and risk meeting the cops.

"You think he's still in there?" I asked Louis.

"Who? Stritch? If he is, it's because he's dead, and I don't believe Tony Celli has anyone that good on his side, assuming anyone was left alive in there," replied Louis. Again, I caught that thoughtful look in his eyes as he examined my face in the rearview mirror.

"I tell you this," he said. "He knows now that Abel is dead, and he's gonna be real pissed."

CHAPTER FIFTEEN

LOUIS AND ANGEL dropped me at my Mustang, and then followed me to Java Joe's. I felt drained, and sick inside. I thought of the look in Abel's eyes before he died, and the sight of the young gunman violated at the moment of his death, and an old man loaded with sneakers and copper wiring running into the cold, wet night.

At the coffee shop, Louis and Angel decided to stay outside in the Mercury drinking take-out mochas. Lee Cole was seated by the window, her jeans tucked into shin-high fur-lined boots and a white wool top buttoned to the neck. As she stood to greet me, the light caught the streaks of silver in her hair. She kissed me softly on the cheek and held me tightly. Her body started to shake and I could hear her sobbing into my shoulder. I pushed her gently away, my hands on her shoulders, and watched as she shook her head in embarrassment and searched through her pockets for a tissue. She was still beautiful. Walter was a lucky man.

"She's gone, Bird," she said, as she sat. "We can't find her. Help me."

"But she was with me only a few days ago," I said. "She stopped off here for a few hours with her boyfriend."

She nodded. "I know. She called us from Portland, told us she was heading on with Ricky. Then she rang us one more time on the way to some place farther north and that was the last we heard from her. She was under strict instructions to call us each day, just so we'd know she was okay. But when we didn't hear . . ."

"Have you been in touch with the police?"

"Walter has. They think she may have run off with Ricky. Walter argued with her about him last month, about how she should be concentrating on her study and not on chasing boys. You know how Walter can be, and retirement hasn't made him any more tolerant."

I nodded. I knew how he could be. "When you get back, call Special Agent Ross in the FBI's Manhattan office. Mention my name. He'll make sure that Ellen's name is in the NCIC database." The National Crime Information Center kept records of all missing persons, adults and juveniles, reported to the police. "If it isn't, it means that the police aren't doing what they should be doing, and Ross may be able to help you with that as well."

She brightened up a little. "I'll ask Walter to do it."

"Does he know you're here?"

"No. When I asked him to contact you, he refused. He's already been up there, trying to put pressure on the local police. They told him that the best thing to do would be to wait, but that's not Walter. He drove around, asking in the other towns, but there was no sign. He got back yesterday, but I don't think he's going to stay. I told him I had to get out of the house for a while, and that my sister would stay by the phone. I had the flight already booked. I'd tried calling you on the cell phone, but I could never seem to get through. So I came up here, and the police in Scarborough told me where you lived. I don't know . . ." She trailed off, then began again. "I don't know all that happened between you and Walter. I know some of it and I can guess at more, but it has nothing to do with my daughter. I left him a note on the refrigerator. He'll have found it by now." She stared out the window, as if visualizing the discovery of the note and Walter's response to its contents.

"Is there any chance that the police might be right, that she has run away?" I asked. "She never seemed like that kind of kid and she didn't seem troubled at all when I met her, but people get funny sometimes when love enters the equation."

She smiled for the first time. "I remember what that feels like. I may be older than you, but I'm not dead yet." The smile disappeared as her words set off a chain reaction in her head, and I knew she was trying not to picture what might have happened to Ellen. "She didn't run away. I know her and she would never do that to us, no matter how badly we had fought with her."

"What about the kid—Ricky? I get the impression that their eyes met from opposite sides of the track."

Lee didn't seem to know much about Ricky beyond the fact that his mother had left the family when he was three and his father had raised him and his three sisters by holding down two dead-end jobs. He was a scholarship student—a little rough and ready, she admitted, but she didn't believe that there was any malice in him or that he would have been party to some elopement.

"Will you look for her, Bird? I keep thinking that she's in trouble somewhere. Maybe they went hiking and something went wrong, or somebody . . ." She stopped abruptly and reached out to take my hand. "Will you find her for me?" she repeated.

I thought of Billy Purdue and of the men hunting him, of Rita and Donald, of a hand emerging from a mass of wet, rotting leaves. I felt a duty to the dead, to the troubled young woman who had wanted to create a better life for herself and her child, but she was gone and Billy Purdue was drifting toward some kind of reckoning from which I couldn't save him. Maybe my duty now was to the living, to Ellen, who had looked after my little girl for the brief span of her life.

"I'll look for her," I said. "You want to tell me where she was going when she made the call?"

As she spoke, the world seemed to shift on its axis, throwing strange shadows across familiar scenes, turning everything into an off-kilter version of its former self. And I cursed Billy Purdue because, somehow, in some way that I couldn't yet comprehend, he was responsible for what had happened. In Lee's words, once-distant worlds eclipsed one another and indistinct shapes, like plates moving beneath the earth, came together to form a new, dark continent.

"She said she was heading for a place called Dark Hollow."

I brought her to the Portland Jetport in time to catch her flight to New York, then drove back to the house. Angel and Louis were in the front room, watching a sleazy talk show marathon on cable.

"It's 'I Can't Marry You, You're Not a Virgin,'" said Angel. "At least they're not claiming to be virgins, else it'd be 'I Can't Marry You, You're a Liar.'"

"Or 'I Can't Marry You, You're Ugly,'" offered Louis, sipping a bottle of Katahdin ale, his feet stretched out before him on a chair. "Man, how they get the freaks for this show? They trawl the crowds at truck pulls?" He hit the remote, muting the sound on the TV.

"How's Lee doing?" asked Angel, suddenly serious.

"She's holding together, but only just."

"So what's the deal?"

"I've got to head north again, and I think I'm going to need you two to come with me. Ellen Cole was last heard from on the way to Dark Hollow, the same place Billy Purdue grew up, for a time, and the place I think he's heading back to now."

Louis shrugged. "Then that's where we going,"

I sat down in an easy chair beside him. "There may be a problem."

"Jeez, Bird," said Angel, "we're not exactly starved for problems as it is."

"This problem have a name?" asked Louis.

"Rand Jennings."

"And he would be?"

"Chief of police in Dark Hollow."

"And he doesn't like you because?" said Angel, taking up the baton from Louis.

"I had an affair with his wife."

"You the man," said Louis. "You could fall over and make hitting the ground look complicated."

"It was a long time ago."

"Long enough for Rand Jennings to forgive and forget?" asked Angel.

"Probably not."

"Maybe you could write him a note," he suggested. "Or send him flowers."

"You're not being helpful."

"I didn't sleep with his wife. In the helpful stakes, that puts me a full length clear of you."

"You see him last time you were up there?" asked Louis.

"No."

"You see the woman?"

"Yes."

Angel laughed. "You're some piece of work, Bird. Any chance you might keep the mouse in its hole while we're up there, or you planning to renew old acquaintances?"

"We met by accident. It wasn't intentional."

239

"Uh-huh. Tell that to Rand Jennings. 'Hi Rand, it was an accident. I tripped and fell into your wife.'" I could still hear him laughing as he headed for his bedroom.

Louis finished his beer, then lifted his feet from the chair and prepared to follow Angel. "We screwed up tonight," he said.

"Things got screwed up. We did what we could."

"Tony Celli ain't gonna give up on this thing. Stritch neither."

"I know."

"You want to tell me what happened on the top floor?"

"I felt him waiting, Louis. I felt him waiting and I knew for sure that if I went in after him, I'd die. Despite evidence to the contrary, I don't have a death wish. I wasn't going to die at his hands, not there, not anywhere."

Louis remained at the door, considering what I had told him. "If you felt it, then that's the way it was," he said at last. "Sometimes, that's all the difference there is between living and dying. But if I see him again, I'm taking him down."

"Not if I see him first." I meant it, regardless of all that had taken place and the fear that I had felt.

His mouth twitched in one of his trademark semismiles.

"Bet you a dollar you don't."

"Fifty cents," I replied. "You've already earned half your fee."

"I guess I have," he said. "I guess I have."

Louis and Angel left early the next morning, Louis for the airport and Angel to scout around Billy Purdue's trailer to see if he could find anything that the cops might have missed. I was about to lock up the house when Ellis Howard's car bumped into my drive and then Ellis himself stepped heavily from the car. He took a look at my bag and gestured at it with a thumb.

"Going somewhere?"

"Yep."

"You mind telling me where?"

"Yep."

He slapped his hand gently on the hood of my Mustang, as if to transfer his frustration into the metal of the car. "Where were you yesterday evening?"

"On my way back from Greenville."

"What time'd you get back into town?"

"About seven. Should I call a lawyer?"

"You come straight home?"

"No, I parked up and met someone in Java Joe's. Like I said: should I call a lawyer?"

"Not unless you want to confess to something. I was going to tell you what happened out at the Portland Company complex last night, but maybe you already know, seeing as how your Mustang was down by the harbor last night."

So that was it. Ellis was fishing. He had nothing, and I wasn't about to break down and beg for mercy.

"I told you: I was meeting someone."

"This person still in town?"

"No."

"And you don't know anything about what happened at the complex last night?"

"I try to avoid the news. It affects my karma."

"If I thought it would help, your karma would be kicking its heels in a cell. We found four bodies in that complex, all of them associates of Tony Celli, plus two dead feds and a mystery caller."

"Mystery caller?" I asked, but I was thinking of something else. By my count, there should have been five bodies in the complex. One of Tony's men had survived and escaped, which meant there was a good chance that Tony Celli knew Louis and I had been in the building.

Ellis looked closely at me, trying to assess how much I knew. As he spoke, he waited for a reaction. He was disappointed.

"We found the Toronto cop, Eldritch, dead. Three bullets,

two different guns. The one to the head was an execution shot."

"I'm waiting for the *but*."

"The *but* is that this guy wasn't Eldritch. His ID says he was, his prints and his face say he wasn't. Now I've got the Toronto PD howling at me to find their missing man, I've got a bunch of feds who are very interested in the John Doe who killed two of their agents, and I have four members of Boston's finest crew using up morgue space that the morgue can't afford to give them. The ME is considering relocating here permanently, seeing as how we're such good customers and all. Plus Tony Celli hasn't been seen since his night at the Regency."

"He stiff on the bill?"

"Don't, Bird. I'm not in the mood. Don't forget that Willeford is still missing and, until you came along, he knew as much about Billy Purdue as anyone."

I let it pass without comment. I didn't want to think of what I might have brought down on Willeford. Instead, I said: "Bangor turn up anything on Cheryl Lansing?"

"No, and we're no further on the killing of Rita Ferris and her son. Which brings me to my second reason for calling. You want to tell me again what you were doing in Bangor? And then Greenville?"

"Like I told Bangor, Billy Purdue hired someone to trace his parents. I thought that maybe he might try to follow that trail now that he's in trouble."

"And is he following that trail?"

"Someone is."

Ellis moved toward me, his bulk menacing, his eyes more so. "You tell me where you're going, Bird, or I swear to God I'll arrest you here and now and let ballistics take a look at that gun of yours."

I knew that Ellis wasn't kidding. Even though the silenced guns now lay at the bottom of Casco Bay beside Mifflin, I couldn't afford to delay the search for Ellen Cole. "I'm heading north to a place called Dark Hollow. The daughter of a friend of mine has gone missing. I'm going to try to find her. Her mother was the person I met at Java Joe's last night."

Some of the anger went out of his face. "Is it a coincidence that Dark Hollow is Billy Purdue's country?"

"I don't believe in coincidences."

He patted the hood one more time, and seemed to reach a decision. "Neither do I. You stay in touch now, Bird, y'hear?"

He turned and walked back to his car.

"Is that it?" I said. I was surprised to see him let it go so easily.

"No, I guess it isn't, but I don't see what more I can do." He stood at the open door of the car, and watched me. "Frankly, Bird, I'm balancing the benefits of hauling you in and grilling you, assuming you'd tell us anything, against the benefits of having you wandering around and looking under rocks. So far, the scales are tipping in favor of the second option, but only just. You remember that."

I waited a heartbeat.

"Does this mean you've decided against recruiting me, Ellis?"

He didn't reply. Instead, he shook his head and drove away, leaving me to think about Tony Celli and Stritch and an old man in a harbor bar, drinking beers and waiting for the new world to sweep him away.

I had told Ellis some of the truth, but not all. I was going to Dark Hollow, and would be there by nightfall, but first Louis and I would pay a visit to Boston. There was a slight possibility that Tony Celli might have taken Ellen Cole, perhaps in the hope of using her as leverage if I found Billy Purdue before he did. Even if that was not the case, there were some things to be clarified before we went up against Celli again. Unlike the members of his crew, Tony was a made guy. It was important that everybody understood the potential repercussions if we were forced to confront him.

Before I left to meet Louis at the airport, I stopped off at the Kraft Mini-Storage at Gorham. There, in three adjoining units, was what I had retained of my grandfather's possessions: some furniture; a small library of books; some silver plates; a brass screen for a fireplace; and a series of boxes filled with old paperwork and files. It took me fifteen minutes to locate what I was looking for and take it back to the car: a manila expanding file, held closed by a piece of red ribbon. On the index tab, written in my grandfather's ornate script, were the words *Caleb Kyle*.

CHAPTER SIXTEEN

AL Z OPERATED out of an office above a comic book store on Newbury Street. It was an odd location, but it suited him to be in a place where tourists browsed among chichi clothes stores, sipped exotic teas or browsed in galleries. It was busy, there were too many people around for anyone to cause trouble, and he could send out for flavored coffees or scented candles anytime he wanted.

Louis and I sat outside a Ben & Jerry's ice cream parlor across from Al Z's brownstone office, eating chocolate chip cookie dough ice cream and drinking large coffees. We were the only people sitting outside, mainly because it was so cold that my ice cream hadn't even begun to melt yet.

"You think he's noticed us?" I asked, as my fingers gave up their efforts to hold the spoon without shaking.

Louis sipped his coffee thoughtfully. "Tall, handsome black male and his white boy sittin' outside eatin' ice cream in the fuckin' winter? I think someone must have noticed us by now."

"I'm not sure I like being called 'boy,'" I mused.

"Get in line, whitey. We got a three-hundred-year start on that particular grievance."

At a window above the comic book store, a shadow moved.

"Let's go," said Louis. "It wasn't for the damn cold, brothers be running the world by now."

At the top of a flight of steps, next to the window of the store, there was a buzzer beside a wooden, windowless door. I pressed the buzzer and a voice answered simply: "Yes?"

"I'm looking for Al Z," I said.

"No Al Z here," replied the voice, all in a fast flow of heavily accented English so that it came out as "Noalseeher." It was followed by a click and the intercom went silent.

Louis hit the buzzer again.

"Yes," said the same voice.

"Man, just open the damn door, okay?"

The intercom clicked off, then buzzed, and we passed through, the reinforced door springing shut behind us. We walked up four flights of stairs to where a plain, unvarnished door stood open. A figure leaned against the window beyond, small and bulky, its hand resting midway between its neck and its belt, ready to move for the gun if necessary. The only ornamentation on the wall was a cheap-looking black and white clock, which softly ticked away the seconds. I figured the surveillance camera was probably hidden behind it. When we entered the room and saw the television screen on Al Z's desk showing only an empty stairwell, I realized I was right.

There were four men in the room. One was the short bulky guy, his skin yellow as a beeswax candle, who had watched us from the doorway. An older man, his flesh heavy at the jowls like a basset hound's, sat on a worn leather sofa to the left of the doorway, his legs crossed, a white shirt and red silk tie beneath his black suit. His eyes were hidden by small, round-framed sunglasses. Against the wall, a young buck leaned with his thumbs hooked into the empty belt loops of his pants, holding his silver-gray jacket away from his sides to reveal the butt of a

H&K semiautomatic at his waist. His gray suit pants were baggy, narrowing to pipe-cleaner thinness where they met his silver-tooled cowboy boots. The eighties revival was obviously still in full flow where he came from.

Louis was looking straight ahead as if the room was empty apart from the fourth man who sat behind a teak desk inlaid with green leather, the desktop clean apart from a black telephone, a pen and notebook and the TV screen, which kept up its unceasing vigil on the stairs.

Al Z looked like a well-groomed undertaker on vacation. His thin silver hair was swept back from the broad expanse of his forehead and slicked tightly to his skull. His face was craggy and wrinkled, the eyes dark like opals, the lips thin and dry, the nostrils on his long nose slim and strangely elongated, as if he had been bred for his powers of smell. He wore a three-piece suit of autumn hues, the fabric a mix of reds and oranges and yellows, finely interwoven. His white shirt was open at the neck, the collar narrow pinpoint, and there was no tie. In his right hand he held a cigarette; his left lay flat on the desk, the nails short and clean, but not manicured. Al Z acted as the buffer between the upper reaches of the organization and the lower. He solved problems, when they arose. It was his gift to be a problem solver, but there was no point in a manicure if your hands were always going to be dirty.

There were no chairs in front of his desk, and the man in the dark suit remained spread across the sofa, so we stayed standing. Al Z nodded at Louis, then looked long and appraisingly at me.

"Well, well, the famous Charlie Parker," he said at last. "If I knew you were coming, I'd have worn a tie."

"Everybody knows you, how you gonna make any money as a private dick?" muttered Louis. "Hiring you for undercover work be like hiring Jay Leno."

Al Z waited for him to finish before turning his attention

from me to Louis. "If I knew you were bringing equally distinguished company, Mr. Parker, I'd have made everybody else wear a tie too."

"Long time no see," said Louis.

Al Z nodded. "I got bad lungs." He waved the cigarette gently as he spoke. "The New York air don't agree with me. I prefer it up here."

But there was more to it than that: the mob was no longer what it once had been. The world of *The Godfather* was history before the film ever hit the screen, the image of the Italians already sullied by their involvement in the heroin epidemic of the seventies, and since then walking disaster areas like John Gotti Jr. had debased it even further. RICO—the racketeer-influenced and corrupt organization laws—had put an end to the construction shakedowns, the garbage collection monopolies, and the mob control of the Fulton Street Fish Market in New York. The heroin-smuggling business that had operated out of pizza parlors was gone, busted by the FBI in 1987. The old bosses were dead, or in jail.

Meanwhile, the Asians had spread from Chinatown, crossing the divide of Canal Street into Little Italy, and the blacks and the Latinos now controlled operations in Harlem. Al Z had smelled death in the air and had receded even further into the background, to the north, watching events in New York while dealing with the problems of the troubled New England operation. Now he sat in a bare office above a comic book store in Boston, and tried to maintain some element of stability in what little remained. That was why Tony Clean was so dangerous: he believed the old myths and still saw the potential for personal glory in the tattered remnants of the organization. His actions threatened to bring down heat on his associates at a time when the organization was in a weakened position. His continued existence endangered the survival of everyone around him.

To our left, the young gun eased himself from the wall.

"They're carrying, Al," he said. "You want me to lighten their load?"

From the corner of my eye, I saw Louis's eyebrow raise itself about a quarter of an inch. Al Z caught the gesture, and smiled gently.

"I wish you luck," he said. "I don't think either of our guests are the kind to give up their toys so easily."

The young gun's glow of confidence flickered, as if he was unsure whether or not he was being tested. "They don't look so tough," he said.

"Look harder," said Al Z.

The gunslinger looked but his powers of perception left a lot to be desired. He glanced once again at Al Z, then made a move toward Louis.

"I wouldn't, if I were you," said Louis softly.

"You ain't me," said the younger man, but there was a hint of wariness in his voice.

"That's true," said Louis. "I was you, I wouldn't be dressed like no crack pimp."

A bright light flashed in the young man's eyes. "You talk to me like that, you fuckin' nig . . ." The word died in a kind of gasp in his throat as Louis's body twisted, his left hand closing tightly on the man's neck and propelling him backward, his right quickly slipping the gun from the Italian's belt holster and tossing it to the floor. The young man gurgled once as he hit the wall, spittle flying from his lips as the air was forced from his body. Then slowly, his feet began to lift from the floor; first his heels, then his toes, until the only thing holding him upright was Louis's unyielding left hand. His face turned pink, then deep red. Louis did not release his grip until a hint of blue began creeping into his lips and ears, then the fingers of his hand opened suddenly and the gunman sank to the ground, his hands fumbling at the collar of his shirt as he struggled to draw painful, choking breaths into his parched lungs.

During the whole incident, nobody else in the room had moved, because Al Z hadn't given any indication that they should. He looked at his struggling soldier the way he might have looked at a one-clawed crab dying on a beach, then returned his attention to Louis.

"You'll have to excuse him," he said. "Some of these boys, they learn their manners and their speech patterns in the gutter." He turned his attention to the bulky man at the door, waving his cigarette at the figure on the floor, who now lay with his back against the wall, his eyes dazed and weak. "Take him to the bathroom, get him a glass of water. Then try to explain to him where he went wrong."

The bulky guy helped the younger man to his feet, and accompanied him outside. The big man on the sofa didn't move. Al Z got to his feet and walked over to the window where he stood for a moment, watching the street below, before turning and resting against the windowsill. The three of us were now on the same level, and I recognized the gesture of good manners after what had taken place.

"Now, what can I do for you gentlemen?" he asked.

"A girl came to visit me a few days ago," I began.

"Lucky you. The last time a girl came to visit me, it cost me five hundred dollars."

He smiled at his joke.

"This girl is the daughter of a friend of mine, an ex-cop."

Al Z shrugged. "Forgive me, but I don't understand how this concerns me."

"I had an encounter with Tony Clean after the girl's visit. It kind of hurt, but I don't think Tony got much more satisfaction out of it than I did."

Al Z took a long drag on his cigarette, then exhaled the smoke in a noisy sigh through his nose. "Go on," he said, wearily.

"I want to know if Tony took the girl, as leverage maybe. If he has her, he should hand her back. He doesn't need cop trouble. Not on top of everything else," I added.

Al Z rubbed the corners of his eyes and nodded without speaking. He looked to the fat man on the sofa. The fat man's head moved slightly, the eyes impossible to see behind his shades.

"Let me get this straight," said Al Z at last. "You want me to ask Tony Clean if he has kidnapped an ex-cop's daughter and, if he has, you want me to tell him to hand her back?"

"If you don't," said Louis quietly, "we have to make him do it ourselves."

"You know where he is?" replied Al Z. I was aware of the air in the room quickly becoming charged.

"No," I said. "If we knew that, maybe we wouldn't be here. We figured you might." But something in the way Al Z had asked that last question told me that he didn't know, that Tony Clean was operating in some place beyond Al Z's control, and I guessed that Al Z was weighing up his position even before we arrived. That was the purpose of the fat man on the sofa. That was why he had not been asked to leave, because he wasn't the kind of man anyone asked to leave a room. He was the kind who did the asking. Things were coming apart for Tony Clean, a fact that Al Z seemed to confirm with his next words.

"Under the circumstances, it would be unwise for you to involve yourselves in this matter," he said softly.

"Under what circumstances?" I replied.

He puffed out some smoke. "Private business matters, the kind you should leave private. If you don't back off, we might have to push you."

"We might push back."

"You can't push back if you're dead."

I shrugged. "Getting us there might be the hard part." It was handbags at ten paces, but the underlying threat in Al Z's voice was coming through loud and clear. I watched as he stubbed out his butt in a cut glass ashtray with more force than was strictly necessary.

"So you're not going to keep out of our affairs?" he asked.

"I'm not interested in your affairs. I have other concerns."

"The girl? Or Billy Purdue?"

He surprised me for a moment, but not for long. If there was a pulse, then Al Z had his finger on it and he would only remove his finger when the pulse stopped.

"Because if it's Billy Purdue," he continued, "then we may have the seeds of a difficulty."

"The missing girl is a friend, but Rita Ferris, Billy's ex-wife, was my client."

"Your client's dead."

"It goes beyond that."

Al Z pinched his lips. To his right, the fat man on the sofa remained as impassive as a Buddha.

"So you're a man of principle," said Al Z. He tackled the word *principle* like it was a peanut shell he was crushing beneath his heel. "Well, I'm a man of principle too."

I didn't think so. Principles are expensive things to maintain and Al Z didn't look like he had the moral resources to support any. In fact, Al Z didn't look like he could work up the moral resources to take a leak on a burning orphanage.

"I don't think your principles and mine would qualify for the same definition," I said at last.

He smiled. "Maybe not." He turned to Louis. "And where do you stand on all this?"

"Beside him," said Louis, inclining his head gently in my direction.

"Then we have to reach an accommodation," Al Z concluded. "I'm a pragmatist. You step lightly in this matter, and I won't kill you unless I have to."

"Likewise," I said. "Seeing as how you've been so hospitable and all." Then we left.

• • •

Outside, it was cold and overcast.

"What do you think?" asked Louis.

"I think Tony's out there on his own, and maybe he hopes he can sort this mess out before Al Z loses his patience. You think he has Ellen?"

Louis didn't reply immediately. When he did, his eyes were hard. "He does or he doesn't, somehow it all ties in with Billy Purdue. Means it's gonna end bad for someone."

We walked around to Boylston and hailed a cab. As it pulled up, Louis slid in and said, "Logan," but I raised a hand.

"Can we take a detour?"

Louis shrugged. The cab driver shrugged too. It was like bad mime.

"Harvard," I said. I looked at Louis. "You don't have to come. I can meet you at the airport."

Louis's eyebrow rose half an inch. "Nah, I'll tag along, 'less you think I'm going to cramp your style."

The cab dropped us off at the monolithic William James Hall, close by Quincy and Kirkland. I left Louis in the lobby and took the elevator to room 232, where the psychology department had its office. My stomach felt tight, and there was sweat on my palms. At the office, a polite secretary told me where Rachel Wolfe's office was located, but she also told me that Rachel wouldn't be in that day. She was at a seminar out of town, and wouldn't be back until the following morning.

"Can I take a message?" she asked.

I considered turning around and walking away, but I didn't. Instead, I reached into my wallet and took out one of my cards. On the back, I wrote the new telephone number for the Scarborough house and handed the card to the secretary. "Just give her this, please."

She smiled. I thanked her, and I left.

Louis and I walked back to Harvard Square to catch a cab. He didn't speak until we were on our way to Logan.

"You do that before?" he asked, with just the faintest hint of a smile.

"Once. I never got that far the last time, though."

"So, you, like, stalking her, right?"

"It's not stalking if you know the person well."

"*Oh.*" He nodded deeply. "Thanks for clearing that one up. Never really understood the distinction before."

He paused before he spoke again. "And what you trying to do?"

"I'm trying to say I'm sorry."

"You want to get back with her?"

I tapped my fingers on the window. "I don't want it to be the way it is between us, that's all. Frankly, I don't know *what* I'm doing and, like I told your significant other, I'm not even sure that I'm ready yet."

"But you love her?"

"Yes."

"Then life will decide when you're ready." He didn't speak again.

CHAPTER SEVENTEEN

A NGEL MET US at the airport, and we drove to the food court at the Maine Mall to eat before we headed north.

"Shit," said Angel, as we drove down Maine Mall Road. "Look at this place. You got your Burger King, your International House of Pancakes, your Dunkin' Donuts, your pizza parlors. You got your four main food groups right here on your doorstep. Live here too long and they'll be rolling you from one place to the next."

We ate Chinese in the food court of the mall and told Angel about our encounter with Al Z. In return, he produced a crumpled letter addressed to Billy Purdue, care of Ronald Straydeer.

"Cops and the feds did a pretty good job, but they didn't deal with your buddy Ronald the right way," he said.

"You talked to him about his dog?" I asked.

"Talked about his dog, then ate some stew." He looked a little queasy.

"Roadkill?" I knew that Ronald wasn't above scavenging, despite the state's laws on taking roadkill. Myself, I couldn't see the harm in using a deer or squirrel for food instead of letting it rot by the side of the road. Ronald did a pretty mean venison steak, served with beets and carrots preserved by burying them in sand.

"He told me it was squirrel," said Angel, "but it smelled like skunk. It didn't seem polite to ask. Seems this letter came for Billy about a week back, but Ronald hadn't seen him to give it to him."

The letter was postmarked Greenville. It was short, little more than an extension of good wishes, some details of renovations to the house and some stuff about an old dog that the writer still had around the place and with which Billy Purdue seemed to have been familiar when it was a pup. It was signed, in his old man's scrawl: "Meade Payne."

"So they stayed in touch all these years," I remarked. It seemed to confirm what I had thought: if Billy Purdue was going to seek help from anyone, it would be Meade Payne.

We drove nonstop to Dark Hollow, Angel and Louis shooting ahead in the Mercury. The mists gathered as I went farther north, so that journeying from Portland to Dark Hollow was like moving into a strange, spectral world, where house lights glowed dimly and the beams of headlights assumed their own, lancelike solidity; where road signs announced towns that existed only as scattered dwellings without any hub or center. There was more snow forecast, I knew, and soon the snowmobilers would arrive in numbers to hurtle along the Interstate Trail system. But for now, Greenville was still quiet as I drove through, sand mixed with snow by the side of the road, and I passed only two cars on the uneven, pitted surface of Lily Bay Road on the way to Dark Hollow.

When I arrived at the motel, Angel and Louis were already checking in. The same woman with the blue-rinse hair who had greeted me earlier in the week stood behind the desk, examining their details on a single registration card. Beside her, a brown cat slept on the counter, curled in on itself with its nose almost touching its tail. Angel was doing the talking while Louis examined a series of battered tourist booklets in a rack. He glanced at me when I came in, but didn't acknowledge my presence further.

"You gentlemen sharing a room?" asked the blue-rinse woman.

"Yes, ma'am," replied Angel, with a look of homely wisdom on his face. "A dollar spared is a dollar made."

The woman glanced at Louis, resplendent in a black suit, black coat and white shirt. "Your friend a preacher?" she said.

"Kind of, ma'am," said Angel. "He's strictly Old Testament, though. An eye for an eye, and stuff like that."

"That's nice. We don't get many religious folks staying here."

Louis's face had the long-suffering look of a saint who has just heard that the rack is to be tightened.

"If you're interested," the woman continued, "we got a Baptist service tonight. You're welcome to join us."

"Thank you, ma'am," said Angel, "but we prepare to engage in our own forms of worship."

She smiled understandingly. "Long as it's quiet and doesn't disturb the other guests."

"We'll do our best," intervened Louis, taking the key.

The woman recognized me as I approached the desk. "Back again? You must like it here in Dark Hollow."

"I hope to get to know it better," I replied. "Maybe you can help me with something."

She smiled. "Sure, if I can."

I handed her a photo of Ellen Cole, the small, ID kind taken in a photo booth. I'd had it blown up on a color copier so that the picture was now eight-by-ten size. "You recognize this girl?"

The woman looked at the picture, squinting her eyes behind the thick lenses of her spectacles. "Yes, I do. She in some kind of trouble?"

"I hope not, but she's missing and her parents have asked me to help them find her."

The woman turned her attention back to the picture, nodding as she did so. "Yes, I recall her. Chief Jennings was asking about her. She stayed here with a young man for one night. I can get you the date, if you like."

"Would you, please?"

She took a registration card from a green metal card box and examined the details. "December fifth," she said. "Paid by credit card made out in the name of Ellen C. Cole."

"Do you recall anything that happened, anything out of the ordinary?"

"No, nothing important. Someone had suggested to them that they visit here, someone they gave a ride to from Portland. That's about all. She was nice, I remember. He was kind of a surly kid, but they can be that way at that age. I should know: raised four of my own and they were meaner than wharf rats until they were twenty-five."

"Did they give any indication of where they might be heading after they left here?"

"North, I guess. Maybe up to Katahdin. I don't know, frankly, but I told them that, if they had some time to spare, they should drive out and watch the sunset on the lake. They seemed to like the idea. It's a pretty sight. Romantic, too, for a young couple like that. I let them check out late in the afternoon, just so they wouldn't have to be rushing to pack."

"And they didn't say who recommended that they see Dark Hollow?" It seemed an odd thing to suggest. Dark Hollow didn't have that much going for it.

"Sure they did. It was an old guy they met along the way. They gave him a ride up here, and I think maybe he met up with them before they left."

I felt my stomach turn a little. "Did they mention his name?"

"No. Didn't sound like anybody from around here, though," she said. Her brow furrowed a little. "They didn't seem concerned about him or nothing. I mean, what harm could an old man do?" I think she meant the question to be rhetorical when she started out, but by the end I don't think it sounded that way to either of us.

She apologized, told me she didn't know any more, then gave me directions to the lakeshore viewing point, about a mile or two outside the town, on a tourist map. I thanked her, left my bag in my room and knocked on the door of the room next door, now occupied by Angel and Louis. Angel opened the door and let me in. Louis was hanging up his suits in the battered brown closet. I put the old man to the back of my mind. I wasn't about to leap to conclusions, not yet.

"What do people do for fun around here?" asked Angel, sitting down heavily on one of the two double beds in the room. "This place sees less action than the pope."

"Endure the winter," I said. "Wait for the summer."

"Fulfilling existence, if you're a tree."

Louis finished arranging his clothes and turned to us. "Find out anything?"

"The manager remembers Ellen and her boyfriend. She told them to go watch the sunset out of town, then reckons they went north."

"Maybe they did go north," said Louis.

"Rangers up in Baxter State Park have no record of them, according to Lee Cole. Apart from that, the options up north are limited. Plus, the woman at the desk says they gave some old guy a ride up here, and it was this old man who suggested that they stay in Dark Hollow."

"Is that a bad thing?"

"I don't know. Depends on who he was. It could be nothing." But I thought of the old man who had tried to take Rita Ferris at the hotel, and the figure of the old man Billy Purdue claimed to have seen the night that his family was taken from him. And I thought too of something Ronald Straydeer had said when he misheard my comment as we stood before Billy Purdue's trailer, discussing a man he might or might not have seen on his property.

You're getting old.

Yuh, he could have been old.

"So what now?"

I shrugged glumly. "I'm going to have to talk to Rand Jennings."

"You want us to come along?"

"No, I have other plans for you two. Take a ride out to the Payne place, see what's going on."

"See if Billy Purdue's turned up, you mean," said Angel.

"Whatever."

"And if he has?"

"Then we go and get him."

"And if he hasn't?"

"We wait, until I'm certain that Ellen Cole isn't in some kind of trouble here. Then . . ." I shrugged.

"We wait some more," finished Angel.

"I guess," I replied.

"That's good to know," he said. "At least I can plan what to wear."

The Dark Hollow Police Department lay about half a mile beyond the northern end of the town. It was a single-story brick building with its own generator in a concrete bunker at its eastern side. The building itself was quite new, a consequence of a fire a couple of years back that had destroyed the original structure just off the main street.

Inside it was warm and brightly lit, and a sergeant in long sleeves stood behind a wooden desk filling in some forms. His shiny name badge said "Ressler," so I figured he was the same Ressler who had watched Emily Watts die. I introduced myself and asked to see the chief.

"Can I ask what it's in connection with, sir?"

"Ellen Cole," I replied.

His brow furrowed a little as he picked up the phone and dialed an extension number. "There's a guy here wants to talk to you about Ellen Cole, chief," he said, then put his hand over the receiver and turned back to me. "What did you say your name was again?"

I hadn't said it the first time, but I gave it to him and he repeated it into the phone. "That's right, chief. Parker. Charlie Parker." He listened for a moment, then looked at me again, sizing me up. "Yeah, that sounds about right. Sure, sure." He put the phone down then reappraised me without saying anything.

"So, does he remember me?" I asked.

Ressler didn't reply, but I got the feeling that the sergeant knew his chief well and had detected something in his voice that put him on his guard. "Follow me," he said, unlocking a dividing door to the left of the desk and holding it to one side to let me pass. I waited while he relocked it, then followed him between a pair of desks and into a small, glass-walled cubicle. Behind a metal desk, on which lay trays of papers and a computer, sat Randall Jennings.

He hadn't changed too much. True, he was grayer and had put on a little weight, his face now slightly puffy and the beginnings of a double chin hanging down below his jawline, but he was still a good-looking man, with sharp brown eyes and wide, strong shoulders. It must have hurt his ego, I thought, when his wife had commenced an affair with me.

He waited for Ressler to leave and close the door of the office before he spoke. He didn't ask me to sit down and didn't seem troubled by the fact that, standing, I could look down on him.

"I never thought I'd see your face again," he said at last.

"I guessed by the way you said good-bye," I replied.

He didn't respond, just rearranged some papers on his desk. I wasn't sure if the gesture was meant to distract him, or me. "You're here about Ellen Cole?"

"That's right."

"We don't know anything about it. She came, she left." He raised his hands in a gesture of helplessness.

"That's not what her mother thinks."

"I don't care what her mother thinks. What I'm telling you is what we know, same thing I told her father when he was up here."

It struck me that I must just have missed Walter Cole, that we might even have been in town at the same time. I felt a twinge of sorrow that he had been forced to come up here alone, fearing for his daughter's safety. I would have helped him, had I known.

"The family's filed a missing person's report."

"I'm aware of that. I had a federal agent chewing my ear over a nonexistent NCIC filing." He looked hard at me. "I told him it was a long way from New York to Dark Hollow. We do things our own way up here."

I didn't respond to his bout of territorial spraying. "Are you going to act on the report?" I persisted.

Jennings stood up, the knuckles of his large hands resting on his desk. I had almost forgotten what a big man he was. There was a gun in a holster at his belt, a Coonan .357 Magnum out of St. Paul, Minnesota. It looked shiny and new. I guessed that Rand Jennings didn't have much cause to use it way up here, unless he sat on his porch and took potshots at rabbits.

"Am I having trouble making myself understood?" he said softly, but with a hint of suppressed anger. "We've done what we can. We have responded to the missing person report. Our view is that the girl and her boyfriend may have run away together and, so far, we have no reason to suspect otherwise."

"The manager of the motel said they were heading north."

"Maybe they were."

"All that's north is Baxter and Katahdin. They never made it there."

"Then they went someplace else."

"There may have been someone else with them."

"Maybe there was. All I know is that they left town. If they were still here, I'd know about it."

"I can see now why you never made detective."

He flinched, and his face flushed red. "You don't know the first damn thing about me," he said. The anger was distinct now as he pronounced his next words slowly and with deliberate emphasis. "If you'll excuse me, we have some real crimes to deal with."

"Really. Someone stealing Christmas trees? Maybe trying to screw a moose?"

He walked around the desk and came close to me as he passed by to open the door of his office. I think he half expected me to take a step back from him, but I didn't.

"I hope you're not planning on looking for trouble here," he said. He could have been talking about Ellen Cole, but his eyes said he was talking about someone else.

"I don't have to look for trouble," I replied. "I stay still long enough, trouble finds me."

"That's because you're dumb," he said, still holding the door open. "You don't pay attention to the lessons life teaches you."

"You'd be surprised how much I've learned."

I prepared to leave his office, but his left hand shot out to block me. "Remember one thing, Parker: this is my town and you're a guest. Don't abuse the privilege."

"So it's not a case of 'what's mine is yours?'"

"No," he said, with menace. "No, it isn't."

•   •   •

I left the building and walked to my car, the wind now howling through the trees and biting at my bare fingers. Above me, the sky was dark. As I reached the Mustang, an old green Nissan Sunny pulled into the lot and Lorna Jennings stepped from the car. She was wearing a black leather jacket with a big fur collar and blue jeans tucked into the same boots she had been wearing the last time we met. She didn't see me until she had begun to walk toward the main entrance. When she did spot me, she stopped short for a moment before coming over, casting an anxious glance at the illuminated doorway as she did so.

"What are you doing here?" she asked.

"Talking to your husband. He wasn't very helpful."

She raised an eyebrow at me. "Are you surprised?"

"No, not really, but it's not about me. A girl and a young man are missing and I think somebody here may know what happened to them. Until I find out who that might be, I'm going to be around for a while."

"Who are they?"

"The daughter of a friend, and the girl's boyfriend. Her name is Ellen Cole. You ever hear Rand mention her?"

She nodded. "He said he'd done what he could. He thinks they may have eloped."

"Young love," I said. "It's a beautiful thing."

Lorna swallowed and ran a hand through her hair. "He hates you, Bird, for what you did. For what we did."

"That was a long time ago."

"Not for him," she said. "Or me."

I was sorry I'd mentioned young love. I didn't like the look in her eyes. It made me nervous. But I surprised myself by asking the next question.

"Why are you still with him, Lorna?"

"Because he's my husband. Because I have nowhere else to go."

"That's not true, Lorna. There's always somewhere else."

"Is that an offer?"

"Nope, it's just an observation. You take care," I began to walk away, but she reached out and stopped me by placing her hand on my arm.

"No, you be careful, Bird," she said. "He hasn't forgiven you, and he won't."

"Has he forgiven you?" I asked.

There was something in her face as she spoke, something that reminded me of that first afternoon we spent together and the warmth of her skin against mine. "I didn't want his forgiveness," she said. Then she smiled sadly and left me.

I spent the next hour wandering around the stores in Dark Hollow, showing Ellen Cole's photograph to anyone who'd take the time to look. They recalled her at the diner, and in the drugstore, but nobody had seen them leave and no one could confirm whether or not they left with another man, or speculate as to whom that person might have been. It grew colder and colder as I walked, my coat wrapped tightly around me, the lights of the stores casting a yellow glow on the snow.

When I had exhausted every avenue of inquiry, at least for the present, I went back to my room, showered, and changed into a pair of denims and a shirt and sweater before pulling on my overcoat and preparing to meet Angel and Louis for dinner. Angel was already outside the room, drinking coffee and blowing puffs of white breath into the air like an unhealthy steam engine.

"You know, it's warmer out here than it is in that room," he said. "I lost a layer of skin from my feet, the tiles in the bathroom are so cold."

"You're too sensitive for this world. Who would have thought it?"

He snorted unhappily and stamped his feet while alternating the coffee cup from hand to hand, each time putting his free hand under the opposite armpit.

"Stop," I said. "You're going to make it rain. Any sign of activity out at Meade Payne's place?"

He came to a relative standstill. "None that we could see without knocking on the door and asking for cookies and a glass of milk. Caught a sight of the young guy and Payne eating supper, but they were alone, far as we could see. You have any luck with Jennings?"

"No."

"You surprised?"

"Yes and no. He's got no reason to help me, but this isn't about me. It's about Ellen and her boyfriend, but I could see in his eyes that he would use them to get at me, if he could. I don't understand him. He's suffered. I know he has. His wife took up with another man behind his back, a man ten years younger than him, but he's still with her, and it's hell for both of them. It wasn't as if Rand was old, or cruel, or impotent. He had what it took; or, maybe, he had it according to his own definition of it. I took something away from him, and he won't ever forgive me for it. But how can he not feel for Ellen Cole, for Ricky, for their families? No matter how much he hates me, they have to matter." I kicked idly at the dirt on the ground. "Sorry, Angel. I'm thinking out loud."

Angel tossed the remains of his coffee into a mound of frozen, compacted snow. I could hear the soft hiss as it hit the ice, as the coffee corrupted the whiteness of its crystals one by one.

"Suffering isn't enough, Bird," said Angel softly. "So he's suffered: big fuckin' deal. Get in line with the rest of us suckers. It's not enough to suffer, and you know that. What matters is that you understand that others suffer, and some of them suffer worse than you could ever do. The nature of compassion isn't coming to terms with your own suffering and applying it to others: it's knowing that other folks around you suffer and, no matter what happens to you, no matter how lucky or unlucky you are, they keep suffering. And if you can do something about that, then you do it, and you do it without whining or waving your own fuckin' cross for the world to see. You do it because it's the right thing to do.

"From what you say, this Rand Jennings doesn't have a compassionate bone in his body. All he feels is self-pity, and he doesn't understand any suffering but his own. I mean, look at his marriage. There are two of them in it, Bird; whatever you may have felt for her, she's stayed with him this long, and if you hadn't turned up like a fire in February then everything would be just the way it was. He'd be unhappy and she'd be unhappy and they'd be unhappy together, and it seems like they've set their own boundaries on what is and is not going to happen to change that situation.

"But he's selfish, Bird. He only thinks of his own hurt, his own pain, and he blames her for it, and you, and, by extension, the world. He doesn't care about Ellen Cole, or Walter, or Lee. He's all full up pissing and cursing at the bum hand he thinks life has dealt him, and that hand ain't never gonna change."

I looked at him, at his unshaven profile, the wisps of dark hair curling out from under his dark wool hat, the empty coffee cup forgotten in his hand. He was a mass of contradictions. It struck me that I was taking life lessons from a five-six semiretired burglar whose boyfriend, not twenty-four hours earlier, had executed a man against a brick wall. My life, I reflected, was taking some strange turns.

Angel seemed to sense what I was thinking, because he turned to me before he spoke again. "We've been friends for a long time, you and me, maybe even without either of us realizing it. I know you and, for a time, you weren't far off becoming like Jennings and a million others like him, but I know now that's not going to happen. I'm not sure how things changed and I don't think I want to know most of it. All I know is that you're becoming a compassionate man, Bird. That's not the same as pity, or guilt, or trying to pay off some debt to fortune or to God.

It's feeling other people's pain as your own, and acting to take that pain away. And maybe, sometimes, you have to do bad things to do that, but life doesn't balance easy. You can be a good man and perform bad actions, because that's the nature of things. People who believe otherwise, well, they're just time-servers, because they spend so much time wrestling with their consciences that nothing gets done, and nothing changes, and the innocent and the defenseless, they just keep getting hurt. In the end you do what you can, maybe what you have to do, to make things better. Your heart isn't going to be weighed against a feather in the next life, Bird. My guess is they use something heavier, otherwise we'll all end up in hell."

He smiled at me, a small, wintry smile that said he knew the cost of following that philosophy. He knew, because he was following it himself: sometimes with me, sometimes with Louis, but always, always according to what he believed was right. I wasn't sure that what he said could be applied to me. I made moral judgments in what I did, but I didn't believe that I was always entitled to do so and I knew that I had not yet managed to purge myself of the guilt and grief I felt. I acted to ease my own pain and, in doing so, I sometimes managed to ease the pain of others. That was as close to compassion as I thought I could get, for the present.

From the far end of town came the sound of sirens, gradually drawing nearer. Red-and-blue lights flashed across the buildings on the main street as a cruiser tore around the corner and headed in our direction at high speed. It screeched a hard left at the intersection and drove by. In the front seat of the car I could see the figure of Randall Jennings.

"Must be a doughnut sale on," remarked Angel.

A second car came down the main street, spun on its rear tires as it made the turn, then headed after the first vehicle.

"With free coffee," he added.

I tossed my keys in my hand, then nudged Angel off the hood

of the Mustang, where he had just taken up a position. "I'm going to take a look. You want to come along?"

"Nah. I'm a-waitin' for Black Narcissus to finish making himself lovely for us. We'll hold off for you, burn some furniture to keep warm."

I followed the lights of the lead cars as they glanced against the trees, the branches like hands outstretched over the road. After a mile I caught up with the cruisers as they headed up into the forest through a private logging company road, the wooden barrier thrown to one side to enable the cars to pass. Beside the barrier stood a man wearing a wool hat and a parka. A path wound down behind him to a small house on the edge of the company land. I figured that maybe it was he who had made the call to the police.

I stayed close behind the rear car, watching its taillights as it swerved and dipped along the narrow, rutted track. Eventually the cruisers came to a halt beside a Ford truck with a Ski-Doo in back, a huge bearded man with a belly like a pregnant woman's standing beside it. Jennings emerged from the lead car, Ressler stepping out of the car behind at the same time accompanied by another patrolman. Flashlights blinked into life and the line of three cops headed over to the back of the truck and peered inside. I took my own Maglite from the trunk and walked over to them. As I went, I heard the bearded man say:

"I didn't want to leave him out there. There's snow coming on, means he might have been lost till the thaw."

Faces turned toward me as I approached, one of them that of Rand Jennings.

"The fuck are you doing here?" he said.

"Collecting berries. What you got?"

I shone my flashlight beam into the bed of the truck, although what was there didn't need the extra illumination. It needed darkness and dirt and a headstone six feet above it.

It was a man's body, laid out on a sheet of tarpaulin, his

mouth wide open and filled with leaves. His eyes were closed and his head was twisted at an unnatural angle. He lay, crumpled and broken, amid the tools and plastic containers in the truck, his hair touching the empty gun rack.

"Who is he?"

For a moment, I didn't think Jennings was going to answer. Then he sighed and said:

"It looks like Gary Chute. He was a surveyor for the timber company. Daryl here found him when he was out checking some traps. Came upon his truck back a ways as well, couple of miles from the body."

Daryl looked like he was about to deny the traps part of the statement. His mouth opened briefly then closed again at a look from Jennings. Daryl looked kind of slow, I thought. His eyes were dull and his brow low, and his mouth, though closed, was in continual motion, as if he was worrying at the inside of his bottom lip with his teeth.

Beside him, Ressler was flicking through the dead man's wallet.

"It's Chute all right," he said. "No cash in the wallet, though. Credit cards are still here. You take it, Daryl?"

Daryl shook his head wildly from side to side. "No, I didn't touch nothin'."

"You sure?"

Daryl nodded his assent. "Sure," he said. "I'm sure." Ressler didn't look like he believed him, but he didn't say anything more.

"Why didn't anyone look for him?" I asked, although, from what Martel had told me, I could guess the answer.

"He's a freelance consultant," said Jennings. "He wasn't due to report until next week and his wife only got worried a day or two ago, when he didn't show like he'd promised. I hope you're not trying to imply anything here, Parker. I've had just about my fill of you."

I ignored him and turned to Daryl. "How did you find him?"

"Huh?"

"I mean, what position was he in?"

"Lying at the bottom of a ridge, near buried by the snow and the leaves," replied Daryl. "Looked like he just slipped, hit some stones and trees on the way down, then caught his neck on a root. Must have snapped like a twig." Daryl smiled uneasily, unsure that he had said the right thing.

It didn't sound very likely, especially with the money missing from his wallet. "You say there was snow *and* leaves on him, Daryl?"

"Yessir," said Daryl eagerly. "Branches too."

I nodded, and shone my flashlight on the body once again. Something caught my attention at his wrists and I let the light linger for a moment before flicking it off. "It's a shame he was moved," I said.

Even Jennings had to agree. "Shit, Daryl, you should have left him where he was, then let the wardens go and get him."

"I couldn't leave him out there," said Daryl. "It weren't decent."

"Maybe Daryl's right. If it snows, and it will, we could have lost him until the spring," said Ressler. "Daryl says he found the body at Island Pond, wrapped it in the tarp and hauled it back ten miles to his truck with his Ski-Doo. Island Pond's quite a ways from here and, according to Daryl, the road turns into one big snowdrift way before you reach the pond."

I glanced at Daryl with new respect; there weren't many men who'd haul the body of a stranger for miles. "No way anyone can head out there in the dark, assuming we could even find the place," concluded Jennings. "Anyway, this is a matter for the wardens and the state police, but not us. We'll arrange to have him taken to Augusta in the morning, let the ME take a look at him, but that's the end of our responsibility."

I looked up, beyond the trees and into the black night sky.

There was a sense of heaviness, as of a weight above us about to fall. Ressler followed my gaze.

"Like I said, Daryl was right. Snow's coming."

Jennings gave Ressler a look that said he didn't want any more details of the discovery spoken of in front of Daryl and, especially, me. He slapped his hands together sharply. "Okay, let's go." He leaned into the bed of the truck and covered Gary Chute's body with the tarp, using pieces of scrap metal, a wheel iron and the butt of a shotgun to hold it in place. He crooked a finger at the patrolman.

"Stevie, you ride in the bed here, make sure that tarp doesn't come off." Stevie, who looked about eleven, shook his head unhappily then climbed carefully into the truck, squatting down beside the body. The other cops went back to their cars, leaving only Jennings and me.

"I'm sure we all appreciate your assistance, Parker."

"Funny, but I don't think you mean that."

"You're right, I don't. Stay out of my way, and out of my business. I don't want to have to tell you that again." He tapped me once on the chest with a gloved finger, then turned and walked away. The cruisers started almost in unison and formed a convoy with the truck—one ahead, one behind—as Gary Chute was brought back to Dark Hollow.

Leaves and branches, as well as snow, had covered Chute's body, according to Daryl. If his death was accidental, and Daryl had taken the money from his wallet, then that didn't make too much sense. The trees were bare, and it had been snowing pretty regularly over the last week or so. Snow would have covered the body, but not leaves and branches. Their presence indicated that someone could have been trying to hide Gary Chute's body.

I walked back to my car and thought of what I had seen in the flashlight's glow: red marks on the dead man's wrists. Those marks weren't made by a fall, or by animals, or frost.

They were rope burns.

• • •

When I got back to the motel, Angel and Louis were gone. There was a note under my door, written in Angel's strangely neat hand, telling me that they had gone to the diner and would see me there. I didn't follow them. Instead, I went down to the motel reception desk, filled two plastic cups with coffee and returned to my room.

Chute's death continued to bother me. It was unfortunate that it had been Daryl who found the body, even if he had acted with the best of intentions. Chute's truck could probably have served as a rough marker for the crime scene but now its integrity had been fatally compromised by Daryl's removal of the body.

Maybe it was nothing, but on a map I marked roughly where Gary Chute's body had been found at Island Pond. Island Pond was about forty miles northeast of Dark Hollow. The only way to reach that area was along a private road, which required a permit for use. If someone had killed Gary Chute, he'd have to have taken that road to get to him, following him into the wilderness. The other possibility was that whoever killed him was in the wilderness already, waiting for him. Or . . .

Or maybe Chute was unlucky enough to see someone, or something, that he shouldn't have. Maybe whoever killed him didn't go into the wilderness after him, but was coming back out again. And, if that was the case, then the first place that person would arrive at was Dark Hollow.

But that was all speculation. I needed to get my thoughts in order. On a page of my notebook, I noted all that had happened since the night that Billy Purdue had stuck his knife in my cheek. Where there were links, I formed dotted lines between the names. Most of them came back to Billy Purdue, except Ellen Cole's disappearance and the death of Gary Chute.

And in the center of the list was a white space, empty and

clean as new-fallen snow. The other names and incidents circled around it, like planets around a sun. I felt the old instinct, the desire to impose some pattern on incidents that I did not yet fully understand, some form of explanation that might begin to lead me to an ultimate truth. When I was a detective in New York, dealing with the deaths of those whom I had not known, with whom I had no direct connection, to whom I had no duty beyond that of the policeman whose task it is to find out what happened and to ensure that someone pays for the crime, I would follow the threads of the investigation as I had laid them out and when they led nowhere, or proved simply to be false assumptions, I would shrug and return to the core to follow another thread. I was prepared to make mistakes in the hope that I would eventually find something that was not an error.

That luxury, the luxury of detachment, was taken away from me when Susan and Jennifer died. Now they all mattered, all of the lost, all of the gone, but Ellen Cole mattered more than most. If she was in trouble, then there was no room for error, no time to make mistakes in the hope that they would lead to some final reckoning. Neither could I forget Rita Ferris and her son, and at the thought of her I looked instinctively over my shoulder and toward the dark rectangle of the window, and I recalled a weight on my shoulder, cold but not unyielding; the touch of a familiar hand.

There was too much happening, too many deaths revolving around the white space at the center of the page. And in that space, I put a question mark, dotted it carefully, then extended the dots down to the bottom of the page.

And there I wrote the name *Caleb Kyle*.

I should have gone out to eat then. I should have found Angel and Louis and gone to a bar where I could have watched them drink and flirt oddly with each other. I might even have had a drink, just one drink . . . Women would have gone by, swaying gently as the alcohol took hold of their bodies and minds. Perhaps one of them might have smiled at me, and I might have smiled back and felt the spark that ignites when a beautiful woman focuses her attention on a man. I could have had another drink, then another, and soon I would have forgotten everything and descended into oblivion.

The anniversary was approaching. I was aware of it as a dark cloud on the horizon, moving inexorably to engulf me in memories of loss and pain. I wanted normality, yet it continued to hang beyond my reach. I wasn't even sure why I had gone to Rachel's office, except that I knew that I wanted to be with her even though my feelings for her made me feel sick and guilty, as if I was somehow betraying Susan's memory. With these thoughts, after all that had happened over the past few days, and after allowing my mind to explore the nature of the killings that had occurred in both the recent and distant past, I should not have remained alone.

Tired and so hungry that my appetite had faded entirely away to be replaced by a deeper, gnawing unease, I undressed and showered, then climbed into my bed, pulling the sheets over my head and wondering how long it would take me to fall asleep. Just long enough, it emerged, to get that thought out.

I awoke to a noise, and a faint, unpleasant odor that took me a few moments to identify. It was the smell of rotting vegetation, of leaves and mulch and standing water. I rose from my pillow and wiped the sleep from my eyes, my nose wrinkling as the smell of decay grew stronger. There was a clock radio on the nightstand—the time read 12:33 A.M.—and I checked it in case the alarm might somehow have switched itself on during the night, but the radio was silent. I looked around the room, conscious now of a strangeness to the light, a tinge of unfamiliar color that should not have been present.

There was singing coming from my bathroom.

It was low but sweet, the sound of two voices combining to sing the same song, a song that sounded like a nursery rhyme, the words muffled by the closed bathroom door.

And from beneath the door, a green light seeped, its form rippling across the cheap carpet. I pushed back the covers and stood naked on the floor, but felt no cold, no chill, and began to walk toward the bathroom. As I did so, the smell grew stronger. I could feel it adhering to my skin and hair, as if I were bathing in its source. The singing rose in volume, the words now clear, the same three syllables repeated over and over again in high, girlish tones.

Caleb Kyle, Caleb Kyle

I was almost at the point where the tendrils of light from beneath the door reached their farthest extension. From behind the door came the sound of water softly lapping.

Caleb Kyle, Caleb Kyle

I stood for a second at the periphery of the green light, then placed one bare foot in its pool.

The singing stopped as soon as my foot touched the floor, but the light remained, moving slowly, viscously, across my bare toes. I reached forward and carefully turned the handle of the door. I pulled it open and stepped onto the tiles.

The room was empty. There were only the white surfaces, the neat pile of towels above the toilet, the sink with its low-grade soaps still wrapped, the glasses with their paper covers, the flower-speckled curtain over the bath pulled almost completely across . . .

The light came from the behind the curtain, a sickly, green glow that shone with only a vestige of the power of its original source, as if it had fought its way through layers and layers of obstacles to offer what little illumination it could. And in the quiet of the room, broken only by the soft lapping of water from behind the curtain, it seemed as if something held its breath. I heard a soft giggle, smothered by a hand, the laugh echoed by another, and the water behind the curtain lapped more loudly.

I reached out a hand, gripped the plastic and began to pull it quickly across. There was some resistance, but I continued to open the curtain until the interior of the bath was completely exposed.

The bath was full of leaves, so full that they reached up to the faucets. They were green and red, brown and yellow, amber and gold. There was aspen and birch, cedar and cherry, maple and basswood, beech and fir, and their shapes twisted and overlapping in a riot of decay.

A shape moved beneath the leaves, and bubbles broke upward. The vegetation shifted and something white began to rise to the surface, a long, slow ascent as if the water was far deeper than it could possibly be. As it neared, it seemed to separate into two figures, their hands held as they rose, their long hair spreading and flowing as they came, their mouths open, their eyes blind.

Then a doll's head broke through the leaves and I glimpsed, once again, gray skin and a stained blouse.

I let the curtain drop and backed away, but the wet tiles betrayed me. And as I fell, their shades moved behind the curtain and I backed away on my hands and heels, my fingers and toes scrabbling for purchase until I awoke once again, the sheets in a pile at the end of the bed, the mattress exposed and a bloody hole in its fabric where I had torn through it with my nails.

A hammering came at the door.

"Bird! Bird, you okay in there?" It was Louis's voice.

I crawled from my bed and found that I was shivering uncontrollably. I struggled with the chain on the door, my fingers fumbling at the catch, and then, at last, it was open and Louis was standing there before me in a pair of gray sweatpants and a white T-shirt, his gun in his hand.

"Bird?" he repeated. There was concern in his eyes, and a kind of love. "What's the matter?"

Something bubbled in my throat, and I tasted bile and coffee.

"I see them," I said. "I see them all."

CHAPTER EIGHTEEN

I SAT ON THE EDGE of my bed, my head in my hands, and waited while Louis went to the office and poured two cups of coffee from the eternally brewing pot. As he passed by his own room I heard him exchange words with Angel, although he was still alone when he closed the door behind him, shutting out the cold night air. He handed me one of the cups, and I thanked him before sipping from it silently. From outside came the soft tapping of snow falling on my window. He didn't talk for a time, and I felt him considering something in his mind.

"I ever tell you about my Grandma Lucy?" he said at last.

I looked at him in surprise. "Louis, I don't even know your surname," I replied.

He smiled dimly, as if it was all he could do to recollect what it might have been himself. "Anyways," he continued, and the smile faded, "Lucy, she was my gran'momma, my daddy's momma, not much older than I am now. She was a beautiful woman: tall, skin like day fading into night. She wore her hair down, always. I never recall her wearing it no other way but down, it tumbling over her shoulders in dark curls. She lived with us until the day she died, and she died young. The pneumonia took her, and she faded away in shakes and sweats.

"There was a man who lived in the town, and his name was Errol Rich. Ever since I knew him, he just wasn't a man to turn the other cheek. When you were black, and you lived in that kind of town, that's the first thing you learned. You always, always, turned the other cheek, 'cause if you didn't, weren't no white sheriff, no white jury, no bunch of redneck assholes with ropes ready to tie you to the axle of a truck and drag you along dirt roads till your skin came off, weren't none of them going to see it no other way but a nigger gettin' above himself, and settin' a bad example to all the other niggers, maybe gettin' them all riled up so's that white folks with better things to do would have to go out some dark night and teach them all a lesson. Put some manners on them, maybe.

"But Errol, he didn't see things that way. He was a huge mother. He walked down the street and the sun wasn't big enough to shine around his shoulders. He fixed things—engines, mowers, anything that had a moving part and the hand of man could find a way to save. Lived in a big shack out on one of the old county roads, 'long with his momma and his sisters, and he looked them white boys in the eye, and he knew they was afraid.

"Except, this one time, he was driving by a bar out by Route 101 and he heard someone call out "Hey, nigger!" and the cracked old windshield of his truck, it just exploded in. They threw a big old bottle through it, full of all the piss those assholes could work up between 'em. And Errol, he pulled over, and he sat there for a time, covered in blood and glass and piss, then he climbed out of the cab, took him a length of timber maybe three feet long from the bed of his truck, and he walked over to where them good ol' boys were sitting on the stoop. There was four of 'em, including the owner, a pig of a man called Little Tom Rudge, and he could see them freeze up as he came.

"'Who threw that?' says Errol. 'You throw that, Little Tom?

'Cause if you did, you better tell me now, else I'm gonna burn your shit-heap down to the ground.'

"But nobody answered. Them boys, they was just struck dumb. Even together in a bunch and all liquored up, they knew better than to mess with Errol. And Errol, he just looked at them for a time, then he spat on the ground and he took that length of timber and threw it through the window of the bar, and Little Tom, there wasn't nothing he could do. Least of all, not then.

"They came for him the next night, three truckloads of 'em. They took him in front of his momma and his sisters and brought him to a place called Ada's Field, where there was a black oak tree that was maybe a century old. And when they got there, half the town was waitin' for 'em. There was women there, even some of the older children. Folks ate chicken and biscuits, and drank soda pop from glass bottles, and talked about the weather, and the coming harvest, and maybe the baseball season, like they was at the county fair and they was waitin' for the show to start. All told, there was more than a hundred people there, sittin' on the hoods of their cars, waitin'.

"And when Errol came, his legs and hands were tied and they hauled him up onto the roof of an old Lincoln that was parked under the tree. And they put a rope around his neck, and tightened it. Then someone came up and poured a can of gasoline over him, and Errol looked up, and he spoke the only words he said since they took him, and the only words he would ever say again on this earth.

"'Don't burn me,' he said. He wasn't asking them to spare him, or not to hang him. He wasn't afraid of that. But he didn't want to burn. Then I guess maybe he looked up into their eyes and saw that what was to be would be, and he bowed his head and he started to pray.

"Well, they grabbed the rope around his neck and they pulled it so that Errol was balancing on the tips of his toes on the roof of the car, and then the car started and Errol hung in the air, twisting and thrashing. And someone came forward with a burning torch in his hand and they burned Errol Rich as he hung, and those people, they listened to him scream until his lungs burned and he couldn't scream no more. And then he died.

"That was at ten after nine, on a July night, maybe three miles away from our house, right on the other side of town. And at ten after nine, my Grandma Lucy, she rose from her chair by the radio. I was sittin' at her feet. The others, they was in the kitchen or in bed asleep, but I was still with her. Grandma Lucy, she walked to the door and stepped out into the night, wearin' nothin' but her nightdress and a shawl, and she looked out into the woods. I followed her, and I said: 'Miss Lucy, what's the matter?' But she didn't say nothin', just kept on walkin' until she was about ten feet away from the edge of the trees, and there she stopped.

"And out in the darkness, among the trees, there was a light. It didn't look like no more than a patch of moonlight but, when I tried to find it, there was no moon, and the rest of the woods was dark.

"I turned to Grandma Lucy and I looked at her eyes." Louis stopped, and his own eyes flickered closed briefly, like a man recalling a pain that has been forgotten for a long time. "Her eyes were on fire. In her pupils, right in the deepest blackness at the center, I could see flames. I could see a man burning, like he was standing before us, sheltered by the trees. But when I looked into the darkness, there was only that patch of light, nothin' more.

"And Lucy, she said: 'You poor boy, you poor, poor boy,' and she started to cry. When she cried, it was like her grief put out the flames, because the burning man in her eyes started to fade until, in the end, he was gone, and the patch of light in the woods, that was gone too.

"She never spoke about what happened to nobody else, and

she told me not to tell either. But I think my momma knew. Least, she knew that Lucy had some kind of gift that nobody else had. She could find the shades in the places nobody else could find, the places where nobody else would look. And the things that moved through the shadows, the folks passing on their way, she saw them too."

He stopped. "Is that what you see, Bird?" he asked softly. "The shades?"

I felt cold at my fingertips and in my toes. "I don't know," I replied.

"Because I recall what happened back in Louisiana, Bird," he continued. "You saw things back there that nobody else saw, I know that. I could sense it from you, and it scared you."

I shook my head slowly. I couldn't admit to what I didn't want to believe myself. I sometimes thought—maybe even hoped—that I had been unhinged by grief, that the loss of my wife and child had made me mentally ill, emotionally and psychologically disturbed, so troubled by guilt that I was haunted by images of the dead conjured up by my sick mind. Yet I had seen Jennifer and Susan first after meeting Tante Marie Aguillard in Louisiana, after she had told me what had happened to them when she could not possibly have known. The others came later, and they spoke to me in my dreams.

Now, as I saw Rita and Donald, my own Jennifer, felt my Susan's hand upon me, I half hoped that it was the fact that the anniversary was almost on me, that remembered grief had wormed its way into the recesses of my mind and had started to trouble me again. Or maybe it was a product of guilt, the guilt I felt at wanting Rachel Wolfe, the guilt I felt at wanting the chance to start over again.

There is a form of narcolepsy in which sufferers literally daydream, the dreams of REM sleep coming upon them in the course of their daily lives, so that the real and the imagined become one and the worlds of sleeping and waking collide. For a time, I thought I might have been a victim of something similar but I knew, deep down inside, that this was not the case. Two worlds came together for me, but they were not the worlds of sleeping and waking. No one slept in these worlds, and no one rested.

I told some of this to Louis, as he watched me quietly from a chair in the corner. I now felt a little ashamed at my outburst, at bringing him in here to listen to my ravings. "Maybe I just have bad dreams, that's all. But I'll be okay, Louis. I think I'll be okay. Thank you."

He looked me hard in the eyes, then stood and walked to the door. "Anytime." He opened the lock, then paused.

"I'm not the superstitious kind, Bird. Don't go makin' that mistake about me. But I know what happened that night. I could smell burning. I could smell the leaves on fire."

And with that he returned to his room.

Still the snow fell, the crystals turning to ice on my window. I watched them form, and thought of Cheryl Lansing's granddaughters, and Rita Ferris, and Gary Chute. I didn't want Ellen Cole to join them, or Billy Purdue either. I wanted to save those who remained.

In an effort to distract myself, I tried to read. I had just about finished a biography of the earl of Rochester, an English dandy who had boozed and whored his way to an early grave in the time of Charles II, writing some great poetry while he did so. I read the final pages lying on my bed beneath the yellow light from the wall lamp, warm air humming into the room. It seemed that in 1676, Rochester had been involved in the slaying of a constable and had gone into hiding, disguising himself as a quack physician named Dr. Alexander Bendo who sold medicines made out of clay, soot, soap and pieces of old wall to the suckers of London, none of whom ever guessed the true identity of the man they trusted with their most intimate secrets, and with the most private parts of their wives' bodies.

Old Saul Mann would have liked Rochester, I thought. He

would have appreciated the element of disguise, the possibility of one man taking on the identity of another in order to protect himself, then conning the very people who were searching for him. I fell asleep to the soft patter of snow on glass and dreamed of Saul Mann, wrapped in a cloak of moons and stars, his cards spread on a table before him, waiting quietly for the great game to begin.

CHAPTER NINETEEN

THE SNOWS that came that night were the first heavy falls of the winter. They fell on Dark Hollow and Beaver Cove, on Moosehead Lake and Rockwood and Tarratine. They sugarcoated Big Squaw Mountain and Mount Kineo, Baker Mountain and Elephant Mountain. They turned the Longfellows into a white scar that ran across the back of Piscataquis. Some of the smaller ponds froze, creating a layer of ice as thin and treacherous as a traitor's blade. The snow sat heavy on the evergreens and the ground below lay silent and undisturbed, save for the sound of branches giving way reluctantly beneath the weight they carried, the compressed flakes falling heavily to the drifts below as snow welcomed back snow. In my disordered, disturbed sleep, I felt the snow falling, sensed the change in the atmosphere as the world was shrouded in white and the night waited for the exquisite perfection of winter's work to be revealed in the slow-dawning light of day.

Quite early, I heard a snowplow moving down the main street of the town and the slow, careful progress of the first cars, their chains making a distinctive noise on the road. The room was so cold that beads of moisture turned the windows to shattered glass, miraculously restored by the sweep of a hand. I looked out on the world, at the tracks of the cars, at the first people walking on the streets, their hands deep in their pockets or by their sides, the bulk of their layers of sweaters and shirts, thermals and scarves, forcing them to move with a comical unfamiliarity, like children thrust into new boots.

I approached the bathroom with unease, but all was quiet and clean within. I showered, keeping the water as hot and powerful as I could stand, then dried myself quickly, my teeth already chattering as the temperature cooled the drops on my body. I pulled on jeans, boots, a thick cotton shirt and a dark wool sweater, added a coat and gloves, and stepped out into the crisp, cold morning air. Beneath my feet, the snow crunched and shifted, my progress marked by the impression of my footsteps behind me. I knocked twice, sharply, on the door of the next room down.

"Go away," said Angel's voice, the force of his words undiminished by the fact that they came through about four layers of blankets. I felt a moment of guilt at having woken them the night before, and tried to keep my mind off the conversation I had had with Louis.

"It's me," I replied.

"I know. Go away."

"I'm heading over to the diner. I'll see you there."

"I'll see you in hell first. It's cold outside."

"It's colder in there."

"I'll take my chances."

"Twenty minutes."

"Whatever. Just go away."

I was about to head for the diner when something about my car distracted me. From the window of my room it had seemed that its red lines were only partially obscured by the snow, for flashes of color showed through as if a hand had wiped away some of the snowfall. But that wasn't why the snow on my car was streaked with red.

There was blood on the windshield. There was blood also on the hood, and a long line of it ran from the front of the car, across the driver's door and the rear window, before pooling below the trunk. I walked through the snow, feeling it crunch beneath my feet. At the back of the car, beside the right rear wheel, lay a pile of mangled brown fur. The cat's mouth was open, and its tongue hung over its small white teeth. A red wound ran across its belly, but most of its blood seemed to be on my car.

To my left, I heard the office door slam and watched as the manager walked over to me. Her eyes were red from crying.

"I already called the police," she said. "I thought, when I saw her first, that you'd hit her with your car, but then I saw the blood and knew that couldn't be. Who'd do something like that to an animal? What kind of a person could take pleasure in hurting it so?" She began to cry again.

"I don't know," I said.

But I did know.

It took me three knocks to get Angel to the door. He stood shivering as I told him about the cat, Louis behind him listening silently.

"He's here," said Louis, finally.

"We don't know that for sure," I replied, but I knew he was right. Somewhere close by, Stritch was waiting.

I left them and walked across to the diner. It was ten after eight, and it was already almost full, warm air circulating with the smell of fresh coffee and bacon, voices raised at the counter and in the kitchen. For the first time, I noticed the Christmas decorations, the Coca-Cola Santa Claus, the tinsel and the stars. It would be my

second season without them. I felt almost grateful for Billy Purdue, maybe even for Ellen Cole, for giving me something on
which to concentrate my mind. All of the energy I might have
poured into grieving, into anger and guilt, into fearing the anniversary, I now put into the search for these two people. But that
gratitude was a brief, passing thing, an ugly betrayal of the people involved, and I quickly felt disgusted with myself for using
someone else's sufferings to alleviate my own.

I took a booth and watched the people passing by. When the
waitress came, I ordered only coffee. The sight of the cat and the
thought of Stritch trailing us had ruined my appetite. I found
myself closely examining the faces of the people in the diner, as
if Stritch might somehow have mutated himself, or stolen their
form. There were a couple of timber company men across from
me, eating plates of ham and eggs and already talking about
Gary Chute.

I listened and learned, for the world of the northern wilderness was on the verge of change. An area of almost one hundred
thousand acres of forest, owned by a European paper company,
was about to be harvested. The area had last been logged in the
thirties and forties and now it had matured again. For the last
decade, the company had been restoring roads and bridges in
preparation for the big lumber trucks with their claw-shaped
hydraulic lifts that would move into the wilderness, enabling
the transportation of the pine, spruce and fir, the maple and
birch, to begin. Chute, a graduate of the University of Maine at
Orono, was one of those responsible for checking the roads, the
tree growth and the likely boundaries for the logging.

The laws relating to forestry had changed since the last cutting. Then, the companies had cleared all of the land, causing
silting that killed fish, displaced animals and led to serious ero-
sion. Now they were obliged to cut in a checkerboard pattern,
leaving half the forest for another twenty to thirty years so that
the habitats could grow again. Already there were signs of early

cuts, where the deer and moose would feed on the raspberries, willow and alders that sprang up to fight for the new light. And so the days of the undisturbed northern wilderness were now numbered, and soon men and machines would be making their way into its vastness. Gary Chute had been the first of many, and it struck me that his job must have taken him into areas where few people had set foot in decades.

Across the street, Lorna Jennings stepped from her green Nissan, wearing a white padded jacket buttoned and tied over black denims and black, calf-length boots. I wondered how long she had been there: there were no exhaust fumes around the car, and despite the fact that there was little traffic on the street, the tracks of her tires had been crossed by a number of other vehicles.

She stood at the curb, her hands in the pockets of her jacket, and looked over at the diner. Her eyes moved along the windows until they came to where I sat, a mug of coffee in my hand. She seemed to consider me for a moment, then walked across the road, entered the diner and took a seat opposite me, unbuttoning her jacket as she sat. Beneath it, she wore a red, turtleneck sweater that tightly followed the sweep of her breasts. One or two people looked over at her as she sat, and words were exchanged.

"You're attracting attention," I said.

She blushed slightly. "The hell with them," she said. She wore a trace of pink lipstick and her hair hung loose to the nape of her neck, strands falling gently near her left eye like dark feathers from a bird's wing. "Some of them know you were out there last night, when they found the body. People have been asking why you're here."

She ordered, and a waitress brought her coffee and a bagel, with some thin slices of bacon on a separate plate, then gave each of us a sly look before stepping away. Lorna ate the bagel unbuttered, holding it in her left hand while her right picked up pieces of bacon that she nibbled at daintily.

"And what answer have they got?"

"They've heard that you're looking for a girl. Now they're trying to figure out if you had any reason to be interested in the disappearance of the timber company man." She stopped and took a sip of coffee. "Well, have you?"

"Is that you asking, or Rand?"

She grimaced. "You know that's a low blow," she said quietly. "Rand can ask his own questions."

I shrugged. "I don't think Chute's death was accidental, but that's for the ME to confirm and I don't see any connection between him and Ellen Cole." That wasn't completely true. They were connected by Dark Hollow and the dark line of a road drawn through the wilderness upon which Chute's death hung like a single red bead.

"But there have been other deaths as well, some of them tied up with a guy called Billy Purdue. He was one of Meade Payne's boys, once upon a time."

"You think he might be here?"

"I think he might try to get to Payne. There are people after him, bad people. He took money that didn't belong to him and now he's running scared. I think Meade Payne is one of the only people left whom he can trust."

"And where do you fit in?"

"I was doing some work for his wife. Ex-wife. Her name was Rita Ferris. She had a son."

Lorna's brow furrowed, then her eyes closed briefly and she nodded as she remembered the name. "The woman and child who died in Portland, that was them, wasn't it? And this Billy Purdue, he was her ex-husband?"

"Uh-huh, that's them."

"They say he killed his own family."

"They say wrong."

She was silent for a time, then said: "You seem very sure of that."

"He wasn't the kind."

"And do you know 'the kind?'" She was watching me carefully now. There were conflicting emotions in her eyes. I could sense them coming from her, just as I had sensed the snow falling softly in the night. There was curiosity, and pity, and something else, too, something that had lain dormant for many years, a feeling repressed and now gradually being released. It made me want to draw back from her. Some things were best left in the past.

"Yes, I do. I know the kind."

"You know, because you've killed them."

I waited a heartbeat before I answered. "Yes."

"Is that what you do now?"

I smiled emptily. "It seems to be part of it."

"Did they deserve to die?"

"They didn't deserve to live."

"That's not the same thing."

"I realize that."

"Rand knows all about you," she said, pushing away the remains of her food. "He spoke about you last night. Actually, he shouted about you, and I shouted back." She sipped her coffee. "I think he's afraid of you." She looked out on to the street, refusing to look directly at me and instead staring at my reflection in the glass. "I know what he did to you, in that men's room. I always knew. I'm sorry."

"I was young. I healed."

She turned back to me. "I didn't," she said. "But I couldn't leave him, not then. I still loved him, or thought I did. And I was young enough to believe that we had a chance together. We tried to have children. We thought it might make things better. I lost two, Bird, the last one only a year ago. I don't think I can carry to term. I was so useless, I couldn't even give him a child." She tensed her lips, and brushed her hair back from her forehead. There was a deadness about her eyes.

"Now I dream about walking away, but if I leave, I leave with nothing. That's the understanding we have, and maybe that's the way it'll have to be. He wants me to stay, or so he says, but I've learned a lot too these last few years. I've learned that men hunger. They hunger and they want, but after a while they stop feeling that hunger for what they have so they look elsewhere. I've seen the way he stares at other women, at the girls in their tight dresses when they come through town. He thinks that one of them will fill whatever he aches for, but they can't and then he comes back and says that he's sorry, that he knows now. But he only knows for as long as the guilt is sharp and alive, and then it passes and he starts to want again.

"Men are so stupid, so self-absorbed. Each of them thinks he's different, that this ache, this emptiness inside him, is unique to him and him alone, and that it somehow excuses whatever he does. But it doesn't, and then he blames the woman for somehow holding him back, as if, without her, he would be better than he is, more than he is. And the hunger grows and, sooner or later, it starts to feed on itself and the whole sorry mess falls apart like muscle and tendon separated from the bone."

"And don't women hunger too?" I asked.

"Oh, we hunger all right. And, most of the time, we starve. At least, we do around these parts. You hunger too, Charlie Parker. And you want, maybe more than most. You wanted me, once, because I was different, because I was older and because you shouldn't have been able to have me, but you could. You wanted me because I seemed unobtainable."

"I wanted you because I loved you."

Lorna smiled at the memory. "You'd have left me. Maybe not immediately—it might have taken years—but you'd have left me. As I got older, as the wrinkles started to appear, when I dried up inside and you found I couldn't have children, when some pretty thing came along and flashed you a smile and you started to think, 'I'm still young, I can do better than this.' Then you'd have gone, or strayed and come back with your tail between your legs and your dick in your hand. And I couldn't have taken that pain, Charlie, not from you. I'd have died. I'd have curled up and died inside."

"That shouldn't have been the reason that you stayed with him." I stopped myself, because no good could come of this. "Anyway, that was in the past. What's done is done."

She looked away, and there were furrows of hurt at her brow. "Were you ever unfaithful to your wife?" she asked.

"Only with a bottle."

She laughed softly, and looked up at me from beneath her hair. "I don't know whether that's better or worse than a woman. Worse, I think." The smile disappeared but a kind of tenderness stayed in her eyes. "You were full of pain, even then. How much more pain have you taken on since?"

"It wasn't of my choosing, but I was to blame for what led to it."

It seemed as if all of the other people around us had faded away, had become mere shadows, and the small circle of daylight around the table represented the boundary of the world, with darkness beyond in which pale figures drifted and flickered like the ghosts of stars.

"And what did you do?" And softly, so softly, I felt her hand touch my own.

"Like you say, I hurt people. And now I'm trying to make up for what I've done."

And in the gloom around us, the figures seemed to draw closer, but they were not the folks eating in a small-town diner, filled with gossip and the tiny tendernesses of a close-knit community. They were the figures of the lost and the damned, and there were those among them whom I had once called friend, lover, child.

Lorna stood and around us the diner came into focus again,

and the specters of the past became the substance of the present. She looked down upon me and my hand burned gently where she had touched me.

"'What's done is done,'" she said, repeating my words. "Is that how you feel about us?"

It seemed that the lines between our past and our present had become blurred, somehow, and we were digging at old wounds that should have healed long before. I didn't reply, so she shrugged on her jacket, took five bucks from her purse and left it on the table. Then she turned and walked away, leaving me with the memory of her touch and the faint lingering of her scent, like a promise made but not yet fulfilled. She knew that Rand would hear that we had been seen together, that we had spoken at length in the diner. I think, even then, she was pushing him. She was pushing us both. I could almost hear the clock ticking, counting down the hours and minutes until their marriage finally self-destructed.

In front of her, the door opened and Angel and Louis stepped into the diner. They glanced at me, and I nodded back. Lorna caught the gesture as she left, and as she passed, she acknowledged them with a small smile. They sat opposite me as I watched her cross the street and head north in her white jacket, her head low like a swan.

Angel called for two coffees and whistled softly as he waited for them to arrive. He was whistling "The Way We Were."

After they had eaten breakfast, I went over with them in detail the discovery of Chute's body the night before and we divided out what we were going to do that day. Louis would head up to the lake and try to find a vantage point from which to continue watching the Payne house, since the previous night's scouting party had proved unproductive. Before heading out, he would drop Angel in Greenville, where we had arranged for him to rent an ancient Plymouth at a gas station. From Greenville, he would head out to Rockwood, Seboomook, Pittston Farm and

Jackman, West Forks and Bingham, all of the towns to the west and southwest of Moosehead Lake. I would take Monson, Abbot Village, Guilford and Dover-Foxcroft to the south and southeast. In each town, we would show photographs of Ellen Cole, checking stores and motels, coffee shops and diners, bars and tourist information offices. Wherever possible, we would talk to local law enforcement and the old-timers who occupied their favorite booths in the bars and diners, the ones who would be sure to notice strangers in town. It would be tiring, frustrating work, but it had to be done.

I noticed Louis was edgy as we spoke, his eyes moving swiftly around the diner and out onto the street beyond.

"He won't come at us in daylight," I said.

"Could have taken us last night," he replied.

"But he didn't."

"He wants us to know he's here. He likes the fear."

We said nothing more about him.

Before heading down to my assigned towns, I decided to follow the route Ellen and her boyfriend might have taken on the day they left town. On the way, I stopped off at a service station and got a mechanic to fit the Mustang with chains. I wasn't sure how bad the roads might get as I headed north.

I kept glancing in my rearview mirror as I drove, conscious now that Stritch might be somewhere in the area, but no cars followed me and I passed no other vehicle on the road. A couple of miles outside the town was a sign for the scenic ridge. The road up to it was steep and the Mustang struggled a little on some of the bends. Two minor roads snaked east and west at one point but I stuck with the main route until it came to a small parking lot that looked out over an expanse of hill and mountain, with Ragged Lake shimmering to the west and Baxter State Park and Katahdin to the northeast. The parking lot marked the end of the public access road. After that, the roads were for the use of the timber company, and would have played hell with the shocks of most cars. The land was startling in its whiteness, cold and beautiful. I could see why the woman at the motel had sent them up here, could imagine how wonderful the lake looked when it was bathed in gold.

I came back down to the intersection, where the minor road to the east was thick with snow. It went on for about a mile before ending in fallen trees and thick scrub. The land at either side was heavily wooded, the trees dark against the snow. I drove back and took the western road, which gradually veered northwest to skirt the edge of a pond. The pond was maybe a mile long and half a mile wide, its banks surrounded by skeletal beech and thick pine. By its western bank, a small trail wended its way through the trees. I left the car and followed it on foot, the ends of my jeans quickly becoming heavy and wet.

I had walked for maybe ten minutes when I smelled smoke and heard a dog barking. I left the trail and climbed an incline through the trees, which revealed, at its peak, a small house, maybe no more than two rooms wide. It had an overhanging roof and a narrow porch and square, four-pane windows from which old paint flaked. The house itself might have been white once but most of the paint had now disappeared, leaving only patches below the eaves and on the window frames. Three or four large rubber garbage cans, the kind used for recycling by businesses, stood to one side of the house. On the other was an old yellow Ford truck. The rusting hulk of a blue Oldsmobile, its tires long gone, its windows thick with dirt, stood about five feet from the Ford. I caught some movement inside, and then a small black mongrel dog, its tail docked and its teeth bared, sprang through the open window from the backseat and moved quickly toward me. It stopped two or three feet from me and barked loudly.

The door of the house opened and an old man with a thin beard appeared. He wore blue overalls and a long, red raincoat. His hair was straggly and matted and his hands were almost black with dirt. I could see the hands clearly, because they were clutching a Remington A-70 pump-action shotgun, which was pointing in my direction. When the dog saw the old man emerge, its barking increased in volume and ferocity and its stumpy tail wagged frenziedly from side to side.

"What do you want here?" said the old man, in a voice that was slightly slurred. One side of his mouth remained immobile when he talked, and I figured he had some kind of nerve or muscle damage to his face.

"I'm looking for someone, a young woman who may have been around here a couple of days back."

The old man almost grinned, exposing a mouthful of yellow-stained teeth, broken, on both the top and bottom rows, by gaps. "Don't get young women around here no more," he said, the gun not moving from me. "Don't got the looks."

"She was blonde, about five-five. Her name was Ellen Cole."

"Didn't see 'em," said the old man, and he waved the gun at me. "Now get off my property."

I didn't move. Beside me, the dog lashed out and nipped at the end of my pants. I was tempted to kick it, but I figured it would latch on to my leg in an instant. I didn't take my eyes from the old man as I considered what he had just said.

"What do you mean 'them'? I only mentioned the girl."

The old man's eyes narrowed as he realized his mistake. He jacked a shell into the shotgun, driving the small dog wild. It gripped the wet end of my jeans tightly and tugged with its sharp white teeth.

"I mean it, mister," he said. "You just take your leave and don't come back, else I'll shoot you now and take my chances with the law." He whistled to the dog. "Come away now, boy, I don't want you gettin' hurt." The dog instantly turned and ran back to the Oldsmobile, its powerful back legs propelling it through the open window. It watched me from the front seat, still barking.

"Don't make me come back, old man," I said quietly.

"I didn't make you come here to begin with, and I sure ain't makin' you come back. I got nothing to say to you. Now I'm tellin' you for the last time: get off my land."

I shrugged, turned and walked away. There was nothing more to be done, not without the risk of getting my head shot off. I looked back once to find him still standing on the porch, the shotgun in his hands. I had other people to talk to, but I figured I'd be back out to see that old man again.

That was my first mistake.

CHAPTER TWENTY

AFTER I LEFT the old man I drove south. His words bothered me. It could have been nothing, I supposed; after all, he might have seen Ricky and Ellen together in town, and the news that someone was concerned that they were missing would have spread pretty quickly, even as far as the boondocks where the old man lived. If it turned out there was more to it than that then I knew where to find him, if I needed to.

I made my tour of the towns, Guilford and Dover-Foxcroft taking more time than the others, but I came up with nothing. I stopped at a pay phone to call Dave Martel in Greenville and he agreed to meet me at St. Martha's in order to pave the way with Dr. Ryley, the director. I wanted to talk to him about Emily Watts.

And Caleb Kyle.

"I hear you've been asking about the Cole girl," he said, as I prepared to hang up.

I paused. I hadn't been in contact with him since I arrived back in Dark Hollow. He seemed to detect my puzzlement.

"Hey, it's a small place. News gets around. I had a call from New York early this morning, asking about her."

"Who was it?"

"It was her father," continued Martel. "He's on his way back up here. Seems he got into a shouting match with Rand Jennings, and Jennings told him to keep away from Dark Hollow if he wanted to help his daughter. Cole called me to see if I could tell him anything that Jennings wouldn't. Probably called the county sheriff and CID as well." CID was the Criminal Investigations Division of the state police.

I sighed. Giving Walter Cole an ultimatum was like telling the rain to fall up instead of down.

"He say when he was going to arrive?"

"Tomorrow, I guess. I think he's going to stay here, instead of in the Hollow. You want me to give you a call when he gets here?"

"No," I said. "I'll find out soon enough." I told him a little about the background to the case, and how I had become involved at Lee's instigation, not Walter's. Martel gave a small laugh.

"Hear you were out there when they found Gary Chute as well. You sure lead a complicated life."

"You hear anything more about it?"

"Daryl brought the wardens out to where he found Chute—hell of a trip, from what I hear—and the truck's being brought back for examination, soon as they can clear a road through the snow. The body's on its way to Augusta. According to one of the part-timers who was down here this morning, Jennings seemed to think there was some bruising to the body, like he'd been beaten before he died. They're going to question the wife, see if she might have run out of patience with him and sent someone to take care of him."

"Pretty lame."

"Pretty," he agreed. "I'll see you at the home."

· · ·

Martel's car was already pulled up outside the main entrance to St. Martha's when I arrived, and he and Dr. Ryley were waiting for me by the reception desk.

Dr. Ryley was a middle-aged man with good teeth, a well-cut suit and the oily manner of a casket salesman. His hand was soft and moist when I shook it. I had to resist the temptation to dry my palm on my jeans when he had detached himself from me. It wasn't hard to see why Emily Watts had taken a shot at him.

He told us how much he regretted what had happened and advised us on the new security measures that had been introduced as a result, which seemed to consist of nothing more than locking the doors and hiding anything that could be used to knock out the guards. After some to-ing and fro-ing with Martel, he agreed to let me speak to Mrs. Schneider, the woman who occupied the room next to that of the late Emily Watts. Martel decided to wait in the lobby, in case we spooked the old lady by arriving as a team. He sat, drew a second chair in front of him with the tip of his shoe, then put his feet up and seemed to fall asleep.

Mrs. Erica Schneider was a German Jew who fled to America with her husband in 1938. He was a jeweler and brought enough gems with him to enable him to set up in business in Bangor. They had been comfortable too, she told me, at least until he died and the bills that he had been hiding from her for the best part of five years resurfaced. She was forced to sell their house and most of her possessions, then fell ill from stress. Her children had put her in the home, arguing that most of them were within visiting distance anyway, although this didn't mean that any of them actually bothered to visit her, she said. She spent most of her time watching TV or reading. When it was warm enough, she walked in the grounds.

I sat beside her in her small, neat room with its carefully made bed, its single closet filled with old, dark dresses, its dressing table covered with a limited selection of cosmetics that the old woman still carefully applied each morning, as she turned to me and said: "I hope I die soon. I want to leave this place."

I didn't reply. After all, what could I say? Instead, I said: "Mrs. Schneider, I'll try to keep what's said here today between us, but I need to know something: did you call a man named Willeford in Portland and talk to him about Emily Watts?"

She said nothing. I thought for a moment that she might start to cry, because she looked away and seemed to be having trouble with her eyes. I spoke again. "Mrs. Schneider, I really need you to help me. Some people have been killed, and a young girl is missing, and I think that maybe these things are connected to Miss Emily in some way. If there's anything at all you can tell me, anything that might assist me in bringing this thing to a close, I would appreciate it, I truly would."

She gripped and twisted the cord of her dressing gown in her hands, wincing. "Yes," she replied, at last. "I thought it might help her." The cord drew tighter and there was fear in her voice, as if the rope was tightening not around her hands, but around her neck. "She was so sad."

"Why, Mrs. Schneider? Why was she sad?"

The hands still worked at the cord as she replied. "One night, perhaps a year ago, I found her crying. I came to her, and I held her, and then she spoke to me. She told me that it was her child's birthday—a boy, she said, but she had not kept him, because she was afraid."

"Afraid of what, Mrs. Schneider?"

"Afraid of the man who fathered the child," she said. She swallowed and looked to the window. "What harm can it do to talk of these things now?" she whispered softly, more to herself than to me, then turned her face to mine. "She told me that, when she was young, her father . . . Her father was a very bad man, Mr Parker. He beat her and forced her to do things, you understand? Sex, *ja?* Even when she was older, he would not let her leave him, because he wanted her near him."

I nodded, but stayed silent as the words tumbled out of her like rats from a sack.

"Then another man came to her town, and this man made love to her, and took her to his bed. She did not tell him about the sex, but, in the end, she told him about the beatings. And this man, he found her father in a bar and he beat him, and told him that he must never touch his daughter again." She emphasized each word with a wag of her finger, carefully spacing each syllable for maximum emphasis. "He told her father that if anything happened to his daughter, he would kill him. And because of this, Miss Emily fell in love with this man.

"But there was something wrong with him, Mr. Parker, in here—" She touched her head. "—and in here." Her finger moved to her heart. "She did not know where he lived, or where he came from. He found her when he wanted her. He went missing for days, sometimes weeks. He stank of wood and sap and once, when he came back to her, there was blood on his clothes and under his nails. He told her that he hit a deer in his truck. Another time, he told her that he was hunting. Two different reasons he gave, and she started to feel afraid.

"That was when the young girls began to disappear, Mr. Parker: two girls. And once, when she was with him, she smelled something on him, the smell of another woman. His neck, it was scratched, torn, as if by a hand. They argued, and he told her that she was imagining things, that he had cut himself on a branch.

"But she knew it was him, Mr. Parker. She knew it was him who was taking the girls, but she could not tell why. And now, now she was pregnant by him, and he knew this. She had been so scared to tell him, but when he learned about it he was so pleased. He wanted a son, Mr. Parker. This he told her: 'I want a son.'

"But she would not hand over a child to such a man, she told me. She grew more and more afraid. And he wanted the child, Mr. Parker, he wanted it *so* badly. Always, always he was asking her about it, warning her against doing anything that might damage it. But there was no love in him or, if there was, it was a strange love, a bad love. She knew that he would take the child, if he could, and she would never see it again. She knew he was a bad man, worse even than her father.

"One night, when she was with him, in his truck by her father's house, she told him that she was in pain. In the toilet outside, she had a newspaper, and in the newspaper was—" She struggled for the words. "Guts, blood, waste. Again, you understand? And she cried and smeared the blood on herself and put it in the bowl and called for him and told him, told him that she had lost his baby."

Mrs. Schneider stopped again, and took a blanket from her bed, which she wrapped around her shoulders to ward off the cold. "When she told him this," she continued, "she thought that he would kill her. He howled, Mr. Parker, like an animal, and he raised her by the hair, and he hit her, again and again and again. He called her 'weak' and 'worthless.' He told her that she had killed his child. Then he turned and walked away and she heard him in the woodshed, moving among the tools her father kept there. And when she heard the sound of the blade, she ran away from the house and into the woods. But he followed her, and she could hear him coming through the trees. She stayed quiet, not even breathing, and he went past her, and he did not come back again, not ever.

"Later, they found the girls hanging from the tree, and she knew that he had left them there. But she never saw him again and she went to the sisters here, at St. Martha's, and I think that she told them why she was afraid. They sheltered her until she had the boy, and then they took the child away from her. After that, she was never the same and she came back here, after many years, and the sisters, they took care of her. When the home was sold, she used what little money she had to stay here. It is not an expensive place, this, Mr. Parker. This you can see." She waved her hand at the dull little room. Her skin was thin as paper. Sunlight dripped like honey through her fingers.

"Mrs. Schneider, did Miss Emily tell you the name of the man, the man who fathered her child?"

"I do not know," she replied.

I sighed softly but, as I did so, I realized that I had not given her time to finish, that she had more to say.

"I know only his first name," she continued. She moved her hand gently in the air before me, as if conjuring up the name from the past.

"He was called Caleb."

Snow falling, inside and out; a blizzard of memories. Young girls turning in the breeze, my grandfather watching them, rage and grief welling up inside him, the smell of their decay wrapped around him like a rotting cloak. He looked at them, a father and husband himself, and he thought of all the young men that they would not kiss, the lovers whose breath they would not feel against their cheeks in the dead of night and whom they would never comfort with the warmth of their bodies. He thought of the children they would never have, the potential within them for the creation of new life now stilled forever, the gaping holes at their bellies where their wombs had been torn apart inside them. Within each one, there had existed possibilities beyond imagining. With their deaths, an infinite number of existences had come to an end, potential universes lost forever, and the world shrank a little at their passing.

I stood and walked to the window. The snowfall made the grounds look less forbidding, the trees less bare, but it was all an illusion. Things are what they are, and changes in nature can only hide their true essence for a time. And I thought of Caleb, moving into the comforting darkness of the forest as he raged at the death of his unborn child, betrayed by the too-thin, too-weak body of the woman he had protected and then inseminated. He took at least three after her in rapid succession, fueling his fury until it was spent, then hung them with his earlier victims like trimmings on a tree to be found by a man who was not like him, a man who was so far removed from him that he felt the deaths of each of these young women as a personal loss. For Caleb's was a world in which things mutated into their opposites: creation into destruction, love into hate, life into death.

Five deaths, but six girls missing; one remained unaccounted for. In my grandfather's file, her name had been marked on a sheaf of pages, upon which her movements on the day she disappeared had been minutely reconstructed. A picture of her was stapled to the corner of the bundle: plump, homely Judith Mundy, a hardness to her passed down by generations of people who had worked thin, unforgiving soil to create a foothold and scratch a living from this land. Judith Mundy, lost and now forgotten, except by the parents who would always feel her absence like an abyss into which they shouted her name without even an echo in reply.

"Why would this man do such a thing to these girls?" I heard Mrs. Schneider ask, but I had no answer for her. I had stared into the faces of people who had killed with impunity for decades, and still I did not know the reasons for what they did. I felt a pang of regret at the loss of Walter Cole as a colleague. This was what Walter could do: he could look inside himself and, secure in his sense of his own innate rightness, he could create an image of that which was not right, a tiny tumor of viciousness and ill will, like the first cell colonized by a cancer from which he could construct the progress of the entire disease. He was like a mathematician who, when faced with a simple square on a page, plots its progress into other dimensions, other spheres of being beyond the plane of its current existence, while remaining ultimately detached from the problem at hand.

This was his strength and also, I thought, his weakness. Ultimately, he did not look deeply enough because he was afraid of what he might find within himself: his own capacity for evil. He resisted the impulse to understand himself fully that he might understand others better. To understand is to come to terms with one's potential for evil as well as good, and I did not think that Walter Cole wanted to believe himself capable, at whatever level, of doing deeds of great wrong. When I had performed acts that he found morally unacceptable, when I had hunted down those who had done evil and, by doing so, had done evil myself, Walter had cut me adrift, even though he had used me to find those individuals and knew what I would do when I found them. That was why we were no longer friends: I acknowledged my culpability, the deep flaws within myself—the pain, the hurt, the anger, the desire for revenge—and all of these things I took and used. Maybe I killed a little of myself each time I did so; maybe that was the price that had to be paid. But Walter was a good man and, like many good men, his flaw was that he believed himself to be a better one.

Mrs. Schneider spoke again. "It was the mother, I think," she said, softly.

I leaned against the windowpane and waited for her to continue.

"Once, when this man, this 'Caleb,' was drunk, he told Miss Emily of his mother. She was a hard woman, Mr. Parker. The father, he had left them out of fear of her. She beat her boy, beat him with sticks and chains, and she did worse things too. And later, when she was done, she would hurt him. She would drag him by the legs, or the hair, and kick him until he coughed blood. She chained him outside, like a dog, naked, in rain, and snow. All this, he told Miss Emily."

"Did he tell her where all this took place?"

She shook her head. "Maybe south. I don't know. I think . . ."

I didn't interrupt as her brow furrowed and the fingers of her right hand danced in the air before me.

"*Medina*," she said at last, her eyes ablaze in triumph. "He said something to Miss Emily about a Medina."

I noted down the name. "And what happened to his mother?"

Mrs. Schneider twisted in her chair to look at me. "He killed her," she said simply.

Behind me, the door opened as a nurse brought in a pot of coffee and two cups, along with a tray of cookies, presumably at the instigation of Dr. Ryley. Mrs. Schneider looked a little surprised, then took on the role of hostess, pouring my coffee, offering sugar, cream. She pressed cookies on me, which I refused, since I figured she might be grateful for them later. I was right. She took one for herself, carefully put the rest in two napkins from the tray and placed them in the bottom drawer of her dressing table. Then, as the snow clouds gathered once again in the skies above and the afternoon grew dark, she told me more about Emily Watts.

"She was not a woman who talked very much, Mr. Parker, only that one time," she said in her carefully pronounced English, which still carried traces of her roots in her *w*'s—"vas," "voman"—and in some of her vowels. "She said 'hello,' or 'good-night,' or spoke of the weather, but no more. She never again talked of the boy. The others here, if you ask them, even if you step into their rooms for a moment, they will talk of their children, their grandchildren, their husbands, their wives." She smiled. "Just as I did to you, Mr. Parker."

I was about to say something, to tell her that I didn't mind, that it was interesting, the least I could do, something half-meant and well intended, when she raised a hand to stop me. "Don't even begin to tell me that you enjoyed it. I am not a young girl who needs to be humored." The smile remained as she said it. There was something in her, some relic of old beauty, that told me that in her youth many men had humored her, and had been glad to do so.

"So she did not talk of such things," she went on. "There were no photographs in her room, no pictures, and since I have been here, since 1992, all she has ever said to me is, 'Hello, Mrs. Schneider,' 'Gutt Morning, Mrs. Schneider,' 'Is a fine day, Mrs. Schneider.' That was all, nothing else, except for that one time, and I think she was ashamed of it later, or perhaps afraid. She had no visitors, and never spoke of it again, until the young man came."

I leaned forward, and she imitated the movement, so that we were only inches apart. "He came some days after I made the call to Mr. Willeford, after I saw his notice in the newspaper. We heard shouting from downstairs and then the sound of running. A young man, a big man, with large, wild eyes, came past my door and burst into Miss Emily's room. Well, I was afraid for her, and for me, but I took my stick—" She pointed to a walking stick with a head carved into the shape of a bird and a metal tip at the end. "—and I followed him.

"When I came to the room, Miss Emily was sitting at her window, just as I am now, but her hands were like, *ach,* like this." Mrs. Schneider put her hands flat on her cheeks and opened her mouth wide in an expression of shock. "And the young man, he looked at her and he said only one word. He said to her: 'Momma?' Like that, like a question. But she only shook her head and said, 'No, no, no,' again and again. The boy, he reached out for her, but already she was moving away from him, back, back, until she was in the corner of her room, down on the floor.

"Then I heard from behind me the sound of the nurses. They brought with them the fat guard, the one Miss Emily hit on the night she ran off, and I was bundled out of the room while they took the boy away. I watched him as they took him, Mr. Parker, and his face . . . Oh, his face was like he had seen someone die, someone he loved. He cried and called out again, 'Momma, Momma,' but she did not reply.

"The police arrived, and they took the boy away. A nurse, she came to Miss Emily and she asked her if it was true, what the boy had said. And Miss Emily told her, 'No,' that she does not know what he is talking about, that she has no son, no child.

"But that night, I heard her crying for so long that I thought she would never stop. I went to her and held her. I told her that it was okay, that she was safe, but she said only one thing."

She paused and I saw that her hands were shaking. I reached out and stilled them and she moved her right hand, slipping it over mine and holding it tightly, her eyes closed. And I think, for a moment, I became her son, her child, one of those who never visited and who had left her to die in the cold north as surely as if they had hauled her into the forests of Piscataquis or Aroostook and abandoned her there. Her eyes reopened and she released my hand. Her own hands were still once again when she did so.

"Mrs. Schneider," I said gently. "What did she say?"

"She said: 'Now he will kill me.'"

"Who did she mean? Billy, the young man who came to her?" But I think I already knew the real answer.

Mrs. Schneider shook her head. "No, the other. The one she was always afraid would find her, and nobody could help her, or save her from him."

In her words, I heard the echo of other words, words heard in a dream on a dark night, words whispered to me by someone who no longer had a voice.

"It was the one who came later," concluded the old woman. "He learned of what had happened, and he came."

I waited. Something brushed softly against the window and I

watched a snowflake drift down the pane, melting as it went. "It was the night before she ran away. It was cold that night. I remember, I had to ask for an extra blanket, it was so cold. When I woke, it was dark, black, with no moon. And I heard a noise, a scraping from outside.

"I climbed from my bed and the floor was so chilly that I—ah!—I gasped. I went to the window and drew the curtain a little, but I could see nothing. Then the sound came again, and I looked straight down and . . ."

She was terrified. I could feel it coming off her in waves, a deep abiding fear that had shaken her to her core.

"There was a man, Mr. Parker, and he was climbing up the pipe, hand over hand. His head was down, and turned away from me, so I could not see him. And, anyway, it was so dark that he was only a shadow. But the shadow reached the window of Miss Emily's room and I could see him pushing at it with one hand, trying to force it up. I heard Miss Emily scream, and I screamed too, and ran into the hallway calling for a nurse. And all the time, I can hear Miss Emily screaming and screaming. But when they came, the man was gone and they could find no trace of him in the grounds."

"What kind of man was he, Mrs. Schneider? Tall? Short? Big? Small?"

"I told you: it was dark. I could not see clearly." She shook her head in distress as she tried to remember.

"Could it have been Billy?"

"No." She was definite about that. "It was the wrong shape. It was not as big as him." She lifted her hands in imitation of Billy's large shoulders. "When I told Dr. Ryley about the man, I think he believed that I was imagining things, that we were two old women frightening each other. But we were not. Mr. Parker, I could not see this man clearly, but I could *feel* him. He was no thief come to steal from old women. He wanted something else.

He wanted to hurt Miss Emily, to punish her for something she did long ago. The boy Billy, the boy who called her 'Momma,' he started something by coming here. Perhaps, Mr. Parker, I started it, by calling this man Willeford. Perhaps it is all my fault."

"No, Mrs. Schneider," I said. "Whatever happened to cause this started a long time ago."

She looked at me then with a kind of tenderness before she reached out and laid a hand softly on my knee to emphasize what she said next. "She was afraid, Mr. Parker," she whispered. "She was so afraid that she wanted to die."

I left her, alone with her memories and her guilt. Winter, the thief of daylight, caused lights to twinkle in the distance as Martel and I walked to our cars.

"Did you learn anything?" he asked.

I didn't reply immediately, but thought back on all that I had learned. In my mind, I saw newspaper reports of the disturbance at the home and heard the gossip of locals as they spoke of the man who had come looking for his lost mother. And their whispers traveled north on the wind, into the forest, into the wilderness.

"Could a man survive out there?" I asked Martel at last.

Martel's brow furrowed. "Depends on how long he's out there, what kind of clothing and supplies—"

"That's not what I mean," I interrupted. "Could he survive for a long time, for years, maybe?"

Martel thought for a moment. When he spoke, he didn't mock the question but answered it seriously, and he rose in my estimation for doing so. "I don't see why not. People have been surviving out there since the country was settled. There are still the remains of farmhouses to prove it. It wouldn't be an easy existence, and I guess he'd have to go back to civilization once in a while, but it could be done."

"And no one would disturb him out there?"

"Most of it hasn't been touched in the best part of fifty years. Go far enough into the forest and not even hunters or wardens are likely to bother you. You think someone went in there?"

"Yes, I do." I shook his hand and opened the door of the Mustang. "Trouble is, I think he's come out again."

CHAPTER TWENTY-ONE

I HAD THE SCENT of him then, had begun to feel the knowledge of him creep over me, but I needed more if I was to understand him, if I was to hunt him down before he found Billy Purdue, before he killed again. I was so close to making the connection: it hung just beyond my reach like the name of a half-remembered melody. I needed someone who could take my own half-formed suspicions and mold them into a coherent whole, and I knew of only one person whom I trusted that much.

I needed to talk to Rachel Wolfe.

I drove back to Dark Hollow, packed an overnight bag and placed the file on Caleb Kyle at the top. Louis and Angel returned in their separate cars as I was leaving. I explained what I was doing then started to drive to Bangor to catch the flight to Boston.

I was just outside Guilford when, three cars ahead of me, I spotted a yellow Ford truck, its exhaust belching dirty fumes onto the road. I accelerated past it, glancing idly at the driver as

I did so. In the cab sat the old man who had threatened me with his shotgun. I stayed ahead of him for a time, then pulled into a gas station at Dover-Foxcroft to let him pass. I stayed four or five cars behind him all the way to Orono, where he drove into the parking lot of a run-down mall and stopped outside a store called "Stuckey Trading." I checked my watch. If I delayed any longer, I'd miss my flight. I watched the old man as he removed a couple of black sacks from the bed of his truck and headed into the store, then I slapped the steering wheel once in frustration and accelerated toward Bangor and the airport.

I knew that Rachel Wolfe was holding tutorials at Harvard while the college funded research she was conducting into the link between abnormal brain structures and criminal behavior. She no longer engaged in private practice and, as far as I knew, was no longer assisting with criminal profiling.

Rachel had acted as an unofficial adviser on a number of cases for the NYPD, including the Traveling Man killings. That was how I met her, how we became lovers, and it was what eventually tore us apart. Rachel, whose policeman brother had died at the hands of a disturbed gunman, believed that by exploring the criminal mind she could prevent the same thing happening to others. But the Traveling Man's mind had been unlike any other, and the hunt for him had almost cost Rachel her life. She had made it known that she did not wish to see me, and until recently, I had respected that wish. I did not want to cause her any more pain, yet now I felt that I had nowhere else to turn.

But there was more to it than that, I knew. Twice in the last three months I had gone to Boston with the intention of finding her, or trying to reestablish what we had lost, but each time I had turned back without talking to her. Leaving my card on that last visit, with Louis waiting downstairs in the lobby, was as close as I had come to contacting her. Perhaps, in some way, Caleb Kyle would provide a bridge between us, a professional conduit that might also allow the personal to run alongside it. I think, also, that I was afraid, fearful of facing the winter on my own.

On the flight, I added what I had learned from Mrs. Schneider to my grandfather's file, writing carefully in block capitals. I scanned the photos as I went, noting the details of these young women now long dead, their lives more carefully documented by my grandfather after they were gone than by anyone while they were alive. In many ways, he knew them and cared about them as much as their own parents. In some cases, he cared about them more. He outlived his own wife by almost twenty years, and outlived his daughter by twelve. He had lived to mourn a lot of women, I thought.

I remembered something he said to me, after I became a policeman. I sat beside him in the Scarborough house, matching coffee mugs on the table, and watched as he examined my shield, the light reflecting on his spectacles as he twisted and turned it in his hand. Outside, the sun shone, but the house was cool and dark.

"It's a strange vocation," he said at last. "These rapists, and murderers, thieves and drug peddlers, we need them to exist. Without them, we'd have no purpose. They give our professional lives meaning.

"And that's the danger, Charlie. Because, somewhere down the line, you'll meet one who threatens to cross over, one you can't leave behind when you take off your badge at the end of the day. You have to fight it, or else your friends, your family, they all become tainted by his shadow. A man like that, he makes you his creature. Your life becomes an extension of his life, and if you don't find him, if you don't bring him to an end, he'll haunt you for the rest of your days. You understand me, Charlie?"

I understood, or thought I did. Even then, as he came to the end of his life, he was still tainted by his contact with Caleb Kyle. He hoped that it would never happen to me, but it did. It happened with the Traveling Man and, now, it was happening again. I had inherited the monkey on my grandfather's back, his ghost, his demon.

After I made my additions, I went through the file again, trying to feel my way into my grandfather's mind and, through his efforts, into the mind of Caleb Kyle. At the end of the file was a folded sheet of newspaper. It was a page from the *Maine Sunday Telegram* dating from 1977, twelve years after the man my grandfather knew as Caleb Kyle had blinked out of existence. On the page was a photograph taken in Greenville of a representative of the Scott Paper Company, which owned most of the forest north of Greenville, presenting the steamboat *Katahdin* to the Moosehead Marine Museum for restoration. In the background people grinned and waved, but farther back a figure had been caught, his face turned to the camera, a box containing what might have been supplies held in his arms. Even from a distance, he appeared tall and wiry, the arms holding the boxes long and thin, the legs slim but strong. The face was nothing more than a blur, ringed carefully in red felt-tip.

But my grandfather had enlarged it, then enlarged it again, and again, and again, each enlargement placed behind the preceding picture. And from the page a face grew, bigger and bigger until it took on the size and dimensions of a skull, the ink turning the eyes into dark pits, the face a construct of tiny black and white dots. The man in the picture had become a specter, his features indistinguishable, unrecognizable to anyone except my grandfather. For my grandfather had sat beside him in that bar, had smelled him, had listened as this man directed him to a tree where dead girls twisted in the breeze.

This, my grandfather believed, was Caleb Kyle.

At the airport, I called the psychology department at Harvard, gave them my ID number and asked them if Rachel Wolfe was due to teach that day. I was informed that Ms. Wolfe was due to give a tutorial to psychology students at 6 P.M. It was now 5:15 P.M. If I missed Rachel on campus, or if she canceled her tutorial, there were people who could get a residential address for me but it would take time, and time, I was rapidly coming to realize, was something I just didn't have. I climbed into a cab and my fingers beat an impatient tattoo on the window all the way to Harvard Square. A UC election banner hung outside the Grafton pub and a lot of the kids on the streets wore student election badges on their bags and coats as I headed across the campus to the junction of Quincy and Kirkland. I sat in the shadow of the Church of the New Jerusalem, across from the William James Hall, and waited.

At 5:55 P.M. a figure dressed in a black wool overcoat, ankle-length boots and black trousers, her red hair tied back with a black and white ribbon, walked down Quincy and entered the James Hall. Even at a distance, Rachel still looked beautiful and I caught one or two male students sneaking looks at her as she passed. I kept a short distance behind her as I followed her into the entrance hall and watched her take the stairs to seminar room 6 on the lower ground floor, just to make sure that she wasn't going to cancel and leave. I followed her as she entered the seminar room and closed the door, then I took a seat in a plastic chair with a view of the door and waited.

After an hour, the tutorial ended and students began to stream out, notebooks clutched to their chests or poking out of their bags. I moved aside to let the last student leave, then stepped into a small classroom dominated by a single big table, with chairs arranged around it and against the walls. At the head of the table, beneath a blackboard, sat Rachel Wolfe. She was dressed in a dark green sweater with a man's white shirt beneath it, the collar turned up around her neck. As always, she wore some light makeup, carefully applied, and a dark red lipstick.

She looked up expectantly, a half-smile on her face that froze as soon as she saw me. I closed the door gently behind me and took the first vacant seat at the table, which was just about as far away from her as I could get.

"Hi," I said.

She didn't speak for a moment before very deliberately putting her pens and notes away in a leather attaché case. Then she stood and started to shrug on her coat. "I asked that you not try to contact me," she said, as she struggled to find her left sleeve. I stood and walked over to her, and held the sleeve out so she could get her arm in. I felt kind of sleazy intruding on her space that way, but I also felt a momentary twinge of resentment: Rachel had not been the only one hurt in Louisiana in the hunt for the Traveling Man. The resentment quickly passed, to be replaced by guilt as I recalled the feel of her in my arms, her body racked by sobs after she was forced to kill a man in the Metairie cemetery. Once again, I saw her raising the gun, her finger tightening on the trigger, fire leaping from the muzzle as the gun bucked in her hands. Some deep, unquenchable instinct for survival had kicked in on that awful summer day, fueling her actions. I think that now, when she looked at me, she recalled what she had done, and she felt a fear of what I represented: that capacity for violence that had briefly exploded into existence within her and whose embers still glowed redly in her dark places.

"Don't worry," I said, lying a little. "I'm here for professional reasons, not personal ones."

"Then I certainly don't want to hear about it." She turned, her case beneath her arm. "Excuse me, I have work to do."

I put out a hand to touch her arm, and she glared at me. I withdrew it. "Rachel, please. I need your help."

"Please, let me leave. You're blocking my way."

I moved back and she shuffled past me, her head down. She had the door open when I spoke again. "Rachel, listen to me, just for a moment. If not for me, then for Walter Cole."

She stopped at the door, but didn't turn around. "What about Walter?"

"His daughter Ellen is missing. I'm not sure, but it may have something to do with a case I'm working on. It may also be connected somehow to Thani Pho, the student who was killed last week."

Rachel paused, then took a deep breath, closed the door and sat down in the seat I had previously occupied. Just to keep things equal, I sat down in her seat.

"You have two minutes," she said.

"I need you to read a file, and give me an opinion on it."

"I don't do that anymore."

"I hear you're working on a study about the connection between violent crime and brain disorders, something involving brain scans."

I knew a little more than that. Rachel was involved in research into dysfunctions in two areas of the brain, the amygdala and the frontal lobe. As I understood it from reading a copy of an article she had contributed to a psychology journal, the amygdala, a tiny area of tissue in the unconscious brain, generates feelings of alarm and emotion, allowing us to respond to the distress of others. The frontal lobe is where emotions are registered, where self-consciousness emerges and plans are constructed. It is also the part of the brain that controls our impulses.

In psychopaths, it was now believed, the frontal lobe failed to respond when confronted with an emotional situation, possibly due to a failure in the amygdala itself or in the processes used to send its signals to the cortex. Rachel, and others like her, were pressing for a huge brain-scan survey on convicted criminals, arguing that they could reveal a connection between brain damage and psychopathic criminal behavior.

She frowned. "You seem to know a lot. I'm not sure that I like the idea of you keeping tabs on me."

I felt that twinge of resentment again. I felt it so strongly that my mouth twitched involuntarily. "It's not like that, but I see your ego is still strong and healthy."

Rachel smiled slightly, a tiny, fleeting thing. "The rest of me isn't quite so robust. I'm going to be scarred for life. I'm in therapy twice weekly and I've had to give up my own practice. I still think of you, and you still frighten me. Sometimes."

"I'm sorry." Maybe it was my imagination, but there was something in that pause, in that *sometimes,* that implied she thought of me in other ways too.

"I know. Tell me about this file."

And I did, giving her a brief run through the history of the killings, adding some of what Mrs. Schneider had told me and some of what I suspected, or had guessed, myself. "Most of it is in here." I raised the battered manila folder. "I'd like you to take a look, see what you can come up with."

She reached out and I slid the file to her across the long table. She flicked quickly through the handwritten notes, the carbon copies, the photographs. One of them was a crime scene photo taken by the banks of the Little Wilson. "Oh my God," she whispered, and closed her eyes. When she opened them again, there was a new light in them, the spark of professional curiosity but also something else, something that had attracted me to her in the first place.

It was empathy.

"It could take a couple of days," she said.

"I don't have a couple of days. I need it tonight."

"Not possible. I'm sorry, but I couldn't even begin to do it in that time."

"Rachel, no one believes me. No one will accept that this man could ever have existed or, worse, could still be alive now. But he's out there. I can *feel* him, Rachel. I need to understand him, in however small a way. I need something, anything, to make him real, to bring him out of that file and to form a recognizable picture of him. Please. I've got this jumble of details in my head, and I need someone to help me make sense of it. There's no one else I can turn to and, anyway, you're the best criminal psychologist I know."

"I'm the *only* criminal psychologist you know," she said, and that smile came again.

"There's that as well."

She stood. "There's no way I'll have anything for you tonight, but meet me tomorrow at the Coop bookstore, at, say, eleven o'clock. I'll give you what I have then."

"Thank you," I said.

"You're welcome." And with that she was gone.

I stayed where I always stayed when I was in Boston, in the Nolan House over on G Street in south Boston. It was a quiet bed-and-breakfast, with antique furniture and a couple of okay restaurants close by. I checked in with Angel and Louis, but there was no movement in Dark Hollow.

"You see Rachel?" asked Angel.

"Yes, I saw her."

"She okay?"

"She didn't seem too pleased to see me."

"You bring back bad memories."

"Story of my life. Maybe someday, someone will see me and think happy thoughts."

"Never happen," he said. "Hang loose, and tell her we were asking after her."

"I will. Any move out at the Payne house?"

"The younger guy went into town to buy milk and groceries, that's about all. No sign of Billy Purdue, or Tony Celli, or Stritch, but Louis is still acting funny. Stritch is around here somewhere, that much we can be sure of. Sooner you're back here, the better."

I showered, put on a clean T-shirt and jeans, and found a

copy of the Gousha deluxe road atlas from 1995 among the guidebooks and magazines in the hallway of the Nolan House. The Gousha listed eight Medinas—Texas, Tennessee, Washington, Wisconsin, New York, North Dakota, Michigan and Ohio— and one Medinah, in Illinois. I ruled out all of the northern towns in the hope that my grandfather was right about Caleb's southern roots, which left Tennessee and Texas. I tried Tennessee first. No one in the Gibson County sheriff's office recalled a Caleb Kyle who might or might not have killed his mother on a farm sometime in the 1940s but, as a deputy told me helpfully, that didn't mean it didn't happen, it just meant that nobody around could *recall* it happening. I made a call to the state police, just on the off chance, but got the same reply: no Caleb Kyle.

It was approaching eight-thirty when I started calling Texas. Medina, it emerged, was in Bandera County, not Medina County, so my first call to the Medina County Sheriff didn't get me very far. But I hit lucky on the second call, real lucky, and I couldn't help wondering how my grandfather would have felt had he got this far and learned the truth about Caleb Kyle.

CHAPTER TWENTY-TWO

HE SHERIFF'S NAME was Dan Tannen, a deputy told me. I waited to be transferred to the sheriff's own office. After a couple of clicks on the line, a female voice said: "Hello?"

"Sheriff Tannen?" I asked. It was a good guess.

"That's me," she said. "You don't sound surprised."

"Should I be?"

"I've been mistaken for the secretary a couple of times. Pisses me to hell, I tell you. The Dan is short for Danielle, for what it's worth. I hear you're asking about Caleb Kyle?"

"That's right," I said. "I'm a private investigator, working out of Portland, Maine. I'm—"

She interrupted me to ask: "Where did you hear that name?"

"Caleb?"

"Uh-huh. Well, more particularly Caleb *Kyle*. Where'd you hear *that* name?"

That was a good question. Where did I begin? With Mrs. Schneider? With Emily Watts? With my grandfather? With Ruth Dickinson and Laurel Trulock and the three other girls who ended up dangling from a tree by the banks of the Little Wilson?

"Mister Parker, I asked you a question." I got the feeling that

Sheriff Tannen was likely to be holding on to her post for some time.

"I'm sorry," I said. "It's complicated. I heard it for the first time when I was a boy, from my grandfather, and now I've heard it twice in the last week." And then I told her what I knew. She listened without making any comment, and when I had finished telling my story there was a long pause before she spoke.

"It was before my time," she said, at last. "Well, some of it was. The boy lived out in the Hill Country, maybe four miles southeast of here; him and his momma. He was born, best as I can recall without looking up a file, in 1928 or '29, but he was born Caleb Brewster. His pappa was a Lyall Brewster who went off to fight Hitler and ended up dying in North Africa and the two of them, Caleb and his mother, were left to fend for themselves. Plus, Lyall Brewster never got around to marrying Bonnie Kyle, Bonnie Kyle being his mother's name. You see, that was why I was interested in hearing you say Caleb *Kyle*. There aren't many people who'd know him by that name. Fact is, I've never heard him called by that name. He was always Caleb Brewster here, right up until the time he killed his mother.

"She was the devil's own bitch, according to those that knew her. Kept herself to herself, and the boy beside her. But the boy was smart, Mr. Parker: at school, he raced ahead in math, reading, just about anything he put his mind to. Then his mother decided that she didn't like the fact that he was attracting attention to himself and took him out of school. Claimed she was teaching him herself."

"You think there was abuse?"

"I think there were stories. I recall someone telling me that they once found him wandering naked on the road between here and Kerrville, covered in dirt and hog shit. Police brought him home to his momma in a blanket. Boy couldn't have been more than fourteen or fifteen. They heard him yelpin' as soon as the door closed behind 'em. She sure took the stick to him, I reckon, but as for anything else . . ."

She paused again, and I heard her gulping liquid at the other end of the line. "Water," she said, "case you're wondering."

"I wasn't."

"Well, whatever. Anyway, I don't know about sexual abuse. It came up at the trial, but it came up at the Menendez brothers' trial as well, and look where it got them. Like I said, Mr. Parker, Caleb was smart. Even at sixteen, seventeen, he was smarter than most of the people in this town."

"You think he made it up?"

She didn't answer for a time. "I don't know. But if there was abuse, then he was smart enough to try to use it as mitigation. You have to remember, Mr. Parker, that people didn't talk about it so much in those days. The fact of someone bringing it up was unusual. In the end, I guess we'll never know for certain what happened in that house.

"But there was more to Caleb Brewster than intelligence. People around here recall that he was mean, or worse than mean. He tortured animals, Mr. Parker, and hung their remains from trees: squirrels, rabbits, even cats and dogs. There was no evidence to tie him to it, you understand, but folks knew it was him. Maybe he got tired of killing animals, and decided to move up a step. There was other stuff too."

"What do you mean?"

"Well, let's take this in the order it happened. Two or three days after that incident on the road, Caleb Brewster killed his mother and fed her remains to the hogs. Sheriff Garrett and another deputy came up to check on the boy and found him sitting on the porch, drinking sour milk from a jug. There was blood in the kitchen, on the walls and on the floor. Boy still had the knife beside him. Bonnie Kyle's clothing was in the hog pen, along with some bones, which was pretty much all that the hogs had left of her, apart from a small silver ring. One of the hogs had passed it out in its stool. I think they got it in the Frontier Museum over in Banderas now, alongside two-headed lambs and Indian arrowheads."

"What happened to Caleb?"

"He was tried as an adult, then sent down."

"For life?"

"Twenty years. He got out in sixty-three or sixty-four, I think."

"Was he rehabilitated?"

"*Rehabilitated?* Fuck, no. I reckon he was off the scale before he ever killed her, and he never got back on it again. But someone saw fit to release him, taking into account the extenuating circumstances. He'd served his time and they couldn't keep him locked up forever, no matter how good an idea that might have been. And, like I said, he was smart. He kept his nose clean in prison. They thought he was getting better. Myself, I think he was waiting."

"He came back to the Hill Country?" I asked, although I already sensed the answer to the question.

Again, there came that pause. This time, it remained unbroken for what seemed like a long time.

"The house was still standing," began Tannen. "I remember him coming back into town on the Greyhound—I was maybe ten or eleven—and Caleb walking out toward the old house, and folks stepping onto the other side of the street and then watching him as he passed. I don't know how long he spent there. Couldn't have been more than a couple of nights, but . . ."

"But?"

She sighed. "A girl died. Lillian Boyce. They reckon she was the prettiest girl in the county, and they were probably right. They found her down by the Hondo Creek, near Tarpley. She'd been cut up pretty bad. That wasn't the worst of it, though."

I waited, and it seemed to me that I knew what was coming, even before she said it.

"She was hung from a tree," she said. "Like someone wanted her to be found. Like she was a warning to us all."

The line seemed to hum, and the cell phone was hot in my hand, as Sheriff Tannen concluded her story. "When we found her, Caleb Brewster had gone again. There's still a warrant outstanding, far as I know, but I didn't think anyone would ever get to serve it.

"At least, I didn't until now."

After I hung up, I sat on my bed for a time. There was a deck of playing cards on a bookshelf in the room and I found myself shuffling it, the edges of the cards blurring before my eyes. I saw the queen of hearts and drew her from the deck. Hanky-poo, that was what Saul Mann used to call "Find the Queen." He would stand at his felt-covered trestle-table, seemingly talking to himself as he arranged the cards before him, flipping one card over with the rim of another. "Five gets you ten, ten gets you twenty." He didn't even seem to notice the punters slowly gathering, attracted by the sure movement of his hands and the promise of easy money, but he was always watching. He watched and he waited, and slowly, surely, they came to him. The old man was like a hunter who knows that, at some point, the deer must surely cross his path.

And I thought too of Caleb Kyle, staring at the remains of the girls he had torn apart and hung from trees. A memory came to me, a recollection of a legend told of the Emperor Nero. It was said that after Nero killed his own mother, Agrippina the Younger, he ordered that her body be opened, so that he could see the place from which he had come. What motivated this action is unclear: morbid obsession, perhaps, or even the incestuous feelings that the ancient chroniclers ascribed to him. It may even have been the case that he hoped to understand something of himself, of his own nature, by gazing upon the site of his own origin.

He must have loved her once, I thought, before it all turned to fury and rage and hate, before he found it in himself to take her life and rend her to pieces.

And, for a brief moment, I felt a kind of pity for Caleb, a sorrow for the boy he once was and a hatred for the man that he became.

I saw shadows falling from trees, and a figure moving north, ever north, like the needle on a compass. Of course he would have headed north. North was as far away from Texas as he could get after avenging himself on the community that had seen fit to jail him for what he had done to his mother.

But there was more to it than that, it seemed. When my grandfather was a boy, the priest would read the gospels at the north side of the church because north had always been perceived as an area that had not yet seen God's light. It was the same reason why they buried the unbaptized, the suicides and the murderers on northern ground, outside the boundaries of the church walls.

Because north was unknown territory.

North lay the darklands.

The next morning, the bookstore was crowded with students and tourists. I ordered coffee and read a copy of *Rolling Stone* that someone had left on a chair until Rachel arrived, late as usual. She still wore her black coat, this time with blue denims and a sky-blue V-neck sweater. Beneath it, her blue-and-white striped Oxford shirt was buttoned to the neck. Her hair hung loose on her shoulders.

"Are you ever early?" I asked, as I ordered her a coffee and a muffin.

"I was up until 5 A.M. working on your damned file," she replied. "If I was charging you for my time, you couldn't afford me."

"Sorry," I said. "I can barely afford the coffee and muffin."

"You're breaking my heart," she said, but it seemed that her attitude had softened a little since the day before, although it could have been wishful thinking on my part.

"You ready for this?" she asked.

I nodded, but before she went on I told her what I had learned from the sheriff in Medina and how Caleb had taken his mother's name to escape his past.

She nodded to herself. "It fits," she said. "It all fits."

The coffee arrived and she added sugar, then unwrapped the muffin, tore it into bite-sized pieces and began to talk.

"Most of this is guesswork and supposition. Any decent law enforcement officer would laugh me out of his building, but since you're neither decent nor a law enforcement officer, you'll take what you can get. Plus, everything you've given me is also based on guesswork and supposition, with a little superstition and paranoia thrown in." She shook her head in bemusement, then grew serious as she opened her wire-bound notebook. Line upon line of closely written text lay before her, dotted here and there with yellow Post-its. "Most of what I'm going to tell you, I think you know already. All I can do is to clarify it for you, maybe put it into some kind of context.

"If this man does exist—at least, if the same man, Caleb Kyle, is responsible for all of these killings—then you're dealing with a textbook psychopathic sadist. Actually, you're dealing with worse than that, because I've never encountered anything like this in the literature, or in clinical work, certainly not all in one package. By the way, this file doesn't record any killing after 1965. Even allowing for the newspaper photograph, have you taken into account the possibility that he might be dead, or maybe imprisoned again for other crimes? Either could explain the sudden cessation of killing."

"He could be dead," I admitted, "in which case this is all a waste of time and we're dealing with something else entirely. But let's assume that he wasn't imprisoned. If the sheriff was right, and Caleb was as smart as she believed, then he wasn't going back to prison again. Plus my grandfather checked at the time— it's in the file—and I know that he consulted on a random basis in the intervening years, although he would have been looking for Caleb Kyle, not Caleb Brewster."

She shrugged. "Then you have two further possibilities: either he continued to kill, but his victims are all listed as missing persons if they've been missed at all or . . ."

"Or?"

Rachel tapped the top of her pen on her notebook, beside a word encircled in a red ring. "Or else he's been dormant. The possibility that some serial killers, if that's even what he is, enter periods of dormancy is one that's being considered by the FBI's Investigative Support Unit, the folks in the Criminal Profiling and Consultation Program. You know this, because I've told you about it before. It's a theory, but it might explain why some killings just cease without anyone ever being apprehended. For some reason, the killer reaches a point where the need to find a victim isn't so strong, and the killings stop."

"If he's been dormant until now, then something just woke him up," I said. I thought of the timber company surveyor, heading into the wilderness to pave the way for the forest's destruction, and what he might have encountered in that forest. I recalled too Mrs. Schneider's story, followed up by a piece in the newspaper, and Willeford's old-style investigation, where you knocked on doors and pinned up notices and put the word around until it filtered down to the person you were trying to reach; and the newspaper story about Billy Purdue's arrest at St.

Martha's. If you put out honey, you shouldn't be surprised when the wasps come.

"It's tenuous, but those are the possibilities you have to consider," Rachel continued. "Okay, let's look at the original killings. First, although it may only be a minor point, the location where the bodies were found was important. This Caleb Kyle determined how soon they would be found, where they would be found and by whom. It was his way of controlling and participating in the search. The original killings may have been disorganized—we'll never know for sure, since we don't know where they were killed—but the display of the bodies was very organized. He wanted to be part of some element of the discovery. My guess is that he was watching your grandfather right up to the moment when he found the women.

"As for the killings themselves, then if what the Schneider woman told you is true, which depends in turn on the truth of what Emily Watts told her, Kyle was already killing during their relationship. The extent of decay on each of the five bodies differed: Judy Giffen and Ruth Dickinson were killed first, with a gap of almost one month between them. But Laurel Trulock, Louise Moore and Sarah Raines were killed in rapid succession: the ME's report indicated that Trulock and Moore could have been killed in the same twenty-four-hour period, with Raines killed no more than twenty-four hours later again.

"My guess is that each of these girls—or certainly the last three—were physically similar to Emily Watts. They were slim, delicate girls: more passive than Emily, maybe, who was strong when the need arose, but still of a type. You encountered revenge rapes when you were a policeman, didn't you?"

I nodded.

"A man argues with his wife, or his girlfriend, storms out of the house and takes out his anger on a complete stranger," continued Rachel. "In his mind, all women bear collective responsibility for the perceived faults of one woman, and therefore any woman can be disciplined and punished for the real or imagined slight or the overstepping of whatever boundaries the rapist has established in his mind as acceptable behavior for a woman.

"Well, Caleb Kyle is like those men, but this time it went much further. The ME found no evidence of actual sexual assault on the three later victims, but—and here we're into classic morbid fear of female sexuality territory—there was some damage to the sexual organs, presumably inflicted by the same instrument that was used to make stab wounds to the belly and to destroy the womb of each victim. In fact, what's interesting is that, in the cases of Giffen and Dickinson, he stabbed them *after* they had been dead for almost one month, probably after he killed the other three girls, or shortly before."

"He went back to them after he thought she had lost the baby."

"*Exactly*. He was punishing them because Emily Watts's body had betrayed him by losing his child: many women being punished for the faults of one. My guess would be that he had punished other women before, perhaps for different reasons."

She fed herself a piece of muffin and sipped her coffee. "Now, when we go back to the ME's report, we find evidence that each of the girls was tortured before death. There were fingernails missing, toes and fingers broken, teeth removed, cigarette burns, bruising inflicted by what may have been a coat hanger. That might be significant, but not for now. In the case of the last three victims, the torture inflicted is significantly more extreme. These girls suffered a lot before they died, Bird." Rachel looked at me solemnly, and I could see the pain in her eyes, pain for them and the memory of her own pain.

"According to the victim profiles collated by your grandfather, these young women were gentle, from good homes, maybe a little asocial. Most of them were shy, sexually inexperienced. Judy Giffen appeared to have had some sexual experience. My guess is they probably pleaded with him before they died, thinking they could save themselves. But that was what he wanted: he wanted them to cry and to scream. There may be a connection there between aggression and fulfillment. He experienced a sexual excitement from their pleas, but he also hated them for pleading, and so they died."

Her eyes were bright now, her excitement at trying to worm her way into this man's consciousness obvious in the movement of her hands, the speed with which she spoke, her intellectual pleasure in making startling, unexpected connections, yet balanced by her abhorrence of the acts she was discussing. "God," said Rachel, "I can almost see his PET scan: temporal lobe abnormalities associated with sexual deviancy; distortion in the frontal lobe leading to violence; low activity between the limbic system and the frontal lobes, indicating a virtual absence of guilt or conscience." She shook her head, as if she was marveling at the behavior of a particularly nasty bug. "He's not asocial, though. These girls may have been shy, but they weren't stupid. He would have to be skilled enough to gain their trust, so the intelligence fits.

"As for Kyle's social background, if what he told Emily Watts is true, he was abused physically and possibly sexually in childhood by a mother figure who told him that she loved him during or after the abuse, and then punished him afterward. He had little nurture or protection and was probably taught self-sufficiency the hard way. When he was old enough, he turned on his abuser and killed her, before moving on to others. With Emily Watts, something different happened. She was herself a victim of abuse, then she became pregnant. My guess is that he would have killed her anyway, as soon as she had the child. From what she said, he wanted the child."

She took a sip of coffee and I used it as an opportunity to interrupt.

"What about Rita Ferris and Cheryl Lansing? Could he have been responsible for their deaths?"

"It's possible," said Rachel. She regarded me quietly, waiting for me to find a connection.

"I'm missing something," I said at last. "That's why you look like the cat that got the cream."

"You're forgetting the mutilation of the mouths. The damage inflicted on the wombs of those girls in 1965 was meant to convey a message. The mutilations were a signifier. We've seen damage to victims used in that way before, Bird." The smile went away, and I nodded: the Traveling Man.

"So, once again, three decades later, we have mutilations, in this case directed to the mouths of victims and in each case meant to signify something different. Rita Ferris's mouth was sewn shut. What does that mean?"

"That she should have kept her mouth shut?"

"Probably," said Rachel. "It's not subtle, but whoever killed her wasn't interested in subtlety."

I considered what Rachel had said for a moment before I figured out what it might mean. "She called the cops on Billy Purdue and they took him away." That could have meant that he had been watching the house the night Billy was arrested, making him the old man that Billy claimed to have seen the night Rita and Donald were killed, maybe even the same old man who had attacked Rita at the hotel.

"In Cheryl Lansing's case," continued Rachel, "her jaw was broken and her tongue torn out. I'm pushing the envelope a little here, but my guess is that she was being punished for *not* speaking."

"Because she was party to the concealment of the child's birth."

"That would seem to be a plausible explanation. In the end, regardless of what made Caleb Kyle this way, and regardless of signifiers and whatever grievances he may feel, he's a killing machine, completely without remorse."

"But he felt something for the loss of his child."

Rachel almost leapt from her chair. "*Yes!*" She beamed at me the way a teacher might beam at a particularly bright pupil. "The problem, or the key, is the sixth girl, the one who was never found. For a whole lot of reasons, most of which would probably result in me being ostracized by my peers if I stated them in print, I think your grandfather was right when he suspected that she was also a victim, but he was wrong in the *type* of victim."

"I don't understand."

"Your grandfather assumed that she had also been killed but had not been displayed for some reason."

"And you don't." But I could see where she was going, and my stomach tightened at the possibility. It had been at the back of my mind for some time and, maybe, at the back of my grandfather's. I think he hoped that she was dead, because the other option was worse.

"No, I don't believe she was killed, and it comes back to the torture inflicted on those girls. This wasn't simply a means of gaining satisfaction and fulfillment for this man: it was a test. He was testing their strength, knowing at the same time, but perhaps not admitting it to himself, that they would fail his test because they simply weren't strong enough.

"But look at the profile of Judith Mundy. She's strong, well built, a dominant personality. She didn't cry easily, could handle herself in a fight. She would pass that kind of test, to the extent that he probably didn't have to hurt her very much to realize that she was different."

Rachel leaned forward and the expression on her face changed to one of deep abiding sorrow. "She wasn't taken because she was weak, Bird. She was taken because she was strong."

I closed my eyes. I knew now what had happened to Judith Mundy, why she had not been found, and Rachel knew that I had understood.

"She was taken as breeding stock, Bird," she said quietly. "He took her to breed on."

Rachel offered to drive me to Logan, but I declined. She had done enough for me, more even than I felt I had a right to ask. As I walked alongside her across Harvard Square, I felt a love for her made all the more intense by the fact that I believed she was slipping further and further away from me.

"You think this man Caleb may be connected to the disappearance of Ellen Cole?" she asked. Her arm brushed against mine, and for the first time since I had come to Boston, she did not pull away from the contact.

"I don't know for sure," I replied. "Maybe the police are right. Maybe her hormones got to her and she did run away, in which case I'm not sure what I'm doing. But an old man found her and drew her to Dark Hollow and, like I keep telling people, I don't believe in coincidences.

"I have a feeling about this man, Rachel. He's come back, and I think he's returned for Billy Purdue and to avenge himself on everyone who helped to hide him. I think he killed Rita Ferris. It may have been out of jealousy, or to cut Billy off so that he'd have no other ties, or because she was going to leave him and take the boy with her. I don't think that Donald was meant to die. Caleb would have wanted his grandson alive but, somehow, Donald became involved in the struggle. My guess is that he was fatally injured when Caleb tried to push him away."

Something caught in my throat at the memory of Donald, and I didn't speak again until we reached the square. I put out my hand to Rachel. I didn't kiss her because I didn't feel that I had the right. She took my hand and held it tightly.

"Bird, this man feels he has some dispensation to avenge himself on anyone who crosses him because he believes that he's been wronged. I've just labeled him as psychopathic." In her eyes, there was concern, and more.

"In other words, what's my excuse?" I smiled, but it went no deeper than my mouth.

"They're gone, Bird. Susan and Jennifer are dead, and what happened to them and to you was a terrible, terrible thing. But every time you make someone pay for what was done to you, you hurt yourself and you risk becoming the thing you hate. Do you understand?"

"It's not about me, Rachel," I replied softly. "At least, not entirely. Someone has to stop these people. Someone has to take responsibility." There was that echo again.

they are all your responsibility.

Her hand moved gently over mine, her fingers on my fingers, her thumb rubbing lightly on my palm, then she touched my face with her free hand. "Why did you come here? Most of what I told you, you could have figured out for yourself."

"I'm not that smart."

"Don't bullshit a bullshitter."

"So it's true what they say about psychologists."

"Only the New Age ones. You're avoiding the question."

"I know. You're right: some of it I had guessed, or half-guessed, but I needed to hear it back from someone else, otherwise I was afraid that I was going crazy. But I'm also here because I still care about you, because when you walked away you took something from me. I thought that this might be a way of getting closer to you. I wanted to see you again. Maybe, deep down, that's all it was." I looked away from her.

Her grip tightened on my hand. "I saw what you did, back in Louisiana. You didn't go there to find the Traveling Man. You went there to kill him, and anyone who stood in your way got hurt, and got hurt badly. Your capacity for inflicting violence scared me. You scared me."

"I didn't know what else to do, not then."

"And now?"

I was about to answer when her finger touched the scar on my cheek, the mark left by Billy Purdue's blade. "How did this happen?" she asked.

"A man stuck a knife blade in me."

"And what did you do?"

I paused before answering. "I walked away."

"Who was he?"

"Billy Purdue."

Her eyes widened, and it was as if something that had been curled inside her to protect itself gradually began to unfurl. I could see it in her, could feel it in her touch.

"He never had a chance, Rachel. The odds were stacked against him from the start."

"If I ask you a question, will you answer me honestly?" she said.

"I've always tried to be honest with you," I replied.

She nodded. "I know, but this is important. I need to be sure of this."

"Ask."

"Do you need the violence?"

I thought about the question. In the past, I had been motivated by personal revenge. I had hurt people, had killed people, because of what had been done to Susan and to Jennifer, and to me. Now that desire for revenge had dwindled, easing a little every day, and the spaces it left as it receded were filled with the potential for reparation. I bore some responsibility for what happened to Susan and Jennifer. I didn't think that I would ever come to terms with that knowledge, but I could try to make up for it in some small way, to acknowledge my failings in the past by using them to make the present better.

"I did, for a time," I admitted.

"And now?"

"I don't need it, but I will use it if I have to. I won't stand by and watch innocent people being hurt."

Rachel leaned over and kissed me gently on the cheek. Her eyes were soft when she pulled away.

"So you're the avenging angel," she said.

"Something like that," I replied.

"Good-bye, then, avenging angel," Rachel whispered softly.

She turned and walked away, back to the library and her work. She didn't look back, but her head was down and I could feel the weight of her thoughts.

The plane rose from Logan, heading upward and north through the cold air, heavy cloud surrounding it like the breath of God. I thought of Sheriff Tannen, who had promised to hunt up the most recent pictures available of Caleb Kyle. They would be thirty years old, but at least they would be something. I took the blurred newspaper photo of Caleb from my grandfather's folder and looked at it again and again. He was like a skeleton slowly being fleshed out, as if the process of decay were being gradually, irrevocably reversed. A figure that had been little more than a name, a shape glimpsed in the shadows, was assuming an objective reality.

I know you, I thought. I *know* you.

CHAPTER TWENTY-THREE

I ARRIVED IN BANGOR early that afternoon, picked up my car in the airport parking lot and started back for Dark Hollow. I felt like I was being pulled in ten different directions, yet somehow each one seemed to lead me back to the same place, to the same conclusion, by different routes: Caleb Kyle had come back. He had killed a girl in Texas shortly after his release from prison, probably as an act of revenge against a whole community. Then he had assumed his mother's name and headed north, far north, eventually losing himself in the wilderness.

If Emily Watts had told the truth to Mrs. Schneider—and there was no reason to doubt her—then she had given birth to a child and hidden it because she believed its father to be a killer of young women, and sensed that this man wanted the child for his own purposes. The leap required was to accept that this child might be Billy Purdue, and that his father could be Caleb Kyle.

Meanwhile, Ellen Cole and her boyfriend were still missing, as was Willeford. Tony Celli had gone to ground, but was undoubtedly still searching for some trace of Billy. He had no choice: if he did not find Billy, he would be unable to replace the money he had lost and he would be killed as an example to others. I had a suspicion that it was already too late for Tony Clean, that it had been too late from the very moment that he had purchased the securities, maybe even from the time when the thought of using someone else's money to secure his future first crossed his mind. Tony would do whatever he had to do to track Billy down, but everything he did, all of the violence he inflicted and all of the attention it drew to himself and his masters, made it less and less likely that he would be allowed to live. He was like a man who, trapped in the darkness of a tunnel, focuses his mind on the only illumination he sees before him, unaware that what he believes to be the light of salvation is, in reality, the fire that will consume him.

There were other reasons, too, to be fearful. Somewhere in the darkness, Stritch waited. I imagined that he still wanted the money but, more than that, he wanted revenge for the death of his partner. I thought of the dead man in the Portland complex, violated in his last moments by Stritch's foulness, and I thought too of the fear that I had felt, the certainty that I could have allowed death to embrace me in those shadows if I had chosen to do so.

There remained also the old man in the forest. There was still the chance that he knew something more than he had told me, that his remark about the two young people was based on more than gossip he had overheard in the town. For that reason, there was one stop to be made before I returned to Dark Hollow.

At Orono, the store was still open. On the sign above the door, the words "Stuckey Trading" were illuminated from below, the name written in script. Inside, it smelled musty and felt oppressively warm, the AC making a noise as if glass were grinding in its works while it pumped stale air through its vents. Some guys in biker jackets were examining secondhand shotguns while a woman in a dress that was new when Woodstock convened flicked through a box of eight-tracks. Display cases held old watches and gold chains, while hunting bows stood upright on a rack beside the counter.

I wasn't sure what I was looking for, so I browsed from shelf to shelf, from old furniture to almost-new car-seat covers, until something caught my eye. In one corner, beside a rack of foul-weather clothing—old slickers mainly, and some faded yellow oilskins—stood two rows of shoes and boots. Most of them were ragged and worn, but the Zamberlans stood out immediately. They were men's boots, relatively new and considerably more expensive than the pairs surrounding them, and some care had obviously been lavished on them recently. Someone, probably the store owner, had cleaned and waxed them before putting them out for sale. I lifted one and sniffed the interior. It smelled of Lysol, and something else: earth, and rotting meat. I lifted the second boot and caught the same faint odor from it. Ricky had been wearing Zamberlans on the day they came to visit me, I recalled, and it wasn't often that boots so fine turned up in an out-of-the-way secondhand goods store. I brought the pair of boots to the counter.

The man behind the register was small with thick, dark artificial hair that seemed to have come from the head of a department store mannequin. Beneath the wig, at the back of his neck, wisps of his own mousy-colored strands peered out like mad relatives consigned to the attic. A pair of round eyeglasses hung from a string around his neck and lost themselves in the hairs of his chest. His bright red shirt was half unbuttoned and I could see scarring at the left side of his chest. His hands were thin and strong looking, with the little finger and ring finger of his left hand missing from just above the first joint. The nails on the fingers that remained were neatly clipped.

He caught me looking at his mutilated left hand and raised it in front of his face, the twin stumps of the lost fingers making his hand look as if he was trying to form a gun with it, the way little kids do in the school yard.

"Lost them in a sawmill," he explained.

"Careless," I replied.

He shrugged. "Blade damn near took the rest of my fingers as well. You ever work in a sawmill?"

"No. I always thought my fingers looked okay on my hands. I like them that way."

He looked at the stumps thoughtfully. "It's strange, but I can still feel them, y'know, like they're still there. Maybe you don't know how that feels."

"I think I do," I said. "You Stuckey?"

"Yessir. This is my place."

I put the boots down on the counter.

"They're good boots," he said, picking up one with his un-mutilated hand. "Won't take less than sixty bucks for 'em. Just waxed 'em, buffed 'em and put 'em out for sale myself not two hours ago."

"Smell them."

Stuckey narrowed his eyes and put his head to one side. "Say what?"

"I said, 'Smell them.'"

He looked at me oddly for a few moments, then took one boot and sniffed the inside tentatively, his nostrils twitching like a rabbit's before the snare.

"I don't smell nothin'," he said.

"Lysol. You smell Lysol, don't you?"

"Well, sure. I always disinfect 'em before I sell 'em. Don't no-body want to wear boots that stink."

I leaned forward and raised the second boot in front of him. "You see," I said softly, "that's my question. What did they smell of *before* you cleaned them?"

He wasn't a man who was easily intimidated. He thrust his body forward in turn, six knuckles on the counter, and arched an eyebrow at me. "Are you some kind of nut?"

In a mirror behind the counter, I saw that the bikers had

turned around to watch the show. I kept my voice low. "These boots, they had earth on them when you bought them, didn't they? And they smelled of decay?"

He took a step back. "Who are you?"

"Just a guy."

"You was just a guy, you'da bought the durned boots and been gone by now."

"Who sold you the boots?"

He was becoming belligerent now. "That's none of your god-damned business, mister. Now get out of my store."

I didn't move. "Listen, friend, you can talk to me, or you can talk to the cops, but you will talk, understand? I don't want to make trouble for you, but if I have to, I will."

Stuckey stared at me, and he knew that I meant what I said. A voice interrupted before he could respond. "Hey, Stuck," said one of the bikers. "You okay back there?"

He raised his battered left hand to indicate that there wasn't a problem, then returned his attention to me. There was no trace of bitterness when he spoke. Stuckey was a pragmatist—in his line of business, you had to be—and he knew when to back down.

"It was an old fella from up north," he sighed. "He comes in here maybe once a month, brings stuff that he's found. Most of it's junk, but I give him a few bucks for it and he goes away again. Sometimes, he brings in something good."

"He bring these in recently?"

"Yesterday. I gave him thirty bucks for 'em. Brought in a backpack too, Lowe Alpine. I sold it straight off. That was about it. He didn't have nothin' else to offer."

"This old guy from up Dark Hollow way?"

"Yeah, that's right, Dark Hollow."

"You got a name?"

His eyes narrowed again. "Just tell me, mister, what are you: some kind of private cop?"

"Like I said, I'm just a guy."

"You got a lot of questions for someone who's just a guy." I could sense Stuckey digging his heels in again.

"I'm naturally curious," I said, but I showed him my ID anyway. "The name?"

"Barley. John Barley."

"That his real name?"

"The hell do I know?"

"He show you any identification?"

Stuckey almost laughed. "You seen him, you'd know he wasn't the kind of fella carries no ID."

I nodded once, took out my wallet and counted six ten-dollar bills onto the counter. "I'll need a receipt," I said. Stuckey filled one out quickly in sloped capitals, stamped it, then paused before handing it to me.

"Like I told you, I don't want no trouble," he said.

"If you've told me the truth, there won't be any."

He folded the receipt once and put it in a plastic bag with the boots. "I hope you won't take this personal, mister, but I reckon you make friends 'bout as easy as a scorpion."

I took the bag and put my wallet back in my coat. "Why?" I asked. "You sell friendship here too?"

"No, mister, I sure don't," he said, and there was a finality in his tone. "But I don't reckon you'd be buying any even if I did."

CHAPTER TWENTY-FOUR

IT WAS ALREADY DARK when I began the journey back to Dark Hollow. Snow was drifting across the road to Beaver Cove and beyond, where the narrow, winding, tree-lined road led to the Hollow. The snow seemed to glow in the headlights, small golden fragments of light tumbling down, as if heaven itself was disintegrating and falling to earth. I tried to call Angel and Louis on the cell phone, but it was a useless effort. As it turned out, they were already at the motel when I got back. Louis answered the door dressed in black pants with a razor-sharp crease and a cream-colored shirt. I could never figure out how Louis kept his clothes so neat. I had shirts that had more creases than Louis's while they were still in the box.

"Angel's in the shower," he said, as I stepped past him into their room. On the television screen, a reporter mouthed silently before the White House lawn.

"What's seldom is wonderful."

"Amen to that. If it was summer, he'd be attracting flies."

It wasn't true, of course. Angel may have looked like someone who was barely on nodding terms with soap and hot water, but he was, all things considered, remarkably clean. He just looked more crumpled than most people. In fact, he looked more crumpled than just about anyone I knew.

"Any movement over at the Payne place?"

"Nothing. The old man came out, went back in again. The boy came out, went back in again. After the fourth or fifth time, the novelty started to wear off. No sign of Billy Purdue, though, or anyone else."

"You think they knew you were out there?"

"Maybe. Didn't act like it, which could go either way. You got anything?"

I showed him the boots and told him of my conversation with Stuckey. Angel came out of the shower at that moment, wrapped in four towels.

"Shit, Angel," said Louis. "The fuck are you, Mahatma Gandhi? What you use all the towels for?"

"It's cold," he whined. "And I got marks on my ass from that car seat."

"You gonna get marks on your ass from the toe of my shoe, you don't get me some towels. You just dry your scrawny white ass and haul it down to the desk, ask the lady for more towels. And you better make damn sure they soft, Angel. I ain't rubbin' my back with no sandpaper."

While Angel dried himself and dressed, muttering softly as he did so, I told them in detail about my encounters with Rachel, Sheriff Tannen and Erica Schneider, and what I had learned of Billy Purdue's visit to St. Martha's.

"Seems like we accumulatin' a whole lot of information, but we don't know what it means," remarked Louis, when I was done.

"We know what some of it means," I said.

"You think this guy Caleb really exists?" he asked.

"He was real enough to kill his mother, and maybe another local girl the best part of two decades later. Plus, those girls who died in '65 weren't killed by a mentally handicapped man. The display of the bodies was a lot of things—a gesture of contempt, a means to shock—but it was also an attempt at an act of madness. I think it was designed to make people think that only a madman could have done it, and the planting of an item of clothing at Fletcher's house gave them the madman they were looking for."

"So where did he go?"

I sat down heavily on one of the beds. "I don't know," I said, "but I think he went north, into the wilderness."

"And why didn't he kill again?" added Angel.

"I don't know that either. Maybe he did, and we just never found them." I knew that hikers had been murdered on the Appalachian Trail, and I'd heard that others had gone missing and never been found. I wondered if, somehow, they might have left the trail, hoping for a shortcut, and encountered something much worse than they had ever imagined.

"Or it could be he was killing before he ever arrived in Maine, but nobody ever traced the deaths back to him," I continued. "Rachel thought that he might have entered a period of dormancy, but recent events may have conspired to change that."

Angel took one of the Zamberlans and held it in his hands. "Well, we know what this means, assuming these once belonged to Ellen Cole's boyfriend." He looked at me, and there was a sadness in his eyes. I didn't want to answer him, or to acknowledge the possibility that if Ricky was dead, then Ellen could be dead too.

"Any sign of Stritch?" I asked.

Louis bristled. "I can almost smell him," he said. "The woman at the desk is still pretty cut up about her cat, no pun intended. Cops are blaming it on kids."

"What now?" said Angel.

"I go see John Barley," I replied, the obvious falsity of the name grating even as I said it, but Louis shook his head.

"That's a bad idea, Bird," he said. "It's dark, and he knows the woods better than you do. You could lose him, and any way of finding out how he came by these boots. Plus, there's his damn dog: it'll warn the old man, and then he'll start shooting, and could be you'll have to shoot back. He's no good to us dead."

He was right, of course, but it didn't make me feel any better. "At dawn, then," I said, but reluctantly. Unspoken between us was the possibility that I had already encountered Caleb Kyle, and had turned away from him because he had threatened me with a gun.

"Dawn," Louis agreed.

I left them and went back to my own room, where I dialed Walter and Lee Cole's house in Queens. Lee picked up on the third ring, and in her voice was that mixture of hope and fear that I had heard in the voices of hundreds of parents, friends and relatives, all waiting for word of a missing person.

"Lee, it's me."

She said nothing for a moment but I could hear her footsteps, as if she was moving the phone out of earshot of someone. I guessed it was Lauren. "Have you found her?"

"No. We're in Dark Hollow, and we're looking, but there's nothing yet." I didn't tell her about Ricky's boots. If I was wrong about what might have happened to him, or mistaken about the ownership of the boots, it would only be worrying her unnecessarily. If I was right, then we would know the rest soon enough.

"Have you seen Walter?"

I told her I hadn't. I figured he was probably in Greenville by now, but I didn't want to see him. He would only complicate matters, and I was finding it hard enough to keep my emotions in check as it was.

"He was so angry when he found out what I'd done." Lee started to cry, her voice breaking as she spoke. "He said that people get hurt when you get involved. They get killed. Please, Bird, please don't let anything happen to her. Please."

"I won't, Lee. I'll be in touch. Good-bye."

I hung up and ran my hands over my face and through my hair, letting them come to rest eventually at the knots in my shoulders. Walter was right. People had been hurt in the past when I became involved in situations, but they got hurt mainly because those people also chose to involve themselves. Sometimes you can push folks one way or the other, but they take the most important steps on their own initiative.

Walter had principles, but he had never been put in a position where those principles might have to be compromised to safeguard those he loved, or to avenge them when they were taken from him. And now he was close to Dark Hollow, and a situation that was already difficult and complicated was likely to get worse. I sat with my face in my hands for a time, then undressed and showered, my head down and my shoulders exposed to allow the water to work like fingers on my tired, tense muscles.

The phone rang as I was drying myself. It was Angel. They were waiting for me so that we could head off and eat together. I wasn't hungry, and my concerns for Ellen were muddling my thought processes, but I agreed to join them. When we arrived at the diner, there was a sign on the door announcing that it had closed early. There was some kind of charity event in the Roadside Bar that night to raise funds for the high school band and everyone and anyone was going to be in attendance. Angel and Louis exchanged a look of profound unhappiness.

"We got to help the band if we want to eat?" asked Louis. "What kind of peckerwood town is this? Who we got to pay off if we want to buy a beer? The PTA?" He examined the sign a little more closely. "Hey, a country-and-western band: 'Larry Fulcher and the Gamblers.' Maybe this town ain't such a dump after all."

"Lord, no," said Angel, "not more shit-kicker music. Why can't you listen to soul music like anyone else of your particular ethnic persuasion? You know, Curtis Mayfield, maybe a little Wilson Pickett. They're your people, man, not the Louvin Brothers and

Kathy Mattea. Besides, not so long ago people used that country shit as background music when they were hanging your people."

"Angel," said Louis patiently, "nobody ever hung no brother to a Johnny Cash record."

There was nothing for it but to head down to the Roadside. We went back to the motel and I got my car keys. When I came out of my room, Louis had added a black cowboy hat with a band of silver suns to his ensemble. Angel put his hands on his head and swore loudly.

"You got the rest of the Village People in there too?" I asked. I couldn't help but smile. "You know, you and Charley Pride are plowing a pretty lonely furrow with that black country-and-western routine. The brothers see you dressed like that and they may have words to say."

"Brothers helped to build this great country, and that 'country-and-western routine,' as you put it, was the soundtrack to generations of workers. Wasn't all Negro spirituals and Paul Robeson, y'know. Plus, I like this hat." He gave the brim a little flick with his fingers.

"I was kind of hoping you two could maintain a low profile while we were here, unless it's absolutely necessary that you do otherwise," I said, as we got into the Mustang.

Louis sighed loudly. "Bird, I'm the only brother from here to Toronto. Less I contract vitiligo between this motel and the high school band scam, ain't no way that I can be low profile. So shut up and drive."

"Yeah, Bird, drive," said Angel from the backseat, "'else Cleavon Little here will get his posse on your ass. The Cowpokes with Attitude, maybe, or Prairie Enemy . . .'"

"Angel," came the voice from the passenger seat. "*Shut* up."

The Roadside was a big old place done in dark wood. It was long, windowed and single storied at the front with a gabled entrance in the center that rose up above the rest like the steeple of a church. There were plenty of cars parked in the lot, with more around the sides stacked up almost to the woods. The Roadside was at the western edge of town; beyond it was dark forest.

We paid our five-dollar cover charge at the door—"Five dollars!" hissed Angel. "This a mob place?"—and made our way into the bar itself. It was a long cavernous room, almost as dark inside as it was outside. Weak lights hung on the walls and the bar was lit sufficiently so that drinkers could see the labels on the bottles, but not the sell-by date. The Roadside was a lot bigger than it looked from the outside and the light died just beyond the limits of the bar and the center of the dance floor. It stretched maybe three hundred feet from the door to the stage at the far end, with the bar on a raised platform at the center. Tables radiated from it into the dimness at the walls, which were lined in turn by booths. At the edges, the Roadside was so dark that only pale moon faces were visible, and then only when their owners stepped into a pool of light. Otherwise, they were only vague shapes moving against the walls, like wraiths.

"It's a Stevie Wonder bar," said Angel. "The menu's probably in braille."

"It's pretty dark," I agreed. "Drop a quarter here, it'll be worth ten cents by the time you find it."

"Yeah, like Reaganomics in miniature," said Angel.

"Don't say nothing bad about Reagan," warned Louis. "I have good memories of Ron."

"Which is probably more than Ron has," smirked Angel.

Louis led the way to a booth over by the right-hand wall, close to one of the emergency doors that stood halfway down each of the Roadside's walls. There was probably at least one other door at the back, behind the stage. At present, that stage was occupied by what seemed to be Larry Fulcher and the Gamblers. Louis was already tapping his feet and nodding his head in time to the music.

In fact, Larry Fulcher and his band were pretty good. There were six of them, Fulcher leading on the mandolin, guitar and banjo. They played "Bonaparte's Retreat" and a couple of Bob Wills songs, "Get With It" and "Texas Playboy Rag." They moved on to the Carter Family with "Wabash Cannonball" and "Worried Man Blues," "You're Learning" by the Louvin Brothers and then did a neat version of "One Piece at a Time" by Johnny Cash. It was an eclectic selection, but they played well and with obvious enthusiasm.

We ordered burgers and fries. They came in red plastic baskets with a liner on the bottom to hold in the grease. I felt my arteries hardening as soon as I smelled the food. Angel and Louis drank some Pete's Wicked. I had bottled water.

The band took a break and people flooded toward the bar and the bathrooms. I sipped some water and scanned the crowd. There was no sign of Rand Jennings, or his wife, which was probably a good thing.

"We should be out at Meade Payne's place now," said Louis. "Billy Purdue arrives, he ain't gonna do it in a parade float in daylight."

"If you were out there now, you'd be freezing and you wouldn't be able to see a thing," I said. "We do what we can." I felt like the whole situation was slipping away from me. Maybe it had always been slipping away, right from the time I took five hundred dollars from Billy Purdue without ever questioning where he might have found it. I still felt certain that Billy would make his way to Dark Hollow, sooner or later. Without Meade Payne's cooperation there was always the chance that he could slip past us, but my guess was that Billy would hole up with Meade for a time, maybe even try to make for Canada with his help. Billy's arrival would disturb the routine out at the Payne place, and I had faith in the ability of Angel and Louis to spot any such disturbance.

But Billy was still a comparatively minor concern next to

Ellen Cole although, in some way that I hadn't yet figured out, there had to be a connection between them. An old man had guided them up here, perhaps the same old man who had shadowed Rita Ferris in the days before her death, maybe even the same old man who had once been known as Caleb Brewster by the people of a small Texas town. Dark Hollow was just too small a place for those kinds of occurrences to take place randomly.

As if on cue, a woman pushed her way through the throng at the bar and ordered a drink. It was Lorna Jennings, her bright red sweater like a beacon in the crowd. Beside her stood two other women, a slim brunette in a green shirt and an older woman with black hair, wearing a white cotton top decorated with pink roses. It seemed to be a girls' night out. Lorna didn't see me, or didn't want to see me.

There was a burst of applause and Larry Fulcher and his band came back onstage. They burst into "Blue Moon of Kentucky" and the dance floor instantly became a mass of movement, couples swinging each other across the floor, smiles on their faces, the women spinning on their toes, the men twisting them expertly. There was laughter in the air. Groups of friends and neighbors stood talking, beers in hand, enjoying a night of community and kinship. Above the bar, a banner thanked everyone for supporting the Dark Hollow High School Band. In the shadows, younger couples kissed discreetly while their parents practiced foreplay on the dance floor. The music seemed to grow in volume. The crowd began to move faster. The sound of glass breaking came from the bar, accompanied by a burst of embarrassed laughter. Lorna stood beside a pillar, the two women on either side silent now as they listened to the music. In the shadows at the walls, figures moved, some barely more than indistinct shapes: couples talking, young people joshing, a community relaxing. Here and there, I heard talk of the discovery of Gary Chute's body but it wasn't personal and it didn't interfere with the night's festivities. I watched a man and woman seated at the bar across from Lorna as they kissed hard, their tongues visible where their mouths met, the woman's hand snaking down her partner's side, down, down . . .

Down to where a child stood before them, lit by a circle of light that seemed to come from nowhere but within himself. While couples moved close by, and groups of men walked through the crowds carrying trays of beer, the child still held a space to itself and no one came close or broke the shell of light that surrounded him. It lit his blond hair, brought up the color of his purple rompers, made the nails of his tiny hands shine as he raised his left hand and pointed into the shadows.

"Donnie?" I heard myself whisper.

And from the darkness at the far side of the bar, a white shape appeared. Stritch's mouth was open in a smile, the thick, soft lips splitting his face from side to side, and his bald head gleamed in the dim light. He turned in the direction of Lorna Jennings, looked back at me, and drew his right index finger across his neck as he moved through the crowd toward her.

"Stritch," I hissed, springing from my seat. Louis scanned the crowd, already rising, his hand reaching for his SIG.

"I don't see him. You sure?"

"He's on the other side of the bar. He's after Lorna."

Louis went right, his hand inside his black jacket, his fingers on his gun. I moved left, but the crowd was thick and unyielding. I pushed my way through, people stepping back and yelling as their beer spilled. ("Buddy, hey buddy, where's the fire?") I tried to keep Lorna's red sweater in view, but I lost it as people passed into my line of vision. To my right, I could just make out Louis moving through the couples at the edge of the dance floor, his progress attracting curious glances. To my left, Angel was making his way around the bar in a wide arc.

As I neared the counter, the men and women were packed tightly, calling for drinks, waving money, laughing, caressing. I pushed through, spilling a tray of drinks and sending a thin, acned young man tumbling to his knees. Hands reached for me and angry voices were raised, but I ignored them. A barman, a fat, dark-skinned man with a thick beard, raised a hand as I climbed onto the bar, my feet slipping on the wet floor.

"Hey, get down from there," he called, then stopped as he saw the Smith & Wesson in my hand. He backed off, making for the phone at the end of the bar.

Now I could see Lorna clearly. Her head turned as I rose above her, other heads turning too, their eyes wide. I spun to see Louis fighting his way through the pack at the bar, scanning the crowd, trying to catch a glimpse of that white, domed head.

I saw him first. He was maybe ten or twelve people back from Lorna, still moving in her direction. Once or twice people looked his way, but they were distracted by the sight of me on the bar, the gun hanging from my right hand. Stritch smiled at me again, and something flashed in his hand: a short, curved blade, its point wickedly sharp. I made a jump from the bar to the central section where the cash registers and bottles stood, then a second jump, which put me almost beside Lorna, glasses flying from my feet and shattering on the floor. People moved away from me and I heard screaming. I stepped from the bar and pushed my way to her.

"Move back," I said. "You're in danger here."

She was almost smiling, her brow furrowed, until she saw the gun in my hand. "What? What do you mean?"

I looked past her to where I had last seen Stritch, but he was receding from sight, losing himself once again in the crowd. Then a head appeared as Louis stood on a table, trying to keep low enough to avoid making himself a target for a shot. He turned to me and gestured to the center exit. On the stage, the band kept playing, but I could see them exchanging worried looks.

To my left, burly men in T-shirts were moving toward us. I grabbed Lorna by the shoulders. "Take your friends and stay close to the bar. I mean it. I'll explain later." She nodded once, the smile no longer on her face. I think I knew why. I think she had caught a glimpse of Stritch and had seen in his eyes what he had intended to do to her.

Using my shoulders, I started to make my way to the center exit. A small flight of steps led up to it and I could see a waitress at the door, a pretty girl with long, dark hair, frowning uncertainly as she watched what was happening at the bar. Then a figure appeared beside her, and the white, domed head broke into a smile. A pale hand lost itself in her hair and the blade flashed beside her head. The waitress made an attempt to tear herself away and fell to her knees as she did so. I tried to raise my gun but people were jostling me, heads and arms obscuring my vision. Someone—a young man with a football player's build—tried to grab my right arm, but I struck him in the face with my elbow and he moved back. Just as it seemed that we were powerless to prevent the girl from getting her throat cut, a dark object spun through the air and shattered as it struck Stritch's head. To my left, Angel stood on a chair, his hand still raised from where he had released the bottle. I saw Stritch stumble backward, blood already pouring from the multiple cuts in his face and head, as the waitress tore herself away and tumbled down the steps, leaving a garland of hair in her attacker's hand. The door behind Stritch swung open and, in a blur of movement, he disappeared into the night.

Louis and I were only seconds behind him. We reached the steps at almost the same instant. Behind us, blue uniforms appeared at the main door and I could hear shouting and screams.

Outside, beer kegs stood stacked to one side of the door, a green trash can at the other. Ahead of us was the edge of the forest, gilded by the big lamps that lit the side of the bar. Something white moved into the darkness beyond, and we moved after it.

CHAPTER TWENTY-FIVE

THE SILENCE OF THE WOODS was startling, as if the snow had muted nature, stifling all life. There was no wind, no night-bird sounds, only the crunch of our shoes and the soft snap of unseen twigs buried beneath our feet.

I closed my eyes hard, willing them to adjust to the dark light of the forest, my hand supporting me against a tree trunk. Around us, mostly hidden by the snowdrifts, tree roots snaked over the thin soil. Louis had already fallen once, and the front of his coat was speckled with white.

Behind us, noises and shouting came from the direction of the bar, but no one followed as yet. After all, it was still unclear what had happened: a man had waved a gun; another man had thrown a bottle and injured a third; some people thought they had seen a knife, a fact that the waitress would surely confirm. It would take them a while to find flashlights and for the police to organize a pursuit. Occasionally, a weak beam of light flashed yellow behind us, but soon the thickening trees blocked its path. Only a sickly moonlight that fell wearily through the branches over our heads provided any illumination.

Louis was close by me, close enough so that we remained in each other's sight. I raised a hand and we stopped. There was no sound ahead of us, which meant that Stritch was either picking his steps carefully or had stopped and was waiting for us in the shadows. I thought again of that doorway in the Portland complex, that certainty I had that he was there and that, if I went after him, he would kill me. This time, I resolved, I would not back down.

Then, from my left, I heard something. It was soft, like the sound of evergreen leaves brushing against clothing, followed by the soft compression of snow beneath a footfall, but I had heard it. From Louis's expression, I could tell that he had noticed it too. A second footfall came, then a third, moving not toward us, but away from us.

"Could we have gotten ahead of him?" I whispered.

"Doubt it. Could be someone from the bar."

"No flashlight, and it's one person, not a group."

But there was something else about it. The noise was careless, almost deliberately so. It was as if someone wanted us to know that he or she was out there.

I heard myself swallow loudly. Beside me, Louis's breath briefly threw a thin mist across his features. He looked at me and shrugged.

"Keep listening, but we best get moving."

He stepped out from behind the trunk of a fir and the sound of a shot shattered the silence of the forest, sending bark and sap shooting into the air beside his face. He dived for the ground and rolled hard to his right until he was shielded by a natural depression, from which the blunt edge of a rock nosed its way out of the snow.

"Night vision," I heard him say. "Fuck these professionals."

"You're supposed to be a professional," I reminded him. "That's why you're here."

"Keep forgetting," he replied, "what with being surrounded by amateurs and all."

I wondered how long Stritch had been watching us, waiting

to make his move. Long enough to see me with Lorna, and to understand that some kind of bond existed between us. "Why did he try to take her in such a public place?" I wondered aloud.

Louis risked a look around the edge of the stone, but no shots came. "He wanted to hurt the woman, and for you to know it was him. More than that, he wanted to draw us out."

"And we followed him?"

"Wouldn't want to disappoint him," replied Louis. "I tell you, I don't think the man gives a fuck about that money anymore."

I was getting tired of hugging the big fir. "I'm going to make a move, see how far I can get. You want to take another peep out of your hole and cover me?"

"You the man. Get going."

I took a deep breath and, staying low, began to zigzag forward, tripping on two concealed roots but managing to keep my feet as Stritch's gun barked twice, kicking up snow and dirt by my right heel. It was followed by a burst of fire from Louis's SIG that shattered branches and bounced off rocks but also seemed to force Stritch to keep his head down.

"You see him?" I yelled, as I squatted down, my back to a spruce and my breath pluming before me in huge clouds. I was starting to warm up at last, although, even in the darkness, my fingers and hands appeared to be a raw, vivid red. Before Louis could reply, something off-white whirled in a copse of bushes ahead and I opened fire. The figure retreated into the darkness. "Never mind," I added. "He's about thirty feet northeast of you, heading farther in."

Louis was already moving. I could see his dark shape against the snow. I sighted, aimed and fired four shots into the area where I had last seen Stritch. There was no return fire and Louis was soon level with me but about ten feet away.

And then, again to my left but this time farther ahead, there came the sound of movement in the woods. Someone was moving quickly and surefootedly toward Stritch.

"Bird?" said Louis. I raised a hand quickly and indicated the source of the noise. He went silent, and we waited. For maybe thirty seconds nothing happened. There was no noise, not even a footstep or the falling of snow from the trees. There was nothing but the sound of my heart beating and the blood pumping in my ears.

Then two shots came in close succession followed by what sounded like two bodies impacting. Louis and I moved at the same instant, our feet freezing, our legs held high so that they would not drag in the snow. We ran hard until we burst through the copse, our hands raised to ward off the branches, and there we found Stritch.

He stood in a small, stony clearing doused in silver moonlight, his back to us, his toes barely touching the ground, his hands gripping the leafless trunk of a fallen pine that lay at an upward angle in the snow, supported by hidden rocks beneath the drifts. From the back of his tan raincoat, something thick and red had erupted that glistened darkly in the light. As we approached him, Stritch shuddered and seemed to grip the tree harder, as if to force himself off the sharp tip on which he had been impaled. A fine spray of blood shot from his mouth and he groaned as his grip weakened. He turned his head at the sound of our footsteps and his eyes were large with shock, his thick, moist lips spread wide against gritted teeth as he tried to hold himself upright. Blood coursed from the wounds in his head, dark rivers of it flowing over his pale features.

As we were almost upon him, his mouth opened and he cried out as his body shuddered hard for the last time, his grip failing, his head falling forward and coming to rest against the gray bark of the tree.

And as he died, I scanned the glade, conscious that Louis was doing the same, both of us acutely aware that beyond our line of sight someone was watching us, and that there was a kind of joy in what he saw, and in what he had done.

CHAPTER TWENTY-SIX

I SAT IN RAND JENNINGS'S office in the Dark Hollow police department and watched the snow falling on the window-pane against the early morning darkness. Jennings sat across from me, his hands steepled together, the fingertips resting in the small roll of fat that hung beneath his chin. Behind me stood Ressler, while outside the office uniformed patrolmen, mostly part-timers called in for the occasion, ran back and forth down the hallway, bumping into one another like ants whose chemical signalers had been interfered with.

"Tell me who he was," said Jennings.

"I already told you," I said.

"Tell me again."

"He called himself Stritch. He was a freelance operator: murder, torture, assassination, whatever."

"What's he doing attacking waitresses in Dark Hollow, Maine?"

"I don't know." That was a lie, but if I told him it was an attempt to gain revenge for the death of his partner then Jennings would have wanted to know who killed the partner and what part I had played in the whole affair. If I told him that then the chances were that I would be locked up in a cell.

"Ask him about the nigra," said Ressler. Instinctively, the muscles on my shoulders and neck tightened and I heard Ressler snicker behind me. "You got a problem with that word, Mr. Big Shot? Don't like to hear a man being called a buck nigra, especially if he's your friend?"

I took a deep breath and brought my rising temper under control. "I don't know what you're talking about, but I'd like to hear you talk like that in Harlem."

Ressler grew redder as Jennings unsteepled his hands and jabbed an index finger at me. "Again, I'm calling you a liar, Parker. I got witnesses saw a colored follow you out that door; same colored checked into the motel with a skinny white guy in tow the day you arrived; same colored who paid cash in advance on the room, the room he shared with the same skinny white guy who hit this man Stritch with a bottle; and the same colored . . ." His voice rose to a shout. "The same fucking colored who has now left his motel and disappeared into the fucking ether with his buddy. Do you hear me?"

I knew where Angel and Louis had gone. They were at the India Hill Motel on Route 6 outside Greenville. Angel had checked in and Louis was lying low. They would eat out of the McDonald's nearby and wait for me to call.

"Like I said, I don't know what you're talking about. I was alone when I found Stritch. Maybe someone else followed me out, thought that I might need some help catching this guy but, if he did, then I didn't see him."

"You're full of shit, Parker. We got three, maybe four sets of prints running in the direction of that clearing. Now I'm going to ask you again: why is this guy attacking waitresses in my town?"

"I don't know," I lied, again. If the conversation had been a horse, someone would have shot it by now.

"Don't give me that. You spotted the guy. You were moving

after him before he even went for the girl." He paused. "Assuming it was Carlene Simmons he was after to begin with." His face took on a thoughtful expression, and his eyes never left my face. I didn't like him. I never had, and what had passed between us gave neither of us any particular reason to mend our fences, but he wasn't dumb. He stood and went to the window, where he stared out into the blackness for a time. "Sergeant," he said at last, "will you excuse us?"

Behind me, I heard Ressler shift his weight and the soft, deliberate tread of his footsteps as he walked to the door and closed it quietly behind him. Jennings turned to me then and cracked the knuckles of his right hand by crushing them in his left.

"I took a swing at you now, not one man outside this room would try to stop me, even if he wanted to. Not one man would interfere." His voice was calm, but his eyes burned.

"You take a swing at me, Rand, you better hope someone tries to interfere. You might be glad of the help."

He sat on the edge of his desk, facing me, his right hand still cupped in his left and resting on his thighs. "I hear you been seen around town with my wife." He wasn't looking at me now. Instead, all his attention seemed to be focused on his hands, his eyes examining every scar and wrinkle, every vein and pore. They were old man's hands, I thought, older than they should have been. There was a tiredness about Jennings, a weariness. Being with someone who doesn't love you just so no one else can have her takes its toll on a man. It takes its toll on the woman too.

I didn't respond to his statement, but I could tell what he was thinking. Things come around sometimes. Call it fate, destiny, God's will. Call it bad luck if you're trying to keep a dying marriage frozen so that it doesn't decay any further. I think Rand's marriage had been like that: something that he willed to be the way it was, frozen in some half-alive world waiting for the miracle that would bring it back to life. And then I had arrived like the April thaw and he had felt the whole construct start to melt around his ears. I had nothing to offer his wife, at least nothing that I was prepared to give. What she saw in me, I wasn't sure. Maybe it was less to do with me than with what I represented: lost opportunities, paths untaken, second chances.

"You hear what I said?" he asked.

"I heard."

"Is it true?" He looked at me then, and he was scared. He wouldn't have called it that, wouldn't even have admitted it to himself, but it was fear. Maybe, somewhere deep inside, he did still love his wife, although in such a strange way, in a manner that was so disengaged from ordinary life, that it had ceased to have any meaning for either of them.

"If you're asking, then you already know."

"You trying to take her away from me again?"

I almost felt pity for him. "I'm not here to take anyone away from anyone else. If she leaves you, she does so for her own reasons, not because a man from her past bundles her off against her will. You got a problem with your wife, you deal with it. I'm not your counselor."

He shifted himself off the desk and his hands went to his sides, forming fists as they did so. "Don't talk smart to me, boy. I'll . . ."

I rose and moved forward, so that we were face-to-face. Even if he tried to hit me now, there would be no space for him to give the swing momentum. I spoke softly and distinctly. "You won't do anything. You get in my way here and I'll take you down. As for Lorna, it's probably best that we don't even talk about her, because, like as not, it'll get ugly and one of us will get hurt. Years ago, that was me taking your kicks on a piss-covered floor while your buddy looked on. But I've killed men since then, and I'll kill you if you cross my path. You got any more questions, chief, or you want to charge me, you know where to find me."

I left him, collected my gun from the desk, and prepared to

drive back to the motel. I felt raw and filthy, my feet still cold and damp in my shoes. I thought of Stritch, writhing and struggling against the gray wood, raised up on his toes in a vain, futile effort to survive. And I thought of the strength it had taken to force him onto the tip of that dead tree. Stritch had been a squat, powerful man with a low center of gravity. People like that are hard to move. The collar of his raincoat had been torn where his killer had gripped him, using his own body weight against him, building up the momentum necessary to impale him on the tree. We were looking for someone strong and fast, someone who perceived Stritch as a threat to himself.

Or to someone else.

A cold wind rippled the main street of Dark Hollow and sprinkled the car with a fine dusting of snow as the motel drew into view. I walked to my room, put my key in the lock and turned it, but the door was already unlocked. I stepped to the right, unholstered my gun and gently eased the door fully open.

Lorna Jennings sat on my bed, her shoes off and her knees pulled up to her chin, the main illumination in the room coming from the lamp by the bedside. Her hands were clasped around her shins with the fingers intertwined. The television was on, tuned to a talk show, but the volume was down to near zero.

She looked at me with something that was almost love, and nearly hate. The world that she had created for herself there—a cocoon of indifference surrounding buried feelings and the dying heart of a poor marriage—was falling apart around her. She shook her head, her eyes still fixed on me, and seemed on the verge of tears. Then she turned away toward the window that would soon be shedding bleak winter light into the room.

"Who was he?" she said.

"His name was Stritch."

Near her bare feet, her thumb and index finger pushed her wedding ring almost to the end of her finger and spun it there, back and forth, before it eventually slipped off, to be held instead between her fingertips. I didn't think it was a good sign.

"He was going to kill me, wasn't he?" Her voice was matter-of-fact, but something trembled beneath it.

"Yes."

"Why? I'd never seen him before. What had I ever done to him?" She rested her left cheek on her knee, waiting for my response. There were tears running down her face.

"He wanted to kill you because he thought you meant something to me. He was looking for revenge, and he saw his chance to take it."

"And do I mean something to you?" Her voice was almost a whisper now.

"I loved you once," I said simply.

"And now?"

"I still care enough about you not to let anyone hurt you."

She shook her head, lifted it from her knees and put the heel of her right hand to her face. She was crying openly now.

"Did you kill him?"

"No. Someone else got to him first."

"But you would have killed him, wouldn't you?"

"Yes."

Her mouth was curled down in pain and misery, tears falling from her face and gently sprinkling the sheets. I took a tissue from the box on the dresser and handed it to her, then sat beside her on the edge of the bed.

"Jesus, why did you have to come here?" she said. Her body was racked by sobs. They came from so deep inside her that they interrupted the flow of her words, like little caesuras of hurt. "Sometimes, whole weeks went by when I didn't think about you. When I heard you got married, I burned inside, but I thought that it might help, that it might cauterize the wound. And it did, Charlie, it really did. But now . . ."

I reached out to her and touched her shoulder, but she pulled away. "No," she said. "No, don't." But I didn't listen. I moved fully onto the bed, kneeling beside her now, and drew her to me. She struggled, and slapped me open-handed on my body, my face, my arms. And then her face was against my chest, and the struggling eased. She wrapped her arms around me, her cheek hard against me, and a sound came through her gritted teeth that was almost a howl. I moved my hands across her back, my finger-tips brushing the strap of her bra beneath her sweater. It rose up slightly at the end, exposing a moon-sliver of skin above her jeans and the lace decoration of her underwear beneath the blue denim.

Her head moved slightly beneath my chin, her cheek rubbing against the skin on my neck and progressing upward, never los-ing contact, until it was against my own cheek. I felt a surge of lust. My hands were shaking, as much a delayed reaction from the pursuit of Stritch as her closeness to me. It would have been so easy to go with the moment, to re-create, however briefly, a moment of my youth.

I kissed her softly on the temple, then drew away.

"I'm sorry," I said. I stood and moved to the window. Behind me, I heard her move to the bathroom and the door closing, the hiss of the faucets. For a brief instant I had been a young man again, consumed with desire for something I had no right to have. But that young man was gone, and the one who had taken his place no longer had the same intensity of feeling for Lorna Jennings. Outside, the snow fell like years, blanketing the past with the unblemished whiteness of possibilities untold.

I heard the bathroom door reopen. When I turned around, Lorna was standing naked before me.

I looked at her for a moment before I spoke. "I think you left something in the bathroom," I said. I made no move toward her.

"Don't you want to be with me?" she asked.

"I can't, Lorna. If I did, it would be for the wrong reasons and, frankly, I'm not sure I could deal with the consequences."

"No, it's not that," she said. A tear trickled down her cheek. "I've grown old. I'm not like I was when you knew me first."

It was true: she was not as I remembered her. There were dimples on her upper thighs and buttocks, and small folds of fat at her belly. Her breasts were less firm and there was soft flesh beginning to hang on her upper arm. The faint trace of a varicose vein wormed its way across the upper part of her left leg. On her face, there were fine wrinkles around the mouth and a triad of lines snaked away from the corner of each eye.

And yet, while the years had transformed her, were changing her even now, they had not made her any less beautiful. Instead, as she grew older, her femininity had been enhanced. The fragile beauty of her youth had withstood the harsh winters of the north and the difficulties of her marriage by adapting, not fading, and that strength had found expression in her face, in her body, lending her looks a dignity and maturity that had been buried before and had only occasionally displayed itself in her features. As I looked into her eyes and her gaze met mine, I knew that the woman I had loved, for whom I still felt something that was almost love, remained untouched within.

"You're still beautiful," I said. She watched me carefully, trying to be certain that I was not trying to blind her with kind lies. When she saw that I was telling the truth, her eyes closed softly as if she had just been touched deep inside but could not tell whether she felt pain or pleasure.

She covered her face with her hands and shook her head. "This is kind of embarrassing."

"Kind of," I agreed.

She nodded and went back into the bathroom. When she emerged, fully-clothed. she walked straight to the door. I followed her, reaching it as she touched the handle. She turned before opening it, and rested her hand against my cheek. "I don't know," she said, her forehead resting gently against my shoulder for a moment. "I just don't know."

Then she slipped out of the room and into the morning light.

I slept for a time, then showered and dressed. I looked at my watch as I strapped it to my wrist, and a pain lanced through my stomach unlike anything I had felt in months. In all that had happened—the hunt for traces of Caleb Kyle, the encounter with Rachel, the death of Stritch—I had lost track of the days.

It was December eleventh. The anniversary was one day away.

It was past three when I ate dry toast and coffee at the diner, and thought of Susan, and the rage I felt at the world for allowing her and my daughter to be taken from me. And I wondered how, with all of this pain and grief coiled inside me, I could ever begin again.

But I wanted Rachel, I knew, and the depth of my need for her surprised me. I had felt it as I sat opposite her in Harvard Square, listening to her voice and watching the movements of her hands. How many times had we been together? Twice? Yet, with her, I had felt a peace that had been denied me for so long.

I wondered too at what I might bring upon her, and upon myself, if the relationship was allowed to develop. I was a man moon-haunted by the ghost of his wife. I had mourned for her, and I still mourned for her. I felt guilt at my feelings for Rachel, at what we had done together. Was it a betrayal of Susan's memory to want to start over? So many feelings, so many emotions, so many acts of revenge, of attempted recompense, had been concentrated into the last twelve months. I felt drained by them, and tormented by the images that crept unbidden into my dreams and my waking moments. I had seen Donald Purdue in the bar. I had seen him as clearly as I had seen Lorna naked before me, as clearly as I had seen Stritch impaled on a tree.

I wanted to start again, but I didn't know how. All I knew was that I was moving closer and closer to the edge, and that I had to find some way to anchor myself before I fell.

I left the diner then drove down to Greenville. The Mercury was parked at the back of the motel beneath a copse of trees, making it almost invisible from the road. I didn't think Rand would come after Angel and Louis, not as long as he had me, but it didn't hurt to take precautions. As I parked, Angel opened the door to room six, moved aside to let me in, then closed the door behind him.

"Well, look at you," he said, a wide grin on his face.

Louis lay on one of the room's two double beds, reading the latest issue of *Time*. "He right, Bird," he said. "You the man. Pretty soon, you and Michael Douglas both be in one o' them sex clinics and we be reading about you in *People* magazine."

"We saw her arriving as we left," said Angel. "She was in kind of a state. I didn't see there was anything else I could do but let her in." He sat alongside Louis. "Now I just know you're going to tell us that you and the chief sat down and talked this thing out and he said, 'Sure, you can sleep with my wife, because she really loves you, not me.' Because, if you didn't, then, pretty soon, you're going to be even less welcome there than you are already. And, frankly, you're currently about as welcome as a dead man's feet in summertime."

"I didn't sleep with her," I said.

"She come on to you?"

"You ever hear of sensitivity?"

"It's overrated, but I'll take that as a yes and assume that you didn't respond. Jeez, Bird, you got the self-restraint of a saint."

"Let it go, Angel. Please."

I sat on the edge of the second bed, and put my head in my hands. I breathed deeply and closed my eyes tightly. When I looked up again, Angel was almost beside me. I lifted my hand to let him know that I was okay. I went to the bathroom and soaked my face with cold water before returning to them.

"As for the chief, I haven't been run out of town yet," I said, picking up the conversation where we had left off. "I'm a witness-cum-suspect in the unsolved murder of an unidentified man in the Maine woods. Jennings asked me to stick around, shoot the breeze. He did tell me something else as well: the ME hasn't officially delivered his report yet, but it's likely to confirm that Chute was beaten badly before he was killed. From the marks on his wrists, it looked like someone hung him from a tree to do it." The investigation into the death would be conducted out of CID III's headquarters in Bangor, Jennings had told me, but Dark Hollow itself was likely to be crawling with cops by the following morning.

"Louis made some calls, touched base with a few of his associates," said Angel. "He found out that Al Z and a contingent of Palermo irregulars flew into Bangor last night. Seems like Tony Celli just ran out of time."

So they were closing in. There was a reckoning coming. I could feel it. I went to the door and looked out on the quietness of the India Hill Mall, at the tourist information office and the deserted parking lot. Louis came over and stood beside me.

"You called that boy's name in the bar last night, just before you saw Stritch," he said.

I nodded. "I saw something, but I don't even know what it was." I opened the door and stepped outside. He didn't pursue the subject.

"So what now?" said Louis. "You dressed up like you ready for an Arctic adventure."

"I'm still going after the old man to find out how he came to sell Ricky's boots to Stuckey."

"You want us to tag along?"

"No. I don't want to spook him any more than I have to, and it's better if you stay out of Dark Hollow for a while. After I've spoken to him, maybe then we can decide how to proceed. I can handle this one on my own."

But I was wrong.

"Midway in our life's journey, I went astray
from the straight path and woke
to find myself in a dark wood."
—Dante, *Inferno*

CHAPTER TWENTY-SEVEN

A S I DROVE to the house of the old man known as John
Barley, the image of Stritch impaled on a tree returned to
me. He couldn't have known about Caleb Kyle, couldn't
have suspected that he was being hunted on two sides. He
had reckoned on killing Louis and me, avenging his partner
while simultaneously ending the contract on his life, but he had
no inkling of Caleb.

It seemed certain to me that Caleb had killed Stritch, although how he had learned of his existence I didn't know. I
guessed that he might have encountered Stritch when both of
them were closing in on Billy Purdue. In the end, maybe it came
down to the fact that Caleb Kyle was a predator, and predators
are attuned not only to the nature of their prey but also to the
nature of those who might prey upon them in turn. Caleb hadn't
survived for over three decades without a highly developed ability to sense impending danger. In this case, Stritch had posed a
potentially lethal threat to Billy Purdue, and Caleb had sniffed
him out. Billy was the key to Caleb Kyle, the only one who had
seen him and survived, the only one left who could describe
what he looked like. But as I approached the road to John Bar-

ley's shack, I knew that Billy's description might prove unnecessary. When I stepped from the car, my gun was already in my hand.

It was early evening when I reached the old man's house. There was a light burning in one of the windows as I ascended the hill that sloped gently upward to his yard. I came from the west, against the wind, keeping the house between me and the dog in its makeshift automobile kennel. I was almost at the door when a sharp yelp came from the car and a blur moved fast across the snow as the dog at last caught my scent and tried to intercept me. Almost immediately, the door of the house swung open and the barrel of a shotgun appeared. I grabbed the gun and yanked the old man through the gap. Beside me, the dog became frenzied, alternately leaping at my face and nipping at the cuffs of my pants. The old man lay on the ground, winded by his fall, his hand still on the gun. I lashed out at the dog and put my gun to the old man's ear.

"Ease off the shotgun, or I swear to God I'll kill you where you lie," I said. His finger lifted from the trigger guard and his hand moved slowly away from the stock of the shotgun. He whistled softly and said: "Easy, Jess, easy. Good boy." The dog whined a little then moved away a distance, contenting itself with circling us repeatedly and growling as I hauled the old man to his feet. I gestured at a chair on the porch and he sat down heavily, rubbing his left elbow where he had banged it painfully as he landed.

"What do you want?" asked John Barley. He didn't look at me, but kept his gaze on the dog. It moved cautiously over to its master, giving me a low growl as it did so, before sitting down beside him where he could rub it gently behind the ear.

I had my Timberland pack over my shoulder and I threw it at him. He caught it and looked dumbly at me for the first time.

"Open it," I said.

He waited a moment, then unzipped the pack and peered in.

"You recognize them?"

He shook his head. "No, I don't believe I do."

I cocked the pistol. The dog's growling rose an octave.

"Old man, this is personal. You don't want to cross me on this thing. I know you sold the boots to Stuckey over in Orono. He gave you thirty dollars for them. Now you want to tell me how you came by them?"

He shrugged. "Found 'em, I guess."

I moved forward and the dog rose up, the hairs on its neck high and tight. It bared its teeth at me. I kept the gun on the old man then, slowly, moved it down to his dog.

"No," said Barley, his hand reaching down to hold the dog back and to cover its bared breast. "Please, not my dog."

I felt bad threatening his dog, and the feeling made me wonder if this old man could possibly be Caleb Kyle, if he could have some hidden reserve of strength that might have made him a match for Stritch. I thought that I would know Caleb when I found him, that I would sense his true nature. All I got from John Barley was fear: fear of me and, I suspected, fear of something else.

"Tell me the truth," I said softly. "Tell me where you got those boots. You tried to get rid of them after we spoke. I want to know why."

He blinked hard and swallowed once, his teeth worrying his bottom lip until he seemed to reach a decision within himself, and spoke.

"I took 'em from the boy's body. I dug him up, took the boots, then covered him again." He shrugged once more. "Took me his pack too. He didn't have no need for 'em anyways."

I resisted pistol-whipping him, but only just. "And the girl?"

The old man twice shook his head, as if trying to dislodge an insect from his hair. "I didn't kill 'em," he said, and I thought for a moment that he might cry. "I wouldn't hurt nobody. I just wanted the boots."

I felt sick inside. I thought of Lee and Walter, of times spent with them, with Ellen. I did not want to have to tell them that their daughter was dead. I once again doubted that this raggedy old man, this scavenger, could be Caleb Kyle.

"Where is she?" I asked.

He was rubbing the dog's body methodically now, hard sweeps from the head almost to its rump. "I only know where the boy is. The girl, I don't rightly know where she might be."

In the light from the window, the old man's face glowed a dim yellow. It made him look sickly and ill. His eyes were damp, the pupils barely pinholes. He was trembling gently as the fear took over his body. I lowered the gun and said: "I'm not going to hurt you."

The old man shook his head and what he said next made my skin crawl. "Mister," he whispered, "it ain't you I'm afraid of."

He saw them near the Little Briar Creek, he said, the girl and the boy in front and a figure, almost a shadow, in the backseat. He was walking with his dog, on his way home from hunting rabbits, when he saw the car pull in below him, harsh noises like stones grinding coming from the engine. It was not yet evening, but darkness had already fallen. He caught a glimpse of the two young people as they passed before the headlights of the car, the girl in blue jeans and a bright red parka, the boy in black, wearing a leather jacket that hung open despite the cold.

The boy lifted the hood of the car and peered inside, using a pocket flashlight to illuminate the engine. He could see him shake his head, heard him say something indistinguishable to the girl, then swear loudly in the silence of the forest.

The rear door of the car opened and the third passenger stepped out. He was tall, and something told John Barley that he was old, older even than Barley himself. And for reasons that, even now, he did not fully understand, he felt a chill cross him and, from close by, he heard the dog give a low whine. Beside the car, the figure stopped and seemed to scan the woods, as if to ascertain the source of the unexpected noise. Barley patted the dog lightly: "Hush, boy, hush." But he could see the dog's nostrils working quickly, and felt the animal shivering beside him. Whatever he scented, it spooked him badly and the dog's unease communicated itself to his owner.

The tall man leaned into the driver's side of the car and the headlights died. "Hey," said the boy. "What're you doing? You killed the lights." His flashlight beam moved and illuminated first the face of the man approaching and then the gleam of something in his hand.

"Hey," said the boy again, softer now. He moved in front of the girl, forcing her back, protecting her from the blade. "Don't do this," he said.

The knife slashed and the flashlight fell. The boy stumbled back and Barley heard him say, "Run, Ellen, run." Then the old man was upon him like a long, dark cloud and Barley saw the knife rise and fall, rise and fall, and heard the sound of its cutting against the noise of the trees gently swaying.

And then the figure moved after the girl. He could hear her stumbling, awkward progress through the woods. She did not get far. There was a scream, followed by a sound as of a blow heavily falling, and then all was silent. Beside him, the dog shifted on the ground, and gave a low, soft keen.

It was some time before the tall figure returned. The girl was not with him. He lifted the boy beneath the arms and hauled him to the rear of the car, where he bundled him into the trunk. He opened the driver's door and slowly, surely, began to push the car down the dirt road that led to Ragged Lake.

Barley tied his dog to a tree and gently wrapped his pocket handkerchief around its muzzle, patting it once and assuring it that he would be back. Then he followed the sound of the car as its wheels crunched on the trail ahead.

About half a mile down the road, just before Ragged Lake, he came upon a clearing next to a patch of beaver bog, dead trees fallen and twisted in the dark water. In the clearing, a pit had been dug and newly excavated earth lay in piles like funeral mounds. There was a slope at one end of the pit, and the old man used it to push the car into the earth. It came to rest almost level, the right rear wheel slightly raised. Then the figure climbed onto the roof and, from there, made its way to the lip of the hole. There was the sound of a spade being removed from the earth and then the soft shifting as it plunged deep once again, followed by a scraping as the first load hit the roof of the car.

It took the old man two hours, all told, to bury the car. Soon, snow would cover the ground and the drifts would hide any subsidence in the earth beneath. He lifted and threw methodically, his pace never varying, never once stopping to take a breath, and, despite all that he had seen, John Barley envied him his strength.

But just as the old man had finished circling the area to make sure that he had done his job well, Barley heard a bark from nearby followed by a long howl and he knew that Jess had managed to remove the binding from his muzzle. Below him, the figure stopped and cocked its head, then swung the spade hard into the beaver bog and began to move, his long legs eating up the incline, heading toward the sound of the dog.

But Barley was already moving, quickly and silently. He picked his way over fallen logs, following deer paths and moose trails so that he might avoid alerting the man behind by breaking new branches. He reached the dog to find it pulling from the rope, its tail wagging, emitting gentle yips of joy and relief. It struggled a little as he restored the binding, then he untied it, took it in his arms and ran for home. He stopped once to look back, certain almost that he had heard sounds of pursuit from close behind, but he could see nothing. When he got back to his cabin, he locked his door, reloaded his shotgun with lethal number-one shot and sat in a chair, never resting until dawn broke, when he fell into a bad, fitful sleep, punctuated by dreams of earth falling into his open mouth.

"Why didn't you tell someone what you saw?" I asked him. Even then, I was not sure whether or not to believe him. How could I believe that he was who he said he was, that such a story could be true? But when I looked in his eyes there was no trace of guile, only an old man's fear of approaching death. The dog now lay beside him, not asleep, its eyes open, sometimes casting glances at me to make sure that I had not moved during the telling of the old man's tale.

"I didn't want no trouble," he replied. "But I went back to see if there was any trace of the girl, and for those boots. They were fine boots and maybe, maybe I wanted to be sure that I hadn't imagined what I saw. I'm an old man, and the mind plays tricks. But I didn't imagine nothing, even though the girl was gone and there wasn't even blood on the ground to tell where she might have been. I knew that I hadn't imagined it as soon as I saw the dip in the ground and the spade hit metal. I was going to keep the boots and the pack, maybe had half a notion to take them to the police so they wouldn't think I was crazy when I told them the story. But . . ." He stopped. I waited.

"The next night, after what happened, I was sitting here on the porch with Jess and I felt him trembling. He didn't bark or nothing, just began to shake and whine. He was staring out into the woods, just there."

He raised a finger and pointed to a place where the branches of two striped maples almost touched, like lovers reaching out to each other in the dark. "And there was someone standing there, watching us. Didn't move or nothing, didn't speak, just stood watching. And I knew it was him. I could feel it deep in me, and I could sense it in the dog. Then he just seemed to fade into the woods, and I didn't see him again.

"But I knew why he had come. It was a warning. I don't think he knew for certain what I might have seen, and he wasn't going to kill me unless he knew, but right then and there I wished I'd never gone back for them boots. And if I said anything, he'd find out and he'd come for me. I knew that. Then you came around asking questions and I thought for sure I had to get rid of them. I emptied the pack and sold it and the boots to Stuckey and I was glad for what he gave me. I burned the boy's clothes out back. There was nothing else for it."

"You ever see this man before?" I asked.

Barley shook his head. "Never. He wasn't from around these parts, else I'd have recognized him." He leaned forward. "You didn't ought to have come here, mister." There was a tone almost of resignation in his voice. "He'll know, and he'll come for me. He'll come for us both."

I looked out into the gathering night, into the shadows of the trees. There were no stars visible in the sky and the moon was obscured by cloud. The forecast was for more snow; twelve inches were promised over the next week, maybe more. And suddenly I was seized with a fearful regret that my car was back down the road, and that we would have to walk through the darkness of the woods to get to it.

"You ever hear the name Caleb Kyle?" I asked him.

He blinked once, as if I had struck him on the cheek, but there was no real surprise in it. "Sure I heard it. He's a myth. There was never a man by that name, least not around these parts." But just by asking him I had sown doubts in his mind, as I could almost hear the tumblers falling into place, as I watched his eyes widen in realization.

So Caleb had tracked Ellen and Ricky, had wormed his way into their trust. He was the one who had advised them to visit Dark Hollow, just as the hotel manager had told me, and I didn't doubt that it was Caleb who had sabotaged the engine of their car and then told them where to pull in, close by Ragged Lake where there was a grave already waiting. What I couldn't understand was why he had done this. It made no sense, unless . . .

Unless he had been watching me all along, ever since I began helping Rita Ferris. Anyone who sided with Rita would automatically be perceived as taking a stand against Billy. Did he take Ellen Cole, maybe even kill her as he killed her boyfriend, to punish me for interfering in the affairs of a man whom he believed to be his son? If Ellen was still alive, then any hope of finding her now rested on understanding the mind of Caleb Kyle, and perhaps finding Billy Purdue. I thought of Caleb watching me as I slept, after he had killed Rita and Donald, after he had placed the child's toy on my kitchen table. What was he thinking then? And why didn't he kill me when he had the chance? Somewhere, just beyond my reach, lay an answer to these questions. I tightened my fists in frustration at my inability to grasp it, and then it came to me.

He knew who I was, or, more importantly, he knew whose grandson I was. It would appeal to him, I thought, to torment the grandson as he had tortured the grandfather. More than thirty years later, he was beginning the game again.

I motioned to John Barley. "Come on, we're leaving."

He stood slowly and looked out at the trees, as if in expectation of seeing that figure once again. "Where are we going?"

"You're going to show me where that car is buried, and then you're going to tell Rand Jennings what you told me."

He did not move, but remained staring fearfully into the trees. "Mister, I don't want to go back there," he said.

I ignored him, picked up his shotgun, unloaded it and tossed the empty gun back into the house. I motioned him to go ahead of me, my gun still in my hand. After a moment's hesitation, he moved.

"You can bring your dog," I said, as he passed me. "If there's something out there, he'll sense it before we will."

CHAPTER TWENTY-EIGHT

THE FIRST SNOW began to fall almost as soon as we lost sight of the old man's house, thick, heavy concentrations of crystal that covered the road and added their weight to the earlier falls. By the time we reached the Mustang our shoulders and hair were white, and the dog gamboled beside us, trying to catch snowflakes in its jaws. I sat the old man in the passenger seat, took a pair of cuffs from the trunk and cuffed his left hand across his body to the armrest on the door. I didn't trust him not to take a swing at me in the car, or to run off into the woods as soon as he had a chance. The dog sat on the back seat, leaving muddy paw prints on my unholstery.

Visibility was poor as I drove and the windshield wipers struggled to remove the snow. I stayed at thirty at first, then slowed to twenty-five, then twenty. Soon, there was only a veil of white before me and the tall shapes of the trees at either side, pine and fir standing like the spires of churches in the snow. The old man said nothing as he sat awkwardly beside me, his right hand holding on to the dashboard for support.

"You better not be lying to me, John Barley," I said.

His eyes were blank, their gaze directed inward, like those of a man who has just heard his death sentence pronounced and knows that it is fixed and inalterable.

"It don't matter," he said, and behind him the dog began to whine. "When he finds us, won't matter what you believe."

Then, perhaps fifty feet ahead of us, the driving snow playing games with perspective, I saw what looked like headlights. As we drew closer, the shapes of two cars appeared as they pulled fully into the road, blocking our path. Behind us, more headlights gleamed, but farther back, and when I continued to move forward, they seemed to recede, then disappeared, their glare reflected now from the trees to my right, and I realized the car behind had turned sideways and stopped, boxing us in.

I slowed about twenty feet from the cars ahead. "What's going on?" said the old man. "Maybe there's been an accident."

"Maybe," I said.

Three figures, dark against the snow and the lights, moved toward us. There was something familiar about the one in the center and the way he moved. He was small. An overcoat hung loose over his shoulders and, from beneath it, his right arm protruded in a sling. As he moved into the glare of the car's lights, I saw the dark threads of stitching in the wounds on his forehead, and the ugly twisting of his harelip.

Mifflin smiled crookedly. I was already reaching for the keys to the cuffs with one hand while with the other I removed my Smith & Wesson from its holster. Beside me, the old man sensed we were in trouble and began yanking at the cuffs.

"Cut me loose!" he screamed. "Cut me loose!"

From behind came the barking of the dog. I tossed the keys to the old man and he reached down to free his hand as I slapped the car into reverse and hit the accelerator, my gun against the wheel. We slammed into the car behind us with the sound of crunching metal and breaking glass, the impact straining the belts as we jerked toward the windshield. The dog tumbled forward into the space between the seats and yelped as it hit the dash.

Ahead of us, five figures now moved through the snow in our direction, and I heard the sound of a door opening behind us. I moved the car into drive and prepared to hit the accelerator again, but the Mustang cut out, leaving us in silence. I leaned down to turn the key in the ignition, but the old man was already opening his door, the dog on his lap nosing at the gap. I reached out to stop him—"No, don't"—and then the windshield exploded and a black and red spray, star-studded with glass shards, filled the car, splashing my face and body and blinding my eyes. I blinked them clear in time to see the old man's ruined face sliding toward me, the remains of the dog lying across his thighs, and then I was pushing my door open, staying low as I hurled myself from the car, more shots tearing into the hood and the interior, the rear window shattering as I tumbled onto the road. I sensed movement behind and to my left, spun and fired. A man in a dark aviator's jacket, a stunned look on his face and blood on his cheek, twisted in the snow and fell to the ground ten feet away from me. I glanced at the point of collision where the Mustang had hit their Neon and saw the body of a second man forced upright between the driver door and the shell of the Dodge, crushed by the impact as he tried to get out of the car.

I turned and broke for the side of the road, sliding down the slope and into the woods, bullets striking the road above me and the snow and dirt around me, shouts and cries following me as I found myself among the trees, twigs snapping beneath my feet, branches scraping my face, twisted roots pulling at my legs. Flashlight beams tore through the night and there came the staccato rattle of an automatic weapon, ripping through the leaves and branches above me and to my right. The old man's blood was still warm on me as I ran. I could feel it dripping down my face, could taste it in my mouth.

I kept running, my gun in my hand, my breath sounding harsh and ragged in my throat. I tried to change direction, to work my way back to the road, but flashlights shone almost level with me to my right and left as they moved to cut me off. Still the snow fell, trapping itself on my lashes and melting on my lips. It froze my hands and almost blinded me as it billowed into my eyes.

And then the terrain changed and I stumbled on a rock, wrenching my ankle painfully, and half slid, half ran down a final incline until my feet splashed in icy cold water and I found myself looking out on the dark expanse of a pond, the winter light drowning in its blackness. I turned, trying to find a way back, but the flashlights and cries drew nearer. I saw a light to my far left, another approaching through the trees to the right, and knew that I was surrounded. I took a deep breath, wincing at the pain as I tested my ankle. I drew a bead on the beam to my right, aimed low and fired. There was a cry of pain and the thrashing of a body falling. I fired twice more, straight ahead at the men approaching through the darkness, and heard a call to, "Kill the lights, kill the lights."

Automatic fire raked the bank as I plunged into the water, keeping the gun extended at shoulder level. The pond was not deep, I figured. Even in the darkness, I could see a chain of rocks breaking the water about half a mile out, midway across its width at its narrowest point. But those rocks were deceptive; I was maybe twenty-five feet out from the bank, cutting diagonally across to the far shore, when the bed sloped and I lost my footing with a splash. I surfaced, gasping, and a flashlight scanned across me, then returned, freezing me in its beam. I took another deep breath and dived as shots dashed the surface of the water like raindrops. I could feel the slugs tearing by me as I dived, deeper and deeper, into the black waters, my lungs bursting and the cold so intense that it felt like a burning.

And then something tugged at my side and a numbness began to spread, slowly mutating into a new, bright red pain that spread fingers of hurt through my body. I twisted like a fish caught on a line as warm blood spilled from my side into the water. My mouth opened in agony, precious oxygen bubbling to the surface, and my gun slipped from my fingers. I panicked, scrambling madly upward, only barely calming myself enough so as not to make a noise when I broke the surface. I took a deep breath, keeping my face almost level with the water, as the pain swept over me. There was numbness in my legs, in my arms and at the tips of my fingers. The gunshot wound burned, but not as badly as it would when exposed to the air.

On the banks, figures moved, but only one light was visible now. They were waiting for me to appear, still fearful of the gun I no longer had. I took a breath and dived again, keeping barely below the surface as I swam, one-handed, away from them. I did not rise again until my hand brushed the bottom of the pond in the shallows by the bank. Keeping my injured side raised, I dragged myself through the shallows, looking for a point where I could safely climb onto land. The automatic spoke again, but this time the bullets struck far behind me. Other shots came, but they were random, unfocused, hoping for a lucky hit. I kept moving onward, my eyes on the deeper darkness ahead where the woods lay.

To my right, I saw a break in the bank and water falling over stones: the river. And that river, I knew, flowed through Dark Hollow. I could have headed for the farthest shore and the woods beyond, but if I fell down among the trees or lost my sense of direction, the best I could hope for would be death from freezing, because no one would know I was there except for Tony Celli's men. If they found me, I would not have to worry about the cold for long.

I found a footing at the mouth of the river, where it flowed from the lake, but I did not stand, preferring instead to keep pulling myself along until an outcrop of trees masked me enough from the men behind to enable me to rise and move into the river itself. My side ached badly now, and every movement sent a fresh surge of pain through me. Water tumbled over a small bank of stones and it took me two attempts to gain a foothold. I pulled myself up and lay, once again, in the water as a flashlight beam moved by and shone in my direction before continuing on past the mouth. I counted to ten, then stumbled for the bank.

The snow had eased a little as the wind dropped. It was less driving now but still falling thickly, and the ground around me was completely white. The pain in my left side grew as I struggled through the deep snow, and I stopped against the trunk of a tree to examine the wound. There was a ragged hole in the back of my jacket, and the sweater and shirt beneath, with a small entry hole around the tenth rib, and a larger exit hole close by at more or less the same level. The pain was bad but the wound was shallow: the distance between the entry and exit holes was little more than two inches. Blood dripped through my fingers and pooled on the snow below. That should have warned me, but I was scared and hurt and was not as careful as I should have been. I reached down, gasping at the pain it caused, and took two handfuls of snow. I packed the snow into the wounds and moved on, slipping and sliding on the bank but remaining close to the water so I would not lose my way. My teeth were chattering uncontrollably and my clothes clung damply to my body. My fingers burned from the icy water. I was nauseous with shock.

It was only when I had traveled some distance, stopping occasionally to rest against a tree, that I recalled where I was in relation to the town. Ahead of me and to my right, perhaps two hundred yards away, I could see the lights of a house. I heard the noise of a set of falls, saw before me the steel skeleton of a bridge and I knew where I was, and where I could go.

A light burned at the kitchen window of the Jennings house as I fell against the back door. I heard a noise from inside and Lorna's voice, panicked, saying: "Who's there?" The curtains at the door parted a little and her eyes widened as she saw my face.

"Charlie?" There came the sound of a key turning in the lock and then the support of the door was taken away from me and I fell forward. As she helped me to a chair, I told her to call room six at the India Hill Motel and no one else, and then I closed my eyes and let the pain wash over me in waves.

Blood bubbled from the exit hole as Lorna cleaned the wound; the skin around it had been wiped down and she had removed some tattered pieces of cloth from within with a pair of sterilized tweezers. She passed a swab over the wound and the burning sensation came again, causing me to twist in the chair.

"Hold still," she said, so I did. When she was done, she made me turn so that she could get at the entry hole. She looked a little queasy, but she kept going.

"Are you sure you want me to do this?" Lorna asked when she was done.

I nodded.

She took a needle and poured boiling water on it.

"This will hurt a little," she said.

She was being optimistic. It hurt a lot. I felt tears spring from my eye at the sharpness of the pain as she put stitches in each wound. It wasn't textbook medical care, but I just needed something to get me through the next few hours. When she had finished, she took a pressure bandage and applied it, then took a longer roll and wound it around my abdomen.

"It'll hold until we can get you to a hospital," she said. She gave me a small, nervous smile. "Red Cross first-aid classes. You should be grateful I paid attention."

I nodded to let her know that I understood. It was a clean wound. That was about the only good thing that could be said for it.

"You want to tell me what happened?" asked Lorna. I stood up slowly and it was only then that I noticed the blood on the tiles.

"Damn," I said. A wave of nausea swept over me, but I held on to the table and closed my eyes until it had passed. Lorna's arm curled around my upper body.

"You've got to sit down. You're weak, and you've lost blood."

"Yeah," I said, as I pushed myself away from the table and walked unsteadily to the back door. "That's what I'm worried about." I lifted the curtain and looked outside. It was still snowing but in the light from the kitchen I could see the telltale trail of red leading from the direction of the river to the door of the kitchen, the blood so thick and dark that it simply absorbed the falling snow.

I turned to Lorna. "I'm sorry, I shouldn't have come here."

Her face was solemn, her lips pinched, and then she gave another small smile. "Where else could you have gone?" she said. "I called your friends. They're on their way."

"Where's Rand?"

"In town. They found that man, Billy Purdue, the one they've been looking for. Rand's holding him until the morning. Then the FBI and a whole lot of other people will arrive to talk to him."

That was why Tony Celli's men were here. Word of Billy Purdue's capture would have spread like wildfire through the agencies and police departments involved, and Tony Celli would have been listening. I wondered how quickly they had spotted me when they arrived. As soon as they saw the Mustang, they must have known and decided that it would be less trouble to kill me than to risk my interference.

"The men who shot me, they want Billy Purdue," I said quietly. "And they'll kill Rand and his men if they won't hand him over."

Something flickered on the window, like a falling star reflected. It took me a second to figure out what it was: a flashlight beam. I grabbed Lorna by the hand and pulled her to the front of the house. "We've got to get out of here," I said. The hallway was dark, with a dining room leading off to the right. I stayed low, despite the pain in my side, and peered through the space beneath the window blinds into the front yard.

Two figures stood at the end of the yard. One held a shotgun. The other had his arm in a sling.

I came back to the hallway. Lorna took one look at my face and said: "They're out front as well, aren't they?"

I nodded.

"Why do they want you dead?"

"They think I'll interfere, and they owe me for something that happened back in Portland. You must have guns in the house. Where are they?"

"Upstairs. Rand keeps them in the dresser."

She led the way up the stairs and into their bedroom. It contained a large, country pine bed, with a yellow bedspread and yellow pillows. A matching pine dresser stood across from a large closet. In one corner was a small bookshelf packed with books. A radio played softly in another corner, The Band singing "Evangeline," with Emmylou Harris's vocals snaking in and out of the verse and chorus. Lorna pulled some old T-shirts from a drawer and threw them on the floor, revealing the guns. The first was a Charter Arms Undercover .38 with a three-inch barrel, a real lawman's weapon. There was a speed loader beside it, fully packed. Close by, in a Propex holster, lay a second gun: a Ruger Mark II with a tapered barrel. There was an almost empty box of .22 Long Rifle rimfire cartridges in the corner of the drawer.

"God bless the paranoid," I said. I took the .38, loaded it and tucked it into my belt, then picked up the Ruger and examined it. The bolt was open, the chamber was empty and the safety was on.

"Rand sometimes uses it for target practice," Lorna explained, as I released the bolt, ejected the magazine and began loading it with cartridges. On the bedside cabinet stood a large plastic bottle of water, almost empty now. I steadied myself against the dresser. In the mirror facing me, my skin appeared deathly pale. There were smudges of hurt and exhaustion under my eyes and my face was pockmarked by glass cuts and smeared with sap and the old man's blood. I could smell him on me. I could smell his dog.

"Do you have tape; adhesive tape?"

"Maybe downstairs, but there's a roll of adhesive bandage in the bathroom cabinet. Will that do?"

I nodded, took the plastic bottle and followed her into the yellow-and-white tiled bathroom. She opened the cabinet and handed me the roll of inch-wide bandage. I emptied the last of the mineral water into the sink, inserted the slim barrel of the Ruger into the bottle and held it in place by wrapping the bandage repeatedly around it.

"What are you doing?" asked Lorna.

"Making a suppressor," I replied. I figured that if Celli's men searched the house, I could take one of them out with the suppressed .22 if I had to and buy us five, maybe ten seconds of time. In a gunfight at close quarters, ten seconds is an eternity.

From below came the sound of the back door being kicked in, followed by the shattering of glass and the sound of the front door being opened. I inserted the magazine and pulled the bolt, jacking a cartridge into the chamber.

"Get in the tub and keep your head down," I whispered. She slipped off her sandals and climbed silently into the bathtub. I removed my shoes and left them behind the door, then moved softly onto the landing and back into the bedroom. The radio was still playing, but The Band had now been replaced by Neil Young, his high, plaintive tones echoing around the room.

"Don't let it bring you down . . ."

I took up a position in the shadows by the window. The gun felt awkward in my hand after the Smith & Wesson, but at least it was a gun. I released the safety, and waited.

"It's only castles burning . . ."

I heard him on the stairs, watched his shadow moving ahead of him, saw it stop and then begin to step into the room, following the music. I tightened my grip on the trigger, and took a deep breath.

"Just find someone who's turning . . ."

He pushed the door open with his foot, waited a moment, then darted fully into the bedroom, his shotgun raised. I swallowed once, then exhaled.

" . . . And you will come around."

I pulled the trigger on the .22 and the top of the bottle exploded dully with a sound like a paper bag bursting. He stumbled back and I shot him again as I advanced, the light leaving his eyes as he slid slowly down the wall. I caught the shotgun, a pistol-grip Mossberg, as it slipped from his grasp. Dropping the .22, I stepped over his body, my stocking feet soundless on the floor, and moved back into the hallway.

"Terry?" called a voice from below, and I saw a man's hand, a .44 Magnum held in its grip, then his arm, his body, his face. He looked up and I took him in the head, the noise of the shotgun like a cannon's roar. His features disappeared in a red haze and he tumbled backward. I pumped and was already moving onto the stairs when a bullet struck the wall close to my left ear, a muzzle flashing in the darkness of the dining room. I fired, pumped, fired, pumped: two shots into the darkness. Glass broke and plaster disintegrated, and no more shots came. The front door now stood ajar. What remained of its glass burst and wood splinters flew as more shots came from the kitchen. I stayed on the stairs, jammed the shotgun between the supports of the banisters, turned it and fired the last round.

In the kitchen, a shadow detached itself from the wall and moved to the edge of the long hallway, firing a barrage of shots, sending wood singing from the banisters and yellow dust clouding from the wall beside me as his aim gradually grew closer and closer. I reached for the .38, yanked it from my belt and fired three shots. There was a cry of pain as, from the corner of my eye, I saw movement at the front door. It distracted me and, as I turned, the wounded gunman in the kitchen exposed himself fully and moved into the hall, his gun hand raised, the other hand holding onto his shoulder. He bared his teeth and then a noise came, louder than any gunshot I had ever heard before, and a hole appeared in his torso, big enough for a man to put his fists through if he chose. I thought I could see the kitchen through it, the glass on the floor, the sink unit, the edge of a chair. The gunman remained upright for a split second longer then tumbled to the ground like a puppet with its strings cut.

At the door stood Louis, a huge Ithaca Mag-10 Roadblocker shotgun in his hands, the rubber stock still fast against his shoulder. "Man just had himself a 10-gauge handshake," he said. From the back of the house came more shots and the sound of a car accelerating fast. Louis jumped over the corpse, with me close behind. We headed through the ruined kitchen to the back door and looked out on the yard beyond. Angel stood at the gate, a Glock 9mm in his hand, and shrugged at us.

"He got away, the ugly fuck. I didn't even see him until he was in the car."

"Mifflin," I said, wearily.

Louis looked at me. "That freak still alive?" He shook his head in wonder.

"Maybe we could blast him into space and hope he burns up on reentry," mused Angel.

I shivered in the cold, with only the bandages to cover my upper body. They were already soaked with red. My ears rang from the noise of the gunfire in the enclosed space of the house. Louis slipped off his overcoat and put it over my shoulders. Despite the cold, I felt like I was burning up.

"You know," said Angel. "You oughta be more careful. You're gonna catch your death like that."

The three of us started at a noise from behind, but only Lorna stood at the door. I walked up to her and placed a hand on her shoulder. She wrapped her arms around herself, keeping her eyes on me and away from the bodies on the floor behind her.

"What are you going to do now?" she asked.

"We're going back to Dark Hollow. I need Billy Purdue alive."

"And Rand?"

"I'll do what I can. You better call him, tell him what's happened."

"I tried. Our phone is dead. They must have cut the wires before they came in."

"Go to a neighbor's house and make the call. With a little luck, we'll get to Dark Hollow shortly after." All of which assumed that the lines hadn't been cut from outside town, in which case Dark Hollow itself would be cut off. My cell phone had failed to raise a signal here, so I doubted if anyone else would have better luck.

Already there were neighbors appearing at their gates, trying to figure out what all the noise was about. It was time to go, but Lorna raised a hand. "Wait," she said, and went back upstairs. When she returned she had my shoes in her arms, along with a thick cotton shirt, a pair of dark pants, a sweater and a padded jacket from LL Bean. She helped me to put on the clothes, glancing away when I stripped off my wet pants, then touched my hand gently as I prepared to leave.

"You take care."

"You too."

Behind me, Angel started up the Mercury, Louis in the front seat. I climbed in back and we moved off. I looked back to see Lorna standing in her yard, watching us until we were gone from her sight.

CHAPTER TWENTY-NINE

THE ROADS WERE DESERTED as we drove, the silence around us broken only by the purr of the Mercury's engine and the soft thud of snowflakes impacting on the windshield. The pain in my side burned fiercely, and once or twice, I closed my eyes and seemed to lose a couple of seconds. I caught Louis taking careful glances back at me in the rearview mirror, and I raised a hand to let him know that I was okay. It might have looked more convincing if the hand hadn't been covered in blood.

When we pulled into the parking lot in front of the police department there were two cruisers parked ahead of us, along with an orange '74 Trans-Am that looked like it would take a miracle to start it and a couple of other vehicles that had remained stationary long enough for the snow to blur their lines, including a rental Toyota out of Bangor. There was no sign of Tony Celli, or any of his men.

We entered through the front door. Ressler stood behind the desk, examining the jack on the telephone. Behind him was a second, younger patrolman whom I didn't recognize, probably another part-timer, and farther back again, standing across from

John Connolly

the station house's two holding cells, was Jennings himself. In a chair beside the desk sat Walter Cole. He looked shocked at my appearance. I was kind of unhappy about it myself.

"The fuck do you want?" said Jennings, causing Ressler to rise from his position and cast a wary eye first over Louis and Angel, then me. He didn't look too happy at the sight of our guns and his hand hovered near his own side arm. His eyes widened a little as he saw the marks on my face and the blood on my clothing.

"What's wrong with the phones?" I returned.

"They're out," Ressler said, after a moment's pause. "All communications are down. Could be the weather."

I moved past him to the cells. One was empty. In the other, Billy Purdue sat with his head in his hands. His clothes were filthy and his boots were stained with mud. He had the haunted, desperate look of an animal caught in a snare. He was humming to himself, like a little boy trying to block out the world around him. I didn't ask Rand Jennings's permission to talk to him. I wanted answers, and he was the only one who could provide them.

"Billy," I said sharply.

He looked up at me. "I fucked up," he said, "didn't I?" Then he went back to humming his song.

"I don't know, Billy. I need you to tell me about the man you saw, the old man. Describe him to me."

Jennings's voice came from behind me. "Parker, get away from the prisoner."

I ignored him. "You listening to me, Billy?"

He was rocking back and forth, still humming, his hands wrapped around his body "Yeah, I hear you." He screwed his face up in concentration. "It's hard. I didn't but hardly see him. He was . . . *old.*"

"Try harder, Billy. Short? Tall?"

The humming started again, then stopped. "Tall," he said, during the pause. "Maybe as tall as me."

"Slim? Stocky?"

"Thin. He was a thin guy, but lean, y'know?" He stood, interested now, trying hard to picture the figure he had seen.

"What about his hair?"

"Shit, I don't know from hair . . ." He went back to his song, but now he added the words, only half forming some of them as if he was not entirely familiar with them.

"Come all you fair and tender ladies
Take warning how you court your man . . ."

And I remembered the song at last: "Fair and Tender Ladies." Gene Clark had sung it, with Carla Olson, although the song itself was much older. With the recognition came the remembrance of where I had heard it before: Meade Payne had been humming it as he walked back to his house.

"Billy," I said. "Have you been out at Meade Payne's place?"

He shook his head. "I don't know no Meade Payne."

I clutched the bars of the cell. "Billy, this is important. I know you were heading out to Meade. You won't get him into trouble by admitting it."

He looked at me and sighed. "I didn't get out there. They picked me up before I even got into town."

I spoke softly and distinctly, trying to keep the tension out of my voice. "Then where did you hear that song, Billy?"

"What song?"

"The song you're humming, "Fair and Tender Ladies." Where did you hear it?"

"I don't recall." He looked away, and I knew that he did remember.

"Try."

He ran his hands through his hair, gripping the tangled locks at the back as if afraid of what his hands might do if he didn't find some way to occupy them, and began to rock back and forth again. "The old man, the one I saw at Rita's place, I think he might have been singing it to himself. I can't get the damned thing out of my head." He started to cry.

I felt my throat go dry. "Billy, what does Meade Payne look like?"

"What?" he asked. He looked genuinely puzzled. From behind me, I heard Jennings say: "I'm warning you for the last time, Parker. Get away from the prisoner." His footsteps sounded on the floor as he walked toward me.

"That's Meade over there, in that picture on the wall," said Billy, standing up as he spoke. He pointed to the framed photograph of three men which hung on the wall near the front desk, a similar version of that which hung in the diner but with only two faces instead of three. I walked over to it, nudging Rand Jennings out of my way as I went. In the middle of the group was a young man in a U.S. Marines uniform, his right arm around Rand Jennings, his left arm around an elderly man who grinned back with pride at the lens. A plaque below the photograph read "Patrolman Daniel Payne, 1967–1991."

Rand Jennings. Daniel Payne. Meade Payne. Except the old man in the picture was short, about five-six, stooped and gentle-eyed, with a crown of white hair surrounding a bald head marked with liver spots. His face was mapped with a hundred lines.

He was not the man I had met at the Payne house.

And slowly, tumblers began to fall in my mind.

Everybody had a dog. Meade Payne had mentioned it in his letter to Billy, but I had seen no dog when I was out there. I thought of the figure Elsa Schneider had seen climbing the drainpipe. An old man couldn't climb a drainpipe, but a young man could. And I recalled what Rachel had said about Judith Mundy, about her being used as breeding stock.

Breeding stock.

Breeding a boy.

And I remembered old Saul Mann, his hands moving over the cards, swiftly palming the lady, or slipping the pea from under a soda pop cap to take five bucks from a sucker. He never pushed

them, never hailed them or tried to force them to come, because
he knew.

Caleb knew Billy would come back to Meade Payne. Maybe
he got Meade's name from Cheryl Lansing before he killed her,
or it could have come up during Willeford's investigations. However he found out, Caleb knew that if he took away all the obstacles and all the options, Billy would have to turn to Meade
Payne.

Because Caleb understood what con men and hunters all understood: that, sometimes, it's best to lay the bait, wait, and let
the prey come to you.

I turned to find Jennings with his Coogan in his hand, pointing in my direction. I guessed that I had ignored him for just
that little too long. "I'm tired of your shit, Parker. You and your
buddies just drop your weapons and get on the ground," he said.
"Now."

Ressler, too, drew his weapon and, in the rear office, the
younger policeman was already holding a Remington pump to
his shoulder.

"Looks like we just crashed a nervous cops' convention," said
Angel.

"Jennings, I don't have time for this," I said. "You have to listen to me—"

"Shut up," said Jennings. "I'm telling you for the last time,
Parker, put . . ." Then he stopped suddenly and looked at the
gun in my belt.

"Where did you get that gun?" he asked, and menace
stepped softly into his voice like a gunman at a funeral. He eased
back the hammer on his pistol and took three steps toward me,
his gun now inches from my face. He had now recognized the
jacket and sweater as well. Behind me, I heard Angel sigh loudly.

"You tell me where you got that gun, dammit, or I'll kill you."

There was no good way to tell him what had taken place, so I
didn't even try. "I was ambushed on the road. The old man who

lived out by the lake, John Barley, he's dead. He died in my car. I was chased, I got to your house and Lorna gave me a gun. You may find some bodies in your living room when you get back but Lorna's okay. Listen to me, Rand, the girl—"

Rand Jennings let the hammer fall gently, hit the safety and then pistol-whipped me with the barrel of the gun, catching me a hard blow on the left temple. I staggered backward as he drew his arm back to hit me again, but Ressler intervened and caught his arm.

"I'll kill you, you fuck. I'll kill you." His face was purple with rage, but there was grief there too, and the knowledge that things could never be the same again after this, that the shell had finally been broken and the life he had lived up to then was escaping even as we spoke, dissipating into the air like so much stale gas.

I felt blood running down my cheek and my head ached badly. In fact, I ached all over, but I figured that was the kind of day it was. "You may not get the chance to kill me. The men who ambushed me work for Tony Celli. He wants Billy Purdue."

Jennings's breathing slowed, and he nodded at Ressler, who cautiously released his hold on Jennings's arm. "Nobody is taking my prisoner," said Jennings.

Then the lights went out, and all hell broke loose.

For a few moments, the station house was in total darkness. Then the emergency lighting kicked in, casting a dim glow from four fluorescents on the walls. From the cells, I heard Billy Purdue shouting: "Hey! Hey out there, what's happening? Tell me what's going on. What happened to the lights?"

From the rear of the station came the sound of three loud bangs like hammer blows, followed by the sound of a door hitting a wall. But Louis was already moving, the huge Roadblocker still in his hand. I saw him pass Billy Purdue's cell and wait at the corner, where the corridor leading down to the back door began. I felt him count three in his head, then he turned, stood to one side and fired two shots down the corridor. He moved out of sight, fired one more shot, then moved back into our line of vision. Jennings, Ressler and I ran to join him, while the young cop and Angel bolted the front door, Walter beside them.

In the corridor, two men lay dead, their faces concealed beneath black ski masks, both wearing black denims and short black jackets.

"They picked the wrong camouflage gear," said Louis. "Ought to have checked the weather forecast." He pulled up one of the masks and turned to me: "Anyone you know?"

I shook my head and Louis released his hold on the mask. "Probably not worth knowing anyways," he said.

We advanced cautiously to the open door. Wisps of snow flew into the corridor, blown by the wind outside. Louis took a broom and used it to nudge the door closed, its lock splintered by the impact of the blows it had received. No more shots came. He then helped Ressler to carry a desk down the corridor from the office and they used it to block the entrance. We left Louis to watch the door and returned to the main office, where Angel and the young cop were each at one side of a window, trying to catch a glimpse of the men moving outside. There couldn't have been many of them left, I figured, although Tony Celli was still among them.

Walter stood farther back. I noticed he had his old .38 in his hand. I was certain now that I knew where Ellen was, assuming she was still alive, but if I told Walter he would run hell-for-leather into Tony Celli's men in an effort to get to her, and that would serve no purpose at all, apart from getting him killed.

A voice came. "Hey, inside. We don't want nobody to get hurt. Just send Purdue out and we'll be gone." It sounded like Mifflin.

Angel looked at me and grinned. "Just promise me, whatever happens, that you'll finish off that gimpy fuck for good this time."

I took up a position beside him and looked out into the darkness. "He is kind of irritating," I agreed. I turned around to find Louis beside me.

"The door's okay. They try to come in again, we'll hear them before they can do any damage." He took a quick look out of the window. "Man, never thought I'd hear myself say this, but I feel like John Wayne."

"*Rio Bravo,*" I said.

"Whatever. That the one with James Caan?"

"No, Ricky Nelson."

"Shit."

Behind us, Jennings and Ressler seemed to be attemping to come up with a game plan. It was like watching two children trying to hold chopsticks with their toes.

"You got a radio?" I asked.

It was Ressler who acknowledged the question. "We're getting white noise, nothing else."

"They're blocking you, or they've taken out your transmitter."

Jennings spoke. "We stay here, they'll give up. This isn't the frontier. They can't just attack a police station and take a prisoner."

"Oh, but this is the frontier," I said. "And they can do what they want. They're not going to leave without him, chief. Celli wants the money Purdue took from him, or his own people will kill him." I paused. "Then again, you could always give them the money."

"He didn't have any money when we found him," said Ressler. "Didn't even have a bag."

"You could ask him where it is," I suggested. I could see Billy Purdue looking at me curiously. Ressler looked at Jennings, shrugged and moved across to the cell. As he did so, Angel dived sideways while Louis pushed me to the floor. I cried out as my injured side hit the carpet.

"Heads up!" shouted Angel.

The front window of the station house exploded inward and bullets tore into the walls, the desks, the filing cabinets, the light fittings. They shattered glass partitions, blew up the watercooler and turned reports and files to confetti. Ressler fell to the ground, the back of his leg already ragged and red. Beside me, Angel rose and opened fire with the Glock. Louis's Roadblocker thundered as he took up a position beside him.

"We're going to be torn apart here," shouted Angel. The firing from outside ceased. Behind us, there was only the sound of paper settling, glass crunching and water still dripping from the remains of the ruined cooler. When the pain in my side at last began to subside a little, I looked at Louis. "We could bring the fight to them," I said.

"Could do," he said. "You up to it?"

"Just about," I lied. On the floor, Jennings was cutting the leg of Ressler's pants to get at the wound. "You got a window that leads out into somewhere dark, maybe concealed by a tree or something?" I asked.

Jennings looked up at us and nodded. "Window of the men's john, down that corridor. It's right beside the wall, too narrow for anyone to fit through the space but someone could get onto the surrounding wall itself from there."

"Sounds good," said Louis.

"What about me?" said Angel.

"You doing a bang-up job with that Glock," replied Louis.

"You think?"

"Yeah. You actually hit anybody I'll start believing in God, but you sure scaring the hell out of Tony's boys."

"What about me?" said Walter. They were the first words he had spoken to me since the funeral in Queens.

"Stay here," I said. "I think I've figured something out."

"About Ellen?" The pain in his eyes made me wince.

"It's no good to any of us while Tony Celli's men are out there," I told him gently. "When this is done with, we'll talk."

We turned to leave, but it seemed like it was going to be one obstacle after another. Rand Jennings was still kneeling by Ressler. His gun was still in his hand. It was still pointing at me.

"You're not going anywhere, Parker."

I looked at him, but continued walking. The muzzle of the gun followed me as I moved past him.

"Parker . . ."

"Rand," I said. "Shut up."

Surprisingly, he did.

With that, we left them and headed to the men's toilet. The window was frosted and opened out above a pair of sinks. We listened carefully for movement outside, then slipped the latch, pulled the window open and stepped back. There were no shots, and within seconds we were hauling ourselves over the wall and into a patch of waste ground behind the north wall of the station, the shells in Louis's coat pockets jangling dully as he hit the ground. My side hurt, but by now I was past caring. I reached out for Louis as he prepared to move away.

"Louis, the old man out at Meade Payne's house is Caleb Kyle."

He almost looked surprised. "What you say?"

"He was waiting for Billy. If something happens to me, you take care of it, okay?"

He nodded, then added. "Man, you be takin' care of it yourself. They ain't killed you yet, then they ain't never gonna kill you."

I smiled and we separated, slowly making our way in a pincer movement toward the front of the station house, and Tony Celli's men.

CHAPTER THIRTY

I DO NOT REMEMBER CLEARLY much of what happened as I stumbled into the darkness. I recall that I was shivering constantly, but my skin was hot to the touch and my face was shiny with sweat. I had Jennings's gun, and had restocked the speed loader from the box of shells, but it still felt strange and unfamiliar in my hand. I vaguely regretted the loss of the Smith & Wesson. I had killed with it and, in doing so, had killed something inside me, but it was my gun and its history over the previous twelve months had mirrored my own. Perhaps it was for the best that it now lay deep in the water.

Snow was falling and the world was mute, its mouth stifled with flakes. My feet sank deep as I followed the wall, the station house to my left, cold piercing my boots and numbing my toes. On the other side of the station, I knew, Louis was moving steadily, the big shotgun in his hands.

I stopped where the wall fell suddenly at the edge of the building, becoming instead a three-foot-high surround for the parking lot. I glanced into the lot, saw no movement and made for the cover of a late-model Ford, but my responses were sluggish and I made more noise than I should have. My hands now shook continuously, so much so that I had to reach up with my left and still the barrel of my gun as I went. The pain in my side was unrelenting but, when I looked down, I saw only small bloodstains on the sweater.

The snow was being urged on by a wind that seemed to have gathered renewed vigor as the night drew on. Great swaths of white were swept into my face, and flakes crowded on my tongue. I tried to find Louis's dark form, but could see nothing beyond the lot. I knelt down, breathing heavily, sick to my stomach. For a moment, I felt that I might faint. I took a handful of snow and, crouching carefully, rubbed it into my face. It didn't make me feel much better, but the gesture saved my life.

Above me, and to my left, a shape moved behind one of the cruisers. I saw a black, patent leather shoe rise from the snow, flakes still clinging to the cuff of the dark pants above it, the tail of a blue overcoat dancing and waving in the wind. I rose, and the gun rose with me, up, up, until my head and the gun were above the hood of the Ford. And as the figure turned, registering the movement, I fired a single shot into his chest and watched dispassionately as he fell back into the drift that had built up against the wall. There he remained slumped, his chin resting on his breast, his blood turning the snow black.

And in that instant, something happened inside me. My world turned dark as the blood-drenched snow and my mind began to lose its general focus. The universe blurred at its edges, leaving me with only a pinhole of perspective. And as the world shifted and tilted I seemed to both feel and hear the sound of a blade entering flesh and then a noise like a melon being halved with a single blow. I followed the tiny lens of clarity across the wall and over the road, where a small bank sloped down to the trees. In the snow a man lay in a heap, his body split from chest to navel and snowflakes gathering in his ruined head. There were footprints around his body, deep and firm. The footsteps veered away from the body and headed toward town, following a second trail of prints whose footfalls were distorted by a limp. There was blood between the marks of Mifflin's shoes. As I followed the tracks, more shots came from the direction of the station house, among them the sound of Louis's gun.

I walked south for five, ten minutes, maybe a little more, before I found myself at the end of a residential street. A woman and a man, both elderly and wrapped tightly in overcoats and blankets, stood on their porch, the old man with one arm around the woman's shoulders. There were no more shots now, but still they waited, and still they looked. Then they caught sight of me and both drew back instinctively, the man pulling his wife, or perhaps his sister, back through the open door and closing it behind them, all the time never taking his eyes from me. There were lights on in some of the other houses, and here and there curtains moved. I could see faces haloed with dim light, but no one else appeared.

I reached the corner of Spring Street and Maybury. Spring Street led on into the center of town, but there was darkness at the end of Maybury, and the twin trails of prints moved in that direction. About halfway down the street, they separated, the distorted set moving on into the shadows, the second set veering northwest through the boundary between two properties. I guessed that Mifflin had got there first and found himself a position in the darkness from which he could view the street below him, and his pursuer had veered off to circle him when he guessed what was happening. I turned south and made my way around the backs of the houses until I came to the edge of a copse of trees where the western verge of the forest began. There I halted.

Perhaps thirty feet from me, at the edge of a pool of light shed by the last streetlamp on the road, a cloud formed and then disappeared. Something moved in a startled, frightened gesture. A face scanned to the left, then to the right, and a figure peered from behind a tree. It was Mifflin, one arm still shrouded in a sling. As I drew nearer, shielded by the shadows and my footfalls silenced by the snow, I saw blood drip thickly from his fingers and join a growing pool at his feet. I was almost upon him when some small sound caused him to turn. His eyes grew wide and he rose swiftly, a knife flashing in his good hand. I shot him in the right shoulder and he spun, his feet twisting beneath him, falling on his back and loosing a loud cry of pain as he landed. I moved forward quickly with the gun trained on him. He blinked hard and tried to focus as the light illuminated my features fully.

"You," he said at last. He tried to rise but he had no strength. Only his head moved before the effort proved too much and it fell back into the snow. As I looked at him, I saw that a long gash had been torn across the front of his coat. Something shone wetly within.

"Who did this?" I said.

He tried to laugh, but it came out as a cough and blood sprayed from his mouth and flecked his teeth with red. "An old man," he said. "A fucking old man. He came out of nowhere, slashed me, then took Contorno before we even knew what was happening. I fucking ran, man. Fuck Contorno." He tried to move his head, to look back to the town. "He's out there now, watching us. I can tell."

Maybury was quiet, and nothing moved on the street, but he was right: there was a watchfulness about the darkness as if, somewhere in its depths, someone held his breath, and waited.

"There'll be help here soon," I said, although I was unsure even as I spoke that things had gone our way back at the police department. At least we had Louis, I thought, otherwise we'd all be dead. "We'll get you to a doctor."

He shook his head once. "No, no doctor," he said. He glared at me. "It ends here. Do it, you fuck, do it!"

"No," I said softly. "No more."

But he was not going to be denied. With all the strength left in his body, he reached into the breast of his coat, his teeth gritted with the effort. I reacted without thinking and killed him where he lay, but when I drew his hand from his coat it was empty. How could it be otherwise, when he had only a knife to defend himself?

And as I stood back something seemed to flicker in the darkness across the street, and then was gone.

I headed back to the police department and had almost reached it when a figure appeared to my right. I twisted toward it, but a voice said: "Bird, it's me." Louis appeared from the shadows, his shotgun cradled in his arms like a sleeping child. There was blood spray on his face, and his coat was torn at the left shoulder.

"You tore your coat," I said. "Your tailor's going to shed a tear."

"It was last season's anyways," said Louis. "Made me feel like a bum wearing it." He stepped closer to me. "You don't look so good."

"You are aware that somebody shot me?" I asked, in a pained tone.

"Somebody always shooting you," he replied. "Weren't somebody shooting at you, beating up on you or electrocuting you, you'd be listless. Think you can hold it together?" His tone had changed, and I guessed there was bad news coming.

"Go on," I said.

"Billy Purdue's gone. Looks like Ressler collapsed from his wounds and Billy dragged him by the cuff of his pants over the cell while Angel and the others were distracted. Took his keys from his belt and a shotgun from the rack, then let himself out. Probably left the same way we did."

"Where was Angel? He okay?"

"Yeah, Angel and Walter both. They was helping Jennings to reinforce the back door. Seems like the last of Tony's guys made a second attempt on it after we left. Billy just walked out, clean and free."

"After we'd helped him by clearing the way." I swore vi-
ciously, then told him about Mifflin and the eviscerated man in
the snow.

"Caleb?" asked Louis.

"It's him," I said. "He's come for his boy, and he's killing anyone who threatens him or his son. Mifflin saw him, but Mifflin's
dead."

"You kill him?"

"Yes," I said. Mifflin had given me no choice but to kill him,
yet there had been a kind of dignity to him in his last moments.
"I have to get out to Meade Payne's place."

"We got more immediate problems," said Louis.

"Tony Celli."

"Uh-huh. It's got to end here, Bird. His car's parked maybe
half a mile east, just on the edge of town."

"How do you know?" I said, as we began walking in that direction.

"I asked."

"You must have a very persuasive manner."

"I use kind words."

"That, and a big gun."

His mouth twitched. "A big gun always helps."

A black Lincoln Towncar stood on a side road, its lights dimmed,
as we approached. Behind it were two other cars, big Fords, also
with their lights dimmed, and a pair of black Chevy vans. In
front of the Lincoln, a figure knelt in the snow, its head down,
its hands tied behind its back. Before we could get any closer a
gun cocked behind us and a voice said: "Put them down, boys."

We did as we were told, but didn't turn around.

"Now walk on."

The driver's door of one of the Fords opened, and Al Z
stepped out. As the interior light came on I saw another figure,

fat and silver-haired, dark glasses on his eyes and a cigarette in his hand. Then he faded into the gloom again as Al Z closed the door. He walked to the kneeling figure as three other men appeared from the second Ford and stood, waiting. The kneeling figure raised its head, and Tony Celli looked at us with dead eyes.

Al Z kept his hands stuffed firmly in the pockets of his gray overcoat and watched us as we approached. When we were ten feet from Tony Celli he raised a hand, and we stopped. Al Z looked almost amused.

Almost.

"I asked you to stay out of our business," he said.

"Like I told you, it was the 'our business' part that I had a problem with," I replied. I felt myself swaying, and willed my body to remain still.

"It's your hearing you have a problem with. You should have picked somewhere else to start your moral crusade."

He withdrew his right hand to reveal a Heckler & Koch 9mm, shook his head gently, said, "You fucking guys," in his soft, clipped tones, then shot Tony Celli in the back of the head. Tony slumped face first on the ground, his left eye still open and a hole where his right eye used to be. Then two men came forward, one with a plastic sheet over his arms, and they wrapped Tony Celli and placed his body in the trunk of one of the cars. A third man ran a gloved hand through the snow until he found the bullet, then slipped it into his pocket along with the ejected case and followed his comrades.

"He didn't have the girl," said Al Z. "I asked him."

"I know," I said. "There's someone else. He took a blade to two of Tony's men."

Al Z shrugged. The money was now his primary concern, not the ultimate fate of those who had chosen to follow Tony Celli. "The way I figure it, you've done worse than that," he said.

I didn't respond. If Al Z decided to kill us for what we'd done to Tony Clean's machine, there wasn't a whole lot I could say that would make him change his mind.

"We want Billy Purdue," he went on. "You hand him over, we'll forget what happened here. We'll forget that you killed men you shouldn't have killed."

"You don't want Billy," I replied. "You want your money, to replace what Tony lost."

Al Z took his left hand from his pocket and moved it in a gesture that indicated: "Whatever." Discussing the circumstances of the money's retrieval was just an exercise in semantics as far as he was concerned.

"Billy's gone. He got away in the confusion, but I'll find him," I said. "You'll get your money, but I won't hand him over to you."

Al Z considered this, then looked to the figure in the car. The cigarette moved in a gesture of disregard, and Al Z turned back to us.

"You have twenty-four hours. After that, even your friend here won't be able to save you." Then he walked back to the car, the men around him dispersing into the various vehicles as he did so, and they drove away into the night, leaving only tire tracks and a smear of blood on the snow.

CHAPTER THIRTY-ONE

THE STATION HOUSE looked like it had been attacked by a small army. Its front windows were almost entirely shattered. The door was pitted with bullet holes. Angel opened it as we arrived, and glass tinkled to the floor. Walter stood behind him. Behind us, some of the braver locals were approaching from the southern end of the town.

"Now we go find Caleb," said Louis, but I shook my head.

"There are going to be more cops on their way here soon. I don't want you or Angel here when they arrive."

"Bullshit," said Louis.

"No, it isn't, and you know it. If they find you here, no amount of explaining is going to get you out of trouble. Anyway, this part is personal—for me and for Walter. Please, get going."

Louis paused for a moment, as if he was going to say more, then nodded. "Tonto," he called. "We leavin'." Angel joined him and they headed for the Mercury together. Walter stood beside me as we watched them go. I reckoned I had about an hour left in me, maybe an hour and a half, before I collapsed.

"I think I know where Ellen is," I said. "You ready to go get her?"

He nodded.

"If she's still alive, we're going to have to kill to get her back."

"If that's what it takes," he said.

I looked at him. I think he meant it.

"Okay. You'd better drive. It hasn't been my best day behind the wheel."

We left the car a quarter of a mile beyond the Payne house and approached it from the rear, using the trees as cover. Two lights burned inside, one in a front room, the other in an upper bedroom. There was still no sign of life when we reached the verge of the property, where a small hut, its roof fitted with a sheet of corrugated iron, stood decaying slowly. There were footsteps in the snow that were not entirely obscured by the snowfall. Someone had been moving about recently, and the engine of the truck parked close by was still warm.

A smell came from the hut, the desolate odor of decaying flesh. I moved to the corner, reached around and carefully slipped the bolt. It made a little noise, but not much. I opened the door and the smell became stronger. I looked at Walter, and saw hope die in his eyes.

"Stay there," I said, and I slipped inside.

The smell was so strong now that it made my eyes water, and the stink was already clinging to my clothes. In one corner stood a long chest freezer, its corners eaten by rust which had left holes in its structure, its unconnected lead twisted around one support like a tail. I covered my mouth and lifted the lid.

Inside, a body lay curled. It was dressed in blue overalls, its feet bare, one hand behind its back with the rotting fingers splayed, the other obscured by the body. The face was bloated and the eyes were white. They were an old man's eyes. The cold had preserved him somewhat, and despite the ravages that had been visited on his body I recognized him as Meade Payne, the man in the photo back at the diner, the man who had died so Caleb Kyle could take his place and wait for Billy Purdue to come to him. Beneath his body, I saw a tail and black fur: the remains of his dog.

Behind me, I heard the door creak on its hinges and Walter entered slowly and fearfully, his eyes following my stare into the freezer. He could not keep the relief from his features when he saw the body of the old man.

"This the guy in the picture?" he asked.

"That's him."

"Then she's still alive."

I nodded, but I didn't say anything. There were worse things than being killed and I think, in the dark, shuttered places of his mind, Walter knew that.

"Front or back?" I said.

"Front," he replied.

"Okay, let's do it."

The house smelled sour when I opened the front door quietly and stepped into the large kitchen. There was a pine table with four matching chairs, the surface of the table covered with bread, some of it days out of date, and opened cartons of milk that even the temperature in the room had not prevented from going off. There were also some cold cuts, their edges curling and hard, and a dozen empty Mickey's Big Mouths, along with half a bottle of cheap grain whiskey. In one corner stood a black trash bag, from which the worst smells of all came. I reckoned it contained over a week's worth of rotting food.

Through the open kitchen door I saw Walter enter the house, his nose wrinkling at the smell. He moved to his right, his back to the wall and his gun panning across the front dining room, which was connected to the kitchen by a half-open door. I moved forward and did the same with the TV room on the left side of the house. Both rooms were littered with discarded potato chip bags, more beer bottles and cans, and half-eaten food on dirty plates. The TV room also contained a green knapsack, all strapped up and ready to be taken away. I gestured to the stairs and Walter led, keeping to the wall to avoid any creaking steps, his gun high in a two-handed grip.

On the first landing was a bathroom that stank of urine and excrement, with damp, filthy towels lying across the toilet or piled on the floor by the door. Up two steps was the first bedroom, the bed unmade and more scattered food on the floor and dresser, but with no other indication that it had recently been occupied. There were no clothes, no shoes, no bags. It was in this bedroom that the light still burned.

Ellen Cole lay on the bed in the second bedroom, her hands tied to the bed frame with ropes. There was a black rag tied over her eyes and ears, cotton padding stuffed beneath the band to muffle her hearing. Her mouth was taped, with a small hole torn in its center. Two blankets covered her body. On a small bedside table sat a plastic water bottle.

Ellen didn't move as we entered the room although, as we drew closer, she seemed to sense us. Walter reached out to touch her, but she drew away with a small sound of fear. I pulled back the blankets gently. She had been stripped to her underwear, but she didn't appear to be hurt. I left them there as I searched the third bedroom. It, too, was empty, but the bed had obviously been slept in. When I returned to the second bedroom, Walter was gently holding Ellen's head and working the blindfold free. She blinked, her eyes narrowed even in the comparative darkness of the room. Then she saw him and started to cry.

"All empty," I said.

I walked to the bed and cut the ropes holding her hands with my pocketknife while Walter stripped away the tape. He held her in his arms as she cried, her body heaving against him. I found her clothes in a pile by the window.

"Help her to get dressed," I told him. Ellen still had not spoken, but while Walter slipped her feet into her jeans I took her hand and drew her attention to me.

"Ellen, there are just two of them, right?"

It took her a moment or two to respond, then she nodded. "Two," she said. Her voice was strained from lack of use, and her throat was dry. I gave her the water bottle and she took a small sip through the straw.

"Did they hurt you?"

She shook her head, then began to cry again. I held her, then moved away as Walter put her sweater over her arms and drew it down. He put an arm around her shoulders and helped her from the bed, but her legs collapsed almost immediately.

"It's okay, honey," he said. "We'll get you down."

We were about to make our way down when, from below, there came the sound of the front door opening.

My stomach tightened. We listened for a moment or two, but no sound came from the stairs. I indicated to Walter that he should leave Ellen. If we tried to move her again, we would alert whoever was downstairs. She made a tiny, mewing sound as he drew away from her and tried to hold him back, but he kissed her gently on the cheek to reassure her, then followed me. The front door hung open, and snow billowed in from the darkness beyond. As we approached the final steps, a shadow moved in the kitchen to my right. I turned and put a finger to my lips.

A figure moved across the doorway, not looking in our direction. It was the young man I had met on my first visit to the house: Caspar, the man I believed to be Caleb's son. I swallowed hard and moved forward, my hand up to let Walter know that he should hang back near the front door. I counted three and stepped into the kitchen, my gun raised and pointing to my left.

The kitchen was empty, but the connecting door into the dining room was now fully open. I sprang back to warn Walter, just in time to see a shape move behind him and a knife gleam in the dimness. He saw the look on my face and was already moving when the knife came down and caught him in the left shoulder, causing his back to arch and his mouth to contort in pain. He brought his gun across his body and fired beneath his left arm, but the knife rose and caught him again, this time in a slashing movement across his back as he fell. Caspar pushed Walter hard from behind, and his head impacted with a loud smack on the end of the banisters. He fell to his hands and knees, blood running down his face and his eyes heavy and dazed.

The young man turned to me now, with the knife held blade down in his right hand. There was a fresh bullet wound at his hip, staining his filthy chinos a deep red, but he did not seem to notice the pain. Instead, he curled himself and hurled his body down the hallway toward me. His mouth was open, his teeth were bared and the knife was ready to strike.

I shot him in the chest as he ran and he stopped hard, his body teetering on the soles of his shoes. He put a hand to the wound and examined the blood, as if only then would he believe that he had been shot. He looked at me one more time, cocked his head to one side and then made as if to move at me again. I fired a second shot. This time, the bullet took him straight through the heart and he fell back onto the bare floor, his head coming to rest close to where Walter was trying to raise himself onto his hands and knees. I think he was dead before he hit the ground. Above me, I heard Ellen cry out, "Daddy," and saw her appear at the top of the stairs, dragging herself across the steps toward him.

Ellen's cry saved my life. As I turned to look at her, I heard a whistling sound at my back and saw a shadow move on the floor ahead of me. Something caught me a painful glancing blow to the shoulder, missing my head by inches, then the blade end of a spade swept by me. I grabbed at the wooden handle with my left hand, striking back with my right elbow at the same time. I felt it connect with a jaw, then used the momentum of the spade to pull the man behind me forward, using my right foot to trip him as he moved. He stumbled ahead of me, then fell to his knees. He stayed on all fours for a couple of seconds, then rose up and turned to face me, framed against the night by the open door behind him.

And I knew that this, at last, was Caleb Kyle. He was no longer posing as twisted and arthritic but stood tall and straight, his thin, wiry limbs encased in blue denims and a blue shirt. He was an old man, but I felt his strength, his rage, his capacity to inflict pain and hurt, as almost a physical thing. It seemed to radiate from him like heat and the gun in my hand almost wavered with the impact. His eyes were fierce and glowed with a deep, red fire, and I thought instinctively of Billy Purdue. I thought too of the young women left hanging from a tree and the pain they had suffered at his hands, and of my grandfather, forever haunted by his dreams of this man. Whatever pain Caleb himself had endured, he had visited it a hundredfold on the world around him.

Caleb looked at his dead boy lying close by his feet, then at me, and the intensity of his hatred rocked me on my heels. His eyes shone with a deep, malevolent intelligence. He had manipulated us all, evading capture for decades, and had almost succeeded in evading us again, but it had cost his son his life. Whatever happened after, some small measure of justice had been achieved for those poor, dead girls left hanging from a tree, and for Judith Mundy, who, I believed, had been taken deep into the darkness of Great North Woods by this man.

"No," said Caleb. "No."

It was only then that I began to understand why he had wanted so badly to beget a boy. I think if Judith Mundy had given birth to a daughter then his hatred would have led him to kill the child, and try again for a son. He wanted what so many men wanted: to see himself replicated upon the earth, to see the best part of himself live on beyond him. Except, in Caleb's case, that which he desired to see continue was foul and vicious and would have consumed lives just as its father had before it.

Caleb moved forward a step and I cocked the pistol. "Back up," I said. "Keep your hands where I can see them."

He shook his head, but moved back a few steps, his hands held out from his sides. He didn't look at me but kept his eyes fixed on his dead son. I advanced and stood beside Walter, who had raised himself to a sitting position, his uninjured right shoulder against the wall and blood thick on his face. He held his gun loosely in his right hand, but he was unable to focus and was obviously in severe pain. I wasn't doing so good myself. By now, Ellen was halfway down the stairs, but I held up a hand and told her to stay back. I didn't want her anywhere near this man. She stopped moving, but I could hear her crying.

In front of me, Caleb spoke again. "You'll die for what you did to him," he spat. His attention was now fully directed at me. "I'll tear you apart with my bare hands, then I'll fuck the slut to death and leave the body in the woods for the animals to feed on."

I didn't reply to his taunt. "Keep moving back, old man," I said. I didn't want to be with him in an enclosed space; not in the hallway, not on the porch. He was dangerous. I knew that, even with the gun in my hand.

He retreated again, then slowly moved down the steps until he stood in the yard, snow falling on his exposed head and his outstretched arms, light from the front room bathing him. His hands were held away from his sides and I could see the butt of a gun protruding from the back of his pants.

"Turn around," I said.

He didn't move.

"Turn around or I'll shoot you in the legs." I couldn't kill him, not yet.

He glared at me, then turned to his right.

"Reach around. Use your thumb and forefinger to take the butt of the gun, then throw it on the ground."

He did as I told him, tossing the gun into some pruned rosebushes below the porch.

"Now turn back again."

He turned.

"You're him, aren't you?" I said. "You're Caleb Kyle."

He smiled, a gray, wintry thing like a blight on the living organisms around him. "It's just a name, boy. Caleb Kyle is as good as any other." He spat again. "You afeared yet?"

"You're an old man," I replied. "It's you who should be afraid. This world will judge you harshly, but not as harshly as the next."

He opened his mouth, and the saliva made a clicking sound at the back of his teeth. "Your granddaddy was afeared of me," he said. "You look the spit of him. You look afeared."

I didn't reply. Instead, I tossed my head in the direction of the dead man on the floor behind me. "Your dead boy, was his mother Judith Mundy?"

He bared his teeth at me and made as if to move in my direction, and I fired a shot into the ground in front of him. It kicked up a flurry of dirt and snow, and brought him to a halt.

"Don't," I said. "Answer me: did you take Judith Mundy?"

"I swear I'll see you dead," he hissed. He stared beyond me to where his son lay, the muscles in his jaw tightening as he gritted his teeth against the pain he felt. He looked like some strange, ancient demon, the tendons on his neck standing out like cables, his teeth long and yellowed. "I took it to breed on, after I thought my other boy was lost to me, lost down a shithouse sewer."

It. "Is she dead?"

"Don't see how it's any of your business, but it bled to death after it had the boy. I let it bleed. It weren't of no account anyways."

"Now you're back."

"I came back for my boy, the boy I thought was lost to me, the boy that bitch kept from me, the boy all them bitches and sonsofbitches kept from me."

"And you killed them all."

He nodded proudly. "Them as I could find."

"And Gary Chute, the forestry worker?"

"He had no business being there," he said. "I don't spare them that cross my path."

"And your own grandson."

His eyes flickered for a moment, and there was something close to regret in them. "It was a mistake. He got in my way." Then: "He was a sickly one. He wouldn't have survived, not where we were going."

"You've got nowhere to go, old man. They're taking back their forest. You can't kill every man who comes in."

"I know places. There are always places a man can go."

"No, not anymore. There's only one place you're going."

Behind me, I heard a movement on the stairs. Ellen had ignored me and gone to Walter. I guessed that she would.

Caleb looked over my shoulder at her. "She your'n?"

"No."

"Shit," he drawled. "I saw you, and I saw your granddaddy in you, but my eyes must have deceived me when I saw you in her."

"And were you going to 'breed on her' too?"

He shook his head. "She was for the boy. For both my boys. Fuck you, mister. Fuck you for what you did to my boy."

"No," I said. "To hell with you." I raised the gun and pointed it at his head.

Behind me, I heard Walter groan and Ellen shouted "Bird" in her strange, cracked voice. Something cold buried itself in the soft flesh at the back of my head. Billy Purdue's voice said: "Your finger moves on that trigger, and it'll be the last thing you ever do."

I hesitated for an instant, then released my grip on the trigger and moved my finger away from the guard, raising the gun to show him that I had done so.

"You know what to do with it," he said.

I slipped the safety and threw the gun onto the porch.

"Down on your knees," he said.

The pain in my side surged as I knelt. Billy moved in front of me, Walter's gun tucked into the waistband of his pants and a Remington shotgun in his hand, then stepped back so that he could keep both Caleb and me in view.

Caleb Kyle looked upon him with admiration. After all that had happened, after all that he had done, his son had come back to him.

"Kill him, boy," said Caleb. "He killed your half brother, shot him like a dog. He was kin to you. Blood calls for blood, you know that."

Billy's face was a mass of confusion and harsh, conflicting emotions. The shotgun moved toward me. "Is that true? Was he kin to me?" he said, unconsciously adopting the phrasing of the older man.

I didn't reply. His nostrils flared and he brought the butt of the gun down in a glancing blow across my head. I fell forward and from in front of me I heard Caleb laugh. "That's it, boy, kill the sonofabitch." Then his laughter subsided, and dazed as I was, I could see him move forward a step.

"I came back for you, son. Me and your brother, we came back to find you. We heard you was lookin'. We heard about the man that you hired to find me. Your momma hid you away from me, but I came lookin' for you and now the lamb that was lost is found again."

"You?" said Billy, in a soft, bewildered tone I had never heard from him before. "You're my father?"

"I'm your daddy," said Caleb, and he smiled. "Now you finish him off for what he did to your brother, the brother you never got to meet. You kill him for what he did."

I rose to my knees, my knuckles supporting my weight, and spoke: "Ask him what *he* did, Billy. Ask him what happened to Rita and Donald."

Caleb Kyle's eyes glittered brightly, and spittle shot from his mouth. "You shut up, mister. Your lies ain't going to keep me from my boy."

"Ask him, Billy. Ask him where Meade Payne is. Ask him how Cheryl Lansing and her family died. You ask him, Billy."

Caleb sprang onto the steps and his right foot kicked me hard in the mouth. I felt teeth break, and my mouth filled with pain and blood. I saw the foot come forward again.

"Stop," said Billy. "Stop it. Let him be." I looked up and the pain in my mouth seemed as nothing to the agony etched in Billy Purdue's face. A lifetime's hurt burned in his eyes; a lifetime of abandonment, of loss, of fighting against a world that was always going to beat him in the end, of trying to live a life that had no past and no future, only a grinding, painful present. Now a veil had been pulled back, giving him a glimpse of what might have been, of what might still be. His daddy had come back for him, and all of the things he had done, all of the hurt this man had inflicted, he had done for love of his son.

"Kill him, Billy, and be done with it," said Caleb, but Billy did not move, did not look at either of us, but stared into a place deep inside himself, where all that he had ever feared and all that he had ever wanted to be now twisted and coiled over each other.

"*Kill him,*" hissed the old man, and Billy raised his gun. "You do as you're told, boy. You listen to me. I'm your daddy."

And in Billy Purdue's eyes, something died. "No," he said. "You ain't nothin' to me."

The shotgun roared and the barrel leaped in his hands. Caleb Kyle hunched over and tumbled back as if he had been struck hard in the pit of his stomach, except now there was only a dark, spreading stain in which viscera shone and from which intestines protruded like hydra heads. He fell over and lay on his back, his hands raised to try to cover the hole at the center of his being, and then, slowly and agonizingly, he hauled himself to his knees and stared at Billy Purdue. His mouth hung open and blood bubbled over his lips. His face was filled with hurt and incomprehension. After all that he had done, after all that he had endured, his own boy had turned on him.

I heard the sound of another shell being jacked into the gun, saw Caleb Kyle's eyes widen, and then his face disappeared and a warm, red hand obscured my vision, winter light dancing through it like thoughts through the mind of God.

From Dark Hollow the sound of sirens came, carrying on the cold air like the howls of wounded animals. I looked at my watch. It was 12:45 A.M., on the twelfth of December.

My wife and child had been dead for exactly one year.

EPILOGUE

I T IS DECEMBER TWENTIETH. Soon Christmas will be here. Scarborough is a place of ice cream fields and sugar-frosted trees, with colored illuminations at the windows of the houses and holly wreaths at the doors. I have cut a fir in the yard, one of a crop my grandfather planted in the year that he died, and have placed it in the front room of the house. I will add small white lights to it on Christmas Eve, as an act of remembrance for my child, so that if she is watching me from the darkness among the trees she may see the lights and know that I am thinking of her.

Above the fireplace, there is a card from Walter and Lee and a small, gift-wrapped box from Ellen. Next to it is a postcard from the Dominican Republic, unsigned but with a message written by two different hands: "This communicating of a man's self to his friends works two contrary effects; for it redoubleth joys, and cutteth griefs in halves." The quotation is not attributed. I will call them when they return, when the interest in the events that took place in Dark Hollow has begun to recede.

Finally, there is a note. I recognized the handwriting on the envelope when it arrived and felt a kind of wrench in my heart as I opened it. The message said only: "Call me when you can. I miss you." Beneath this line, she had written her home telephone number and the number of her parents' house. She had signed it: "Love, Rachel."

I sit by my window and I think again of the winter dead, and of Willeford. He had been found two days before, and I felt the news of his loss with a sharp pain. For a time, after he disappeared, I had half suspected the old detective. I had done him an injustice, and I think, in a way, I had brought death upon him. His body had been buried in a shallow grave at the back of his property. According to Ellis Howard, he had been tortured before he died, but they had no indication of who might have been responsible. It could have been Stritch, I thought, or it could have been some of Tony Celli's crew, but I think, deep down, that he died because of the old man, Caleb Kyle, and I guessed that maybe it was Caleb's son Caspar who had killed him.

Willeford's name had been attached to the search for Billy Purdue's parents. It was his number that the old woman, Mrs. Schneider, had called. If she could find him, then so could Caleb, and Caleb would have wanted to know all that Willeford knew. I hoped that the alcohol had dulled his pain, had made him a little less frightened as the end came. I hoped that he had told all that he knew as quickly as he could, but I knew that was probably a false hope. There had been something of the old honor, the old courage, about Willeford. He would not have given up the boy so easily. I had a vision of him, sitting in the Sail Loft, his whiskey and his beer before him, an old man adrift in the present. He thought that it was progress that would spell his end, not some demon from the past that he had raised by doing a good turn for a lost, troubled young man.

And I think of Ricky, and the grinding noise that the trunk of the car made as it was opened, and the sight of him huddled beside the spare tire, and of how he had tried to save Ellen in the last moments before he died. I wished him peace.

Lorna Jennings left Dark Hollow, and Rand. She called me to tell me she was leaving for Florida to spend Christmas with her mother before looking for a new place to live. The machine took the message, although I was in the house when she called and could hear her voice against the soft whirring of the tape. I didn't pick up. It was better that way, I thought.

And the man known as Caleb Kyle has been buried in a patch of ground to the north of a churchyard outside Augusta, alongside the boy he called Caspar, and prayers were said for their souls. A few days later, a man was seen at the graveside, a big man with pain in his eyes. He stood in the snow and looked at the shape of the newly disturbed earth beneath it. To his left, the sun faded from the sky, leaving streaks of red across the clouds. The man had a small pack on his back, and a piece of paper with the date of his court appearance written upon it by his bail bondsman. It was an appearance he would never make, and the bondsman knew it. Some of Al Z's money had bought his complicity, and his silence. Al Z could take the loss, I thought.

This was the second cemetery that Billy Purdue had visited that day, and he would never be seen in either again. Billy Purdue would never be seen anywhere again. He would disappear, and no trace of him would ever be found.

But I think I know where Billy Purdue went.

He went north.

Two days after the anniversary of Susan and Jennifer's death, I attended mass at St. Maximilian Kolbe and listened as their names were read out from the altar. The next day, the fifteenth, I visited the grave. There were fresh flowers laid upon it—from Susan's parents, I supposed. We had not spoken since her death, and I think they still blamed me for what had happened. I blamed myself, but I was making reparation. That was all that I could do. That was all any of us could do.

On the night of the fifteenth, they came to me. I awoke to the noise of them in the woods, sounds that were not sounds but the slow joining of worlds within worlds, and I walked to my porch and stood, but I did not descend to them.

Among the shadows, behind the trees, a host of figures moved. At first, they might have been the light shifting as the wind stirred the branches, phantasms of hands and faces, for they were silent as they came forward for me to bear witness. They were young girls, and their dresses, once torn and stained with blood and dirt, were now intact and glowed from within, clinging to soft, slightly rounded bellies that might, once before and long ago, have caused the young men to twist in the seats of their bright red cars, to whistle at them from their vinyl booths, to lean across and whisper to them, to playfully block their escape as they basked in the light from their eyes. The moonlight shone on the soft down of their arms, the gentle movement of their hair, the soft glistening at their lips; the girls in their summer dresses, gathered together in the new-fallen snow.

And farther behind them, others emerged: old women and old men, nightdresses fluttering, stained dungarees war-painted with flecks and dashes of enamel, their gnarled hands traced with thick veins like the roots of the trees clinging to the earth beneath their feet. Young men stood aside for them, their hands joined with those of their women; there were husbands and wives, and young lovers, once violently separated, now together once more. Children moved between their legs, solemn and watchful, carefully making their way to the boundary of the woods; children with the broken bones in their fingers now miraculously restored, children who had been wrenched apart in dark, pain-filled cellars now restored to beauty, their eyes bright and knowing in the winter darkness.

A whole host of the dead gathered before me, their numbers stretching back into the shadows, back into the past. They did not speak but only watched me, and a kind of peace came over me, as if the hand of a young woman had touched me gently in the night, whispering to me that I should sleep.

for now

And beside the rail, where the old man had sat with his dog, where my mother had leaned, still beautiful despite the years, I stood and felt their eyes upon me. A small hand gripped mine and when I looked down I could almost see her, radiant and new, a small beauty revealed against the gentle luminosity of the snow.

And a hand touched my cheek and soft lips met mine, and a voice said:

sleep

And I slept.

ACKNOWLEDGMENTS

A NUMBER OF INDIVIDUALS assisted me with information and advice in the course of writing this book. I wish to particularly thank Rodney Laughton, historian and proprietor of the Breakers Inn at Higgins Beach, Scarborough; Bullwinkle's Guide Service in Greenville, Maine; Chief Duane Alexander of the Greenville Police Department; and Quark, Inc., in New York, for providing details of security technology. Bernd Heinrich's *A Year in the Maine Woods* (Addison-Wesley, 1994); *The Coast of Maine* by Louise Dickinson Rich (Down East Books, 1993); *Coastal Maine: A Maritime History* by Roger F. Duncan (Norton, 1992); and *Fiasco* by Frank Partnoy (Profile, 1997) also proved especially valuable. Any mistakes are my own.

On a more personal note, I would like to thank Anne and Catherine, who read this book in its early stages, and my family and Ruth, for their advice and support. I am indebted, as always, to my editor at Hodder & Stoughton, Sue Fletcher; Emily Bestler, my editor at Simon & Schuster; and, finally, to Kerith Biggs, my foreign rights agent, and my agent and friend, Darley Anderson.

ABOUT THE AUTHOR

JOHN CONNOLLY'S first novel, *Every Dead Thing,* received the Shamus Award for Best First Novel in 1999 and was lauded a *Los Angeles Times* Book of the Year. It was also a bestseller in Britain and Ireland. John Connolly is a regular contributor to *The Irish Times* and has traveled extensively in the United States. He lives in Dublin, Ireland, where he is at work on his next book. For more information, see his Web site at www.johnconnolly.co.uk.